DARK WATER

ROBERT BRYNDZA

GRAND CENTRAL
PUBLISHING

NEW YORK   BOSTON

Copyright © 2016 by Robert Bryndza

Cover design and art by Henry Steadman
Cover copyright © 2019 by Hachette Book Group, Inc.

Grand Central Publishing
Hachette Book Group
1290 Avenue of the Americas, New York, NY 10104
grandcentralpublishing.com
twitter.com/grandcentralpub

Originally published in 2016 by Bookouture
First Grand Central Publishing Mass Market Edition: July 2020

Grand Central Publishing is a division of Hachette Book Group, Inc.
The Grand Central Publishing name and logo is a trademark of Hachette Book Group, Inc.

The publisher is not responsible for websites (or their content) that are not owned by the publisher.

The Hachette Speakers Bureau provides a wide range of authors for speaking events. To find out more, go to www.hachettespeakersbureau.com or call (866) 376-6591.

Library of Congress Control Number: 2019936548

ISBN: 978-1-5387-0193-5 (mass market)

Printed in the United States of America

OPM

10 9 8 7 6 5 4 3 2 1

"A gripping and an edge of your seat read. It made my heart and pulse race with every page I turned. It is one of those books that when you finish, you sit back and just think, wow! There is just so much more I want to say but I think I will just end up gushing and not do this fantastic book the justice it deserves. An outstanding read by an author who is one of my firm favourites."   —*By the Letter Book Reviews*

The Night Stalker

"*The Night Stalker* is dark, fast-paced, and shot through with wit and psychological insight. I couldn't put it down."
—Mark Edwards, bestselling author of *Follow You Home*

"Erika is fast becoming one of my favourite detectives... I absolutely loved this heart-pounding, fast-paced, chilling crime thriller."   —*Book Review Café*

"Just when I thought it couldn't get any better... From the first page, we're sucked in with tension that had me holding my breath."   —*Suspense Is Thrilling Me*

"A truly brilliant crime series... *The Night Stalker* made me feel like I had been swept up in a whirlwind and had me clinging on for dear life, only letting me go right at the very end."
—*By the Letter Book Reviews*

"Intense, suspenseful, and clever... a gripping page-turner that is disturbingly real, and I highly recommend it."
—*What's Better Than Books?*

"Absolutely brilliant...impossible to put this book down!...
A must read."   —*Quiet Knitter*

"A truly fantastic and exciting serial killer chiller!"
   —Booklover Catlady

"*The Night Stalker* is a very gripping, engaging read full
of nail-biting tension. Once I started reading it, I couldn't
stop!...an amazing work of fiction no reader of the crime
genre should miss."   —*Relax and Read Reviews*

"I think any fans of a good police procedural will become
completely engaged in this series featuring a gritty and
determined strong female lead."   —*Carries Book Reviews*

"This book grabbed me by the throat and didn't let go till I
got to the end."   —*Sincerely Book Angels*

The Girl in the Ice

"Compelling at every turn! *The Girl in the Ice* grabs us from
the first page and simply won't let go, as we follow the bril-
liantly drawn Detective Erika Foster in her relentless hunt
for one of the most horrific villains in modern crime fiction."
   —Jeffrey Deaver, #1 internationally
bestselling author

"A riveting page-turner. An astonishingly good plot with
perfectly drawn characters and sharp, detailed writing. *The
Girl in the Ice* is a winner."
   —Robert Dugoni, #1 *Wall Street Journal*
bestselling author

"Robert Bryndza's *The Girl in the Ice* has everything I look for in a mystery: an evil antagonist, a clever detective, and a plot that kept me guessing until the very end!"

—T. R. Ragan, *New York Times* bestselling author

"I loved, loved, loved this book and Erika Foster is most definitely my kind of heroine. She is smart, tenacious, direct, and passionate...I found the writing tight, evocative, and enthralling. I CANNOT wait for the next installment."

—Angela Marsons, *USA Today* bestselling author

"A compelling read—once you've started, it's hard to put down." —Rachel Abbott, author of *Sleep Tight*

"An intriguing web of lies, secrets, and suspense. I really enjoyed getting to know DCI Foster and am already looking forward to the next book."

—Mel Sherratt, author of *Taunting the Dead*

"[A] crime novel that you can easily pick up and get swept up in...you'll find Bryndza's world instantly accessible, his characters compelling and endearing, and his story's central mystery wholly engrossing." —CrymeByTheBook.com

"Once in a while a book stops you in your tracks...this is THAT book." —*Crime Book Junkie*

"A nonstop, edge-of-your-seat, roller coaster of a thriller! The ending, oh the ending! My mind is still blown! This book does not disappoint!" —*Book Addicted Boy*

Also by Robert Bryndza

The DCI Erika Foster crime thriller series
The Girl in the Ice
The Night Stalker
Dark Water
Last Breath
Cold Blood
Deadly Secrets

The Coco Pinchard romantic comedy series
The Not So Secret Emails of Coco Pinchard
Coco Pinchard's Big Fat Tipsy Wedding
Coco Pinchard, the Consequences of Love and Sex
A Very Coco Christmas
Coco Pinchard's Must-Have Toy Story

Standalone Romantic Comedy Novels
Miss Wrong and Mr. Right
Lost In Crazytown

For Marta

Death lies on her, like an untimely frost
Upon the sweetest flower of all the field.

William Shakespeare, *Romeo and Juliet*

PROLOGUE

AUTUMN 1990

It was a cold night in late autumn when they dumped the body in the disused quarry. They knew it was an isolated spot, and the water was very deep. What they didn't know was that they were being watched.

They arrived under the cover of darkness, just after three o'clock in the morning—driving from the houses at the edge of the village, over the empty patch of gravel where the walkers parked their cars, and onto the vast common. With the headlights off, the car bumped and lurched across the rough ground, joining a footpath, which was soon shrouded on either side by dense woodland. The darkness was thick and clammy, and the only light came over the tops of the trees.

Nothing about the journey felt stealthy. The car engine seemed to roar; the suspension groaned as it lurched from side to side. They slowed to a stop as the trees parted and the water-filled quarry came into view.

What they didn't know was that a reclusive old man lived by the quarry, squatting in an old abandoned cottage which had almost been reclaimed by the undergrowth. He was outside, staring up at the sky and marveling at its beauty, when the car appeared over the ridge and came to a halt. Wary, he moved behind a bank of shrubbery and watched. Local kids, junkies, and couples looking for thrills often appeared at night, and he had managed to scare them away.

The moon briefly broke through the clouds as the two figures emerged from the car, and they took something large from the back and carried it toward the rowing boat by the water. The first climbed in, and as the second passed the long package into the boat there was something about the way it bent and flopped that made him realize with horror that it was a body.

The soft splashes of the oars carried across the water. He put a hand to his mouth. He knew he should turn away, but he couldn't. The splashing oars ceased when the boat reached the middle. A sliver of moon appeared again through a gap in the clouds, illuminating the ripples spreading out from the boat.

He held his breath as he watched the two figures deep in conversation, their voices a low rhythmic murmur. Then there was silence. The boat lurched as they stood, and one of them nearly fell over the edge. When they were steady, they lifted the package and, with a splash and a rattle of chains, they dropped it into the water. The moon sailed out from behind its cloud, shining a bright light on the boat and the spot where the package had been dumped, the ripples spreading violently outwards.

He could now see the two people in the boat, and had a clear view of their faces.

The man exhaled. He'd been holding his breath. His hands shook. He didn't want trouble; he'd spent his whole life trying to avoid trouble, but it always seemed to find him. A chill breeze stirred up some dry leaves at his feet, and he felt a sharp itching in his nostrils. Before he could stop it a sneeze erupted from his nose; it echoed across the water. In the boat, the heads snapped up, and began to twist and search the banks. And then they saw him. He turned to run, tripped on the root of a tree and fell to the ground, knocking the wind out of his chest.

Beneath the water in the disused quarry it was still, cold, and very dark. The body sank rapidly, pulled by the weights, down, down, down, finally coming to rest with a nudge in the soft freezing mud.

She would lie still and undisturbed for many years, almost at peace. But above her, on dry land, the nightmare was only just beginning.

CHAPTER 1

Detective Chief Inspector Erika Foster crossed her arms over the bulky life jacket against the icy wind, wishing she'd worn a thicker coat. The small inflatable Met Police Marine Recovery boat churned across the water of Hayes Quarry, dragging behind it a compact transponder, scanning the bottom deep below. The disused quarry was in the center of Hayes Common, 225 acres of woodland and heath situated next to the village of Hayes on the outskirts of South London.

"Water depth is 23.7 meters," said Sergeant Lorna Crozier, the Dive Supervisor. She was hunched over a screen at the front of the boat, where the results of the sonar were beamed back and displayed in inky purple shades, blooming across the screen like a bruise.

"So, it's going to be tough to salvage what we're looking for?" asked Erika, noting her tone.

Lorna nodded. "Anything beyond a depth of thirty meters is tough. My divers can only stay down for short periods. The average pond or canal is a couple of meters deep. Even at high tide, the Thames is ten to twelve meters."

"There could be anything down there," said Detective Sergeant John McGorry, who was squashed in the small plastic seat beside Erika. She followed his youthful gaze across the rippling surface of the water. The visibility couldn't have been more than a couple of feet before it became a swirl of dark shadows.

"Are you trying to sit on my lap?" she snapped as he leaned across her to peer over the edge.

"Sorry, boss." He grinned, shifting back along the seat. "I saw this show on the Discovery Channel. Did you know, only five percent of the ocean floor is mapped. The ocean occupies seventy percent of the Earth's surface, that leaves sixty-five percent of the Earth, excluding dry land, *unexplored...*"

At the water's edge, twenty meters away, clumps of dead reeds swayed in the breeze. A large support lorry was parked on the grassy bank, and beside it the small support team were preparing the diving gear. Their orange life jackets were the only dots of color in the dingy autumn afternoon. Behind them, gorse and heather stretched away with a mix of grays and browns, and a clump of trees in the far distance were bare. The boat reached the end of the quarry and slowed.

"Turning about," said PC Barker, a young male officer sitting at the rudder of the outboard motor. He performed a sharp turn so they could double back and cross the length of the water for the sixth time.

"Do you think some of the fish or eels down there could have grown to, like, super proportions?" asked John, turning to Lorna, his eyes still shining with enthusiasm.

"I've seen some pretty big freshwater crayfish when I've been on dives. Although, this quarry isn't a tributary, so whatever is down there would have been introduced," replied Lorna, one eye on the sonar screen.

"I grew up down the road, in St. Mary Cray, and there was a pet shop near us that, apparently, sold baby crocodiles…" John's voice tailed off, and he looked back at Erika raising an eyebrow.

He was always upbeat and chatty, which she could just about cope with. Although she dreaded working the early shift with him.

"We're not looking for a crocodile, John. We're looking for ten kilos of heroin packed into a waterproof container."

John looked back at her and nodded. "Sorry, boss."

Erika checked her watch. It was coming up to three thirty.

"What's that worth on the street, ten kilos?" asked PC Barker from his spot by the rudder.

"Four million pounds," replied Erika, her eyes back on the sonar image shifting across the screen.

He whistled. "I take it the container was dropped in deliberately?"

Erika nodded. "Jason Tyler, the guy we've got in custody, was waiting for things to quieten down before he came back for it…"

She didn't add that they could only hold him in custody until midnight.

"Did he really think he'd get it back? We're an experienced dive team, and we're going to find this a tough one to salvage," said Lorna.

"With four million quid on the line? Yes, I think he was going to come back for it," replied Erika. "We're hoping to lift his prints off the layers of plastic wrapping inside."

"How did you find out he'd dropped it in here?" asked PC Barker.

"His wife," replied John.

PC Barker gave him a look only another guy could understand, and whistled.

"Hang on. This could be something; kill the motor," said Lorna, leaning closer in to the tiny screen.

A small shape glowed black amongst a swirl of purple hues. PC Barker switched off the outboard motor and the silence rang out, replaced by a swish of water as the boat slowed. He got up and joined her.

"We're scanning an area of four meters each side of the boat," said Lorna, her small hand moving over the smudge on the screen.

"So the scale is correct," agreed Barker.

"You think that's it?" asked Erika, hope rising in her chest.

"Could be," said Lorna. "Could be an old fridge. We won't know for sure till we're down there."

"Will you dive down there today?" Erika asked her, trying to stay positive.

"I'll stay on dry land today. I was on a dive yesterday, and we have to have rest periods," said Lorna.

"Where were you yesterday?" asked John.

"Rotherhithe. We had to recover a suicide from the lake at the nature reserve."

"Wow. It must add a whole new level of freakiness, finding a body deep underwater?"

Lorna nodded. "I found him. Ten feet down. I was searching in zero visibility, and suddenly my hands close around a pair of ankles, and I feel up, and there's the legs. He was standing on the bottom."

"Jeepers. Standing up, underwater?" said John.

"It does happen; something to do with the composition of the gas in the body and the progress of decay."

"It must be fascinating. I've only been in the force for a few years. This is my first time with a dive team," said John.

"We find tons of horrible stuff. The worst is when you find a bag of puppies," added PC Barker.

"Bastards. I've been a copper for twenty-five years, and I still learn something new every day about how sick people can be." Erika noticed how they all turned to her for a moment; she could see them mentally working out how old she was. "So, what about this anomaly? How quick can you get down there and bring it up?" she asked, drawing their attention back to the sonar on the screen.

"I think we'll mark it up with a buoy, and take another pass on it," replied Lorna, moving to the side of the boat and preparing a small orange marker buoy with a weighted line. She dropped the weight over the edge, and it quickly vanished into the deep, dark water, the thin rope playing out over the edge. They left the marker floating as PC Barker fired up the outboard motor, and they moved off across the water.

Just over an hour later they had covered the surface of the quarry, and identified three possible anomalies. Erika and John had come ashore to warm up. The late October day was now fading as they huddled outside the dive lorry with Styrofoam cups of tea. They watched the dive team at work.

Lorna stood on the bank, holding one end of a weighted rope called the jackstay line. It led down into the water and along the bottom of the quarry, where it resurfaced twenty yards from the shore. The boat was anchored beside the first marker buoy, and manned by PC Barker, who was keeping the other end of the jackstay taut. Ten minutes had passed since two divers had entered the water. They'd started at opposite ends of the jackstay, and were searching along the bottom of the quarry to meet in the middle. Beside Lorna another member of the dive team was crouched over a small comms unit the size of a briefcase. Erika could hear the divers' voices as they communicated through the radios in their diving masks.

"Zero visibility, nothing yet . . . We must be close to meeting in the middle . . ." came the tinny voice over the radio.

Erika took a nervous inhale on her e-cigarette, the LED light at the end glowing red. She exhaled a puff of white vapor.

It was three months since she'd been transferred to Bromley Police Station, and she was still trying to find her place and fit in with her new team. Only a few miles from her old borough of Lewisham, in South London, but she was becoming used to the vast difference a few miles can make between the outskirts of London and the edge of the county of Kent. It had a townie feel to it.

She looked over at John, who was twenty yards away, talking on his phone; he was grinning as he chatted. Whenever he had the chance he called his girlfriend. A moment later he finished the call, and came over.

"The divers still looking?" he asked.

Erika nodded. "No news is good news . . . But if I have to release that little bastard . . ."

The little bastard in question was Jason Tyler, a low-level drug dealer who had risen rapidly to control a drug dealing network covering South London and the Kent borders.

"Keep the line taut, I'm getting slack . . ." said the diver's voice through the radio.

"Boss?" asked John awkwardly.

"Yeah?"

"That was my girlfriend, Monica, on the phone . . . She, we, wanted to invite you over for dinner."

Erika glanced at him, with one eye still on Lorna as she looped in a little slack from the jackstay, bracing her feet on the bank. "What?" she replied.

"I've told Monica lots about you . . . Good stuff, of course. Since I've been working with you, I've learned loads; you've made the job so much more interesting. Made me want to be a better detective... Anyway, she'd love to make you her lasagne. It's really good. And I'm not just saying that cos she's my girlfriend. It really is..." His voice tailed off.

Erika was staring at the twenty-foot gap between Lorna on the shore and the boat out on the water. The light was fading rapidly. She thought the divers must be about to meet in the middle, and if they met that would mean they had nothing.

"So what do you say, boss?"

"John, we're right in the middle of a big case," she snapped.

"I didn't mean tonight. Some other day? Monica would love to meet you. And if there were anyone else you'd like to invite, that's cool. Is there a Mr. Foster?"

Erika turned to him. She'd spent the last couple of years hearing herself gossiped about in the force, so she was surprised that John didn't know. She went to answer, but was cut off by a shout that went up from the support team at the water's edge.

They hurried over to Lorna and the dive officer, who was crouched down at the small comms unit. They heard one of the divers say: "There's something packed in under the mud... I need help if I'm going to pull it out... How am I doing for time?" The tinny voice cut through the cold air, and there was interference, which Erika realized were bubbles from the diver's respirator as the officer replied to the diver thirty feet down in the quarry.

Lorna turned to Erika. "I think we've found it. This could be it."

CHAPTER 2

The temperature plummeted by the water as darkness fell. Erika and John paced up and down within the arc of light spilling out of the support vehicles, and the trees behind them had vanished in a darkness which seemed to press down on them all.

One of the divers, slick in his drysuit, finally emerged up the steep banks of the quarry carrying what looked like a large molded plastic suitcase streaked in mud. Erika and John moved over to join the dive team helping him up and onto dry land. John held a small digital camcorder and began to film the diver with the box. It was placed on the grassy bank, on a square of plastic sheeting. They all stood back as John moved in and took several still images of the box intact.

"Okay, boss," he said. "I'm filming."

Erika had pulled on a pair of latex gloves and was holding a pair of bolt cutters. She knelt in front of the box and began to inspect it.

"There's two padlocked latches either side of the carry handle, and there's a pressure equalization valve on the case," she said, indicating a mud-covered button underneath the handle. She clipped both locks with the bolt cutters as John filmed. The dive team watched from a little way back, illuminated by the arc of light from the digital camcorder.

Erika gently turned the pressure valve, which was followed by a hissing noise. She unclipped both latches and pulled up the lid. The light from the digital camcorder shone inside, bouncing off rows of small neat packages, each filled with the rose-gray colored powder.

Erika's heart leapt at the sight of it.

"Heroin with a street value of four million pounds," she said.

"It's horrific, but I can't take my eyes off it," muttered John as he leaned in to get a close-up of the interior.

"Thank you, all of you," said Erika, turning to the silent faces of the dive team standing around in a small semicircle. Their tired faces grinned back.

A crash of interference came through the comms unit from one of the divers still in the water. Lorna went over and started talking to the diver over the radio.

Erika carefully closed the lid of the case.

"Okay, John, put in a call to control. We need this moved securely to the nick, and tell Superintendent Yale we need the fingerprint team ready to pull this apart the moment we get back. We're not taking our eyes off it until it's safely locked up, you understand?"

"Yes, boss."

"And get me one of the large evidence bags from the car."

John went off as Erika stood up and stared down at the case.

"I've got you, Jason Tyler," she muttered. "I've got you, and you're going down for a long time."

"DCI Foster," said Lorna, coming over from where she'd

been talking on the comms unit. "One of our divers was just doing a sweep of the area. He's found something else."

Fifteen minutes later, Erika had bagged up the plastic case of heroin, and John was back with the digital camcorder, filming another diver as he emerged from the water. He had something dark and misshapen cradled in his arms. He brought it over to a fresh square of plastic sheeting which had been laid out on the grass. It was a mud-streaked bundle of plastic entwined in thin rusting chains which were looped through and weighed down by what looked like exercise weights. It was no more than five feet long, and had folded over on itself. The plastic was old and brittle and seemed bleached of color.

"It was found four feet away from the plastic case, partially submerged in silt on the quarry bed," said Lorna.

"It's not heavy. There's something small inside; I can feel it shifting," said the diver.

He placed it on the square of plastic sheeting, and a hush descended over the team, broken only by the branches in the far-off trees creaking in the wind.

Erika felt a cold dread pooling in her stomach. She stepped forward, breaking the silence.

"Can I please have those bolt cutters again?"

She tucked them under her arm, pulled on a fresh pair of latex gloves, then stepped forward, and gently set to work, clipping the rusty chains, which were thin but woven over and under several times. The plastic was so brittle it had become rigid, and it crackled as she unwound the chains and water began to seep out onto the grass from inside.

Despite the cold, Erika realized she was sweating. The plastic was folded repeatedly and rolled over, and as she unwrapped the layers she thought whatever was inside was

small. It smelt only of pond water: stale and a little unpleasant, which set alarm bells off in her mind.

As she reached the last fold in the plastic, she saw the
team around her were completely silent. She had forgotten to
breathe. She took a deep breath, and unfolded the last roll of
the brittle plastic.

The light from the camcorder illuminated its contents.
Inside lay a small skeleton: a jumble of pieces amongst a
layer of fine silt. Little remained of the clothes, just a few
scraps of brown material clung to a piece of ribcage. A small
thin belt with a rusted buckle was looped around the spinal cord, which was still attached to the pelvis. The skull
was loose, and nestled in a curved pile of ribs. A few murky
wisps of hair remained attached to the top of the skull.

"Oh my God," said Lorna.

"It's very small...It looks like a child's skeleton," said
Erika softly.

They were plunged into darkness as John darted away
with the camcorder and over to the banks of the quarry,
where he kneeled down and was violently sick in the water.

CHAPTER 3

It was raining hard when Erika climbed into the driver's seat of her car. It hammered down on the roof, and the blue light from the surrounding squad cars and dive lorry caught in the raindrops on the windscreen.

The pathologist's van was the first to pull away from the edge of the quarry. The black body bag had looked so small when it was loaded into the back. Despite her years in the force, Erika felt shaken. Every time she closed her eyes she saw the tiny skull with its wisps of hair and empty staring eye sockets. The question kept swirling around in her mind. *Who would dump a small child in the quarry? Was it gang related? But Hayes was an affluent area with a low crime average.*

She ran her hands through her wet hair and turned to John.

"Are you all right?"

"Sorry, boss. I don't know why I...I've seen plenty of dead bodies before...There wasn't even any blood."

"It's okay, John."

Erika started the engine as the two backup vehicles and

the one escorting the case of heroin pulled away. She put the car in gear and followed. They rode in silence as the somber convoy's headlights illuminated the dense woodland rolling past on both sides of the gravel track. She felt a pang of regret she was no longer in her old job on the Murder Investigation Team at Lewisham Row. She was now working in conjunction with the Projects Team, fighting organized crime. It would be another officer's job to find out how the small skeleton ended up thirty feet down in the freezing blackness.

"We found the case. It was where Jason Tyler's wife said it would be," said John, trying to sound positive.

"We need to match his fingerprints; without them we have nothing," said Erika.

They left the common, and drove through Hayes. Lights blazed in the windows of the supermarket, chip shop, and the newsagent, where a row of Halloween rubber masks hung limp in the window, all blank eyes and grotesque hooked noses.

Erika couldn't seem to summon up any feelings of triumph about finding the case of heroin. All she could think about was the tiny skeleton. During her time in the force, she'd spent several years heading up anti-drug squads. The names seemed to change—Central Drug Unit, Drug and Organised Crime Prevention, the Projects Team—but the war on drugs rumbled on, and it would never be won. The moment one supplier was taken out there was another ready and waiting to take his place; filling the vacuum with even more skill and cunning. Jason Tyler had filled a vacuum, and in a short space of time someone would take his place. Wash, rinse, repeat.

Murderers, however, were different; you could catch them and lock them up.

The squad cars in front came to a halt at a set of traffic

lights by Hayes train station. Commuters carrying umbrellas streamed out across the road.

Rain clattered on the roof of the car. Erika closed her eyes for a moment. The small skeleton lying on the bank of the quarry rushed at her. There was a honk from the car behind, and she jumped and opened her eyes.

"It's green, boss," said John quietly.

They crept forward slowly, the roundabout up ahead still clogged. Erika looked out at the people hurrying past, searching their faces.

Who was it? Who would do that? she thought. *I want to find you. I'm going to find you. I want to lock you up and throw away the key—*

The car honked twice from behind. Erika saw the traffic had cleared and she pulled off around the roundabout.

"You asked earlier if I was married," said Erika.

"I just wanted to know if you'd like to bring anyone for dinner—"

"My husband was in the force. He died during a drugs raid, two and a half years ago."

"Shit. I didn't know. I wouldn't have said anything... Sorry."

"It's okay. I thought everyone knew."

"I'm not really into gossip. And you're still welcome to come for dinner. I meant it. Monica's lasagne is really good."

Erika smiled. "Thank you. Maybe when this is over."

John nodded. "The skeleton, it's a little kid, isn't it?" he said softly.

Erika nodded. As they approached the roundabout, the pathologist's van peeled off ahead, and turned to the right. They turned and watched as it drove away and vanished amongst the houses. The police cars carrying the heroin turned left, and Erika reluctantly followed.

*   *   *

Bromley Police Station was a modern three-story brick building at the bottom of Bromley High Street opposite the train station. It was just after 7 p.m., and commuters were hurrying under the awning of Bromley South train station, torrential rain and the promise of the weekend to come hastening their rush. The first groups of Friday night drinkers were moving in the other direction. Young girls held tiny jackets over their heads to keep their even tinier dresses dry, and boys in shirts and smart trousers used free copies of the *Evening Standard.*

Erika drove past the station and turned in to the slip road that wound down to the police station's underground car park, following the two squad cars, their lights still flashing, and flanking the car carrying the heroin.

The ground floor of Bromley Station housed the uniform division, and the corridor was busy with officers arriving for the night shift, pensive and gloomy at the prospect of the night ahead dealing with underage drinkers. Her boss, Superintendent Yale, met Erika, John, and the six uniformed officers accompanying the case at the main staircase leading up to CID Division. He joined them as they climbed the stairs. He had a ruddy face, a shock of bristly red hair, and he always looked as if someone had stuffed him into his uniform: it was a size too small for his bulky frame.

"Good work, Erika," he said, beaming at the case wrapped in the evidence bag. "The fingerprint technicians are waiting upstairs."

"Sir, in addition to the case we found—" started Erika.

Yale frowned. "Human remains, yes. Let's hold off talking about that."

"Sir. The skeleton was wrapped in plastic sheeting. It was a child—"

"Erika, we're at a crucial stage here, don't lose focus."

They reached the door to an office where a plain-clothes officer was waiting; his eyes lit up when he saw the uniformed officer carrying the plastic case in its evidence bag.

"Here it is, let's see if we can get some prints off this and nail Jason Tyler!" said Superintendent Yale. He pulled up his sleeve to check his watch buried in his hairy wrist, adding, "We've got until 8:30 a.m. tomorrow. It's going to be tight, so let's get cracking!"

CHAPTER 4

There was relief and elation at 1 a.m. on Saturday morning when Jason Tyler's prints came back from one of the tightly packed bags of heroin in the case. They had a match.

Erika's team worked through the weekend until Tyler's court appearance on Monday morning, where he was charged and denied bail.

On Monday afternoon Erika knocked on the door of Yale's office. He was just grabbing his coat and about to leave.

"Coming for a drink, Erika? You deserve one. The first round is on me," he grinned.

"I just read the Jason Tyler press statement, sir," she said. "You omitted the discovery of the skeletal remains."

"I don't want it to cloud our case against Tyler, and judging by what you found, it's a historical case. Nothing to do with him. The great thing is that it's not our problem. It's been passed to one of the Murder Investigation Teams."

He pulled on his coat and went over to a filing cabinet by the door, where a tiny hand mirror was fixed with sticky tape, and ran a comb through his unruly mass of red hair.

Erika knew he wasn't being harsh; he was being realistic.

"We going for a drink then?" he asked, turning to her.

"No, thanks. I'm shattered. Think I'll just head home," she said.

"Right-o. Good work," he said, patting her on the shoulder as they left.

Erika returned to her flat in Forest Hill and took a shower. When she emerged from the bathroom wrapped in a towel the afternoon was gray and gloomy, and through the patio window fog hung low in her small square of garden. She pulled the curtains closed, switched on the TV and settled back on the sofa.

Over the next few hours the small skeleton haunted her dreams, replaying the moment she unwrapped the final layer of plastic and saw the skull with the wisps of long hair attached... the thin belt looped around the spinal column—

She was woken by her phone ringing.

"Erika, hi. It's Isaac," said a smooth male voice. "Are you busy?"

Since she'd moved to London two and half years ago, Forensic Pathologist Isaac Strong had become a friend and trusted colleague.

"No. I'm watching some film," she said. She rubbed her eyes as the screen came into focus. "Sarah Jessica Parker and Bette Midler are on broomsticks, followed by another witch on a vacuum cleaner."

"Ah, *Hocus Pocus*. I can't believe it's Halloween again."

"This is my first Halloween in Forest Hill. I'm thinking being on the ground floor might put me at a disadvantage for trick or treaters," said Erika, pulling the towel off her head with her free hand and finding her hair was almost dry.

Isaac paused. "This isn't a social phone call. It's about the remains you recovered on Friday, at Hayes Quarry."

She froze with the towel in her hand. "What about them?"

"I was called in for an urgent post-mortem on Saturday morning, and when I finished, I saw them, and your name on the paperwork, so I took a look."

"I thought one of the Murder Investigation Teams was now in charge?"

"They are, and I've been dealing with them, but now no one is answering my calls. I figured you'd answer, and that you would be interested in what I've found out."

"I am. What can you tell me?"

"I'm at the morgue in Penge. How soon can you get here?" he asked.

"I'm already on my way," she said, dropping the towel and hurrying to get dressed.

CHAPTER 5

Erika's footsteps echoed on the stone floor in the long corridor of the morgue leading down to the autopsy room. She reached a door at the end, and a video camera high on the wall above the door whirred as it turned, almost greeting her. The thick metal door buzzed and clicked open and she went through.

The room was chilly and devoid of natural light. Stainless steel refrigeration units lined one wall, and in the center of the room four autopsy tables glinted under the fluorescent light. The one closest to the door was laid with a blue sheet, and on it, the small skeleton had been pieced together, laying intact, the bones a dark shade of brown.

Dr. Isaac Strong had his back to Erika, and when he heard her enter he straightened up, and turned. He was tall and thin and wore blue scrubs, a white face mask and a tight-fitting blue cap. His assistant, a young Chinese girl, worked quietly and respectfully, moving along a series of bagged-up samples on a bench behind the steel autopsy table. Her latex gloves crackled as she picked up a small bag containing a piece of hair and checked its label against her list.

"Hello Erika," said Isaac.

"Thank you for calling me," she said, looking past him to the skeleton.

There was an unpleasant smell: stale water, decay, and a meaty aroma of bone marrow. She looked back to Isaac's pale, tired face. He pulled down the white mask, raised his immaculately shaped eyebrows, and smiled, breaking through the formality. She smiled back briefly. She hadn't seen him for several weeks. Their friendship was strong, but faced with death, and in this formal setting, they were professional. They nodded, reverting to their roles of Forensic Pathologist and Detective Chief Inspector.

"Procedure dictates that I've had to put through a call to the officer heading the MIT and the SCIT at Scotland Yard, but I thought you would like to know my findings."

"You've contacted the Specialist Casework Investigation Team? That means you've identified who this is?" asked Erika.

He put up his hand. "Let me start from the beginning," he said. They moved closer to the autopsy table, where the grime on the bones contrasted with the pristine sterile sheet where they were neatly arranged. "This is Lan, my new assistant," he said, indicating the elegant young woman. She turned and nodded, just her eyes showing over her mask.

"Okay. You can see the skull is intact, no breaks or abrasions," said Isaac, gently lifting a matted swirl of coarse brown hair and pulling it away, exposing the smooth bone of the skull. "One of the teeth is missing, the top front left incisor," he said, moving his gloved hand down to the upper set of browny-yellow teeth. "And three of the ribs on the upper left side, close to the heart, are broken." His hand moved down to where pieces of the three ribs were laid out. "The body had been wrapped tightly in plastic, which has kept much of the skeleton intact. Typically, in waterways, lakes, or quarries there are pike, freshwater crayfish, eels, and all manner of bacteria and microbes, which will feast and break a corpse down. The plastic protected the skeleton from all but the smallest of microbes which would have consumed the body."

Isaac retrieved a small stainless steel trolley. On it there were some personal effects removed from the skeleton, placed in plastic evidence bags.

"We found several scraps of woolen clothing; a line of buttons to indicate this may have been a cardigan," said Isaac, holding up one of the bags to show where some brown threadbare pieces had been reassembled into a vague shape. He placed it down and picked up another bag. "There is also a belt made from a mix of synthetic plastics; you can see the color has gone but the buckle remains tied." Erika saw just how tiny the waist that it encircled must have been. "And there was a small piece of nylon material, still attached to and tied amongst the hair; I think this was a ribbon..." His voice trailed off as he picked up the smallest bag, which contained a swirl of coarse brown hair tied with a dirty thin strip of material.

Erika paused for a moment and swept her eyes across it all. The skeleton, small and vulnerable, stared back at her with empty eye sockets.

"I had a belt just like this when I was eight. These are the belongings of a young girl?" said Erika, indicating the bag.

"Yes," said Isaac softly.

"Do you have any idea of age?" Erika looked up at him, expecting a blunt response, and for him to give his usual scalding reply that it was too early to know for sure.

"I believe that the skeleton is of a seven-year-old girl called Jessica Collins."

Erika looked between Isaac and Lan, momentarily stunned. "What? How do you know?"

"It can be very hard to determine the sex of skeletal remains, in particular, if death occurred before the age of puberty. The small amount of clothing encouraged the officer heading the MIT to take a leap, and he requested files on missing girls between the ages of six and ten reported in the past twenty-five years. We focused on the missing child reports in the South London area and Kent borders. Obviously, children are reported missing every day, but thankfully most of them are found. When the names came back, the dental records were requested and studied by a Forensic Odontologist. The teeth matched the records of a girl who went missing in August 1990. Her name was Jessica Collins."

Lan went over to the bench and returned with a folder. Isaac took it and slid out an X-ray, holding it up to the light.

"This came through with the report from the Forensic Odontologist. I don't have a light box anymore; the old one has conked out and I'm waiting for new bulbs," he said ruefully. "One of the hazards of X-rays going digital... This was taken from dental records dated July 1989. Jessica Collins was playing croquet in the garden and was hit in the jaw by the ball. She was six years old. If you can see here, there was nothing broken, but the X-ray showed that the front teeth are indented and slightly twisted, and the bottom set too is uneven. It's a perfect match."

They looked back at the skeleton; the top teeth, brown and crooked, the jawbone lying neatly beside it, giving up the secrets of the skeleton's identity.

"During the autopsy I managed to extract a small amount of bone marrow, and it's going off to the lab shortly, but I'm just covering all the bases. I can confirm this is Jessica Collins." There was a pause.

Erika ran her hand through her hair. "Do you have any idea of cause of death?"

"We have the three broken ribs on the left-hand side of the ribcage, clean breaks, and this could indicate blunt force trauma to the heart or lungs. There are no marks or scrapes on the bone, which would have told me that a knife or sharp object was used. We also have the front left incisor missing, but it's not broken off. The whole tooth came loose, but I can't confirm how this was lost. We could expect a seven-year-old to be losing milk teeth..."

"So that's a 'no'?"

"That's correct. But coupled with the fact the body was wrapped in plastic and weighted down, we have to take foul play into account."

"Of course."

"When did you come to the UK, what year?" he asked.

"It was September 1990," she replied.

"Do you remember the Jessica Collins case?"

Erika paused for a moment and raked through the memories of when she moved from Slovakia to the UK, aged eighteen, to work in Manchester as an au pair for a family with two small children.

"I don't know. I didn't speak much English, and it was all a culture shock. For the first few months I was working in their house, and I stayed in my room, didn't have a TV—" she stopped and saw that Isaac's assistant was watching her closely. "No, I'm not aware of the case."

"Jessica Collins went missing on the afternoon of the seventh of August 1990. She left her parents' house to go to her friend's birthday party in the next street. She never arrived at the party. They never found her. It was as if she'd vanished into thin air. It was a major headline story," said Isaac.

He took another piece of paper from the file. It was a

photograph of a young blonde girl with a wide smile. She wore a pink party dress with matching thin belt, a blue cardigan, and white sandals with a multicolored pattern of flowers. In the picture she posed in front of a dark wooden door in what looked like a living room.

There was something about her toothy grin, with the crooked bottom teeth in the picture, which she could see replicated on the jawbone lying on the autopsy table, that made Erika gasp.

"Yes, I remember," she said softly, now recognizing the picture. It had been used in every newspaper story.

"And, right now, we're the only three people in the world who know what happened to her," said Lan, speaking for the first time.

CHAPTER 6

It grew dark as Erika drove back to her flat from the mortuary in Penge. There was little traffic. As the light faded, the low fog swirled, forming a canopy between the terraced houses and shops on either side of the road. The gloom in her heart intensified. Throughout her career, cases came and went, but there were always ones which affected her. Jessica was seven years old when she died.

Erika had become pregnant, quite by accident, late in 2008. She'd fought with her husband, Mark; he'd wanted to keep the baby, but she didn't, and she'd had the pregnancy terminated. Mark hadn't given his blessing, but he had told her that he would support her in whatever she wanted to do. The termination was very early on in the pregnancy, but she had been sure it was a girl. If she'd kept the baby, she'd now be seven.

The roads slid past, grim and gray, and the tears poured down Erika's face. It had been a rough year in the aftermath; she'd lurched between relief and revulsion. She'd blamed herself, and she'd blamed Mark for not fighting her hard enough. A baby would have changed so many things in her life. Mark had offered to be a stay-at-home dad. If he'd given up his job to be a father, he wouldn't have been there at work that fateful day when he was gunned down.

She gulped and sobbed, and as she took one hand off the steering wheel to wipe her eyes, a woman with a small child darted out from behind a line of parked cars along the curb to cross the road. Erika slammed on the brakes just in time, and came screeching to a halt.

The woman was young and dressed in a thick pink bomber jacket. She waved that she was sorry and pulled the little kid—who was dressed in a skeleton Halloween costume—by the arm. It turned its little head and a tiny skeleton face stared into the bright headlights. Erika closed her eyes tight, and when she opened them, they were gone.

When she arrived home, she flicked on the central heating and kept her coat on as she made herself a large coffee and then settled down on the sofa with her laptop. She went straight to Google and typed in "Jessica Collins Missing Girl." A whole page of results came up, and she clicked on the first: a *Wikipedia* entry.

Jessica Marie Collins (born 11 April 1983) disappeared on the afternoon of 7 August 1990, shortly after leaving her parents' house in Avondale Road, Hayes, Kent to attend the birthday party of a school friend.

On the afternoon of 7 August at 13:45 Jessica left 7 Avondale Road, alone, to make the short walk to a neighboring house at 27 Avondale Road, where her friend Kelly was having a birthday party. She never arrived. It wasn't until 15:30, when Kelly's mother phoned Jessica's parents, Martin and Marianne Collins, to check on her whereabouts, that they raised the alarm.

The disappearance quickly attracted wide media coverage in the UK press.

On 25 August 1990, 33-year-old Trevor Marksman was arrested by police and questioned, but was released four days later without charge. Police enquiries continued into 1991 and 1992. The missing person's inquiry was scaled back in late 1993.

No further arrests were made and the case remains open. Jessica Collins's body has never been found, and the case remains unsolved.

Erika checked the location of Hayes Quarry on Google Earth. It was less than one mile from Avondale Road, where Jessica had gone missing.

"Surely the quarry must have been searched when Jessica went missing?" said Erika to herself. She brought up results from Google Images, and found a screenshot of the MET police appeal made in August 1990. Jessica's parents sat behind the obligatory table at the press conference, pale and drawn, and flanked by officers from the MET.

"Twenty-six years," said Erika. She closed her eyes; an image rushed at her. A skull and eye sockets, the jaw and teeth opening wider.

She got up to make some more coffee, when her phone rang. It was Superintendent Yale.

"Sorry to cut in to your evening off, Erika, but I've just had an interesting chat with Jason Tyler's lawyer. Tyler's made an offer to name four of his associates, and hand over emails and records of bank transfers."

"You make it sound like he's buying a house from us!"

"You know the score, Erika. We can hand this over to the CPS knowing we'll get a result and probable conviction. It's a result you should be proud of."

"Thank you, sir. But the prospect of Tyler going down for a reduced sentence doesn't make me feel proud."

"But he'll go down."

"And what's he going to do when he's released? Start up a candle-making business? He'll be back, dealing."

"Erika, where is this coming from? This is the result we wanted. He's out of action; we get to his associates, cut off supply to the dealers."

"What happens to his wife and the kids?"

"They'll testify, probably via video link, and they get a new identity."

"His wife has an elderly mother and two aunts."

"And that's very sad, Erika, but she must have known the score when she hitched her wagon to Jason Tyler. Or did she think all the money coming in to their fancy house was from a candle-making business?"

"You're right. Sorry, sir."

"It's okay."

Erika paused for a moment and scrolled back over the *Wikipedia* article she'd been reading.

"About the skeleton we found in Hayes Quarry. It's been identified. A seven-year-old girl called Jessica Collins. Went missing in 1990."

Yale whistled on the other end of the phone. "Jesus, that's who you found?"

"Yeah. I know the Forensic Pathologist; he's been keeping me in the loop."

"Who's the poor bugger who's been assigned to the case?"

"I don't know, but I'd like to put myself forward as the SIO on this case."

There was a pause. It had come out of Erika's mouth before she could think it through.

"Erika, what are you talking about?" said Yale. "You were assigned to me as part of the Projects Team—as part of Specialist, Organized and Economic Crime."

"But, sir, I discovered the remains. It's on our patch. The missing person case was originally led out of our borough—"

"And a lot has changed since the 1990s, Erika. We don't deal with kidnap or murder. You know that. We deal with proactive contracts to kill, major drugs suppliers, multidimensional crime groups, including ethnically-composed gangs, and serious large-scale firearms trafficking—"

"And when I joined your team, you said I was foisted on you like the aunt that no one wants to have for Christmas!"

"I didn't say it quite like that, Erika, but you are now a *valuable* part of my team."

"Sir, I can solve this case. You know my track record with solving difficult cases. I have unique skills which would benefit a historical murder inquiry—"

"And yet, after all these years you are still a DCI. Have you even considered why?"

Erika was silent on the end of the phone.

"I expressed that wrongly, I'm sorry," he said. "But the answer is still no."

CHAPTER 7

Just before 9 p.m., Erika parked her car and crossed the road to Commander Marsh's house. It was close to Erika, but in a smart, expensive area of South London near Hilly Fields Park. His house looked out over the London skyline, glittering in the darkness. Small groups of little children dressed in Halloween costumes were milling up and down the street with their parents, and their chatter and giggles floated over when Erika opened Marsh's front gate and rapped on the door using the heavy iron door knocker. Up until two months before, Paul Marsh had been Erika's boss at Lewisham Row, and then she had left under a cloud. She was just trying to work out what she was going to say to him when his wife, Marcie, appeared at the gate with their twin girls, Mia and Sophie. They were dressed as identical fairy princesses, each carrying a little plastic pumpkin filled with sweets. Marcie wore black Lycra leggings, a tight black jacket, pointy ears, and her face was painted like a cat. Erika couldn't help but feel irritated by the costume.

"Erika, what are you doing here?" asked Marcie. The two little dark-haired girls looked up at her. Were they five or six? Erika couldn't remember.

"I'm sorry, Marcie. I know you hate me making house calls, but this really is very important. I just need to speak to Paul . . . He's not answering his phone."

"Did you try the station?" she asked, squeezing past her to the door. Erika stepped back.

"He's not answering there either."

"Well, he's not here."

"Trick or treat!" cried one of the girls holding up her pumpkin.

"Trick or treat! We're allowed to stay up late tonight!" screamed the other, bumping the first pumpkin out of the way with her own. Marcie had the door open and looked back at the girls.

"Oh dear. I don't have any sweets," said Erika, fumbling in her pockets. "But here's something to get some more!" She pulled out two five pound notes and dropped one in each pumpkin. They looked between Erika and Marcie, unsure if this was allowed.

"Wow, isn't Erika nice? Say thank you, girls!" said Marcie. Her face not matching the sentiment.

"Thank you, Erika," they both squeaked. They were very cute, and Erika smiled back at them.

"Just remember to brush your teeth after all those sweets."

The girls nodded solemnly. Erika turned her attention back to Marcie.

"I'm sorry. I really need to speak to Paul. Do you know where he is?"

"Hang on . . ." Marcie ushered the two tiny princesses in through the front door, telling them to go and get ready for bed. They waved to Erika and were gone as Marcie pushed the door to.

"Didn't he tell you?"

"Tell me what?" asked Erika, surprised.

"We've separated. He moved out three weeks ago." Marcie crossed her arms, and Erika noticed the long black tail hanging down from the back of her leggings. It swayed in the breeze.

"No. I'm sorry. I really didn't know...I don't work with him anymore."

"Where are you now?"

"Bromley."

"He never tells me anything."

"So, where is he?"

"He's been staying at the flat in Foxberry Road, until we sort something..."

They paused for a moment looking at each other. Erika was having trouble taking Marcie seriously, dressed as a cat. A cold blast of wind wheeled round the side of the house. The girls shrieked from upstairs.

"I have to go, Erika."

"I'm really sorry, Marcie."

"Are you?" she replied pointedly.

"Why wouldn't I be?"

"I'll see you around," said Marcie. She went inside with a swish of her tail, and closed the front door.

Erika walked back to the car, glancing back at the handsome house. The lights going on upstairs.

"What did you do, Paul, you stupid idiot?" she said to herself as she climbed into her car.

CHAPTER 8

Number 85 Foxberry Road loomed over Erika as she pulled up outside. It was at the end of a long line of terraced houses, three stories high, running down from Brockley train station.

She peered up at the top window. Two years earlier she'd rented the top floor flat from Marsh, living there during a long cold winter. As well as the shock of a new city and the loneliness of the sparsely furnished flat, a masked intruder had broken in and nearly killed her.

"You know you could save yourself a lot of hassle and answer your phone," said Erika when Marsh opened the main front door. He wore thick tartan pajama bottoms and a faded Homer Simpson T-shirt. He looked exhausted, and his sandy hair seemed to have grown thinner on top.

"Hello to you too," he said. "Is this work related, or did you bring a bottle?"

"Yes and no."

He rolled his eyes. "You better come in."

The small flat hadn't changed much in the eighteen months since she'd left. It had a smart chilliness with generic IKEA furniture. Erika avoided looking in the open bathroom door as she came through the hall to the living room. This was where the masked intruder had scaled the back wall of the building, punched out the extractor fan and opened the window. That night she had very nearly died as he wrapped his hands around her throat. She had only been saved by her colleague DI Moss. She thought of Moss; she missed working with her and her other colleagues in the Murder Investigation Team at Lewisham Row.

This sharpened Erika's resolve as Marsh indicated she should sit on the small sofa. He went to his phone and switched it on, then moved to the sink to wash a couple of the dirty teacups which were piled up.

"Late on Friday I salvaged four million pounds' worth of heroin from the bottom of Hayes Quarry. We've linked it to—"

"Jason Tyler. Yes, I saw, and just a couple of months into your new job. Good work."

"Thank you. The Marine Unit also found human remains half buried in the silt on the bottom of the quarry. They're unrelated to the Tyler case…" Erika quickly outlined what she knew so far.

"Jesus. You found Jessica Collins?" he said. Erika nodded. "I can sense that you are about to cut to the chase," he added, opening the tiny fridge and pulling out a bottle of milk.

"Yes. I need your help. I want to be SIO on the Jessica Collins case."

Marsh paused with the milk and then slowly opened the carton and began pouring it into two mugs.

"Have you spoken to your superintendent?"

"Yes."

"He said no. Didn't he?"

Erika nodded. "Paul. You should have seen her, the skeleton. So small and vulnerable, three of the ribs were broken. She'd been wrapped in plastic and chucked in the water. We don't know if she was still alive when she went in. Her killer is still out there."

Marsh poured hot water into a small teapot.

"I know one of the MITs have been assigned this, but the investigation hasn't really started yet. It's my borough."

"But with cutbacks, your superintendent is probably pushed to breaking point."

"Every department in the MET is pushed to breaking point, but this case has to go somewhere. We have the manpower and resources at Bromley. I'm the senior officer who found the body. This isn't a stretch by any means. You're a commander now. You can make this happen."

Marsh replaced the milk in the fridge.

"You know Assistant Commissioner Oakley has just taken early retirement? I don't yet have the same rapport with his replacement."

"Who is his replacement?" asked Erika.

"It's not being officially announced until tomorrow morning."

"Come on, you can tell me. It's not as if I'll go and doorstep him..." Marsh raised an eyebrow. "I promise I won't doorstep him."

"Her. The new Assistant Commissioner is Camilla Brace-Cosworthy." Marsh stirred the tea in the pot then poured, adding: "Erika, the look on your face says it all."

"Let me guess. She went to Oxford?"

"Cambridge. Joined the force on the accelerated promotion course."

"So she's hardly walked the beat?"

"That's not what it's about these days."

"What do you mean? There are officers out there every day on the beat, cleaning up the shit and the problems. Once again they've promoted someone to a high rank who knows nothing about life beyond the small sphere of public school and holidays in the Home Counties."

"That's not fair. You don't know her." He handed her a mug of tea, adding, "You've got a chip on your shoulder."

"And?"

"And, I'm enjoying your rant. It's quite entertaining when it's not directed at me." He grinned.

"Look, Paul. I'm aware I can be an idiot. If I wasn't such an idiot at times, I know I could be a superintendent by now; hell, I could even be a chief superintendent—"

"Easy now."

"I've learned a lesson. Please, can you put a good word in the right ear, and help make me SIO on the Jessica Collins case? I know I can catch the bastard who did this. He, or she, is out there and thinks, after all these years, they've got away with it. But I'm going to get them."

Marsh sat on the small sofa beside her and took a sip of his tea.

"You've heard of what happened to the SIO who worked on it as a missing person? DCI Amanda Baker? She was thrown off the case."

"I was thrown off three huge cases, then fought my way back to solve them."

"Amanda wasn't like you. Well, she was, she was a brilliant officer, but she wasn't strong, up here." He tapped his forehead. "She was one of the first female DCIs in the MET, and the first to be assigned to such a high profile case. She had it really tough from her peers, those high up in the MET and the press. They were so suspicious as to how a woman had landed the job of SIO."

"How did she land the job?"

"Damage limitation from top brass. So many mistakes were made in the first few days after Jessica's disappearance; the police were facing a lot of questions. Putting a female DCI in place as SIO was a good story to distract from this, to put the police in a good light."

"But the top brass believed she could do it?"

"Yes, but top brass was unaware that in the months leading up to her being made SIO, she'd been seeing a therapist."

"Why?"

"Back then, in the late eighties, it was a given that if you were a female officer you'd be given the rape cases to deal with. Amanda would take evidence at the scene, and support these women through the whole awful process. The only problem was that she didn't know how to let go, how to separate herself from work. She'd stay in contact with the victims for weeks, months, even years afterward. She saved a lot of women from the abyss. It took an emotional toll, and no one was looking out for her. Amanda was about to be signed off sick when she got the call to say she was going to be SIO on the Jessica Collins case. The case got bigger and bigger as the leads and evidence shrank to nothing. It was as if Jessica Collins vanished into thin air. Eventually, she cracked under the pressure. It's a poisoned chalice, Erika. You're better off out of it, believe me."

"You know me. I won't crack under pressure from anyone," said Erika quietly. "I will crack, however, if I have to spend the next few years on the merry-go-round of taking drug dealers off the street, only for another one to take his place."

They sat for a moment and drank their tea.

"Paul, please. This is a seven-year-old girl who was abducted off the street. God knows what happened to her; what was done to her. And then she was dumped on the bottom of a quarry for twenty-six years. Imagine if someone did that to Mia or Sophie—"

"No! Erika, *do not* bring my daughters into this!" warned Marsh.

"Jessica was someone's daughter... You can make this happen."

Marsh rubbed his eyes, got up and went to the window.

"I can put in a word, but that's all it will be. I can't promise anything."

"Thank you," said Erika, "But as far as Superintendent Yale is concerned, I was never here; I never spoke to you."

"Aren't you going to ask me about Marcie?" he said after a pause.

"No. I figured if you wanted to talk about it, you would."

He leaned against the wall, looking pained.

"Thanks," he said. "We're trying to work things out. We're on a break." Erika raised an eyebrow. "Her words, not mine. She wants to 'go on a break' while she finds out..." His voice cracked and it tailed off. "She met someone else."

"She's the one who cheated?" asked Erika, surprised.

"Yes. Some bloke from one of her art classes. He's twenty-nine. He goes to the gym. How can I...?"

"Paul. Marcie loves you. Hang in there, don't let her forget that you love her."

"Did you think it would be me?" he said suddenly. "Did you think I'd be the one to have an affair?"

"Yes."

He looked hurt.

"Come on, Paul. You know what I mean. You occupy a position of power. There are plenty of nubile young girls at the nick working as support staff, and power like yours is a great aphrodisiac."

"Is it?" he asked, looking at her.

"Power is—for some women it's an aphrodisiac. You must know that?"

He nodded. "Would you like another cup, or something stronger?"

"No. I'd best be getting going."

"If you want, you can stay," he said softly.

"What? I live just up the road—"

"I just meant, that it's late and—"

"No, Paul. I won't be staying," said Erika, standing and grabbing her coat from the back of the sofa.

"You could be politer!"

"You have two small children. And just because Marcie has decided that she wants to shop around doesn't mean you should do the same thing."

His face was now red and angry. "I didn't mean it like that! I meant you could sleep on the sofa."

"I *know* how you meant it. This sofa is barely four-foot long, and this is a one-bedroom flat—"

"Bloody hell!" Marsh began to shout. "It was a kind offer to a friend—"

"I'm not stupid, Paul."

"You are. You're bloody stupid! How can someone be so smart at work and so stupid in life?"

She thundered down the communal stairs, and came out of the front door, slamming it behind her. At the car she fumbled in her pocket for the keys which were caught on a piece of the lining.

"Shit!" she said yanking at them. "Shit, shit, shit!" They came out of her pocket, ripping the lining, and she unlocked and got in. She slammed her hand on the wheel and tipped her head back against the headrest.

"I could have dealt with that much better. I must be stupid," she murmured.

CHAPTER 9

When Erika arrived at Bromley Station early on Tuesday morning she bumped into Superintendent Yale on the ground floor, coming out of the men's toilet with a copy of the *Observer* under his arm.

"Erika, can I have a word?" he said.

She nodded and followed him up to his office. He closed the door and moved round his desk, tucking his shirt in over his expanding belly. He indicated she should sit. He drummed his fingers on the desk, and adjusted the framed picture of his wife and two small sons. His wife was petite and blonde, but his sons had both inherited his unruly red hair, which they both wore Orphan Annie–style.

"I've just had a call from our new Assistant Commissioner," he said after a pause.

"Camilla Brace-Cosworthy?" asked Erika, trying not to show her excitement.

"Yes. I thought she was calling to introduce herself, but no—"

"Why was she calling?"

"She wants to meet you."

"Me? Really?" Erika didn't know how to arrange her face. Should she appear shocked? If so, how shocked? She wasn't known for displaying a huge spectrum of emotions. She settled on wide-eyed surprise.

"Yes. Really. I don't have the ear of the new Assistant Commissioner. She's only been in the position for one day, and yet she wants to meet with you about the Jessica Collins case... Do you know something I don't? You're not going to win an Academy Award for your reaction."

"No, sir," she said, realizing this was partly true.

"I'm your senior officer, Erika, and we had discussed this! I told you we don't have the resources or time to deal with a major historical case such as this. Obviously, it wasn't the answer you wanted, and now I'm getting cold calls from the Assistant Commissioner." Yale was angry now, his face redder than its usual hue.

"I haven't approached her."

"Who did you approach?"

"No one."

Yale sat back in his chair. "You seem to have nine lives, Erika. I'd assumed with the amount of begging that went on from Commander Marsh, begging me to find a place for you on my team, that you and him have a *special* bond."

Erika sat back and tried to stay calm. "We trained together, sir. We were officers on the beat at the same time; he was good friends with my late husband. And he's married."

"Well, Commander Marsh will be attending this meeting too. Did you know that?"

"No, I didn't, sir. And I hope you know that I'm very grateful for the opportunity you've given me."

He nodded, unconvinced. "They're expecting you at eleven. You need to report to her office at New Scotland

Yard." He didn't wait for her to answer, but she could see that the meeting was over when he turned and started working on his computer.

"Thank you, sir."

"And I need your final report on Jason Tyler on my desk by close of play today."

"Yes. Thank you, sir." She got up to leave.

"Erika, even cats run out of lives. Use the ones you have left wisely," he said, looking up at her for a moment before returning to his work.

CHAPTER 10

The Assistant Commissioner, Camilla Brace-Cosworthy, sat at her desk, upright and ready for business. She was an elegant woman in her fifties, and in her prime. She wore the MET dress uniform with its white blouse and checked neckerchief. Her shoulder-length blonde hair was immaculately coiffed, and her makeup was camera-ready.

"Come in, Erika. Do take a seat," she said, her posh accent emphasizing the "do." "Of course, you know Commander Marsh," she added, indicating him beside her with a flutter of red nail-varnished fingers.

"Yes, hello, sir," said Erika, taking the chair in front of the desk. "Congratulations on your new appointment, ma'am."

Camilla batted the compliment away, and slipped on a pair of large designer black-framed glasses.

"Time will tell if I can live up to the hype," she said through magnified eyes. "So, the Jessica Collins case. You recovered her remains on Friday, and they've been officially identified?"

"Yes, ma'am."

Erika saw Camilla had a file on her desk, and was flipping through it.

"You've worked on several Murder Investigation Teams, both in London and in Manchester?"

"Yes, ma'am."

Camilla closed the file, and removed her glasses, and tapped one of the stems on her teeth for a moment.

"Your move to Bromley was clearly a demotion. Why?"

"Erika felt she was being overlooked," said Marsh.

"There was an opportunity for a promotion to superintendent, for which I believe I was overlooked," corrected Erika. "By your predecessor, ma'am. This was at the time when I successfully caught the Night Stalker killer who—"

"Yes! Went on *quite* the rampage," exclaimed Camilla. Erika couldn't tell if it was an exclamation of horror or admiration.

"When I heard that I had been overlooked for the promotion, I challenged Commander Marsh, who was my senior officer at the time, and I threatened to leave. He took me up on it."

Erika looked across at Marsh, who was frowning. She realized this wasn't making her look good.

"But it's Commander Marsh who has been quite insistent that you are put in place as the Senior Investigating Officer on the Jessica Collins case," said Camilla.

"I feel that Erika still has much she can offer..." Marsh began to explain.

Camilla replaced her glasses, and consulted the file.

"You've had quite a checkered career, Erika. Along with the Night Stalker, you were responsible for catching multiple murderer Barry Paton—"

"The York Strangler, ma'am."

"I have it all here. The York Strangler killed eight schoolgirls, and you made quite a leap, identifying him on CCTV from his reflection caught in a shop window across from an ATM."

"Yes, and he still thanks me for it every Christmas and birthday."

Marsh grinned, but Camilla did not. "You weren't so lucky with some of your other cases. You were suspended two years ago pending an investigation."

"I was subsequently cleared, ma'am—"

"If you'll let me finish. You were suspended pending an investigation. You led a drug raid on a house in Greater Manchester, resulting in the deaths of five officers, one of whom was your husband."

Erika nodded.

"How do you come back from that?" asked Camilla, watching her closely.

"I received counseling. I almost lost track of who I was, and I questioned if I wanted to stay in the force. But I did come back, and the results are in the file in front of you."

"I need a safe pair of hands to navigate the reopening of this investigation. Why do you think you're the one for the job?"

"I'm not a career police officer. I dedicate myself totally to my cases. This was a vulnerable seven-year-old girl who disappeared, and someone dumped her like a bag of rubbish in that quarry. I want to find who did this. I want justice for Jessica. I want her family to be able to move on and grieve."

Erika sat back, sweating.

"Justice for Jessica, we could use that," said Marsh.

"No." Camilla shot him a withering look. "Erika, would you mind waiting outside? Thank you."

Erika went back out to the waiting area and took a seat. So many times she thought her career was over, and here she was again, at the start of something exciting. *Was she at the edge of a step up, or a precipice*? Within a few minutes there was a chime from the secretary's phone behind the desk, and she was asked to go back in to the office.

Camilla was pulling her police jacket on and straightening her hair. Marsh stood patiently by her desk.

"Erika, I'm pleased to say that I'd like to put you in as the Senior Investigating Officer on the Jessica Collins case," she said.

"Thank you, ma'am. You won't regret your decision."

Camilla carefully pulled on her braided cap. "I hope not." She came around the desk to shake Erika's hand. "Gosh. You're very tall. Do you have trouble finding trousers that fit?"

For a moment Erika was thrown. "Er, I did, but online shopping has made things easier—"

"It has, hasn't it?" she said, taking Erika's hand in both of hers for a hearty shake. "Right. Well, I have to fly, I'm due at a meeting with the Commissioner. Commander Marsh will brief you on the full details."

"Please give my regards to Sir Brian," said Marsh.

Camilla nodded and showed them to the door.

Erika and Marsh rode down in the lift in silence.

"That felt too easy," said Erika finally.

"No one really wants the case," replied Marsh. "The MIT was glad to hand it over. You'll be running things from the incident room at Bromley; I'll be overseeing, and you'll report to me."

"What about Superintendent Yale?"

"Hasn't he got enough on his plate?"

"He thinks I went behind his back."

"You did go behind his back."

"But it wasn't personal."

"Things always seem personal with you, Erika."

"What does that mean?"

Marsh blew out his cheeks. "I never know what you're thinking. You're direct to the point of being brutal. You don't trust many people."

"And?"

"And, it's tough to work with that."

"If I were a male DCI, would we be having this conversation in a lift? Would you be asking what I'm thinking?"

Marsh scowled and looked away.

"What's going on here? Is this about the other night?"

Marsh looked at the floor for a moment then back up at her. "You need to do your job here, Erika, and you need to do it well."

"Yes, sir."

"I'll be making arrangements for all files and materials relating to the two previous investigations to be sent over to Bromley Station," said Marsh, now sounding businesslike. "You need to get your incident room up and running, and I'll be briefing with your team tomorrow at 3 p.m."

"So are you in charge or am I?"

"You are, but you'll report to me; I'll report to the Assistant Commissioner. You'll also need to work closely with Superintendent Yale as you'll be utilizing his resources."

"Do I get to choose my team?"

"Within reason."

"Good. I want DI Moss and DI Peterson. They're both good officers."

Marsh nodded as the lift reached the ground floor and the doors opened. They stepped out into the large reception area.

"Erika, the screw-ups on the last investigation were huge. One of the suspects successfully sued the MET, and was awarded over three hundred grand in compensation...We only narrowly avoided an official inquiry."

"*Now* you tell me."

"Just make this right, Erika. Find out what happened to Jessica Collins. What's the first thing you're planning to do as SIO?"

"I have to tell the Collins family we've found Jessica," said Erika, her heart sinking.

CHAPTER 11

Marianne Collins unlocked her front door and shuffled into the hallway, carrying food shopping and a small black garment bag. She set the shopping bags down on the dark red carpet by a large wooden staircase, and stopped for a moment to catch her breath. It was a dark and dingy afternoon. She'd left all the lights on, but the bright hallway didn't feel welcoming on her return. It was silent, save for the clock ticking in the living room, and the large house seemed to hang over her with a chill gloom.

She hung the garment bag on the coat stand by the door, and gently unzipped the front. There was a rustle of plastic and the smell of dry cleaning chemicals wafted out. Taking great care, she removed a small red coat on a white padded hanger. It had once been a deep crimson, but after being cleaned several times over the years it was faded.

Marianne looked up at a framed photo on the wall between the coat stand and a full-length mirror. The photo had been taken on the eleventh of April, 1990. Jessica was sitting on a swing in the local park, her long blonde hair catching the sun, and she wore the small red coat over jeans and a Care Bears jumper. Marianne gently hung the coat on the stand and ran her fingers over the buttons, which had retained their crimson shine, she then moved it closer and buried her face in the material. It had been Jessica's seventh birthday present: the last birthday they got to celebrate.

It was a struggle to keep the memories of her daughter fresh after twenty-six years. Upstairs in her dresser drawer she kept one of Jessica's T-shirts in a vacuum packed plastic bag, but over the years it had become stale and had taken on the aroma of Marianne's own hand cream. Time seemed intent on erasing all but her memories.

She pulled away from the coat as the tears came. She wiped her eyes and slipped off the smart black shoes she always wore to the supermarket. She caught herself in the mirror. Her long gray hair was parted and tied back at the nape of her neck, and seemed to drag her deeply lined face down at each side. She took off her jacket, and hung it beside the small red coat. Behind her and reflected in the mirror was a large painting of the Virgin Mary. Marianne reached into the pocket of her skirt and felt her rosary beads, and she twisted the beads around her gnarled fingers; words of prayer came to her lips, but she saw she had ice cream which needed to go into the freezer.

She crossed herself and took the shopping bags through to the kitchen. She filled the kettle and put a teabag in her favorite white mug. The past twenty-six years, the kitchen hadn't had much more than a lick of paint and the odd new appliance. This was the third fridge-freezer, though. Fixed to the door was a large square of white paper covered with a finger painting Jessica had made at nursery school when she was four.

Marianne opened the fridge-freezer and placed inside bacon, cheese, and ice cream. She closed the door, and she paused to look at the finger painting; small hand prints in yellow, red, and green. Fine white lines and creases criss-crossed each tiny palm where the paint hadn't reached. The original was tucked away in a drawer, wrapped in tissue paper. After several years on display, and much to Marianne's horror and dismay, the paint had started to fade, so she'd had it scanned. Even the original scan had been reprinted several times. Marianne ran a finger over it, noting the edges were starting to curl.

Her grief was ingrained; it was part of her now. The tears still came but she had learned to live with the pain, like a constant companion. Looking at the coat, the finger painting, catching sight of the photos of Jessica as she walked past her bedroom on her way to the bathroom—they were all part of her routine, and so was the pain.

The kettle clicked off and she filled her mug, dunking the teabag before fishing it out with a spoon to rest on the draining board. She was about to pour in the milk when the doorbell echoed through the house. She looked at the clock and saw it was just after four.

She wasn't expecting anyone, and people rarely called unannounced.

CHAPTER 12

Erika stood nervously at the stout wooden front door of number 7 Avondale Road with John and retired Detective Constable Nancy Greene, a small, feisty woman whose gray hair had been cut down to short bristles. They'd parked on the road, and walked down the long sloping driveway which opened out into a small courtyard dotted with large terra-cotta pots. In each was a hydrangea, now brown and dry, and they rustled in the wind. A row of bushes at the top of the front garden screened the house from the road above, and through the bare branches an orange streetlight flicked on.

"The nights are really drawing in," said Nancy, breaking the silence, adding, "Someone's at home; I can see light through the front window."

She pressed the bell again, just as the door opened.

"Hello Marianne," smiled Nancy weakly.

Erika had never seen such a pale washed-out woman. Marianne had pasty weathered skin. Her eyes were gray, with deep dark circles underneath. Her steel gray hair hung down past her waist, and was parted and swept back covering her ears. She wore a gray long-sleeved polo neck, black woolen cardigan and an A-line black skirt. A large wooden crucifix hung on a chain from her neck. Her eyes darted between Nancy, Erika and John.

"Marianne, this is Detective Chief Inspector Erika Foster and Detective Constable John McGorry," said Nancy.

John and Erika both held up their IDs. Marianne barely glanced at it.

"Nancy? Why are you here? Is it Laura or Toby...is everyone okay?" Her voice had a hard edge, with the hint of an Irish accent.

"Everyone is fine," said Nancy. "However—"

"Please can we come in, Mrs. Collins?" asked Erika. "It's very important that we speak to you in private. DC Greene, Nancy, has kindly attended, because she was your Family Liaison Officer. Back when your daughter disappeared—"

"What is this? Tell me?" asked Marianne, reaching out a hand to Nancy.

"Marianne, can we please come inside?" said Nancy, as she took the offered hand.

She nodded, and stood to one side to let them in. Marianne showed them through to a large living room. It was elegant but cold, with dark wood furniture, dark red wallpaper, and thick curtains in deep green which matched the furniture.

"Please sit. Would anyone like tea? I've just made a cup," said Marianne, forcing herself to sound bright and happy.

"No, thank you," said Nancy.

They sat on the large sofa under the window. Erika noticed a large painting of the Virgin Mary above the carved wood fireplace, and with a glance around the room counted four crucifixes of varying size on the walls. There were gilt framed pictures of Jessica on every surface: the small tables dotted around, along the windowsill, and a large concentration on a baby grand piano in one corner. Despite this, there were no signs the room was ever used. No magazines, no television or books. Marianne stayed standing, twisting her rosary beads in her fingers.

"We've tried to call your family, but we can't get hold of them," said Nancy.

"They're all out in Spain. Toby and Laura have gone to see their father with his new, well, she's not his wife—"

"We'll need to talk to them…" Nancy started to say.

Marianne's fingers twisted faster, the rosary beads clicking; the small silver cross dangled and swayed against her skirt. Her bottom lip started to tremble and tears pooled in her eyes. "Let me make some tea; would you all like tea?"

"Marianne, please sit down," said Nancy.

"I'll do what I fucking well like in my fucking house!" she suddenly shouted.

"Okay. Please Marianne, please calm down; I need you to listen to what I'm about to say," said Nancy, getting up and taking Marianne by the hands.

"No! No! NO!"

"DCI Foster here phoned me earlier today, because I was here for you when—"

"No!"

"When Jessica—"

"No. Don't say her name. You don't have the right!"

Erika glanced at John. He gulped and was very pale. Nancy went on, gently: "When Jessica disappeared."

"No. No…"

Nancy looked back and nodded to Erika to carry on.

"Mrs. Collins, on Friday night, myself and DC McGorry

were conducting a routine search of Hayes Quarry, and we found some human remains. A skeleton."

Marianne was now silent. Her eyes wide and glassy. She shook her head and started walking backward until her back was against the wall. Nancy stayed with her.

"The skeleton belongs...It was Jessica," said Erika softly.

Marianne shook her head; tears were flowing down her cheeks.

"No. You've made a mistake! She'll come back; someone will find her. She's out there. She probably can't remember who her real family is. I only just had her coat cleaned today..."

Erika and John stayed sitting.

"I'm so sorry, Marianne. They found Jessica." Nancy had tears in her eyes, too. "They've identified her from dental records."

Marianne kept shaking her head, tears streaming silently down her face.

"Mrs. Collins," said Erika softly. "We need to inform your husband, your daughter, Laura, and your son, Toby. They're all in Spain, is that correct? Do you have a number we can call? We'd like the family to be informed before we make a statement to the press."

"Yes," said Marianne softly. Her eyes were wide in disbelief.

"What can I do, Marianne?" asked Nancy.

Marianne turned her head to Nancy, and suddenly pulled her hand back and punched her in the face. Nancy staggered backward, blood pouring from her nose, and crashed onto the coffee table.

"Get out of my house! All of you!" screamed Marianne. "Get out! GET OUT!"

John and Erika leapt up and went to Nancy, whose face

was a bloodied mess. Marianne was screaming, and she sank down against the wall.

Through the front bay window came the sound of cars arriving, and lights began to flare. The press had heard the news and was descending on the house once again.

CHAPTER 13

Ten miles away, in a small terraced house on a quiet residential street in Balham in southeast London, the television buzzed and flickered from the corner of a messy living room. The afternoon was fading behind low gray clouds, and retired DCI Amanda Baker sat slumped in a saggy armchair; her head flopped forward, sleeping. The lights were off, and the light from the TV screen played over her loose jowly face, a burst of studio audience laughter failing to wake her. On a small table at her elbow was an overflowing ashtray and a half-full glass of white wine. This was all that was left of the second bottle she'd opened. She'd pulled the cork on the first at 9:30 a.m., when the breakfast dishes had been stacked in the sink, and the shakes and sweats got too bad.

Her house had been smart. It was decorated in a cold elegant style, much like its owner had looked, but now, like its owner, it was shabby. A fake glow fire rippled in hues of red and orange in the hearth, and a dog's basket beside it was covered in a thick layer of dust.

The phone started ringing in the hall, screeching above

the sound of the TV until it went to voicemail. It was then that Amanda woke.

"What was that?" she said absently.

There was a barking sound, and she rubbed a hand over her face, heaved herself up from the chair and wobbled through to the kitchen, brain foggy, and eyes bleary. She spent a few minutes rummaging through her cupboard full of tinned food, and then it came back to her. Her dog, Sandy, had died a few months ago. She stopped, leaning against the counter. Tears fell onto the crumb-covered work surface with a soft pat. She wiped her face with her sleeve, catching a whiff of her stale breath.

The phone shrieked again from the hallway, and she shuffled through and answered, leaning on the banister for support.

"Is this former Detective Chief Inspector Amanda Baker?" came a young female voice with an edge.

"Who is this?"

"I'm calling for a statement about Jessica Collins, now that the police have recovered her body."

Amanda rocked back on her heels for a moment, unable to speak.

"Hello?" said the voice impatiently. "You were the lead officer investigating, until you were fired from the case—"

"I took early retirement..."

"On Friday, Jessica Collins's skeleton was found in Hayes Quarry—"

"We searched that quarry a few weeks after she went missing. She wasn't there," said Amanda, more to herself than the woman on the phone.

From her spot slumped in the hall against the banister, Amanda could see the television screen in the living room: *BREAKING NEWS* was rolling across the screen.

A ticker tape headline ran underneath, reading: *REMAINS BELONGING TO MISSING GIRL JESSICA COLLINS DISCOVERED*. The sound was off, and the picture changed to show images of Marianne and Martin Collins at a police press conference in 1990, speaking into a microphone, supported by a much younger version of herself; behind them was the old MET police logo on white.

"So, do you have a comment?" asked the voice. She sounded interested, could smell blood. On the TV, a tall blonde officer was reading from a statement. Her name flashed up at the bottom of the screen: **DCI ERIKA FOSTER**.

"DO YOU HAVE A COMMENT?" said the girl, spelling it out; clearly now annoyed at the silence. "They found photos of Jessica in a local sex offender's house; you arrested him, but you let him go though, didn't you?"

"I had no choice! There wasn't enough evidence."

"He's still a free man. Do you think he killed Jessica Collins? Your actions in the months after showed you thought he was guilty. Do you think you've got blood on your hands?"

"Leave me alone!" shrieked Amanda, and she slammed down the phone.

As soon as it hit the cradle it began to ring again. She kneeled down on the floor pushing through piles of old newspapers, magazines, and junk mail. She grabbed the wire and yanked it out of the wall. The phone fell silent. She hurried through to the living room and turned up the sound.

"We'd like to extend our condolences to the Collins family. The case has been reopened, and we are actively pursuing several new leads. Thank you."

The camera zoomed out as Erika Foster went back into the main entrance of Bromley Police Station, flanked by two other officers. The image on the screen flicked back to the BBC news studio and the next news item.

Amanda sat back on her haunches and took deep breaths, her whole body shaking.

"No, no, no . . . this can't be happening," she groaned.

She noticed a small white squeaky toy rabbit peeping out from the piles of old junk. It had belonged to Sandy. She reached out, picked it up, and hugged it to her chest. She began to cry, for Jessica, for her beloved Sandy, and for the life she should have had.

When she finally stopped, she wiped her face with her sleeve, went to the kitchen and opened her third bottle of wine.

CHAPTER 14

It was dark and raining as Erika drove to the main entrance of Accident and Emergency at Lewisham Hospital. It had been a long stressful day, and she felt like she hadn't stopped.

Through the swishing wipers she saw DC Nancy Greene waiting under the canopy. An ambulance pulled away as an elderly lady was stretchered through the automatic doors, a withered arm poking out from under a red blanket and raised in pain.

Erika pulled up, and opened the passenger window. "We have to be quick; there's another ambulance coming up behind."

Nancy had a thick square bandage taped to her nose, spotted with blood. She opened the door and climbed in, clutching a small white paper bag.

"Broken. In two places. And they gave me six stitches," she said, touching the thick white bandage gingerly as she eased herself into the passenger seat.

It gave her nose a beaky quality, and with her large brown eyes looking over she reminded Erika of an owl. She helped Nancy fasten the seatbelt, then put the car in gear and pulled away.

"Thanks for coming. In all the chaos you were the last person I expected," said Nancy.

"I wanted to check you were okay. It was my idea to bring you in to tell Marianne; it backfired a bit . . ."

Nancy shifted in her seat and tilted her head back. "You think?" She laughed darkly. "I saw your statement on the TV in the waiting room. Where are you from? You've got this hint of a northern accent, but you look a bit, I don't know, Polish?"

"I'm Slovak," said Erika, trying to hide her annoyance at being mistaken. "I learned English in Manchester—"

"I couldn't live up North. I'm London born and bred. I can just about bear half an hour of *Coronation Street*, but it's always a relief when the credits start to roll." Erika bit her lip and put the windscreen wipers on a faster speed to deal with the rain pouring down. "Is Marianne okay?" added Nancy.

"DC McGorry called a doctor, and she's been prescribed something so she can sleep. Her family are booked on a flight back to London tonight. We had to tell them over the phone, which wasn't how I wanted to do it, but the press have already got hold of things." They reached the exit, and came to a stop behind a car waiting to pull out. "Where are we going, Nancy?"

"I'm the other side of Dulwich. Head through Forest Hill."

The car in front pulled out, and they could see the road was busy with rush hour traffic. A van slowed and let Erika pull out of the junction, and she waved thanks. The rain came down harder, pounding on the top of the line of cars stretching ahead of them.

"I thought you might help me out too, in return for a lift," said Erika.

"So your lift has an ulterior motive?" said Nancy. She tried to turn her head but winced.

"I'm trying to get up to speed on this case. You were the Family Liaison Officer the whole time from when Jessica disappeared?"

"Yeah, far too long, to be honest. It's all on record, but I can fill you in...Christ this hurts," she said, grimacing. She undid the paper bag, popped a pill out from a foil sheet, and swallowed it dry.

"I have to ask if you intend to press charges?" said Erika, inching the car forward in the traffic.

"Against Marianne? God no, that poor woman has been through enough," said Nancy, leaning back against the headrest. "Although I would like to complain about those bloody doctors. They've given me a pitiful amount of painkillers—"

"She punched you, and she had a string of rosary beads wrapped around her fist."

"A Catholic knuckleduster," grinned Nancy. "Marianne was never violent, in all the years, through all the heartbreak. Sometimes with Family Liaison work you feel like a spare part. You want to be out there on the beat, amongst the action, but you're making tea and answering the phone."

"Family Liaison work is important."

"I know that, but in a strange way I'm pleased I was there today to take the punch. They never write in police reports about all the cups of tea you make, or the advice you give. This will be documented. And, it's closure."

"How long were you there with the family after Jessica disappeared?"

"I spent the first few months, from the August of 1990 onwards, virtually living with them. Marianne and Martin were still together."

"When did they divorce?"

"They're not divorced. You saw the rosary beads around Marianne's fist. Divorce doesn't exist in her world. They separated in '97. They lasted longer than I expected. When a couple loses a child, the strain nearly always rips them apart. But they had little Toby, who was only four when Jessica vanished, and for a time he was the glue that kept them from coming unstuck. Laura is a lot older. She'd already done her first year at university. She delayed going back for her second year, but she should have gone, really. She and Marianne drove each other mad. And Marianne just tuned out everything, poured her energy into trying to find Jessica. Toby was tiny, and Laura ended up having to look after him."

"How old is Toby now?"

"Twenty-nine. He's gay. Not surprisingly, Marianne has never really accepted it."

"Does Toby live locally?"

"No. Edinburgh. Laura is married with two small boys and they live in North London. Martin is in Spain. He let Marianne keep the house. He's a millionaire; I think he makes sure she's taken care of... She just rattles around in that big house all day like she's Miss Havisham. Heartbroken. Although, unlike Miss Havisham, Marianne always pushes the vacuum cleaner around. You saw. The place is spotless."

"What does Martin do in Spain?"

"He builds holiday homes for rich expats. Makes a fortune. Lives in Malaga with his girlfriend, a younger woman, and their two small kids."

Erika was pleased the line of traffic was inching forward. Nancy was a goldmine of information.

"Do you know how Martin and Marianne met?" she asked.

"In Ireland. He's Irish; Marianne is British but she grew

up in Galway. She met Martin when they were in their late teens, at a Catholic youth club. She fell pregnant at seventeen, and they had to marry...I knew I was getting close to Marianne when she told me that story. It was in Ireland in the late seventies. They had a tough start, but he worked his way up on the building sites, and then they made the move to London in 1983 just after Jessica was born. They did it at the right time; made a packet during the property boom. Laura was fourteen when they moved, and I think it was tough for her. She had to leave her friends and her home in Ireland."

"Is that when the problems began?"

Nancy nodded, then winced, again remembering she was bandaged. The traffic was now moving faster, and they inched their way through a set of traffic lights.

"I think Laura found it tough to find her feet when they moved here. When she was growing up they were dirt poor. It wasn't until Laura was in her late teens that they started making money. They were rich enough to spoil Jessica and Toby; they joined so many after-school clubs. Jessica did ballet...She was such a pretty little thing, Jessica."

The traffic inched forward, past the closed shops on Catford High Street. Only a West Indian supermarket was open, and beside it a betting shop. Through the condensation of the brightly lit window they could see a group of old men standing around, peering up at a screen.

"Do you really think you're going to solve it, after all these years?" asked Nancy.

If Erika had any doubts, she wasn't going to share them. "I always solve my cases," she said.

"Well, good luck to you...Just watch out. She went mad—that copper who was on the case before—Amanda Baker."

"How did she go mad?"

"Years in Borough CID dealing with rape victims. It got to her. And then the Jessica case. There were no witnesses. Jessica left the house that afternoon to go to her friend's birthday party down the road, and it was as if she vanished off the face of the earth. She never arrived, no one saw anything. The only suspect was Trevor Marksman, a local sex offender. They found photos and some video he'd taken of Jessica a few weeks earlier, when she was in the park with Marianne and Laura."

"And they arrested him?"

"They did, but he had an alibi. Cast iron. He'd only just been released from prison, and was living in a halfway house. And on the seventh of August, he was there all day. Multiple witnesses could vouch that he didn't leave, including two probation officers. But he was the person with a motive to abduct her. He had a previous conviction for abducting a young girl from the park; she was blonde too, and looked like Jessica. In the end, Amanda had no choice but to release him. They kept surveillance on him, and as time went on she got frustrated and started to harass him. And in return, he enjoyed riling her up, taunting her about her failure to solve the case. In the end she went too far and tipped off a group of local women, vigilantes. Middle of the night they shoved a bottle full of petrol through his letterbox. He survived, but with hideous burns."

"And it came back on Amanda?"

Nancy nodded. "Trevor Marksman found a fancy barrister, and sued the MET. Won three hundred grand. He moved to Vietnam, filthy bastard. Amanda took early retirement, more than she deserved really, but her legacy is that she's a bent copper. The last I heard is that she's virtually dead from cirrhosis of the liver... Here, take the next left."

Erika was disappointed that the journey had come to an

end. She pulled off the main road where the traffic was moving normally. They passed a large pub and some kebab shops before the street became residential.

"This is me, the flats," said Nancy.

There was a gap in the row of terraces, occupied by a drab squat concrete block of flats. Erika pulled up by the curb.

"Thanks for the lift. I'm going to take one more of these strong ones with a nip of something," she said, undoing her seatbelt. It was still raining hard. She winced as she pulled up her hood, catching the edge of the bandage.

"Who do you think did it? Who do you think killed Jessica?" asked Erika, leaning over to peer out of the passenger door.

"God knows... maybe the only motive is that someone randomly snatched her and drove away," said Nancy, ducking down, adding, "you've found Jessica's body, maybe there's only one person who truly vanished into thin air... the person who took her."

CHAPTER 15

It was late when Erika arrived back at Bromley Station. She'd been assigned one of the large open-plan offices on the top floor as her incident room. She couldn't shake off Nancy's parting words, "Now you've found Jessica's body, maybe there's only one person who truly vanished into thin air. The person who took her."

When she came into the incident room, desks were being added to the space, and a technician was busy connecting up their workstations to the Holmes computer system, bringing the hardwiring up from the cables running under the floor. Several officers she hadn't been introduced to yet were on phone calls. Another two officers, a man and a woman, were working to assemble the case evidence gleaned so far onto whiteboards running the length of the back wall.

A huge map of South London and the Kent borders dominated one corner, and a thin female officer with short black hair was pinning up photos beside it, which included Hayes Quarry and 7 Avondale Road. An overweight male officer with sandy-colored hair and rabbit-like teeth was sorting a series of pictures on the table beside her. They were of Jessica Collins dressed in her party outfit, a photo of her skeleton laid out in the mortuary. Another photo showed the brown and tattered remnants of her clothes after years underwater.

"Hello, I'm Detective Chief Inspector Foster," said Erika.

"I'm DC Knight," said the woman, shaking her hand. "And this is DC Crawford."

"I can talk for myself," he snapped. He leaned over and shook Erika's hand. His was cold and clammy.

Knight ignored him and carried on. "We're putting a timeline together: Jessica's movements in the days leading up to the seventh of August when she left 7 Avondale Road. I'm working from the original missing person report and all the statements, but the case notes on the Holmes system are limited."

The Holmes computer system was used by police forces across the country to catalog and index case files. It had been introduced in 1985, and had taken several years for some forces to adopt fully. Knight went on: "DC McGorry has taken delivery of the hard copy case files. He should be back shortly. I think he went to get something to eat."

"Who's this?" asked Erika, picking up a yellowing photo. It was a mugshot of a thirty-five-year-old man with cold blue eyes, greasy blond hair and a pudgy face.

"That's Trevor Marksman," said Crawford, leaning through them to pick it up. "Nasty looking kiddy fiddler, isn't he? Although, this is what he looks like now."

He sifted through the photos and held up another picture of a man with hideous burns to his face and neck. He stared straight into the camera, his skin shiny and red. The only similarity to the first photo was the same cold blue eyes looking out from under the mask of skin grafts. He had no hair, eyebrows or lashes.

"He lives in Vietnam," said Erika, taking the photo. She held it at the edges, not wanting to touch his face.

"Yes, we've got an address in Hanoi, but I don't know if it's up to date," said Knight. "I'm working on more."

"I'm working on it too; we're working together," said Crawford. There was something childish about the way he said it, as if he wanted Erika to know he was working just as hard.

She handed him back the photo.

"Don't say 'kiddy fiddler.' It makes a joke of something horrific. Use sex offender, or pedophile. Okay?" Crawford took it from her, his cheeks flushed, and he nodded. "Do you think this will be ready for tomorrow morning?"

"Yes, ma'am," said Knight.

"Call me boss, please."

"Yes, boss."

John walked through the door with a takeaway box and a can of Coke, and came over to Erika, stuffing some chips in his mouth.

"John, I'm told we've got the hard copies of the Jessica Collins case files?"

John waved his hand in front of his mouth. "Oh, sorry, hot," he said, his mouth full. He swallowed them down with a gulp of Coke. "Sorry, boss. I haven't eaten all day. Yes. We've also had the official autopsy report through from Dr. Strong. I put it on your desk."

"Where is my desk?"

"In your office."

"I've got an office?"

"Up the back there," he said, pointing with a chip.

Erika turned and saw the large glass box at the back of the incident room. It was crammed chest high with white document boxes. She moved over to the door, and John followed. In the middle of the boxes she could just make out a desk.

"Whose idea was it to put them all in here? How am I supposed to get through the door?!" she snapped.

"I didn't know there was so much. I just said to put them in your office—"

"And this is absolutely everything?" she asked.

"Yes. The Specialist Casework Investigation Team sent everything over that they have in storage. Some boxes are marked in date order from 1991 up to 1995, and then some are marked up with the names of locations, and then there are a load with no label at all, where files have been stuffed in with no regard—"

The phone rang from inside Erika's office. John helped her to quickly slide a pile of the boxes out so she could lean through and pick it up. It was Marsh.

"What have you got from the historical case files?" he asked without preamble.

"I've just literally got them, sir."

"Are you putting together a list of suspects? I'd like to see it as soon as possible."

"I had a chat with DC Greene who was the Family Liaison on the case. She gave me a good insight, but I need more manpower to get through this stuff," said Erika, looking around with dismay at it all.

"OK, I'll see what I can do. Did you see the papers?"

As he was speaking, John handed her a slightly rain-splattered copy of the *Evening Standard*, and she saw that the discovery of Jessica Collins had made the front page of the evening edition.

"Yes, I've got a copy."

"Yes, for some reason they forgot to include the number for the incident room. But Colleen Scanlan and the Media Liaison Team is on it, and they should be adding it to the online edition any minute now. Martin Collins is flying in to the UK late tonight with the rest of the family. He's asked for a meeting with the SIO and Media Liaison first thing tomorrow."

"I have a briefing first thing tomorrow, sir," she answered, bristling. "Then I was planning to meet with the family—"

"Well, Martin Collins wants assurances that this case will be dealt with properly after the fiasco it turned into last time. Erika, we need results on this one."

"I'm untangling a web here, sir. I'm serious about more manpower. We need to work through these files fast. Then I can start giving you a list of suspects."

"OK, leave it with me," said Marsh. He hung up.

She leaned through the boxes and replaced the phone. John bit his lip nervously, seeing how annoyed Erika looked.

"Superintendent Yale called. He's still waiting for the Jason Tyler report...Says you promised it to him yesterday?"

"Damn!"

"Sure you don't want a chip?" asked John, offering her the bag. She took one and popped it in her mouth, then pulled out one of the boxes marked "7 August 1990."

"Let's start from the beginning," she said, feeling daunted.

CHAPTER 16

Erika was bleary-eyed when she arrived at Bromley the next morning. She'd stayed late, making a start on the Jessica Collins case files, and finishing the Jason Tyler report, and had only grabbed a few hours' sleep.

When she got out of her car in the underground car park, she heard a whistle and saw two familiar faces coming toward her.

"Boss! Bloody good to see you!" cried Detective Inspector Moss. She was a small compact woman with short red hair tucked behind her ears, and her pale face was a mass of freckles. She rushed forward and grabbed Erika in a bear hug.

"She's very excited to see you," said a tall black officer, joining them a moment later. It was Detective Inspector Peterson, cool and handsome in a sharp black suit.

"Okay. I can't breathe," said Erika, laughing. Moss broke free and took a step back.

"I thought you'd forgotten about us?"

"It's been crazy. I was reassigned here as a spare part and suddenly they piled me high with cases," said Erika, feeling guilty that she hadn't kept in touch with her former colleagues.

"Go on, Peterson, give the boss a hug too," joked Moss.

He rolled his eyes. "Good to see you, boss." He grinned, leaned forward and gave her a pat on the shoulder.

She smiled back and there was an awkward silence.

"Do you need parking permits?" asked Erika.

"Just one, we came in my car; Peterson's waiting to be assigned a new one," said Moss.

"It died at the Sun-in-the-Sands roundabout last week," he said. "Total nightmare, the middle of rush hour. There were cars honking like mad, smoke was pouring out from under my bonnet."

"You should see the bonnet, boss, he looks *really* good in it. I told him not to wear it today—"

"Piss off, Moss," said Peterson.

"He's just being modest, boss. The frills framed his face... Made him look like a baby Idris Elba."

Erika burst out laughing. "Sorry, Peterson," she said.

"'S'alright," he grinned.

Erika had forgotten just how much she enjoyed working with Moss and Peterson, and how much she'd missed them. They reached the lift at the end of the car park, and she pressed the call button.

"It's good to have you both here, thank you. Although, I don't think we'll be laughing much more today. This case is going to be tough."

The incident room was full when they came up to the top floor. Erika introduced Moss and Peterson, and was pleased to see that she'd been assigned six additional CID officers to work on the case files.

Erika stared at the rows of faces waiting expectantly.

"Good morning, everyone. Thank you for making your-selves available so quickly..." She went on to give them a brief outline of the Jessica Collins case, and the develop-ments so far. "With this case we're opening a Pandora's box, or should I say, many boxes," she added, alluding to the case files which were now piled high along the back wall. "What we all need to do is focus in on the facts pertaining to Jes-sica's disappearance. Ignore the fiction. We can't predict how the discovery of Jessica Collins's remains will run in the media, but we have to stay ahead of things. And unlike the 1990s, the challenge may be even greater. We now have rolling news, social media, blogs and online forums, all of which will dredge things up and regurgitate them 24/7. So, these files along the wall need to be revisited, top to tail, and fast. I need all witness statements to be revisited and cross-checked. I want to know everything about Hayes Quarry. What it's been used for over the years. Why was Jessica's body never found? I'm going straight from here to meet with the Collins family, who will no doubt have many questions for me. I need you to hit the ground running with this one."

Detective Constable Knight then stood to take them through the timeline of events leading up to the disappear-ance of Jessica Collins.

"How much do you want me to explain about location, boss?" she asked.

"Imagine we know nothing. We don't live near Hayes. We've never heard of Jessica Collins. We are all hearing this for the first time... And remember," Erika added, "there are never any stupid questions. If you don't understand some-thing, shout."

She leaned against a desk, and Knight moved to a giant four-meter-square map on the back wall.

"This map covers an area of twenty miles from top to

bottom. In the middle is Central London, and the bottom of the map, down south, is the Kent borders, and here we are in Bromley," she said, indicating a large red cross on the map. "We're 2.6 miles from Hayes village. It's a popular commuter belt village; lots of people who live there work in the city of London. It takes thirty minutes to get into the center of London by train, and it has a higher than average population of retired people. Property prices are high, and it's a predominantly white demographic area."

Knight then nodded to Crawford, who moved to a laptop set up on a desk and activated a projector. It shone a larger scale map on a blank square of whiteboard. Knight moved to one side of it and went on: "This is a larger scale map of Hayes Common and village. You can see the high street and the train station. This vast area of green is Hayes Common. It's an area of woodland and heath, crossed by bridleways and footpaths, and several roads. It's one of the largest areas of common land in Greater London, at 225 acres.

"There are multiple access points to the common: Prestons Road, West Common Road, Five Elms Road, Croydon Road, Baston Road, Baston Manor Road, and Commonside. Hayes Quarry, where Jessica's remains were discovered, is situated here." She moved her hand to the southeast area of the common, where Croydon Road, Baston Road and Commonside cut through the green to form a large upside-down triangle.

"The quarry was created between 1906 and 1914, when sand and gravel were excavated. Over the years it has twice been filled and cleared; during the Second World War there was an army base at Hayes Common and anti-aircraft guns. In 1980 the quarry was cleared for the second time by archaeologists as part of a wider dig looking for Bronze Age relics. After this, it was left to fill with water. Bromley

Council twice put forward applications to have the quarry used for commercial fishing, but on both occasions the idea was overturned as the common is a site of nature conservation interest, and is protected."

She paused and moved to the other side of the map, the projection of the roads playing over her tired face like arteries.

"I'll now move on to the timeline of events leading up to the disappearance of Jessica Collins. She lived here with her family in 7 Avondale Road, which is less than a mile from Hayes Quarry; the closest entrance being here on Baston Road. You can see the houses on Avondale Road are all detached with large gardens. It's an affluent area. On Saturday, the seventh of August, 1990, at 1:45 p.m., Jessica left her house to go to a birthday party for her school friend, Kelly Morrison, who lived at number 27 Avondale Road. It was only a short walk of around five hundred meters, but she never arrived. The alarm wasn't raised until 3:30 p.m. when Kelly's mother phoned Marianne to ask where Jessica was."

She nodded at Crawford, who went to the laptop and clicked the mouse. The "Perez Hilton" webpage came up with a photo of Kim Kardashian leaving a Starbucks.

"Whoops!" he chuckled. "My bad. But I bet I'm not the only one in here who is keeping up with the Kardashians!"

There was a deathly silence. Smirks passed between some of the officers dotted around the incident room. Moss caught Erika's eye and raised an eyebrow.

"Here we go," he said, blushing. The projection changed to a Google Street View image; Knight shot him a look and then carried on.

"This is where Baston Road leaves the common and becomes Avondale Road." The Google Street View blurred forward in bursts, the image moving past the houses on

Avondale Road. "You can see that the houses are all large, two or three stories. They're all set back from the street and many of them have high hedges or trees masking them from the road...Here we are passing 7 Avondale Road, the Collins house...and we're moving forward to number 27 Avondale Road. I'm trying to get hold of images of the street from twenty-six years ago."

The Google Street View surged forward past better-appointed houses. A postman was frozen mid-walk, his face blurred, his hand deep in his mailbag. Further along, a woman was emerging from one of the driveways with a small dog. From the back she had short curly blonde hair.

"There we are passing number twenty-seven, home of Jessica's friend, Kelly Morrison. You can see that Avondale Road curves sharply to the left, where it becomes Marsden Road." The Google Street View blurred forward and came to focus on a large manor house painted a buttery yellow with a grand pillared entrance. "This is now the Swann Retirement Home, but twenty-six years ago it was used as a halfway house for convicted sex offenders. Its existence wasn't made public, and it only came to light shortly after Jessica's disappearance. One of its residents, Trevor Marksman, was the main focus for the original investigation. Photographs and home video of Jessica were found in his room on the top floor. He was also spotted by a neighbor hanging around outside their house on the afternoon of the fifth of August, on the sixth around the same time, and on the morning of the seventh. He was arrested two weeks later, and kept in custody for questioning, but no evidence, beyond the photos and video he had taken of Jessica, was found to link him to her disappearance."

"But this was a halfway house *filled* with convicted sex offenders; there must have been more suspects than just Trevor Marksman?" asked Moss.

"Yes, but security at the halfway house was strict, and at 1:30 p.m. on the seventh of August the weekly meeting was called with the residents and the probation officers. A register was called at 1:30 p.m. All the residents were accounted for. The meeting went on for two hours until just after 3:30 p.m. No one left. Kelly Morrison's mother phoned Marianne Collins at 3:30 p.m., asking where Jessica was. Shortly afterward they started searching."

"But now we have a body," said Moss.

"We have Jessica's remains, but there is virtually no forensic evidence after twenty-six years underwater," said Erika.

Knight went on: "All members of Jessica's immediate family have an alibi. Marianne and Martin were both at home with Toby. An elderly neighbor and her husband stopped by at 1:40 p.m., a Mr. and Mrs. O'Shea, now deceased. They were there when Jessica left and they stayed until the alarm was raised. Their oldest daughter, Laura, was two hundred and forty miles away on a camping trip with her boyfriend, Oscar Browne, in the Gower Peninsula in Wales. They'd left early the day before."

She looked at the room. "The results of a door-to-door weren't helpful, most neighbors were out, and those who were in had strong alibis. As you saw in the Google Street Map, most houses are blind to Avondale Road; we have a two-hour period where anything could have happened. There were few tradesmen; there is no post on a Saturday afternoon. Back in 1990 very little of the area was covered by CCTV. No busses travel down Avondale Road."

Silence fell over the room for a moment before Crawford put the lights back on. Erika moved to the front and stood by the map, now faint under the strip lights.

"Thank you. And perhaps, Crawford, you could keep your laptop for work purposes."

"Yes, I'm very sorry. It won't happen again," he sputtered.

Erika went on: "I need everyone's focus, and if any of you feel you're losing focus, take a look at this picture." She indicated the autopsy photo of Jessica's skeleton lying like a completed jigsaw on a blue sheet. "We're having to hit the ground running here with a huge amount of historical case files. However, this should be seen as a positive. The case files could yield much more. We also have the benefit of hindsight. I'd like you to divide the boxes up. DI Moss will be in charge of this. I'd like you to revisit all the evidence on Trevor Marksman; I'd also like you to pay attention to the role of the SIO on the historical case: DCI Amanda Baker—"

"I knew Amanda," interrupted Crawford. "I was a PC on this case back in 1990."

"Why didn't you mention this before?" asked Erika. The officers in the room turned to Crawford, who stood by the door. He blew his cheeks out.

"Um, well, I figured I would when there was time, it's been hectic—"

"I spoke to you and DC Knight yesterday when you were preparing this talk. You didn't think it was relevant? Or that you could have given us some insight?"

Everyone was now staring at Crawford. He blew out his cheeks again, and this habit was getting on Erika's nerves.

"There's been a lot said about DCI Baker..." he started. "I always thought she was dealing with forces from both sides. She had the Collins family criticizing her, and she had a lot of the top brass at the time briefing behind her back. It wasn't right."

"We know this. Can you tell me anything else?"

"Um. I was involved with the searches around Hayes Common and the quarry, in August and September 1990.

The Marine Unit also searched the water. We . . . They didn't find anything," he said.

"So Jessica could have been kept alive, or killed in another location, and her body dumped at a later date," said Erika.

"I didn't have access to anything that went on in the incident room. Back then I was just a uniformed PC, full of enthusiasm . . . Life had yet to sand me down," he said with an awkward chuckle.

It hung in the air for a moment, and he shifted awkwardly by the door. His face still blotchy and red. Erika made a mental note to pull his file. She figured he was in his late forties; she hadn't seen him at Bromley Station in the three months she had been there.

"Okay, everyone, I'd like your main priority to be reviewing the physical evidence. Once we get a hold of what's in all of these boxes we can move forward. We'll reconvene tomorrow morning for a progress report."

The room leapt into life. Erika went over to where Moss and Peterson were sitting next to her office.

"Peterson, you're with me. We're talking to the Collins family. Moss, keep an eye on things here, and—" She tipped her head toward Crawford, who was trying to untie a laptop charger which had become twisted in knots.

"You want me to pull his file?" she said quietly.

"Yeah, but be subtle."

Moss nodded, and Erika left the busy incident room with Peterson.

CHAPTER 17

A tall, lean, tanned man opened the door to 7 Avondale Road. His head was shaved, just a shadow around the edges showed that he was bald on top, and his face had a smattering of black-gray stubble. He wore black chinos and a navy shirt with the sleeves rolled up to show muscular forearms, and expensive black leather loafers. When he introduced himself as Martin Collins it was a shock to Erika. He was a youthful and polished sixty-something in comparison to Marianne, who looked every inch a pensioner.

"We're all in the lounge," he growled; he still had a strong Irish accent.

They followed Martin through; his expensive aftershave cutting through the fusty church-like smell of the house.

Erika introduced herself and Peterson. Marianne sat at the end of the long sofa next to the fireplace. She was dressed head to toe in black, which accentuated her deathly pallor. She was clutching her rosary wrapped so tight around her right hand it dug in to her skin. Next to her sat an attractive dark-haired woman in her forties. She was heavily made-up, and wore a designer trouser suit in black with a white blouse. Her brown eyes were bloodshot and detached.

"Hello, officers, this is my daughter, Laura," said Marianne, indicating the woman.

Laura stood and shook hands with Erika and Peterson. A handsome young man with dark features sat in an armchair beside the long sofa. He too was fashionably dressed in a black suit. He stood and introduced himself as Toby; next to him was a thin handsome Indian man with dark shoulder-length hair. He wore a black silk suit.

"This is my fiancé, Tanvir," Toby added.

They all shook hands. Marianne bit her lip and looked imploringly at Martin.

"What?" said Toby.

"Tobes. Your mother asked that it just be family," said Martin.

"Tanvir is my family, and I'd like him here. It wasn't a problem that Laura have her husband here or her kids—"

"But I didn't bring Todd," snapped Laura. "He's looking after Thomas and Michael."

She took her mother's free hand in hers. Toby opened his mouth to reply.

"I'd like to give you all our condolences. We realize this is a very distressing time," said Erika.

Seeing the rest of the family was a shock; they seemed so vibrant and stylish in comparison to Marianne.

"Yes. Please, take a seat, officers," said Marianne. She indicated a couple of high-backed dining chairs in front of the sofas. Erika and Peterson sat. "Please can I apologize for what happened yesterday. I don't know what came over me."

"I've spoken to Nancy and, while we view striking an officer as a serious matter, she doesn't wish to press charges. The circumstances were extraordinary," said Erika.

"I'm so ashamed..."

"Would you all like some tea, perhaps?" interrupted Tanvir, standing. Everyone froze.

"That would be great," said Peterson.

"You don't know where anything is," snapped Marianne.

"He can use a kettle, and no doubt the cups are still in the same place above the microwave," said Toby.

Tanvir hovered awkwardly.

"Yes, tea would be great," said Erika, giving him a smile.

"Let me make the tea," said Marianne, getting up.

"He's not contagious, Mum," said Toby.

"Toby! For Christ's sake!" snapped Martin.

"Tanvir. I am sure you are a very nice person, but—" started Marianne.

"Enough!" snapped Martin. "Do you want to lose your son as well as your daughter? Let Tan make the bloody tea!"

Tanvir left the room. Marianne pressed a scrunched up ball of tissue to her face. Laura leaned over and gripped her hands.

"How can you say that, Martin?" hissed Marianne.

"For fuck's sake!" said Martin.

He didn't sit and remained pacing up and down in front of the curtains. Erika realized she had to get a grip of this meeting.

"It's fine," said Erika. "I know this must be a difficult time."

"Hear that, Toby," said Martin. "A difficult time. Today was supposed to be just family. I wanted us to all be together for once without—"

"How can you say that, Martin? We'll never *all* be together. How could you forget Jessica!" cried Marianne.

"Jesus. I didn't mean that. Do you really think I've just forgotten about her?" shouted Martin. "You don't have the monopoly on grief...Christ almighty. We all grieve in our own way—"

"Will you stop taking the Lord's name!"

"Dad," interrupted Laura.

"No. I'm not going to be told again that I'm not crying enough, that I'm not doing it right!" He moved over to the sofa and jabbed a finger in Marianne's face. "I loved that little girl, and I would move heaven and earth to spend just one more minute with her, to have her here with us...to have watched her grow up over the past—" His voice broke and he turned away from them all.

"Look, we don't want to intrude on you any more than we need to," said Erika. "You've asked to speak with us. Please let's focus on what we're doing to find the person who did this."

Laura was now crying, along with her mother, and Toby stayed resolute in his chair. His arms crossed over his broad chest.

"Oh I know who did it," said Marianne. "That evil bastard, Trevor Marksman. Have you arrested him?"

"At this stage we're looking in to all aspects of the case," started Erika.

"Don't give me corporate bollocks," said Martin. "Speak like a human!"

"Okay, Mr. Collins. We've inherited a complex case. When Jessica disappeared twenty-six years ago there were few witnesses. We have to go back and pick through the original investigation, which as you know had many flaws."

"Where is he? Marksman?"

"The last we know he was living in Vietnam."

"Vietnam, eh? Teeming with poor young kids. Just think what three hundred grand can buy out there!" started Martin.

"That man, that evil man. How is it fair that he gets to sue the police for all that money, and he walks away, scot free?" said Marianne.

"There wasn't enough evidence at the time," started Erika.

"I've seen these shows on TV. Surely there's more you can do with forensics?" said Martin. "Things that couldn't be done back then?"

"When we discovered Jessica's remains...she'd been underwater for many years. We are limited with what we can do with forensics..."

The family stared back at her, each processing the information that Jessica was dumped underwater.

Erika went on: "I've solved two historical abduction cases, and I've hand-picked the best officers to work with me. I know many people have already given up on Jessica, but I'm not one of them. I'm going to catch this bastard, and bring him to justice. You have my word."

Martin looked between Erika and Peterson, and nodded.

"Okay, well, I'll hold you to that," he said, his eyes beginning to fill up. "You look like a woman I can trust." He turned away and pulled a pack of cigarettes from his pocket and lit up.

"Are you going to screw her too?" said Marianne. There was silence. "Did you know? He was screwing that whore of a detective, Amanda Baker."

"Marianne, quiet—" started Martin.

"No, why should I be quiet? You slept with that woman. A woman who comforted me, who I told private things to about how I felt."

"It was a long time after she joined the case!" shouted Martin.

"And that makes it okay?" said Marianne, standing unsteadily.

"And I'm supposed the one in this family who everyone is ashamed of," said Toby, almost as an aside to Erika and Peterson.

"Shut up!" cried Laura. "All of you. This is about Jessica! My...Our sister; she never got to grow up, she should be here! And all you can do is bicker and fight!" Tears ran tracks down her cheeks through thick foundation, and she wiped at it with the back of her hand.

"It's all right, my darling," said Marianne, putting her arms around Laura, who shook her off.

"When can we see her? I want to see her," said Laura.

"I would like to see her too," said Marianne.

"So do I," said Toby.

"Of course, that can be arranged, but only when the Forensic Pathologist is finished; then Jessica's remains will be returned to you," said Erika.

"What are they doing to her?" asked Laura.

"He's running tests, trying to get as much information as possible to put together a picture of how she died."

"Did she suffer? Please, tell me she didn't suffer," pleaded Marianne.

Erika took a deep breath. "Isaac Strong is one of the best Forensic Pathologists in the country, and as well as this he is very respectful. Jessica is safe in his care."

Marianne nodded and looked up at Martin. He had his back to them, leaning against the wall, his head bowed. The cigarette had burned down in his hand.

"Martin, come here, love," she said. He moved to the sofa, sat on the arm next to Marianne and buried his head in her neck, giving a deep muffled sob. "It's okay, it's all right," she said placing her free hand on his back and pulling him tight to her. Laura turned in to her mother too and they sobbed.

"I hardly remember her," said Toby, with tears in his eyes, looking up at Erika and Peterson.

Tanvir returned with a tray of tea and placed it on the large coffee table. Erika just wanted to leave this oppressive house with its dingy furniture; coupled with the terrible atmosphere, the pictures of the Virgin Mary took on a sinister melancholy.

"We'd like to make a fresh media appeal, and wanted to ask if you would be willing to do that—as a family?" asked Erika. They nodded.

"Our Media Liaison can advise on when and how that happens."

"Do you have any new suspects?" asked Laura.

"Not as yet, but we are working with new information."

"What's that?" asked Laura sharply.

"Well, the obvious one being that we found Jessica in Hayes Quarry. Can I ask what you know about it? Did you spend time there as a family or with Jessica?"

"Why would we go down to that old quarry?" said Marianne. "Jessica loved dancing, and going to pets' corner…"

"I used to go fishing there," said Toby. "When I was twelve or thirteen…Oh Jesus. She must have been down there. I went out on a boat. She was there all the time." Tanvir sat on the arm of his chair and took Toby's hand.

Marianne saw it, and then looked away. Then Peterson spoke.

"I know this is hard, but whose boat was this? Who did you know who had access to a boat?"

"My friend, Karl. It was a rubber dinghy," said Toby. "But me and Karl were thirteen when we went fishing; I was four when Jessica went missing."

"It all leads back to Trevor Marksman," said Martin, looking up and wiping his eyes. "The council seemed to think it was okay to put in a bloody nonce halfway house at the top of our road! Have you seen the photos he took of her, and there's video, *video* from when she was at the park with Marianne and Laura!"

"He is first on our list of suspects, and he will be brought in again for questioning," said Erika.

Martin shook his head. "I wrote to our local MP asking if there could be an inquiry into the first investigation. You know what she did?"

"I don't," said Erika.

"She sent back a fucking template letter. Didn't even have the courtesy to put pen to paper. I employ secretaries for my building firm who don't have much more than the basic qualifications, and even they know to give a proper handwritten response, but an MP? Do you know that to be a Member of Parliament you need no qualifications whatsoever...?" He was now pacing up and down the living room watched by Marianne, Toby and Laura. "What qualifications do you both have?"

"We're police officers," said Peterson.

"Yeah? Well, Marksman, the uneducated fucker, got himself a fancy barrister and legal aid, and sued you all for three hundred grand."

"What happened was regrettable," said Erika. As she heard it come out of her mouth she knew it would anger him even more.

"Well, I've got money, I don't need legal aid, and did you know that Laura's ex-boyfriend is now a bloody good barrister himself?"

"Dad," said Laura, shooting him a look.

"Oscar Browne is a partner at the Fortitudo Chambers, and he's already said he's ready to work for me."

"Oscar Browne," said Erika, remembering the case files

she had seen. "He was your boyfriend at the time of Jessica's disappearance?"

"Yes, he was," said Laura, wiping her eyes.

"And you were both camping in Wales when Jessica vanished?"

"Yes. We came home straightaway when we heard. We saw it on the news..." Her bottom lip began to tremble.

"And you've kept in touch with Oscar?"

"Like me, he's married now with kids, but he's kept in contact. That kind of thing gives you a bond."

Erika could see Martin was now pacing up and down, and red in the face.

"Jessica's killer has been fucking running around, laughing, for the last twenty-six years, cos you lot, you useless fucking lot, have done nothing. You've let stuff slip through your fingers. How could she just disappear? She only went up the bloody road; it takes no time at all, and NO ONE SAW ANYTHING!"

With that he flipped up the tray of tea; the cups and plates went crashing to the floor.

"Please you need to calm down, sir," said Peterson, moving over to Martin.

"You don't tell me to calm down! You don't come in to my house—"

"It's not your house anymore, Martin." screamed Marianne. "And you don't get to come back here and wreck things." She knelt on the floor and began to pick at the large slivers of broken china.

"Mum, you'll cut yourself," said Toby, softly, kneeling down with Marianne and gently pulling her hands away.

Laura looked helplessly between her brother and mother; her father pacing up and down, red in the face.

Martin started kicking at the wall. Marianne screamed at him to stop.

"Mr. Collins, if you don't calm down right now I'll have to cuff you and put you into a police car," said Erika, raising her voice. "Do you really want that to happen? There is press outside and they want nothing more than to find a new angle, and the guilty father will play right into that." This brought Martin up short and he looked at Erika. "So you are going to calm down, please?"

He nodded, chastised. "I'm sorry," he said, rubbing a hand over his head.

"I can't begin to imagine what this has been like for your family," said Erika.

"It ripped us to shreds." He started to cry again and Marianne moved to comfort him, followed by Toby and Laura. Tanvir stood to one side, watching with Peterson.

"Okay, I think we'll leave it there. You need to spend some time together. We will be going over all witness statements again, and we may like to talk to you about certain aspects. One of my officers will be in touch," said Erika.

She signaled to Peterson, and they made a swift exit.

CHAPTER 18

After their meeting with the Collins family, Erika and Peterson sat in the car on the street outside 7 Avondale Road.

"That was terrible," said Peterson, rubbing his eyes wearily. "How did it help, us being there?"

"They're all knotted together with grief. I couldn't even tell them when they could see Jessica's remains. This case is..." Erika stopped herself before she said *unsolvable*. "So, Martin Collins was sleeping with Amanda Baker..."

"Which adds another layer of...complications," agreed Peterson.

"You must be so pleased I requested you for this case," said Erika ruefully.

"I've missed you...I mean I missed working with you, on cases, with Moss too, of course," said Peterson, quickly correcting himself. Erika looked at him for a moment and then turned back to stare out of the car windscreen.

"Jessica went missing, just here." She indicated the street lined with huge, bare oak trees, their branches reaching up above them against the gray sky. "It's cold, isn't it?"

"Do you want the heater on?" asked Peterson.

"No. The street. The area. It feels cold, unwelcoming. All these smart expensive houses, hidden from view."

The group of photographers remained outside on the grass shoulder. They'd taken photos of Erika and Peterson entering and leaving the house. A short graying man started to make his way down the drive, so Erika briefly activated the car's blue lights and siren. He jumped back, noticing them in the unmarked car. She left the blue lights on and put a call in to the station asking for a uniform officer to come down to the house. The photographers trained their lenses on the car for a moment, and then turned back to the house.

"Did you think Martin Collins was a bit theatrical in there?" asked Peterson.

"How do you mean?" asked Erika.

"There was just something hokey about that whole flipping up the tea tray. If he'd thrown something, or...I don't know, hit one of us, I would have expected it."

"You think he has something to hide?"

Peterson shook his head. "How much did the last investigation look into him? His business dealings?"

"He made a lot of money very quickly from the housing boom in the eighties. The Collins family came over from Ireland in 1983, virtually penniless, and by 1990 they were living here..."

"You think someone kidnapped Jessica?"

"I don't know. There was never anything about a ransom?"

"No. She just vanished, and everything disintegrated in the aftermath. Her family, the MET investigation..."

She looked up at the street and undid her seatbelt. "Let's take a walk."

They got out of the car. This briefly caught the attention of the journalists, who snapped away at them with their cameras. Erika and Peterson walked off in the direction of number 27. The houses to their left were lower than the road, each driveway sloped down. To the right the houses sat on a bank, and the driveways led up.

"That's it, we're here, took two minutes," said Peterson. They came to a stop outside number 27. It was a cream-colored two story house with faux pillars out front. The driveway had just been resurfaced and drops of rainwater clung like mercury to the unblemished surface.

"The house has its second lot of new owners since 1990," said Erika. They stood for a moment and looked up and down the street. "The halfway house where Trevor Marksman lived is just up here," she added.

They carried on walking for a few more minutes, and came to where the road turned sharply to the left. A large three-story manor house sat on the other side of the road, nestled in the crease. It was painted a buttery yellow, and its window frames and the pillars out front gleamed white. There was a white painted swing sign on the manicured lawn, and large black letters told them this was now the Swann Retirement Home. The windows gleamed and reflected the gray sky, giving the place a blank stare. A large black crow landed on the sign. His coat gleamed like the painted letters, and he let out a mournful cawing.

They turned and were afforded a clear view of the whole street sloping away and down to their car parked on the curb in the distance where the photographers milled around. The high hedges formed a long wall on each side of the street.

"I just imagine Jessica out here, so close to home, but all alone. Did she scream? Did anyone hear her from behind the thick hedges when she was taken?" said Erika.

"Why dump her in the water less than a mile from her home? What if it was someone on this street? These are big houses. They must have basements."

"I read in the case files that the houses on this street and the surrounding streets were searched; pretty much everyone allowed the police in to look around."

"So she did just vanish," said Peterson. The crow cawed again, as if in agreement. "What now, boss?"

"I think we should pay Amanda Baker a visit," said Erika.

They set off and started to walk back. When they reached the car, the uniformed officer that Erika had called pulled up beside them at the curb. He rolled down his window, and Erika and Peterson went over to speak to him.

They didn't notice, standing amongst the group of journalists, with a camera slung around his neck, there was a tall dark man wearing a long wax jacket. Unlike the rest of the journalists, he wasn't interested in the Collins house. He was intently watching Erika and Peterson, trying to work out their next move.

CHAPTER 19

Amanda Baker lived in an end terrace house in a residential street in Balham, southwest London. The small front garden was an overgrown mess, and graying paint was peeling from the sash windows. The street was quiet, and it had just started to rain when Erika and Peterson parked outside.

The wooden front gate lay broken on the path, and they had to step over it to reach the front door. They rang the bell and waited, but there was no answer. Erika moved to the grimy front window and peered into the living room. She could just make out a television in the corner, showing an afternoon auction show. She jumped when a pair of hooded eyes appeared, framed by wisps of long graying hair. The woman shooed her away with a hand half covered with a long woolen sleeve.

"Hello, Amanda Baker? I'm DCI Foster," said Erika, quickly retrieving her warrant card from her coat and pressing it against the window. "I'm here with my colleague, DI Peterson. We'd like to talk to you about the Jessica Collins case."

The face leaned in and peered at their IDs.

"Nope, sorry," she said, and pulled the curtains closed.

Erika knocked on the window.

"DCI Baker. We're here for your help; it would really help us to hear your thoughts on the case."

The curtains opened a little; the face moved back into view. "I want to see both your warrant cards," she said.

Peterson came to the window and pressed his against the glass. She squinted through the grime. Deep smoker's lines surrounded her lips.

"Go round to the side gate," she said, finally, and pulled the curtains together again.

"What's wrong with the front door?" moaned Peterson as they came out from under the shelter of the front porch into the fine rain.

They hurried alongside a mildewing fence which curved around the front garden. A hand appeared over the top of the fence at the far end, and then one of the panels swung inwards.

Former DCI Amanda Baker was a large woman; she wore a long grubby cardigan over a black T-shirt, dark leggings, and black Crocs with thick gray woolen socks. She had a bloated red face and a large double chin. Her gray hair was long and greasy and tied at the nape of her neck with an elastic band.

"I'll need thirty quid," she said, holding out a hand.

"We'd like to talk to you about the case," said Erika.

"And I'd like thirty quid," repeated Amanda. "I know the score; you'd bung an old prozzie or a dealer a few quid to hear what they have to say. And I know a hell of a lot about this case." She held her hand closer and wiggled her fingers.

"You were a police officer," said Peterson.

Amanda looked him up and down with an appraising eye. "I was, sweetheart. Now I'm just an old bag with nothing to lose."

She went to close the gate.

Erika put out her hand: "Okay," she said, and tipped her head to Peterson.

He rolled his eyes, took out his wallet and handed Amanda a ten and a twenty.

She nodded, tucked them under her bra, and indicated to them to follow her down the dank little alleyway. They passed a bathroom window where a small vent twirled lazily, puffing out the aroma of urine and toilet cleaner. They emerged into a back garden that was overgrown, with sacks of rubbish piled up in one corner.

At the back door Amanda wiped her Crocs on a thin scrap of mat, which Erika thought ironic, as it was the kind of house where you wiped your feet on the way out. The kitchen had once been quite smart, but it was filthy and crammed with dirty dishes and bags of overflowing rubbish. There was a dog bed by a washing machine lurching on spin cycle, but no dog.

"Go through to the front room. You want tea?" she said with a gravelly smoker's voice.

Erika and Peterson looked at the filthy kitchen, then nodded.

They moved through a hallway, past a steep wooden staircase leading up to a gloomy landing. The hallway was crammed with old newspapers piled chest high against the front door. The living room was crowded with furniture, and the walls and ceiling were yellow with nicotine.

"Do you really want to drink her tea?" hissed Peterson.

"No, but if it buys us more time with her…" Erika hissed in reply.

"Well thirty quid should buy us at least an hour," started Peterson.

He was interrupted by a knock at the front window, and a

face pressed against the grimy glass. Amanda came bustling through behind them and went to the window, pulling it up.

"All right Tom?" she said.

A hand passed through a few letters, and then two bottles of Pinot Grigio. Erika moved to the window and saw it was the postman. Amanda pulled the thirty quid from her bra and gave him the twenty. He went off through the front gate, whistling.

"What?" Amanda said to the looks on their faces. "In America they call it bottle service."

"It's not normally delivered by the postman," said Peterson.

"You don't fancy a glass?"

"I'm on duty," he said coldly.

"I'll get your tea then," she said. "Have a seat."

"That answers my question about the front door," said Peterson when she'd left.

"You could be a bit less rude," said Erika.

"What? You want me to get drunk with her on her wine from the postman?"

Despite the situation, Erika laughed. "No, just don't be so stand-offish. A little bit of flirting goes a long way. Look at the bigger picture."

Peterson cleared off a pile of newspapers and chocolate bar wrappers from the sofa and sat down. The living room was crammed with two saggy sofas, a dining table and chairs. The television sat in a large shelving unit dominating one wall, and crammed with books and paperwork. Erika went over to a picture on the wall which stood out. It was in a cheap gold frame with a braid pattern. The color photo was a little spoiled and faded at the bottom where the damp had got inside. A thin young version of Amanda Baker wore the old uniform of the WPC: thick black tights, a skirt, jacket and peaked cap. Her black hair shone from underneath, and she stood outside Hendon Police College with a young male officer in uniform, who wasn't wearing his cap, but had it under his arm. They held up their badges and were grinning at the camera.

"I thought you'd make a beeline for that," said Amanda, shuffling in with a tray of steaming cups of tea and a large glass of white wine.

"I recognize him," said Erika, taking a mug from the tray and peering back at the photo.

"PC Gareth Oakley, as was. We worked in CID back in the seventies. Mc and Oakley were the same rank then. You now know him as retired Assistant Commissioner Oakley."

"That must have been interesting: being a woman in CID in the seventies?"

Amanda just raised an eyebrow.

"Looks like Oakley. He had less hair then than he does now. How old was he?" asked Erika, peering closer at his thinning hair.

Amanda chuckled. "Twenty-three. He started wearing the syrup when he got promoted to the DCI rank."

"That's Assistant Commissioner Oakley?" said Peterson, just catching on.

"We trained together at Hendon, passed out in 1978," said Amanda. She sat heavily in the large armchair by the window. Erika sat next to Peterson.

"Oakley has only just retired, massive golden handshake," said Peterson. It hung in the air for a moment.

"Okay, so we're just here informally to ask you about the Jessica Collins case. I've been assigned it," said Erika.

"Who did you piss off?" chuckled Amanda darkly, taking a large slug of wine and pulling a packet of cigarettes from her cardigan pocket. "It's a poisoned chalice. I always thought they'd dump her in the quarry... although we searched it twice and there was nothing..." She paused to light her cigarette and took a deep drag. "So whether they kept her somewhere, or moved the body. That's your job to find out now, isn't it?"

"You were convinced it was Trevor Marksman?"

"Yeah," she nodded, holding Erika's gaze. "He burned for it though. And you know what? I'd do it again."

"So you freely admit you tipped off the people who put the petrol bomb through his door?"

"Don't you ever want to take justice into your own hands?"

"No."

"Come on, Erika. I've read about you. Your husband was gunned down by that druggie, plus four of your colleagues, and he left you for dead. Wouldn't you love to have an hour in a room with him, just the two of you and a baseball bat covered in nails?" She flicked her cigarette into a large over-flowing ashtray on the table beside her and kept eye contact with Erika.

"Yes, I would," said Erika.

"There you go then."

"But I'd never do it. Our job as police officers is to uphold the law, and not to take it into our own hands. You also had an affair with Martin Collins?"

"I did. Him and Marianne were over; it was eighteen months after Jessica went missing. We got close. I regret that more than Marksman, but I fell in love."

"Did he fall in love?" asked Peterson.

She shrugged and took another large pull on her wine. "I often think it was the only good thing I did for that family. I couldn't bring their daughter back. I made Martin forget, at least when he was with me."

"Now we've found Jessica, do you still think Trevor Marksman did it?" asked Erika.

Amanda took another drag of her cigarette. "I always think that if something is so bloody obvious then it has to be true…He had someone working with him though, and I think that when he took her, he kept her somewhere."

"You had him under surveillance?" asked Peterson.

"We did, but there was a week or so in between her going missing and us getting eyes on him…I think he did it then."

"I had a look at your file," started Erika.

"Oh you did, did you?" said Amanda, squinting through the smoke.

"After the Jessica Collins case, you were moved to the drug squad, and you were charged with selling on cocaine."

"I was a bloody good copper. I paved the way for women like you, and you would have been the token black guy twenty years ago; now you're accepted, taken seriously. You forget about those who fought for your place in the force."

"So it's all down to you is it? Are you the Rosa Parks of the MET?" said Peterson. There was an awkward silence. Erika gave him a look.

"We're not here to do anything more than get your side of things," said Erika.

"My side?"

"Yes, what it was like working on the case, your insight. I'm coming to this blind, with reams and reams of case files."

Amanda was quiet for a moment and lit another cigarette. "When I worked in CID I was the only woman, and I was given every rape case. I looked after those women. I took samples; I cared for them. I never ignored their calls, and I supported them through months of waiting while the bastards who raped them were on remand. Then I held their hand through the court cases. No one gave me any support.

The blokes who used to piss off down the pub early, who used to demand free screws from the sex workers, they got the promotions. And then, when I finally get the Jessica Collins case, I was made to feel like I'd overstepped the mark, had ideas above my station."

"I'm sorry about that," said Erika.

"Don't be sorry. But don't judge me. You get to the point when you find out playing by the rules gets you nowhere..." She indicated the photo on the wall with the butt of her cigarette. "That arsehole, Oakley, ended up as Assistant Commissioner." She stubbed it out in an overflowing ashtray, grinding it down. "We were on the beat a lot together in the old days. One night we were on Catford High Street at 3 a.m., and this lad holds us up at knifepoint in one of the side roads. He was off his head on something...He grabs Oakley and presses the knife against his neck, and Oakley craps himself. I'm not talking metaphorically; he actually shit his pants. The kid with the knife, who's paranoid and wired enough as it is, freaks out at the smell, and runs away. Oakley was saved by his own shit. It's ironic that, years later, he gets a bloody MBE for his work in the force bringing down knife crime...I helped him that night, got him cleaned up, and I kept my mouth shut. We were tight back then. Years later, when it all went wrong for me, and he was Chief Superintendent, he did fuck all. Left me out to fucking dry!"

Amanda was now shaking with rage, and lit another cigarette. They sat in silence for a moment. The clock ticked loudly, a car went past on the road outside, and the sky seemed to have grown darker. Erika looked at Peterson for them to leave.

"There is something," said Amanda. She paused and rubbed at her face. "You found the body in Hayes Quarry. We searched the water twice in August and at the end of

September 1990, and, of course, there was nothing. There was an old guy, a squatter, living in a cottage there. It was tiny, with a cellar. We found nothing. Of course. Then a few months later he hung himself."

"And?" asked Erika.

"I dunno. If Trevor Marksman was working with someone, it could have been him."

"Do you remember his name?"

"Old Bob, he called himself. He wasn't right in the head, but didn't seem violent. They'd shut down one of the local psychiatric hospitals a couple of years before and he'd been turfed out onto the street. He seemed, well, just a bit happy-go-lucky; simple. Then for him to go and drink poison and then hang himself, that stood out for me."

"He drank poison too?" asked Erika.

"Yeah."

Erika's phone rang and she apologized and answered it, and started talking.

"Sure I can't interest you in a glass of wine? Maybe a beer?" asked Amanda, squinting at Peterson through her cigarette smoke.

"No. I'm on duty," said Peterson.

"You don't want to *pump me* for more information?" she said, her eyes going wide.

Peterson was pleased when Erika came off the phone.

"That was Crawford," she said.

"Crawford, Detective Inspector?" asked Amanda, her eyes brightening up.

"Yes. He was on the case back in 1990, wasn't he?"

"Yeah. Annoying little shit. Sort of begs for approval, but does nothing to earn it. Likes to look busy—"

"Well, thank you for what you've told us. We won't take up any more of your time," said Erika. "Is it okay if I call on you again? We're working our way through all the evidence and there may be something I need to run by you, or clarify. If you have time."

"Course, I'm wide open," she said, tapping the ash off her cigarette and directing it to Peterson.

"What do you think?" asked Erika when they were back in the car.

"The house by the quarry is a promising lead. It gives us someone else. Someone who's not Trevor Marksman."

"But he's dead, boss."

They mulled this over for a moment.

"And on a personal level, I feel like I need a shower, that was sexual harassment," he added.

"Horrible, isn't it? But it's all good police training. Now you know how it feels to be a woman," said Erika.

"What did Crawford want?" asked Peterson as she started the engine.

"The Collins family can view Jessica's remains," said Erika.

"Do you think they should? She's just—"

"A skeleton, yes. But they have the right, and Marianne was insistent that she gets to see her daughter."

Erika put the car in gear and they drove away from Amanda's house.

A hundred yards up the road, a blue car was tucked into a row of parked cars lining the pavement. The dark-haired man sat inside. He had followed Erika and Peterson from the Collins house, taking care not to be spotted, and now he watched as they drove away.

He reached inside his long wax jacket, pulled out his phone and dialed a number.

"It's Gerry," he said, speaking with a soft Irish accent. "The officer running the show, DCI Foster, just left Amanda Baker's house. She's with a black officer, dunno his name."

He listened as the voice on the other end spoke; he interrupted, saying: "Just cool it. We knew they'd go and see Amanda... Well, it depends how addled her brain is after all the booze and drugs. There's still a chance she'll put things together now there's a body. And the Foster woman is good, she's shit-hot." He rolled his eyes. "Look, I can arse about following them all week, but we need more, phones and emails hacked... Eyes inside... Okay, I'll sit tight and wait. But remember we're on the clock, in more ways than one, just you remember that."

Gerry hung up his phone as a pretty young blonde girl emerged from the front door of the house level to where he was parked. She pushed a baby in a buggy and, despite the rain, wore tight leggings and her coat was open to show a low-cut top. Gerry looked her up and down, and gave her a wink, and she returned it with a coy smile.

Then he started his car and pulled away.

CHAPTER 20

Later that evening, Erika and Moss stood at the back of the small viewing room at the mortuary in Penge. In front of the glass, waiting for the curtain to open, Marianne Collins waited with Laura, Martin and Toby.

They had dressed smartly for the occasion, all in black, and the only color came from a single red rose Marianne held in her hand. Moss glanced at Erika and frowned. The seconds seemed to draw out; they had been told that things were ready. The room was quiet as they stared, and they could hear the soft buzzing of the bright lights behind the glass. Just as Erika thought she might have to break the silence, the curtain slowly began to open. It caught on the rail above for a moment, before it revealed the skeletal remains of Jessica Collins.

Marianne gave a sob and moved close to the glass, pressing her body flat against it. Jessica's skeleton was neatly laid out on a table with a blue sheet. Isaac had explained to Erika that it was better to use blue. A white sheet would have shown up the discoloration on the bones.

"Hello, darling. We're here for you. We're going to take

care of you now," said Marianne, pressing a hand to the glass. "Daddy and Toby are here; Laura is here too, and I'm here, your mummy." She turned to Martin. "I can see her, she's there. Look, Martin, look, that's her hair. That's my baby's hair."

Isaac had arranged it so the back of the small skull was supported by a thin white pillow, and the coarse wispy hair tumbled off it onto the table. Even though the skeleton was in pieces, it made the remains of Jessica look whole, as if she lay peacefully.

Laura let out a sob and ran from the room. Toby and Martin turned to see where she'd gone, then moved to the glass with Marianne, who was now whispering a prayer; her breath creating an arc of condensation on the glass. Erika nodded to Moss to stay with them and she went outside.

Laura's husband, Todd, was waiting on one of the seats in the corridor with their two small sons. He was a pleasant-looking man with dark hair and soft brown eyes. Laura had her back to Erika, squatting down and hugging the boys, one under each arm. She was sobbing and kissing them, saying: "You're safe. You're mine. I won't let anything happen to you. I promise." Their confused faces looked up at Erika as they were pummeled with Laura's affection.

Toby's partner, Tanvir, returned with cups of coffee from the drinks machine and handed one to Todd, who took it with a smile.

"I will never let you out of my sight. You are too precious," said Laura, hugging the boys tighter.

"Laura," said Todd, leaning over to release her grip on them. "Gently. You'll scare them."

Erika realized from his accent he was American. Laura released the boys and noticed her standing in the corridor.

"What's in that room, Mummy?" said one of the boys. Erika saw they were twins.

"The police found Jessica's—"

"Laura, we said, no details," interrupted Todd.

"No details? Todd. *Details*? Jessica is not just a bunch of details! We're not just going to airbrush her out of existence!" cried Laura, standing.

"Honey, I didn't mean that," said Todd. He stood and took Laura in his arms; she buried her face in his chest and began to howl. The two little boys looked up at Erika with scared wide eyes.

Erika crouched down beside them and smiled. "Hello, I'm Erika. What are your names?"

"Thomas and Michael," said one of them. "I'm Thomas and this is Michael. He's shy." They both nodded sagely, and then looked up at their father. They wore identical blue jeans and green jumpers.

"It's okay, boys, Mommy is really upset, but we're all okay," said Todd, stroking the back of Laura's head.

"Do you boys like chocolate? There's a machine round the corner," said Erika. Todd nodded his thanks over Laura's back.

"Yeah, I've seen that machine, lots of yummy chocolate," said Tanvir.

They moved along the cramped corridor and rounded a corner at the end. There was another group of chairs and a vending machine. The twins moved to the glass and started to choose what they would like to eat.

"Mine's a Mars bar and is number B4," said Thomas.

"I'll have the same," said Michael.

Tanvir fed the change into the machine and pressed the buttons.

"What a time to meet the in-laws," he said.

"You've never met Toby's family?"

"I met Laura and Martin, Kelly and the kids, in Spain—"

"Kelly is Martin's?"

"Yeah she's Martin's...She's very nice. They'd love to get married but Marianne, well, you've met her. She's a very strict Catholic."

"What has Toby told you about Jessica? If you don't mind me asking."

He leaned down to get the Mars bars out of the bottom of the vending machine and gave them to the boys.

"He feels guilty."

"He was only four when she vanished?"

"He feels guilty that he has so few memories of her. He remembers the arguments that Laura and his mother had. Nasty, sometimes physical."

"Who was physical?"

"They both were. Have you seen the kitchen in their house?"

"Briefly."

"There's a big pantry in the back. It used to be a cold room, and it had a refrigeration unit to make it into a huge walk-in fridge. Toby says that one night he came downstairs to get a drink, and he heard sounds coming from the cold room. He opened the door and found Laura. Marianne had locked her inside."

"He's sure?"

Tanvir shrugged. "He told me one night; it was about a year ago. We'd had a few drinks and he opened up to me about his parents."

"Does he have a good relationship with his father?"

"Yeah. Very. You wouldn't know it to look at Martin, you'd think he was a football-loving homophobe, but he's been cool with me, he's cool with Tobes. His girlfriend is lovely."

"Why are you telling me this?" asked Erika.

"I don't know. Maybe I'm sick of my—*our*—lifestyle being invalidated by Marianne on the basis of her religion. And that she's the better person."

"Was she ever cruel to Toby?"

"God no! He was, and is, her baby boy—"

"What's this?" asked a voice. Toby appeared around the corner. And was watching Tanvir with Erika. The boys were now sitting on a bench further down the corridor making a mess of eating their Mars bars.

"DCI Foster was just asking about your mum—if she's going to be okay. She had the police worried that she might be having a breakdown."

Erika was surprised that Tanvir was lying, but she didn't let on and went along with him.

"There are lots of support groups out there. I have the details," she said.

"Mum's got the church; she says they're all she needs... Tan, will you come in and see Jessica? I'd like you to."

"Okay. And your mum?"

"We all lost Jessica, not just her," said Toby.

They went off, and Todd came back to get the boys with Laura, whose eyes were red and puffy.

The secrets seem to run deeper the more I look into this case, thought Erika.

CHAPTER 21

It was late, but Amanda Baker couldn't sleep. She sat in her armchair with a pen and an A4 notebook. After her visit from the detectives she had started to think about the Jessica Collins case again, not in terms of bitter resentment, but how to solve it. She had made a start by writing down everything she could remember, and she had already filled half the notebook. The television was on in the background, but muted, and for the first time in years she felt alive and filled with purpose. She had almost total recall from her time on the case. It was the past fifteen years she struggled to remember, which had passed in a haze of alcohol and frequent dabbling in drugs. She'd even paced herself with the wine, noting as she looked up from her writing that she was only on her third glass.

There was a soft knock on the front room window. She removed her glasses and heaved herself up out of her armchair. Moving to the window she pulled the curtain to one side, and saw a familiar face at the glass. When she pulled it up, the air was crisp and there was a fresh smell of ozone. Crawford squinted at her from the light spilling out of the living room.

"I got your voicemail," he said.

"You look like shit," she replied with a grin.

"You should see yourself."

She gave him a gravelly chuckle and held out her hand. "Climb through. The front door is bust."

He grabbed her hand and hoisted himself up onto the windowsill, his face turning red from the effort of squeezing through the gap. When he was inside he stood for a moment in the middle of the living room catching his breath.

"It's been a while," he said. "Years since we've..."

She nodded in agreement. Where the light hit the top of his head, she could see the last few sandy-colored hairs clinging to the top like spun sugar.

"You want a drink?" she asked.

"Yeah. I could do with one; it's been a hell of a day." He rubbed at his face nervously.

She went out and returned with the bottle and another glass.

"You've let this place go," he said, taking the glass.

"You've let yourself go," said Amanda, clinking his glass and downing hers in one. He nodded in agreement and downed his wine. She took his glass and placed them both on the small table by her armchair. She turned and fixed him with a stare.

"My wife left me," he said.

"Sorry to hear that."

"She's got the kids. The house..."

"Shhhh, kills the mood," said Amanda, moving toward him and pressing a finger to his lips. She half pulled off his coat, trapping his arms down by his side. He looked up at her with slack-jawed desire. She moved her hands down over his protruding belly and back under to his waist where she unbuckled his belt.

"Oh," he said, and she unzipped his trousers and slid her hand into his underwear. He closed his eyes and shuddered. "Oh, Amanda..."

She pulled down his underwear and pushed him back onto the sofa. "Just sit back and be quiet," she said, kneeling on the floor between his legs.

Crawford put his head back and started to breathe heavily.

It was all over a few minutes later. Amanda rose, with difficulty, from the carpet and grabbed her cigarettes from the table.

"I needed that; you've still got it. You give the best head," said Crawford, pulling up his underwear and trousers. "Got any more wine?"

"Sure," she said. She picked up the bottle, topping up his glass.

He took it from her and sat back, sated, and took a long drink.

"I hear you're on the Collins case," said Amanda, lighting up.

"For my sins," he replied, rolling his eyes and taking another pull on his wine. "I like it here, Amanda. I feel like I can relax. My wife, she was so uptight about mess."

"What's happening with the case?" asked Amanda.

Crawford laughed. "You know I can't tell you that."

Amanda took another drag on her cigarette.

"I think you can."

Crawford sat up in the chair. "Hang on, you didn't ask me over for—"

"What? A middle-aged booty call? That was one of the reasons."

"I don't believe you," he said, slamming his wine down. He stood up and grabbed his coat from off the floor.

"I just want to know what's happening with the Collins case. That's all, Crawford."

"Why don't I ever learn? You are just a manipulative bitch."

"Now I'm a bitch; a minute ago I was 'the best.' "

"Yeah, well now I see clearer."

"Ah, you have post-coital clarity, Crawford. What about me?"

"What about you?"

"I'm still feeling unsatisfied. In more ways than one."

Crawford made a move for the window, but she crossed her arms and blocked his way.

"Not so fast. You're forgetting I know your little secrets..."

"They're our secrets, Amanda. You were also involved in selling on the drugs we seized off the street," he hissed.

Amanda shrugged impassively. "But that's the great thing about having absolutely nothing to lose. I'm talking about myself, of course. You've a divorce on the horizon; your cost of living must have gone up since the separation, with maintenance to pay, renting a one-bedroom flat. Then you'll need to negotiate custody of the kiddie-winks. *You* need your job."

"What do you want?" he said, clenching his fists. His face flushing.

"I told you. All I want is to be kept informed about the case... If I need copies of anything, you'll provide those too."

He looked at her for a moment, hate in his eyes.

"Fine. Agreed. Now, are we done?"

"Not quite. I need to feel satisfied that we have an agreement."

"I just told you."

"*Satisfied*," she repeated. She hooked her fingers under

the waistband of her leggings and pulled them down to her ankles.

"You know I don't like that," he said, looking at her naked from the waist down. Her pale flesh. The mass of dark hair.

"We have to do things we don't like, Crawford. It's part of surviving in this life," she said, pushing him down to his knees. "Now get to work."

CHAPTER 22

It was late when Amanda Baker's visitor left. Gerry watched from his car as Crawford made an ungainly exit through the front window, moved despondently to his car, and then drove away.

He waited a little while longer, and then approached Amanda Baker's house. Thick cloud blocked out the moon, and the streetlight outside was broken, shrouding it further in darkness.

He crept up the path and looked through the front window. Inside, Amanda lay slumped, her head back in her armchair, the television on in the corner, showing a nature documentary. Giant stingrays moved through an ocean landscape, accompanied by a soft authoritative narration.

Gerry placed his hands on the bottom of the sash window, and pushed. It wasn't locked. It popped open easily and slid up. He placed a leg over the sill and slipped inside. He closed the window behind him and pulled the curtains.

He now stood over Amanda, looking down at her slack sleeping face, a little drool glistening in the corner of her mouth. Two empty wine bottles were strewn on the carpet beside her. She shifted in her chair, her lips champing together. He reached for the heavy ashtray beside her, prepared to hit her over the head, but she settled back into rhythmic snoring.

He had two options: conceal a small battery-operated listening device in the room, or find a concealed plug for a tiny black box listening device with a SIM card. He saw the messy units, groaning with books and papers, and any plugs would be concealed behind and hard to access. The room stank of smoke, but there was a defunct-looking smoke detector on the ceiling. He stood on the sofa and reached up, quickly fitting the small listening device in the plastic housing of the smoke detector. It was voice-activated, with a battery life of several days.

He stepped down off the sofa and moved through to the hallway. The landline sat on the table, its red charging light glowing in the dark. As he reached out to take the handset from its cradle, the floorboards creaked, and he froze. He moved quickly through a doorway opposite the banister; an empty room filled with junk.

She creaked past him, heavy-footed, to the kitchen. The light came on; he heard the tap running and the crackle of a foil sheet of pills. The light flicked off, and she rumbled past and this time went up the stairs, slowly shuffling.

Gerry came out of the shadows, and worked quickly, taking the landline handset apart and inserting a small listening device.

He paused in the hallway as the sounds of bedsprings creaked upstairs. His eyes had grown used to the dark. He was tempted to go up there, have some fun with her. She was obviously incapacitated. But he had to focus. He could have his fun at a later date. He moved slowly past the base of the staircase, noticing how steep the stairs were.

He made a mental note and then left the house through the front window, melting back into the darkness.

CHAPTER 23

The next morning was clear and gray, but very cold. Erika and Peterson parked in the small gravel car park at the Croydon Road entrance to Hayes Common. They buttoned their coats as they got out, and they followed a gravel path which wound sharply to the left around a bank of trees, then swerved to the right. The trees now blocked out the car park, the view of the houses and road, and it opened out to rolling common land.

"Jeez, how quickly you feel like you're in the middle of nowhere," said Peterson.

"The trees muffle the sound of the road too," said Erika, noting the eerie silence. Their feet crunched on the gravel as they moved past tall bare trees on either side, set so close together that the woods inside were dark.

"This is where I imagine little red eyes watching us from the depths of the wood," added Peterson, "like *The Wind in the Willows*."

The grass and heather were coated with dew, and the sun hadn't yet risen above the trees to evaporate it. A low mist hung in the air, and wisps floated past as they walked.

"What if Jessica was carried this way?" said Erika. They absorbed that thought as their feet crunched along the path.

"Was she wrapped in the plastic before she went in? Or did whoever it was do it by the water?"

"This Croydon Road entrance where we've parked is the closest to the quarry, and we've been walking for—" Erika checked her watch. "Five minutes."

"Maybe it wasn't just one person," said Peterson, plunging his hands in his pockets deep in thought.

The trees on either side seemed to part as the gravel path curved round, and slightly below them sat the quarry. The still water reflected the gray of the sky, and the low mist hung over its surface. The gravel path finished a hundred yards from the water, and they walked across spongy uneven moss to reach its rocky banks. Erika felt it had been longer than a week since she'd been here with the dive team.

"Whoever did this would have needed a boat," she said. "She was found about a hundred yards out."

Peterson picked up a small stone, crouched down and skimmed it across the water.

"Six, not bad," she said as they watched the row of ripples spreading across the water.

"No one would have been able to throw a small child's body that far from here on the shore," said Peterson.

They moved off, their legs as well as their minds working in sync. The path around the quarry was thin in places, and in between there were rocks to clamber over and small gnarled trees, some with their branches hanging into the water's edge, to duck under.

"Okay, I can't see the cottage," said Erika. She pulled out a map.

"In twenty-six years trees would have grown up and—" started Peterson.

"Hang on," said Erika as they came level with a mass of overgrown brambles and reeds. "That's a rooftop, isn't it?" She was pointing at a slice of red tile rising up through a mass of brambles and dried bindweed.

They approached the mass which, as well as being sharp and thick in places, was slick with dew. Now they were closer, Erika could see broken glass glinting in the pale light. They started to make their way through, but the meters of brambles, trees and dense undergrowth were impenetrable.

"Jeez, boss, we need to be better prepared for this; backup, some gloves," said Peterson, wincing as he pulled a large bramble from the soft skin on his thumb.

"You're right; we need this cut down," said Erika, staring back at the small piece of the cottage roof peering through the undergrowth.

They came back out from the undergrowth brushing themselves down, just as a yellow Labrador bounded up with a soggy tennis ball in its mouth. It stopped and sat, placing its paw on the ball.

Erika picked it up and threw it toward the bank of trees in the distance. The dog bounded excitedly away toward it, and brought it back. A woman appeared through the trees and moved slowly down toward them near the water's edge.

"Local old busybody, could be worth a chat," said Peterson.

"Looks a bit eccentric," said Erika as the woman moved closer.

She was dressed in a saggy old green tracksuit, a Chelsea FC bobble hat with long gray hair spilling out, and a Manchester United scarf.

Erika threw the ball a couple more times for the dog, who kept bringing it back. When the woman drew close, they could see she wore a pair of purple trainers; one of the soles was detached and flapping. She carried a beaten up old carrier bag which was full of what looked like sweet chestnuts. Her face was weather-beaten and deeply lined, and she had a scar in the right-hand corner of her mouth which looked as if it had been badly sewn, causing the lip to gather and give her mouth a permanent snarl.

"Serge, heel," she snapped to the Labrador. "Is he bothering you?" She spoke with a refined yet phlegmy upper-class voice. The dog ran to her side as she peered at Erika and Peterson.

"No, he's a lovely dog. Hello, I'm DCI Foster," said Erika, holding out her ID. "This is DI Peterson."

"It's perfectly legal to *glean* chestnuts," she started to say. "Why the bloody hell does it need two of you out here?"

"We're not—" started Erika.

"Bloody police were called when someone was picking blackberries from the hedgerows; did you hear about that? I mean *really*. It belongs to God, and he puts it all on earth for us to eat."

"We're not here about chestnuts or anything that you might be picking," said Erika.

"There's no *might*. I *am* picking. I've picked. Look!" She opened the bag. Chestnuts were packed in tight, all shiny and brown.

"We're investigating the death of Jessica Collins. You may have seen something about her body being recovered from the quarry on the news," said Erika.

"Haven't got a television," said the woman. "But I listen to Radio Four. I heard the news. Nasty business. You found her over yonder," she added, tipping her head toward the quarry.

"Yes. Have you lived around this area for long?"

"I've lived here my whole life: eighty-four years."

"Congratulations," said Peterson, but all this got in return was a scowl.

"What can you tell us about the cottage there, in the undergrowth?" asked Erika.

The woman peered past her, squinting, creasing her face even more.

"Second World War; accommodation and storage for the air base they had here, all quite hush-hush. I think someone stayed on after the war, but then it was empty; it's been empty for years... Old Bob had it for a long time, unofficially, though not long enough to claim squatter's rights, the poor bastard."

A look passed between Erika and Peterson.

"Do you know where he is now?" asked Erika, fishing for more information.

"A few years back. They found him in there. Dead." She tilted her head toward the cottage.

"Do you know what his name was?"

"I told you, Old Bob."

"His legal name?"

"Bob Jennings."

"And what's your name?" asked Erika.

"Why do I have to give you my name? You don't need my name for me to answer questions."

"There are few, if any, witnesses to the death of Jessica Collins. She was only seven when she was dumped in the water. Her body lay weighted down in plastic, and left in the silt, for twenty-six years. We don't know if she was still alive when she was thrown in..."

The old woman was taken aback. "The poor child..."

Peterson stepped forward and gave her his winning smile. "We may have more questions, ma'am. It could be beneficial to us to use your extensive knowledge of the area to help us in our investigation."

She peered up at him for a moment, then said to Erika: "Is he flirting with me?"

"No, of course not," said Peterson, embarrassed.

"I hope not man! Is that your idea of police work?"

Erika stifled a grin, saying: "I can assure you we take police work, and this investigation seriously, any local knowledge will be of great use to us..."

The old lady's faced creased even more as she gave both of them the once-over.

Erika went on: "There were reports of a dark-haired man seen around Jessica's house on the day she went missing. The police never tracked him down, but after the discovery of her body here, we have reason to think it could have been this Bob Jennings."

"Bob? Involved in a murder? No, no, no. He was a queer soul. Rather simple, but murdering a little girl? No. Never."

"How can you be so sure?" asked Erika.

"Because I've lived here all my life. I know a bad egg when I see one. Now, if that's all, good day."

She whistled at the dog and strode off, the Labrador following after her.

"Would you be willing to help us then, if you know so much about the local area?" Erika called after her, but she ignored them and carried on walking.

They watched as she disappeared round the bank of trees, the sole of her shoe flapping.

"Flirting..." muttered Peterson. "She's flattering herself."

"No. She knows more than she's letting on," said Erika. She hurried off to the trees, closely followed by Peterson. When they rounded the corner there was no one there.

"Where did she go?" asked Erika. The thin path between the trees stretched out in front of them. Wisps of fog still hung in the air, and the eerie silence came over them again.

"Maybe she was a ghost," said Peterson.

"The dog too?"

They stopped for a moment. Erika pulled out her phone. "Moss, it's me. See if you can track down whether a boat was kept at Hayes Quarry; look to see if there is any record of a boat being removed by the council. They love to get all pedantic about stuff like that... Also, can you find out exactly what the quarry was used for; the type of sand or gravel that was removed. Maybe something from its history will give us a lead... It's a long shot."

"Sometimes a long shot is all you need," said Peterson when she came off the phone. He turned and looked back to where the quarry was masked by the heather and grass. "To think she was here all this time, less than a mile from home," he said.

CHAPTER 24

That night Erika slept fitfully. In her dreams she was sinking down into the freezing dark waters of Hayes Quarry. The moon was full, and as she slowly sank down, the bottom of the quarry stretched out, lit up like a moonscape. She swam along the bottom, her arms and legs numb, her lungs screaming. The silt billowed up around her, clouding her view, but then it cleared. She saw Jessica standing on the bottom of the quarry but she wasn't a skeleton. She was dressed for her friend's birthday party, her long blonde hair floating around her head like a halo, the fabric of the pink dress billowing lazily in the gentle undercurrents. Her patterned sandals hovered above the silt. Under her arm she held a wrapped gift, a small square of black-and-white polka dots.

Jessica smiled; one of her front teeth was missing and tiny bubbles escaped through the gap. She moved off, floating, without having to move her arms or legs, the gift still tucked under her arm.

Erika could now see that further out on the bottom of the quarry were a row of familiar houses. It was Avondale

Road shrouded in silt, the oak trees in a dark and shadowy line. A light far up ahead blinked once, then twice, and Jessica started to move faster up the underwater avenue. Erika kicked and flailed and swam to catch up, the silt billowing around her. She reached Jessica, grabbed her arm and started to swim for the surface, but as her fingers closed around Jessica's tiny arm and they started to move upward, the skin on Jessica's arm began to fall away, exposing the bones underneath. The skin then fell away from Jessica's face, exposing the skull and gaping eye sockets. By the time Erika broke through to the surface, Jessica was just a skeleton.

Erika took deep breaths of the cold night air, and as her vision cleared, she saw two figures standing at the edge of the quarry.

Erika woke with a yell, her sheets soaked with sweat, but shivering. It was still dark outside her bedroom window, and the clock beside her bed showed it was 4:30 a.m. She got up and took a shower, standing under the hot water for a long time, trying to warm her bones, which still held the chills of the cold water in the quarry. When the water finally ran cold she dried, dressed in her thick robe and came through to the kitchen. She had been reading through a stack of files John had flagged for her attention, and she made some coffee and sat down to work her way through the stack.

Erika arrived at Bromley Station just before 8 a.m., and came out of the lift on the ground floor to a commotion. A group of uniformed officers stood around an old shopping trolley which contained a dummy they'd made for Guy Fawkes Night. It consisted of a comedy policeman's uniform stuffed with old newspaper. The head was a balloon; a mournful face with large eyes had been drawn on in permanent marker. It was topped by a policeman's helmet, where a curly red fright wig poked out from underneath. It looked like the group of officers had been stopped by Superintendent Yale, who was standing at the front of the trolley and was giving them a bollocking.

"So instead of worrying about the terror alert being raised to 'Severe,' you've decided to spend your time pissing about with this?"

"Sir. Tonight is Guy Fawkes Night, and we're collecting for Great Ormond Street," said a small female PC dressed in her stab vest and hi-vis jacket.

"What if top brass were to come in and do a spot check, eh? And they saw all of you standing around with this?"

"We've all just come off shift, sir. We thought if we stayed in uniform we could collect more money," said another officer.

"Would you have time to explain that?"

Erika realized the Guy had an uncanny resemblance to Superintendent Yale.

"Wasn't Guy Fawkes a terrorist?" asked a tall thin officer with a boyish face who had both hands tucked under his stab vest. "We could sort of talk about terrorism too, like a teaching tool."

"Do you want a warning?" snapped Yale. "Now bugger off; get this out of here!"

They turned the trolley and sloped off, the tall officer muttering: "Guy Fawkes tried to blow up the Houses of Parliament, didn't he?"

"Good morning, sir," said Erika, trying to keep a straight face.

"Is it?" he snapped. She opened her mouth, but he didn't wait to hear her answer. "Jason Tyler's legal team are tying us and the CPS in knots. He's now going back on a deal to reveal the location of computer records unless we press for a recommended suspended sentence."

"Bloody hell," said Erika. She wanted to remind him that this is what you get when you start to negotiate with drug dealers, but she didn't. He shook his head and went off down the corridor, muttering.

She took the stairs up to the incident room on the top floor. She was impressed to see that most of her team were already in. It was a Friday, and she was conscious that it was now a week since they had discovered Jessica's remains, and that they had been working flat out for seven days. Phones rang and nearly every desk was full. DC Knight was updating a corner of the whiteboard containing all the information, and a profile of Amanda Baker.

"Morning, boss, can I have a word?" asked Moss. Jumping up from her desk and intercepting her on the way to her glass office, she followed Erika into her office, shoving a piece of a doughnut in her mouth and washing it down with a gulp of coffee.

Erika put her bag on the desk, noticing another pile of case files had been prepared for her.

"How are you finding the team, Moss?"

"Good bunch; DC Crawford is a bit of a tit. Although I've seen bigger tits."

Erika rolled her eyes.

"Not in the mood for humor, boss?"

"Not really." She grinned.

"You had a couple of messages late yesterday from the secretary of an Oscar Browne QC. He wants to meet with you in his chambers."

"Which case is this concerning?" she asked, sitting at her desk.

"The Jessica Collins case, boss."

"Hang on," said Erika, realizing. "Oscar Browne. Is this Laura Collins's ex-boyfriend? The one she was away camping with when Jessica disappeared?"

"Yeah. They were at university together. He went off and is now a high profile barrister."

"And why is he calling me?"

"He wants to talk."

"About what?"

"He's asked if you could talk face-to-face. I pressed him but he wouldn't say any more."

Erika looked out of her office at the incident room. She felt she had hit a dead end already with this case, and she was sure the pile of files on her desk would taunt her further with her inability to find a suspect.

"See if he can do later this morning. Get me anything we have on him from the case files. He must have made a statement at the time. He had an alibi though?"

"He did. He and Laura were away camping in Wales. Marianne waved them off on the day before Jessica went missing. There's a statement from a bloke who worked at the campsite who saw them arrive. Says he remembers Oscar because he was the only black guy he saw all summer."

Erika raised an eyebrow. There was a knock at the door and John entered with some paperwork.

"Morning, boss. I've found some stuff on Bob Jennings, the man who was living in the cottage next to Hayes Quarry. He lived in the Bromley area all his life, spent some time in and out of various mental institutions in Kent. He did have a criminal record, but mostly for petty theft, really petty. In 1986 he stole six bananas from a greengrocer; in 1988 he nicked a necklace in a display case from Ratners. There is no history of violence. The council tried to house him on three occasions but every time he refused."

"So we can presume that's why he ended up squatting in the cottage by the quarry?" said Erika.

"I'll keep looking for more," said John.

"Is that our main suspect? A dead guy who stole six bananas and a crappo necklace?" asked Moss. Erika ignored her. "OK, boss, I'll get that meeting set up with Oscar Browne. And you look like you could use coffee?"

"Thanks, Moss." Erika sat back and rubbed her eyes. This case seemed to be blossoming out of control in all directions.

CHAPTER 25

That afternoon Erika took the fast train from Bromley, arriving half an hour later at London Victoria. The Fortitudo Legal Chambers were housed in a red-brick building a few minutes' walk from the station, a few doors down from the Apollo Theatre.

It felt serious. The stern woman on the front desk; the imposing opulence of the reception area of carved stone and molded high ceilings. Erika was shown to Oscar Browne's office on the top floor, which had a sweeping view of the London skyline.

"Detective Chief Inspector," he said, rising and moving round his desk to welcome her. They shook hands. "Can I get you anything? Tea? Coffee, some water?"

"No, thank you," said Erika.

He was a tall distinguished man with the beginnings of salt-and-pepper in his dark hair. He wore an expensive tailored suit and shoes. He had been eighteen at the time of Jessica's disappearance, which now made him forty-four years old. She sat on the comfortable armchair in front of his desk. It was the office of an expensive lawyer, thick rugs, dark polished wood and the all-seeing secretary. Erika imagined she had been carefully chosen; she was not too easy on the eye to distract the male partners, but attractive enough to show the company was young and dynamic. He waited until the secretary had left, then spoke.

"I was very sad to hear that Jessica's body had been recovered. In some ways twenty-six years has gone so fast, on the other it seems like only yesterday." His voice had a theatrical richness which Erika was sure he used to maximum effect in court.

"I don't think it's gone quickly for the Collins family," she replied.

"No, of course not. Do you have any leads? Suspects?"

Erika tilted her head and looked him square in the eye. "I'm not here to tell you if we have any leads or suspects, Mr. Browne. In fact, why am I here?"

He smiled. His teeth were dazzlingly white. "I'm still in contact with the Collins family, and I witnessed at first-hand how the previous investigation unfolded. It was distressing and damaging for the family."

"I'm aware of what happened."

"I've been asked by the family to act as their spokesperson."

"But you are a barrister, not a PR?"

"Correct."

"Then you must see that there is a conflict of interests. You are a potential witness to the events twenty-six years ago—"

"I could also be a suspect," he finished.

Erika paused.

"Am I a suspect?" He grinned.

"Mr. Browne, I won't be discussing the case with you."

"Then can I speak to you as a concerned citizen?" he asked.

"Of course."

"During the first MET investigation things spun out of control. It seemed that the bad guys won, and they were left with questions, in particular, whether the investigation was mismanaged. If things were missed."

"You were away with Laura Collins weren't you? So you have an alibi?"

He bristled at this. "An alibi?" He sat back and gave her a disarming smile. "I gave the officer at the time a full statement, along with Laura. We were both away camping."

"The Gower Peninsula in Wales?"

"Yes, it's a beautiful part of the country."

"What made you choose Wales?"

"We were both at university in Swansea. It's quite close. We'd been there with friends the previous Easter, and we fancied a proper trip, just the two of us."

"Are you still close to Laura?"

"I wouldn't say we're close. Our relationship didn't last. We split up in early 1991."

"Why?"

"In the September of 1990 we were due to go back for our second year. I was studying Law; she was studying Mathematics. Obviously she didn't return. Did you go to university?"

"No I didn't," said Erika. It came out with more hostility than she intended.

"Well, let me tell you, life at university is very insular and intense. I met another girl; Laura was upset and so was I, but we parted amicably, and I was still there for her."

"So you dumped her?"

"I wouldn't say that. Laura will admit that it was a terrible time; she didn't know how to deal with it, she . . ."

"What?"

"She became impossible to be around. I don't blame her one little bit." He emphasized the last three words with the flat of his palm on the polished surface of the desk.

"You were away camping in the middle of nowhere. How did you find out so fast that Jessica was missing?"

"You're questioning me?"

"I thought I was talking to a concerned citizen?"

He smiled broadly. "There was a coffee shop and bar at the campsite. The next day we saw it on the evening news when we were having a drink. We drove straight back...As I said, I gave all of this in a statement."

"You could have saved me a journey with us doing this over the phone."

"I like to meet people face-to-face...I have spoken several times on the phone with Marianne. She's worried that you won't be willing to re-examine Trevor Marksman's role in Jessica's disappearance. Worried that the civil suit he won against the MET will scare you away."

"I will call Marianne personally and assure her that we are looking at everyone. Trevor Marksman is now living in Vietnam."

"Is he? Where?"

Erika scrambled in her mind for the exact location. "We have an address in Hanoi."

"Are you also aware that he recently spent sixteen months in jail in Vietnam for child sex offenses?"

Erika paused. "We have been working through historical case files; we haven't yet been able to access that information," she said, trying to hide her annoyance.

"Are you also aware that Marksman is now back in the UK and living in London?"

"What?"

"So you're not aware?"

Erika struggled to maintain her composure. He reached into his drawer and pulled out a large Manila envelope and dropped it on the polished desk in front of her. "It's all in there. His address, his temporary address in Hanoi, and he's just incorporated a new company to deal with his real estate assets. He's quite a wealthy man."

Erika pulled the file toward her. "How did you get this?"

"I did some research. I'm a barrister. This is what I do for a living... You see why I thought it best not to do this over the phone? But if you do need to contact me, I'll give you my direct line." He took a compliments slip from his desk, and with a sleek black fountain pen underlined the phone number for his office. Twice. Erika could barely disguise her irritation at this. He held her gaze for a moment and then offered his hand.

"I thank you for your time, officer. I hope I can continue to help you with new information."

"Yes, thank you," she said.

He flashed her the winning smile, but she didn't return it and left his office.

When she'd left the chambers, Erika ducked into an empty doorway and opened the envelope, scanning the papers inside. She then called in to the incident room. Peterson picked up the phone, and she angrily told him what had happened.

"How is it that we didn't know this?" she demanded. "I looked like a complete idiot."

"Boss, we're working through so much of the past. It was on my desk to find out more about him but we're swamped here."

"I know," she said. "You're not going to believe this. Trevor Marksman lives in a fucking penthouse apartment on Borough High Street!"

"You want to pay him a visit?"

"Not yet. I need to think," she said.

"What do you want me to tell the team. Are we coming in tomorrow?"

"Yes," she said. "We can't slack off on this. We're not even close to having a suspect."

She hung up her phone and walked back to the station. She decided to pay another visit to someone who would understand how she felt.

CHAPTER 26

It was growing dark when Erika knocked on Amanda Baker's window. After a moment, the curtain opened, and the sash window was pulled up. Amanda was surprised to see Erika, and the bottle of white wine she had under her arm.

"I thought I'd cut out the middleman," said Erika, holding it up.

Amanda tilted her head suspiciously.

"This is, sort of, a social visit," she added.

"Sort of. Okay. You want to go round?" asked Amanda.

"I'll use the window."

She put out a hand and helped Erika over the sill and inside. Erika took a seat on the sofa and Amanda went off to make tea. When she returned with two steaming cups, she noticed a shift in the woman. She had a spring in her step, her clothes were clean and her long graying hair had been washed and was fastened up in a twist with two pencils. The living room was tidy, and on the small table beside the armchair was a clean ashtray, and a pile of notebooks. One lay open, the pages covered in a black spidery scrawl.

"Sure I can't get you anything stronger? You off-duty?"

"No, thank you," replied Erika, taking the tea. "I don't feel like I'm ever off-duty."

"I've only had two glasses today, whereas about now I would normally be polishing off my second bottle," said Amanda, sitting down in her armchair.

"What's happened?"

"You finding Jessica Collins's body; it's helped. Weirdly."

"How has it helped?"

"Not finding her has haunted me. Weeks, months and then years went by, and I had nothing, there was no evidence, things started to unravel. At one point I thought it was all an elaborate joke. Did you ever see that hidden camera show, *Candid Camera*, when they used to play tricks on people?"

Erika nodded.

"Sometimes I wondered if a guy with a microphone was going to pop up one day with Jessica in tow, and say, 'da-dahhh DCI Baker, we got you!' And she would give me a hug, and the lads at the nick would crowd round, we'd have a laugh, and then go to the pub. Jessica would get to go home to Martin and Marianne."

"It's probably the hardest case I've ever worked," said Erika. "I can deal with complexity, or tracking someone down. But there's *nothing*. I've been reading your case files. Of the sixty houses on Avondale Road, twenty-nine of them were away on holiday, and the residents of a further thirteen houses were out on the afternoon of the seventh of August. In the remaining houses, the neighbors who were at home that afternoon saw nothing."

Amanda nodded, she grabbed the notebook, and one of the pencils from her hair. "I've been writing lots of stuff down; maybe it could help you. It's helping me. I've unlocked a piece of my brain I haven't used in years."

"The detective brain," agreed Erika.

"We did a search of all the front and back gardens in Avondale Road, and looked to see if anywhere had recently been dug over." Amanda flicked through handwritten pages. "On the 13th of August we used a methane probe in the garden of number 34."

"Hang on, there's nothing in the case file about this," said Erika.

"I'm not surprised. The house belonged to the head of Bromley council at the time, John Murray."

"What made you search his garden?"

"A piece of ground in the back had been dug over. It rang some alarm bells."

"Why isn't this in the case files?"

"Local government. They wield more power than you think. A few things went 'missing.'"

"You think this John Murray was involved in Jessica's disappearance?"

"No. He was trying to protect his reputation. The methane probe registered something in his garden, so I had the whole thing excavated. All we found was the body of a decaying cat. A stray that their housekeeper had buried three weeks earlier, without their knowledge. The newspapers got hold of it. They published photos of a digger in his garden. We had to pull up paving slabs, a gazebo. His wife had just had it all landscaped." She lit a cigarette. "They were able to claim on insurance, but his name was linked to Jessica going missing. Bob Jennings had also done the deal with the local authority for the halfway house, and he kept it quiet."

"There's nothing about him in my case files."

"He wasn't a suspect. He did, however, do untold damage by withholding details of the halfway house. I didn't find out the full details of it being there until a few days later, then we lost another couple zeroing in on Trevor Marksman. That's what's always bugged me. He had an alibi, but he could have been working with someone, and he had that window of a few days until we were on to him."

Erika took a sip of her tea, thinking about the Manila envelope in her bag with details of Marksman returning to the UK.

"He taunted me when I interviewed him, after his arrest...I was devastated when I had to let him go."

"But you kept on at him, didn't you?" said Erika. The atmosphere in the room became chilly.

Amanda nodded, fixing her with a stare. "I fucking *hounded* him," she snarled.

CHAPTER 27

Six miles away, in a flat at the top of a high-rise in Morden, South London, Gerry sat in a cramped back bedroom listening at his computer.

Amanda Baker's gravelly voice came through his headphones, loud and close by, uncomfortably close to his ear. He figured she must be sitting in the armchair directly under the smoke alarm.

"We had Marksman under surveillance for a couple of weeks," she said. "He seemed to go on long ridiculous journeys around London. He had a bus saver card and he'd spend his days circling London, climbing off one bus and on to the next. We quickly realized he knew we were on to him...I can see now that he was keeping us away from Hayes..."

There was silence, he heard a clatter of a teacup in a saucer as it was placed on the coffee table.

"What did you do?" It was Erika's voice.

"I struggled to keep morale up. None of my officers wanted to follow Marksman on his wild goose chases, but we had to keep on him, had to be sure that he wasn't doing this to shake us off...Do you know what it was he went down for?"

"No."

Amanda's voice went on: "When Marksman was living in West London, near Earls Court, he abducted a five-year-old girl. He was walking down Cromwell Road, just down from the tube station. There's rows and rows of those old four story terraced houses. In the window of one a small girl was playing. He stopped, got talking to her and persuaded her to leave with him. He said he was a friend of her mother and that he lived a few doors down. He told her he had a puppy. She went with him. He drugged her and took her to an allotment shed about a mile away. He kept her there for three days. He raped her. She was five years old. It was January and the weather was bitterly cold. He thought the allotment was a good bet because of the time of year. There was snow on the ground, and the place was deserted. A dog walker had been past a few days running and he'd seen Marksman going into the shed with a bag of toys...He raised the alarm. When they found her she was dressed only in her night dress, she was terrified and she had pneumonia—"

"What happened to her?"

"She survived. I don't know where she is now. I don't know if she ever recovered, if she was ever able to live a normal life."

There was silence for a moment. Gerry looked at the screen. The tiny colored graph had stopped moving.

"That's why I did it." Amanda broke the silence. "That's why I took the law into my own hands. I wanted that fucker to burn. To burn hotter than the sun, and feel so much pain... I was gutted when I heard he was going to pull through, that the fire hadn't killed him. But I think it's better that he's been left like this. Have you seen how he looks?"

"Yes." Erika's voice, quiet.

"Yeah, he's a scary freak. He looked fairly ordinary before. At least now he can't approach a child without scaring them straight away."

Gerry saw that his iPhone was flashing on the desk beside the laptop. He checked that the audio was recording and he removed the headphones, and answered the call.

"It's working. I'm getting a good audio signal from Amanda Baker's. Erika Foster's there with her now," he said.

"Why is she there? What's happening?" came the voice.

"Chill, man. She's clueless. She's got nothing. She came to see Amanda off her own back, no doubt to make herself feel better."

"What about the phones?" asked the voice.

"I've hacked into Amanda's phone no probs. It's a generic cheapo Android phone, and I gained access with the text message Trojan. I can see why; she plays a lot of games on her phone, and she enters loads of those premium rate phone-in competitions on the TV. She didn't notice the blank text, and I deleted it. I've just done the same with DC Crawford."

"What about DCI Foster. I need ears on her too."

"It's a risk. She's sharp and she's smart. If she susses a hack attempt—"

"I need to know what's going on."

"And I'm fucking telling you, she's got nothing."

"You should be careful. Remember who you're talking to." The voice was icy.

Gerry sat back in his chair and put his feet up on the desk. "I'm your eyes and ears."

There was a pause.

"Hack the Foster woman's phone. If there's any comeback, I'll make sure you're placed far from it. You have my word."

"Okay," said Gerry. "I'll get things started."

CHAPTER 28

It was late when Erika left Amanda Baker's house. She felt she understood a little more about the woman, but she still couldn't condone her actions in tipping off a vigilante group to firebomb Trevor Marksman's house. Her car was parked a little way down the darkened street and she got in, locked the doors and flicked on the light.

The Manila envelope was thick, and she pulled out the paperwork again and looked through the pages. Trevor Marksman was a very rich man. He'd been awarded almost three hundred thousand pounds by a court in 1993. He'd invested it wisely, and was now a millionaire. She looked at the printout of the address where he now lived in London, in an exclusive apartment block in Borough, near London Bridge.

She took out her phone and called Marsh. He answered almost straightaway.

"Sorry to call so late."

"It's only nine o'clock. I'm up," he said.

"Are you okay, you sound a bit down?"

He sighed. "I haven't been sleeping... Marcie wants to

work out official visitation times for when I can see the girls. She's not happy about me just popping in. Popping in. It's my house for Christ sakes!"

"I'm sorry, Paul..."

"It's my own fault. I work too much. I took your call. You haven't phoned me to ask about my marriage, have you?"

"Uh, no..."

"What is it?"

"Trevor Marksman. How were things left after the court case?"

"He won compensation. The MET forked out what was a huge amount in the early nineties. Full apology. There was quite the controversy in the press about having to apologize to a child rapist."

"I want to talk to him."

"No way, Erika. If you bring him in you're opening one hell of a can of worms."

"I don't want to talk to him as a suspect. I want to talk to him as a witness."

"A witness?"

"Yes, no one saw anything, no neighbors, no locals, nothing. The only person who we know had his eye on her in the days leading up to her going missing was Trevor Marksman. Yes, he's a sicko, but if we put that to one side for a moment, he could also have seen something, heard something."

"He never said he did."

"Did anyone ever ask him?"

There was a pause on the end of the line.

"Okay. You'd need to ask him if he'd be willing to talk. You'd need to be diplomatic. Course he lives in Vietnam; you'd have to see about, I don't know, doing it over Skype."

"He's not in Vietnam. He's moved back. He lives in London."

"What the hell? Why didn't we know?"

"He doesn't have to tell us. He was convicted and served time for the rape of the young girl before the Sex Offenders Act in 1997. As you know, it's not retroactive, so doesn't include anyone convicted before 1997."

"So you just want to talk to him?"

"Yes."

"And you're telling me?"

"This is the new me. I'm doing things by the book, keeping my superior officer informed."

"Pull the other one. You almost made me laugh."

"Sounds like you could do with it—"

"Erika…"

"What?"

There was a silence on the end of the phone. Erika thought he was going to ask her something.

"Nothing. Keep me posted, and don't screw it up," said Marsh, and he put the phone down.

CHAPTER 29

Erika and Peterson met on the 9:30 a.m. train into London Bridge. He'd got on at Sydenham, the previous stop, and was saving her a seat when she got on at Forest Hill. He sat by the window, and seemed moody and reluctant to talk, which Erika was glad of after the little sleep she had managed. She'd considered taking Moss to interview Marksman, but she had been invaluable to Erika, running the incident room with startling efficiency. She also thought of John, but his early morning chit-chat would have driven her crazy, and with Peterson she felt she had a more experienced officer.

"It's going to be a bloody long winter," he said as the train slowed and they passed the giant refuse incineration plant after New Cross Gate station. The sky hung low and the blocks of flats seemed to close in around the train tracks.

They left the train at London Bridge, and came out onto Borough High Street. It was bustling with traffic, and tourists were pouring into Borough Market. There was already a line of Christmas stalls selling decorations, and the smell of mulled wine mingled with the chill air and drifted across the road. They passed under the railway bridge and crossed the road, walking for a few minutes through thick crowds, until they came to a tall set of black cast iron gates.

"How the hell has Trevor Marksman ended up living here?" asked Erika, peering through to see a glimpse of a cobbled courtyard. Peterson found his apartment number and pressed call.

"Sometimes it makes you question if there is a God," he replied darkly.

Erika realized this was a question she rarely asked.

"We're here to talk to him as a witness," she said, noting the anger on his face. "He might be helpful."

Peterson went to respond, but there was a crackle from the intercom and a voice asked them to hold some ID to the camera. They pulled out their warrant cards and pressed them toward the tiny lens. After a moment, the huge gates soundlessly swung inwards.

They walked into a large courtyard surrounded by a small landscaped garden. The gates slid closed, and at once they were transported away from the noise of the busy high street.

"That's not him waiting for us?" asked Erika as they approached a tall red-brick building with a large glass entrance. A tall balding man waited in the distance.

"That's not him. He has an assistant," said Peterson.

When they came level the man nodded curtly. He had pale skin, and a bald shiny head. A pink scar wove its way across his forehead and vanished behind his left ear.

"Good morning, officers. May I see your IDs again?" he said politely. He had a clipped South African accent, and Erika could see that underneath his suit he carried considerable bulk. They showed their warrant cards, which he studied carefully, glancing up between them. Satisfied, he smiled and nodded. "Please come in."

They came out of a lift onto the top floor, where there was a small hallway. A large black lacquered table sat between two gleaming blue front doors. On it was a tall and slender white vase with a delicate pattern of roses. It had an almost sinister elegance to it, and it made Erika think fondly of the hallway in her own building; a tiny table covered in copies of the local free newspaper and takeaway leaflets.

"What's your name?" asked Erika. The man had been silent as they traveled up in the lift.

"I'm Joel," he replied. His eyes were gray and distant. "Please remove your shoes," he added as he opened the blue front door on the right.

The front door opened directly out to a large open-plan living area with a beautiful pale blue carpet edged in cream and white roses. It was very warm, and there was an almost overpowering smell of plug-in air freshener. Joel stood over them as they removed their shoes, and Erika noticed how uncomfortable Peterson was.

"Please come through," he said.

They moved through the living area, which was lined with bookshelves and dotted with pale sofas around a large, low coffee table. It was covered in glossy photo books featuring images of young children; one, in particular, was of a young girl in a red swimsuit sitting on a beach. She was making a sandcastle and fixed the camera with large pale blue eyes and a serious pout. The walls were adorned with several large prints of young children. To Erika it was as if their innocence had been caught in the split second of the camera shutter and placed in the apartment to be devoured at leisure. There was nothing illegal about the pictures, but fitting them into the jigsaw of Trevor Marksman's life gave them a disturbing edge.

The room curved to the left and they came to a man

sitting in an armchair by a huge picture window. He looked out over the Thames, the sky low and gray. A small tugboat was the only traffic on the choppy water, pulling a long flat barge.

"Trevor Marksman?" asked Peterson.

The man turned and, for a moment, Erika couldn't speak. His head was covered in skin, but it didn't look as if it had always belonged to him. It looked as if a large flat piece had been rolled out and then carelessly placed over his head. The skin was painfully tight around his eyes, barely affording him eyelids. His lips were non-existent.

"Please sit," he said. He found it difficult to make the plosive "p" sound. He wore loose-fitting trousers, and a shirt which was open at the neck, where his burns continued. His hands were red raw and claw-like, and there were only the remnants of fingernails on his left thumb and right index finger.

"Thank you for agreeing to speak to us," said Erika, placing her bag on the floor and taking off her coat. She looked across at Peterson, who was staring down at Marksman with real rage. She too felt revulsion, but shot him a look to keep a lid on it and focus. She hung her coat on the back of the chair and sat; Peterson sat next to her.

"Would you like some tea or coffee?" asked Trevor. His eyes were cold and very blue, and Erika remembered them from his first mugshot, taken when he was arrested for questioning in August 1990. It was like they were staring out from behind a Halloween mask.

"We'll have coffee," said Erika.

"Joel, would you be so kind?" said Marksman. His voice had a pained hoarse sound. Joel smiled and moved off around a corner to what Erika presumed was the kitchen.

"I don't know what I'd do without Joel. I have heart

problems. I can barely take two steps these days without having to sit."

"So no more prowling kids' playgrounds for you. Or does he do that for you?" asked Peterson.

"We're aware of your history, but we're not here to talk about that," said Erika, turning to stare at Peterson.

"I have only ever been accused of one crime..." said Marksman.

"Yeah. Abducting and raping a young girl," said Peterson. "You drugged her."

"I served seven years for that, and not a day goes by when I don't regret it," he replied hoarsely. He started to cough and brought one of the raw claw hands up to his lipless mouth. He motioned for a beaker with a straw next to Peterson on the sill of the picture window. Peterson sat back and folded his arms. Erika rose and picked it up, holding it up to Marksman's mouth. The sound of him sucking down on the straw filled the room, until there was a gurgle as he emptied the glass.

"Thank you," he said, sitting back. "My voice and throat seem never to have recovered from the smoke damage. The doctor said it was like I'd inhaled ten thousand cigarettes at once."

Erika replaced the glass and sat. He pulled out a tissue nestled in the side of the armchair and wiped at his face. He saw Peterson glaring at him. He put the tissue down and brought his hands to his chest. Slowly, painfully, he used his claws to undo three of his shirt buttons. He splayed the shirt open where a beautiful silver crucifix lay against his burnt chest. Erika noticed he didn't have any nipples.

"I have asked God for forgiveness. I have asked him, and he has forgiven me. Do you believe in forgiveness, Detective Peterson?"

"I'm a detective inspector," he replied coldly.

"Are you a detective inspector who believes in forgiveness?"

"I believe in it, but I think there are some things which should never be forgiven."

"By that you mean people like me."

"You bet I do." Erika shot Peterson a warning look, but he went on. "My sister was raped by our local priest when she was six. He threatened to kill her if she said anything."

Marksman nodded sagely. "The priesthood attracts the best and the worst. Did he repent?"

"Did he repent?"

"Did he ask for forgiveness—"

"I know what it means!" shouted Peterson. "He did it! He raped my sister when she was a child. Words and prayers can't take that away!"

Marksman went to speak, but Peterson was now in full flow: "He died on his own terms, natural causes; he was never brought to justice. My sister, well, she didn't have the luxury of a peaceful death. She killed herself—"

"Peterson, we're here to ask Mr. Marksman questions as a witness," said Erika evenly. "Now sit down."

She had spoken to him before the meeting, telling him to keep his cool. Peterson was breathing heavily and eyeballing Trevor Marksman, small and hunched in his chair.

"I'm sorry for your loss," said Marksman, with an almost maddening calm. Like the photo Erika had seen of him, the skin grafts seemed like a mask, and his cold blue eyes peered through from underneath. His skin crinkled above one eye, and Erika realized he was raising what used to be an eyebrow.

Peterson leapt up, his chair tipping back with a crash, and he had Marksman by the shirt collar before Erika could react. Marksman was lifted out of his chair, but he betrayed no fear and hung loosely in Peterson's grip.

"What was her name?" asked Marksman softly, his face up close to Peterson.

"What?"

"Your sister? What was her name?" repeated Marksman with infuriating calmness.

"You don't get to ask her name!" said Peterson, shaking Marksman hard. "You. Do. NOT GET TO ASK ME HER NAME YOU FUCKING FREAK!"

"Peterson! James. Let him go! NOW," said Erika, placing her hands on his arms. But he carried on shaking Marksman.

"We don't choose to be like this, you know," croaked Marksman, his head flopping back and forward.

Suddenly Joel was at Erika's side, and he had a powerful forearm wrapped around Peterson's upper body.

"Let him go. Or I break your neck," he said calmly.

"We are police officers, we need to calm down here," said Erika, moving to look directly at Peterson.

"This constitutes an assault, and I'd be within my rights," said Joel.

"No one is going to do anything. Peterson, let go, and you, take your hands off him," said Erika. There was a brief stand-off, and then Peterson let go of Marksman, who slumped back in the chair. Joel released Peterson, but stood close, his nostrils flaring.

"Back off," said Peterson.

"No way, mate," said Joel.

"Peterson. I'd like you to leave. I'll call you . . . Go NOW!" said Erika.

Peterson glowered at them all and then left. Moments later the front door slammed.

They settled back down. Joel moved to Marksman and

buttoned his shirt, and helped him get comfortable. Then Marksman motioned with his hand and Joel left.

"I apologize for that," said Erika. "I came here to ask you questions as a witness, and I expected you to be treated that way."

He nodded. "You are kind."

"No. I'm doing my job...I've looked over the statement you gave, and the transcripts of police interviews, in August 1990. You stated that you followed Jessica on the fifth and sixth of August, and you were watching her on the morning of the seventh outside her house?"

"Yes."

"Why?"

Marksman took a ragged breath. "I was in love with her...I can see you grimace. But you have to understand, I can't control how I feel. I'm repulsed by my desires; I cannot control them. She was a beautiful little girl. I first saw her at the newsagent in Hayes, shortly after I was released from prison. She was with her mother. It was maybe early spring in 1990. Jessica was wearing a blue dress and her hair was tied back with a matching ribbon. Her hair was luminous, and she was holding her little brother's hand. She was tickling him and laughing. Her laugh. It was like music. I heard her mother say their address when she was paying the newspaper bill. I started to, well, watch them."

"And how did the Collinses seem, as a family?"

"Happy-go-lucky. Although..."

"What?"

"On two occasions, I was in the park, watching Jessica with her mother and sister."

"Laura?"

"Dark-haired girl?" asked Marksman.

"Yes, that was Laura."

"Jessica was playing on the swings, and the mother and Laura were sat at a bench rowing something chronic."

"What about?"

"I don't know. I couldn't hear from where I was."

"Where was that?"

"A bench on the opposite side of the park."

"That's where you took the pictures of Jessica?"

"And video too. I won a camcorder in a competition at the Co-op..." His eyes lit up and for a moment he smiled at the memory, the skin around his eyes tightening. "The argument got quite vicious. Marianne slapped Laura across the face. I also saw Marianne slap Jessica on the legs, quite frequently. But I suppose it was a long time ago. These days people would be shocked; back then it was usual to slap your children. And those Catholics know all about meting out punishment."

"Laura had just turned twenty, and her mother slapped her around the face?"

Marksman nodded and then rested his chin on his chest, the scar tissue bunching up like crepe paper. "Although she slapped her mother back, gave as good as she got." He gave a wheezing laugh at the memory.

"What happened to your videos and photos?"

"They were seized by the police."

"Did you make copies?" asked Erika.

"No. And they were never returned to me. I don't know why; it was just a video of a park."

"Did you see anyone else suspicious?"

He laughed. "Apart from me?"

"Trevor. I'm asking for your help."

"I don't know. There were always scores of people in that park—parents, children. There was the occasional blackie, but they soon saw which way their bread was buttered—"

"Don't use that word."

"Have you seen Hayes? Very affluent, it's probably just as milky white as it was back in the nineties."

"Can we?..."

"There was a local loon, Bob Jennings."

Erika sat up a little more. "Bob Jennings?"

Trevor nodded.

"What was he doing?"

"You've heard of him?"

"Please, just tell me what he was doing?"

"He was a council gardener. Bit slow, so the council got him cheap no doubt." He gave a wheezing laugh.

"What's so funny?"

"He used to like wanking himself off in the bushes at the park. He had a thing for matronly old ladies with big tits."

"Was he ever arrested?"

Trevor shrugged. "God knows. I know he was already on his third or fourth job with the council. He'd been a road sweeper, binman. His sour-faced old bitch of a sister always used to have a word in the right ear, got things brushed under the carpet. The family is from landed gentry; that kind of posh voice, you know, plum in the gob."

"Who is his sister?"

"The Honorable Rosemary Hooley. A right cunt. I don't know if she's still alive, she probably is. The blue-blooded ones always go on forever."

Erika stopped for a moment. "Hang on, did she live in Hayes?"

Trevor nodded.

"Did she have a scar on her lip?"

"That's her. She had an Alsatian, years back, who bit her on the face. I remember Bob got very upset when I suggested that she'd tried to suck it off...There are people who like that, sucking off animals." Erika could see he was trying to get a rise out of her. He laughed and dissolved into a coughing fit. Joel appeared with a glass of water.

"I think he needs a short break," he said.

"No. I'm done," said Erika, standing and picking up her coat and bag. "Thank you."

She left hurriedly and went to the lift outside; pulling out her phone, she dialed Peterson.

CHAPTER 30

Erika found Peterson leaning on the rail beside the Thames with a takeaway coffee and a cigarette. He was dwarfed by the Golden Hinde II, a museum ship which rose up out of its dock, gleaming black and gold against the gray river. A cold wind roared past, and Erika was glad of it after the clingy, cloying atmosphere of Trevor Marksman's apartment.

"I got you a coffee," he said, reaching down between his feet and handing her a takeaway cup. "Might be cold."

"Thanks," she said, taking a sip.

"Did you drink his coffee? Marksman?"

"No."

"Good."

"Give me a cigarette, would you?"

"I thought you'd given up?" he said.

"I'm starting again."

He pulled out his pack of cigarettes, and she took one and lit up.

"I'm sorry, I shouldn't have asked you to come and speak to him. I didn't think," she said.

"It's okay. He's not worth it."

"No. He did give us a lead, and he did it without realizing."

He turned and looked at her, and for the first time that morning his eyes brightened.

They walked along the Thames Embankment, and Erika filled him in on the rest of the meeting. They grabbed a sandwich at Charing Cross, and took a direct train to Hayes. Typically, the train company had only put on a couple of carriages.

"Why didn't that old woman mention that Bob Jennings was her brother?" said Erika, speaking in a low voice. Every seat was taken and they had to stand, packed in at the back of the crowded carriage.

"She didn't want to give us her name either," said Peterson.

"But she knew we'd just found the skeleton of...you-know-who in the you-know-where," said Erika.

A short woman was crushed in beside them with a magazine, but she was staring. She looked away when they both turned to her.

"I want to talk to her and I don't care if she's from the landed gentry, I hate all that nonsense," said Erika. "Slovakia has many problems but, thankfully, we've escaped having a bloody class system."

It was a short walk up from Hayes train station to the address they'd been sent by control. Rosemary Hooley lived in one of a row of posh-looking cottages next to the Croydon Road entrance to Hayes Common. They overlooked a gravel car park and the common, and were all set back from the quiet road with large gardens. There was a faint smell of wood-smoke, which grew stronger as they approached The Old Vicarage where Rosemary lived. Erika opened the small white front gate. The house was thatched, and the front beautifully kept, with a neat mossy lawn dotted with dead leaves. One of the windows was double aspect, and through a cozy little front room they caught a glimpse of Rosemary Hooley standing in the back garden, raking leaves into a pile. She wore the same old tracksuit with Chelsea FC bobble hat and Man United scarf. The yellow Labrador must have heard them and came bounding round the corner, barking.

"Serge!" cried Rosemary, following moments later through a side gate. She saw Erika and Peterson and took a breath, and leaned on her rake. "Ah... I thought I might see you both again. Tea?"

"Yes, thank you," said Erika.

Rosemary pulled off her battered gloves and indicated they should follow.

A glossy green Aga dominated the kitchen, providing warmth and comfort from the cold outside. Rosemary took off her hat but kept on her coat and wellingtons and crashed about, pulling out cups, milk, sugar, and a Victoria sponge on an old willow-pattern plate. Erika and Peterson sat awkwardly at a wooden table covered in old copies of the *Radio Times*, a car radio with wires hanging out of the back, and a bowl of blackening bananas. Two scrawny cats were asleep in the middle, and Erika could see one had a huge tick on the top of its head.

Rosemary came over and handed the cake plate to Erika. She picked up the first cat and tossed it onto the floor, where it landed expertly on its four paws. She picked up the second cat with the tick and, in a swift movement, twisted it out. She let the cat drop to the floor and held the tick up to the light of the window between her knuckles.

"There, you see, you have to get it out with all the head

intact..." She held it toward Peterson, its black hair-fine legs wriggling, and he turned away looking queasy.

Rosemary moved away to the sink and dropped it down the plughole, activating the garbage disposal with a roar. Erika noted she didn't wash her hands when she returned with a tray of tea things and cut the cake.

"So. Dead girl at the bottom of the quarry...Bad business...Very bad," she said, taking a slurp of her tea. A little dribbled down her chin and she wiped it with the back of her sleeve.

"We asked you about the house by the quarry a few days ago—" started Peterson.

"Yes. I was there, I remember."

"You said that a man squatted in the house...Bob Jennings. Why didn't you mention that he was your brother?" asked Erika.

"You never asked," she replied bluntly.

"We're asking now. And we'd like all the information. The quarry is now a murder scene, and your brother was living beside it. How long did your brother live in the cottage?" said Erika.

Rosemary took another gulp of her tea and looked a little chastised. "Years...I don't know, eleven years. The poor bugger was only a few months off being able to claim squatter's rights. And then he died."

"What were the exact dates he squatted there?" asked Erika.

Rosemary sat back in her chair and thought for a moment. "It would have been 1979 until, I suppose, October 1990."

"And when did he die?"

"He passed away late October 1990." She saw the look that passed between Erika and Peterson. "Is that significant?"

"Do you have a death certificate?"

"Not to hand, no," she said, crossing her arms.

"How was your brother, mentally?" asked Peterson.

Rosemary paused, and for the first time her creased face softened a little. "My brother was a lost soul. One of those people who slipped through the cracks of society."

"Did he have learning difficulties?"

"We never had a complete diagnosis. He was my older brother and, back then, you just sat at the back of the classroom as a troublemaker; there were no child psychologists. The only jobs he held down were with the council... I tried to have him here with me, but he would sleepwalk, or disappear at all hours leaving the door open. This was back when my husband was alive, and our daughter was small. We couldn't have him here. He'd go missing for weeks on end, and then he'd appear, here at the back door. I'd feed him, give him money. He went to prison twice for thieving, silly stuff. He'd see something bright and shiny in a shop, fall in love with it, and slip it in his pocket. No malice."

"I'm sorry to have to ask this but was he ever a suspect in the disappearance of Jessica Collins?" asked Erika.

At this suggestion, her manner changed completely. "How dare you! My brother was many things, but a child killer? No. Never. He didn't have it in him, and even if he did, he could never have masterminded something like that."

"Masterminded?" asked Peterson.

They watched as she lost composure and became flustered. "Well, it was a complex case, wasn't it? She disappeared without a trace...I joined the group of volunteers in the days afterward; we combed every inch of the common; gardens were searched."

"Did the police ever talk to him?"

"I don't know. No! Shouldn't you be the ones telling me that?"

·"As I say, I'm sorry to have to ask this—"

"There was an exhaustive investigation! And you're asking me twenty-six years later if my brother killed a seven-year-old girl?"

"Mrs. Hooley, we are asking questions, nothing more," said Peterson. "And to be honest, we're not sure why you were so evasive when we spoke to you on the common."

"Evasive? How was I evasive? You asked me a question; who lived in the house by the quarry, and I told you that it was Bob Jennings...Why do we all have to act in society like we're at a bloody confessional? I didn't lie to you, I merely answered what you asked."

"But you knew we'd discovered Jessica's remains?"

"And my brother has been dead for many years. You must forgive me...What do you call it these days, a senior moment?"

"Did your brother know or hang around with Trevor Marksman? He was arrested back in 1990 when Jessica Collins disappeared."

"No. My brother did not 'hang around' with convicted pedophiles."

"Do you still have a key to the cottage by the quarry?"

Rosemary rolled her eyes. "No. He was a squatter. I doubt he had one."

"What did you do with your brother's personal effects?"

"He had virtually no possessions. I gave what he had to the local charity shops. There was a silver St. Christopher necklace and it was buried with him."

"Did you think he was suicidal?"

Rosemary took a breath and her face sagged a little. "No. It just wasn't in his nature, and as far as hanging, he had a wild phobia for things being around his neck. As a child he refused to wear a tie or button his shirt. It was one of the reasons he was uneducated. He was expelled from every school. The St. Christopher I mentioned, he wore on his wrist. So for him to fashion a noose and then hang himself..." Her eyes became misty, and she grappled for a tissue in her sleeve. "Now, I think you've taken up more than enough of my time and my hospitality...If you want to ask me any more, I'd like there to be a solicitor present."

The temperature had dropped when Erika and Peterson came out of the gate. They could see Rosemary through the double aspect window, back in her garden. The pile of leaves was now ablaze. In her hand she had a can of what looked like petrol. The road lit up orange.

"Do you think Bob Jennings could have been our man?" asked Peterson as they started to walk back down to the station.

"It's possible, I don't know," said Erika. "We need to track down the tapes Marksman made with his camcorder at the park. Bob Jennings could be in them. It's a long shot, but it could be a lead, we could use it in an appeal."

"If he is our man, it would mean we have to prove a dead guy killed Jessica," said Peterson.

"I want to find out when he died. I also want to see a death certificate."

"You think he's still alive?"

"I don't know what to think," said Erika.

CHAPTER 31

On Sunday, Erika gave her team its first day off in over a week. She'd tried to unwind a little at home, knowing she'd feel refreshed by a little rest, but by late morning she was climbing the walls. She arrived at Bromley Station just after lunch and tried to track down the videotapes which had been seized by police from Trevor Marksman. She spent several hours going through every case file in search of tapes, DVDs or even a Memory Stick, but there was nothing. She then went down to Bromley Station's vast evidence store. The tapes had originally been seized in the borough, and they could have remained gathering dust in the basement of the station. All she had was the evidence number.

She was about to go downstairs when Crawford arrived.

"I wasn't expecting to see you here," he said.

"I can say the same for you," she replied, giving him the once over. He was dressed in jeans and a jumper, with his coat. She stood waiting for an answer.

Sweat glistened on his forehead. "I left my mobile behind..." Just as he said it, a phone started to ring in the pocket of his coat. He pulled it out and canceled the call. "My second phone," he added.

"Okay," said Erika.

She left with her tea, and he followed her up to the incident room. She busied herself with some paperwork, watching him out of the corner of her eye as he searched the floor under his desk.

"I thought I'd dropped it. But it's not here."

"The cleaner was in this morning. What does it look like?"

"Um, it's a Samsung. Smartphone, older model with a cracked case on the back."

"I'll look out for it."

He stood for a moment longer and then left. She waited by the window and watched as he emerged from the front of the station and crossed the road, talking intently into his phone. Making a mental note to keep her eye on him.

She left the station just after six, after a long dusty search in the evidence store in the basement of the station which went nowhere. She'd put a call through to the Specialist Casework Investigation Team, and gave the young girl on the end of the phone the evidence number for the tapes which was listed in one of the case files, but the girl on the end of the phone didn't fill her with hope when she said she'd follow it up.

She stopped by her flat, took a shower, changed, and went to keep a long-standing engagement she'd been looking forward to. Dinner, with Isaac Strong.

She arrived at Isaac's just before eight. He lived in a smart terraced house in Blackheath, which had an effortless elegance that always made her feel calm. She was planning on staying over so they could drink and put the world to rights. Isaac answered the door in jeans, T-shirt and a blue apron.

A delicious smell of roasting chicken mixed with rosemary wafted out.

"Hello. Okay, before I let you in, let's do a doorstep quality control." He grinned. She held up the two bottles of red wine she'd bought and he peered at the labels. "Slovak wine, interesting. This will be a first for me," he said.

"This is from the Radošina vineyard; it's delicious *and* it's drunk by the British royal family. So you could say it's fit for an old Queen like yourself!"

"Cheeky," he said, giving her a hug.

She followed him through to the kitchen, which was pale and elegant with a French-rustic theme: hand-painted white cabinets, work surfaces of pale wood. He pulled an ice bucket from the heavy butler sink in white ceramic, where there nestled a bottle of Prosecco.

"Let's have something fizzy first," he said, pouring her a glass.

She looked around the kitchen and wondered, as she always did, if, as a Forensic Pathologist, Isaac deliberately steered clear of stainless steel. She studied his face as he poured her a glass.

"How are you doing?" she asked. She hadn't had time to talk to him about anything more than the case.

"Fine," he said automatically. "A toast to friendship," he added, and they clinked glasses.

"Are you sure? It's not good to keep it all buttoned up inside," said Erika. She was referring to the death of Isaac's boyfriend, Stephen, a few months earlier.

"I'm finding it difficult to mourn him without feeling angry...It was all a bit one-sided. I loved him and I...I don't know if he really cared much for me," said Isaac softly.

"I think you gave him the stability and love he needed," replied Erika.

"Emphasis on the word 'gave.' All I did was give and I got nothing in return."

There was an awkward silence and he moved to the stove and placed a pan on the gas. "I appreciate you not feeding me with bullshit, but my way of dealing with it all is just to not talk about it...I know it's not healthy."

"There are no rules," said Erika. "I'm here for you, always."

"Thank you...Now let's change the subject."

"Okay, what do you want to talk about?"

Isaac stirred the contents of the pan and placed the spoon in the spoon rest by the hob. "I didn't want to talk shop tonight, but there's something that's come back on the bone marrow sample I took from Jessica Collins," he said.

"What?" said Erika, putting her glass down.

"There were very high levels of a chemical compound called tetraethyl lead present in the bone marrow sample I took from Jessica Collins's right tibia."

"Say that again?"

"Tetraethyl lead. It's an organic lead compound, an ingredient which was added to petrol to improve performance. It's now illegal, and it's been phased out of petrol since 1992."

"When petrol became unleaded," finished Erika.

"Yes. I know you never get the chance to switch off, but I thought you would want to know," he said. He came over to the table and sat topping up her glass.

"Why would so much be showing up in her bone marrow?"

"Obviously, I haven't had any tissue or blood samples to work with, but the conditions in which the body was wrapped and left at the bottom of the lake has preserved the bones."

"She was a healthy young girl and she was eating well, and from what I've read she was a well-cared for child."

"These levels indicate she could have been exposed to high levels of lead petrol before she died, or that it contributed to her death."

"Which puts more credence to my theory that she was abducted and kept in captivity for a period of weeks before her body was dumped in the quarry…She could have been exposed to fumes whilst she was in captivity," said Erika.

"That's up to you to find out."

"I hate it when you say that."

"Always a pleasure to help." He grinned wryly.

She took a long drink, placed it down and traced her finger over the condensation clinging to the glass. "What state is a body in after being buried for twenty-six years?"

"Buried how?" he asked.

"In a grave, conventionally, in a coffin."

"It depends."

"On what?"

"The type of casket, conditions of burial. Sometimes we can see corpses in surprisingly good condition after many years underground. Mahogany lead-lined caskets often slow the progress of decay. The cheaper coffins will erode away, leaving the body at the mercy of the earth and the organisms. Why? Are you thinking of digging someone up?" He got up and went to the counter, bringing back a bowl of roasted almonds.

"I don't know. Possibly. I'd have to justify it, obviously. I'd be looking to prove the cause of death." Erika took a handful and popped them in her mouth, savoring the crunch and the sea salt.

"Was the cause of death proven?"

"I'm still waiting on the death certificate. I have a suspect who died twenty-six years ago…" She quickly told him about Bob Jennings. "His cause of death was down as suicide, but his sister says it was a surprise that he took his own life."

"If it involved poison or broken bones, then traces can remain, but after twenty-six years you'd be risking upsetting family members for no reason."

"He hung himself; that was the documented cause of death."

"Okay, well there's not going to be much to go on for that after all this time. There wouldn't be much left of internal organs. If the neck was broken I would still be able to see that."

"What about his bones? What if he also had high levels of this tetraethyl lead in his bones?"

"But how would you link that specifically to Jessica Collins?"

Erika sighed. "You're right."

"And remember that exhuming anyone, especially after all this time, needs to be justified in court, not just on a hunch…And on a completely different matter, are you hungry?"

"Ravenous," she said with a smile.

"So you'll be eating dessert?"

"I always eat dessert. That's the only thing I'm sure of right now," she said.

CHAPTER 32

Erika took the stairs two at a time up to the second floor at Bromley Station. She clutched a bulging file of notes and checked for the fifth time that she had everything in order.

It was early afternoon on Monday, and just over ten days since Jessica Collins's remains had been discovered, and she now had to go in to a major briefing and give a progress report.

She came through the double doors and ran into Superintendent Yale, making him almost spill his *Who's the Boss?* mug, which was full of tea.

"Whoa! Steady on, Erika," he said, jumping back so that the spillage avoided his shoes and hit the carpet.

"Sorry, sir!" she said.

"You're looking smart," he said, taking in her black suit. "The cavalry is waiting: Commander Marsh, Assistant Commissioner Brace-Cosworthy *and* the Media Liaison with the twitchy eyes—"

"Colleen Scanlan. Sorry about the tea," she said, pulling out a tissue and handing it to him. "And sorry they've thrown you out of your office, sir. Commander Marsh only called me an hour ago to say the Assistant Commissioner was going to be in our borough and wanted to be briefed…"

"Not too hot here, is it? You've got sweat on your top lip," he said, dabbing the drips on his mug.

She wiped it away and moved past him. "Sorry, sir, I have to run—"

"Jason Tyler's henchmen are being rounded up this afternoon," he called after her. "We leaned on him hard. Threatened to take the kids off his wife. He's given us intel on six of his associates, plus access to the PayPal accounts they've been using. Looks like we're going to clean up!"

"Congratulations, sir. That's great to hear. Let's catch up later…"

He watched as she disappeared through the double doors.

" 'Catch up later,' eh? You could have stayed on the case you know, Erika, taken all the glory. This could have earned you a promotion too," he muttered ruefully. He took a gulp of his tea and started down the stairs.

Erika knocked on the office door and went in. The Assistant Commissioner, Camilla, sat behind Yale's desk in her crisp white shirt. Her blonde shoulder-length hair sleek and parted to the left and away from her high forehead. Her pale face was lined, and she wore bright red lipstick so thick and red that Erika imagined if she was thrown against the wall her lips would stick. Marsh perched on a low table to the left; his eyes were tired and his shirt was creased. Erika figured that he was still estranged from Marcie. Colleen Scanlan, the MET's Media Liaison officer sat to the right, her notes balanced on a sliver of desk. Her eyes flitted between Erika, Marsh and Camilla. She wore a gray sensible suit, and like many women in their fifties she'd succumbed to a brutally short haircut. It stuck up in brown tufts.

"Sorry I'm a little late," said Erika.

"Do take a seat, DCI Foster," said Camilla. "I've used this lull in the proceedings to let my coffee cool. It was scalding; don't you agree, Paul?" She picked up a white takeaway cup and took a sip, leaving a pair of bright red lips on the rim.

"Yes, they do do a good cup of coffee in the train station," said Marsh.

"Yes, it's a revelation," she agreed.

Erika could never tell if Camilla was being sarcastic or making conversation. Colleen cautiously took a sip of her takeaway coffee and nodded her agreement.

"Right," said Camilla, watching Erika as she got settled and laid out her paperwork on the table. "Do you have a working list of suspects for me?" She held out a manicured hand, her long red nails waggling in anticipation.

"I'd like to discuss that first before I commit any suspects to paper," said Erika.

"I see," said Camilla. "You'd like us to do your job for you then?"

"That's not what I'm saying, ma'am."

"What are you saying? Do put us in the picture..." She had a habit of drenching everything she said with a synthetic politeness, and it put Erika off her stride.

"In the short time I have had with this case, I've identified a possible suspect. Bob Jennings, a loner who was squatting in a cottage opposite the Hayes Quarry."

"This is good news. Why don't you want to commit him to paper?"

"Robert Jennings died twenty-six years ago; three months after Jessica went missing. He hung himself in the small cottage opposite Hayes Quarry."

"You think he was consumed by guilt?"

"Possibly. I also suspect foul play, which is where my

conflict lies in making him a suspect." Erika went on to tell them what Rosemary Hooley had said about his suicide.

"The quarry was searched twice after Jessica's disappearance. His death came within days of the quarry being searched for the second time."

"But police searched the cottage?"

"Yes, at the same time as the quarry. He still could have kept Jessica captive in the cottage at some point between the seventh of August, 1990, and when she was dumped in the water. I was sent this photo this morning from the Bromley Council records," said Erika, pulling it out of her paperwork.

Camilla took it and popped her glasses on. The thin gold chain swayed as she examined it. In the photo, he had a florid gnomic face, his large nose was bright red, and he had a mass of graying dark hair.

"I've had toxicology results back on Jessica Collins's remains. There were unusually high concentrations of a chemical called tetraethyl lead in samples taken of her bone marrow. It's an organic lead compound—"

"It was added to petrol to improve performance, making it leaded," finished Camilla.

"Yes, ma'am. I spoke to Rosemary Hooley this morning and she has confirmed that Bob Jennings had a petrol generator at the cottage. This would strengthen the theory that Jessica could have been kept captive in the cottage and exposed to petrol fumes."

Camilla pondered this for a moment, then handed the photo to Marsh.

"I understand you met with Trevor Marksman?"

"Yes, and Trevor stated he knew Bob Jennings. I don't know if he was stirring things up, or being provocative, but he mentioned the name to me unprompted. As we know, Trevor had an alibi for the seventh of August, 1990, and a week or so afterward was put under surveillance. No link was ever made to Bob Jennings; Bob could have been working with Trevor and helped him to abduct Jessica." Erika went on to say that she was trying to find the videotape evidence seized from his camcorder.

"It seems you have a great deal here, Erika," said Camilla. "But there are rather too many ifs and buts, and the man is dead, which of course limits any opportunity to interview him."

"Ma'am, I'd like to take a team out and look at the cottage, get forensics in there to pull it apart. I've looked at the plans, and the cottage has a cellar. It's a slim chance, but Jessica Collins's DNA could be present. If it was then we could put forward a request to have Bob Jennings's body exhumed, again in the hope that there is a trace of something. Both are long shots."

"The latter is a very long shot, Erika, but keep me posted. Keep pushing forward with this. Keep your investigation pacey." Camilla turned her attention to Colleen, who sat up, looking flustered.

"I'd like to move for a press conference with the family in the next few days. Make a fresh appeal for any historical information. People's memories may be jogged."

"Erika, if the lost Trevor Marksman video footage could be found in time, it could be something valuable to add to the appeal," said Camilla.

"Yes, ma'am," said Erika.

"Colleen, can you make do with Commander Marsh for the appeal? I'll be away for the next few days. Perhaps he can give his shirt an iron before he goes on camera."

Marsh looked down and smoothed his shirt.

"Yes, ma'am," said Colleen. "I was planning on using the whole Collins family."

"Very good. Unity and family values always play well. I'll be away, but I'll be watching."

When the meeting had finished, Erika walked with Marsh back down to the underground car park. They chatted for a moment, and then were shocked to see Camilla emerge from the lift wearing full motorbike leathers and carrying her briefcase. She moved to a gleaming silver and black Yamaha motorbike, slipped her briefcase into a carrier at the back, and pulled on a black and silver helmet and a pair of thick gloves. She flipped up the visor, and swung her leg over.

"Beats the traffic every time," she shouted as the engine roared to life. With a wave she sped off past them and down the ramp to the slip road.

"She didn't invite you to ride pillion," said Erika.

"Very funny. Riding pillion would be a promotion. She's quite a character," he said.

"There's something quite predatory about her. I can imagine her organizing those swinger parties where everyone throws their keys in a fruit bowl in the middle of the carpet."

"She's married to a high court judge," said Marsh, unlocking his car and opening the door.

"Then they're the ones who probably throw the parties."

"Get the job done. She doesn't mess about, Erika."

"Yes, sir. I'll be in touch about the search of the cottage at Hayes Quarry, and next time, iron your shirt."

He rolled his eyes and got into his car, making a far less impressive exit from the car park.

CHAPTER 33

"So what are you doing here at the end of the line?" asked the dark-haired girl. She leaned on the rail of the balcony holding a cigarette; she flicked her long hair over her shoulder and turned to Gerry. He stood at the other end by the rail wearing just a pair of tracksuit bottoms. She moved her eyes appraisingly down his muscled chest to the dusting of dark hair by his belly button. "Morden, it's the end of the tube line," she added.

"It's not the end of the line," he said, his voice low and menacing. "It's all about perception; it's the start of many."

He looked at the girl he'd picked up at the supermarket on Morden High Street. He hoped she was legal; she certainly looked it. All she wore was a white T-shirt of his, and it barely covered her backside. It was a good arse, he thought, staring. All of her was pretty damn good. She knew it, though. He felt his dick harden.

"Do you always talk in riddles?" she grinned. "What do you do? What's your job?" She took a final draw on her cigarette and flicked it over the balcony. They watched it slowly fall and land, still glowing, on the roof of a BMW. "Shit, that's not yours?" she asked with a giggle, flicking her long hair again.

"No. It's not mine."

She walked over to him; if her bare feet were cold on the concrete she didn't let on. He hadn't offered her any shoes or slippers. She turned to him and slowly pulled up the T-shirt. Her bare breasts rose as she lifted her arms and slipped it over her head. One of her nipples was pierced with a metal bar. The other nipple had the markings of a piercing, and a small scar. He wondered if she liked it rough.

She smiled at him for a moment, enjoying how his eyes played over her naked body, then she held the T-shirt over the balcony and let it go.

"That is mine," he said as it soared down and joined the cigarette butt on top of the car.

"It's just a T-shirt."

He slapped her hard across the face.

"It's not just a T-shirt," he said.

She put her hand to her lip, but her fear quickly vanished, and she pressed herself against him.

"Fuck me, here," she hissed.

"No."

"No?" she sighed. "You sure?" she turned and pressed her arse into his groin. "You can do whatever you want…" She grabbed his hand and pulled it round her waist and pressed it between her legs. His hand was limp but the second it made contact with her pubic hair she started to shriek and writhe. He pulled his hand away.

"What?" she asked.

"All that stupid porno shit, the screams and moans. It's fake. It makes me want to slap you again."

She turned, crossed her arms and the sexy act fell away. She was just a cold naked girl on a balcony.

"Do you want me to go get your T-shirt?" she asked.

"I just want you to go."

She looked at his chest, leaning into the warmth of his body. He saw that she was lonely, and she wanted to stay.

"But I've just got here..." she whined.

He punched her in the face, then grabbed her by the hair and held her face to his. She breathed quickly, and looked at him, dazed. A little blood was seeping from her nostril.

"Now do you get the hint?" he said.

He pushed her away, and she ran inside. He lit another cigarette and watched through the open door as she dissolved into bloody tears, quickly gathering up her jeans and her underwear from where it was strewn around the sofa, pulling her clothes on. With one fearful eye on him she quickly dressed and was gone with a slam of the front door.

He waited a few minutes. She emerged from the stairwell at the bottom, running away into the darkness. The click clacking of her heels fading away.

"Shit," he said. It was four in the morning. He hoped this wouldn't come back on him—that the stupid girl would get home without a hitch.

When he had finished his cigarette he walked slowly down the piss stinking stairwell of the flats past the graffiti on the walls, the broken glass and rubbish on the landings, and he retrieved his T-shirt from the top of the BMW. It was a nondescript white T-shirt, but he'd worn it on two tours of Iraq. It was his lucky T-shirt. He pulled it on and trudged back up the stairs.

When he got back inside the flat, he opened the door and went to the bedroom. He woke up the laptop with a shake of the mouse and sat down.

He found the program with the Trojan horse text message, and seeing it was four thirty, he pressed send.

CHAPTER 34

Early the next morning, when it was still dark, a convoy of police vans rumbled along the gravel path across Hayes Common. Erika had brought her team to search the cottage, with support from uniform division. The convoy parked close to the water, where she had been with the Marine Recovery Unit almost two weeks previously. It was a freezing morning, and everyone was rugged up in winter gear.

The team stood in a circle as Erika briefed them, ten officers in total; they then grabbed cups of tea and coffee, and watched as the darkness receded, moving through shades of blue until the flat expanse of water reflected the gray dawn sky.

A few early morning dog walkers picking their way across the heather in the early dawn light stopped and proceeded to stare before being moved along by a uniformed officer stationed a few hundred yards from the convoy of vans. A police cordon was put up, closing off a large square of grass approaching the quarry, and its perimeter, which included the large swathe of overgrown land around the cottage.

The first part of the morning was spent clearing away

undergrowth and brambles around the cottage, and the cold air was filled with the high-pitched whine of weed trimmers.

Erika waited impatiently outside one of the large support vans with John, Moss and Peterson, drinking tea and stamping her feet to keep warm. Just after 9 a.m., Erika's phone rang, but it cut out as soon as she pulled it from her pocket.

"That's the third call like that this morning: a withheld number," she said, irritably peering at the screen.

"Marketing people, I bet," said Moss, blowing on her tea. "I had a spate of getting them every evening when I sat down for dinner. It drove Celia mad."

"I had a blank text delivered at four thirty. A withheld number," said Erika.

"I'd get that checked out, boss. You didn't open it?"

Erika shook her head.

"I've never had a text message from a withheld number," said Peterson.

"Do all your hotline bling girls leave sultry voicemails?" grinned Moss.

"Piss off," he laughed.

Crawford approached them. "What are we laughing about?" he said, eager to be included.

"Peterson, and his booty calls," said Moss.

"I like a joke, but I'm not really in the mood for stupid humor this morning," snapped Erika.

They all looked down at their feet. Crawford laughed nervously.

"I was here both times we searched the quarry in 1990." He blew out his cheeks theatrically and tipped his head toward the water's edge. "Makes you realize how fast your life goes. I'll be forty-seven in the new year," he said.

"What about the cottage? Can you remember it being involved in either search?" asked Erika.

"We didn't find anything; we presumed it was abandoned."

"But Bob Jennings was squatting there," said Peterson, blowing on his tea.

"Often with squatters you don't know they're there. They live in squalor, don't they? Hence the term squatter." He rolled his eyes for Moss's benefit. "Anyone want more tea? I'm on the way to the kettle."

They shook their heads, and Crawford went off. The drone of the undergrowth being cut carried on.

"He irritates me," said Peterson.

"He talks down to me; we're the same rank," said John.

"Don't worry, mate. Promotion will come, you'll soon be his superior," said Peterson.

"He's got this annoying way of making jokes; always there with a stupid chirpy little know-it-all comment," added Moss.

Erika didn't mention that he'd come back to the station on Saturday, acting suspiciously. She was determined to keep an eye on him.

There was a high-pitched buzz and the sound of wood cracking, and a large lump of the undergrowth fell away, exposing half of the cottage near the water. They turned and watched as more clumps of vegetation were pulled away.

"It looks in a better state than I thought," said Peterson. The chimney stack had collapsed, but the roof looked intact. Most of the windows were broken, but again, the frames remained.

"Have we had any luck from the utility companies?" asked Erika.

"The cottage is effectively off the grid, no power. It did have a water supply and a septic tank. It's not part of the sewage network," said Peterson.

Crawford appeared behind them with a fresh cup of tea, and butted in: "A septic tank could hold evidence. That's if it hasn't been emptied."

"Good point. Can I put you in charge of tracking it down and looking through its contents?" asked Erika.

"Er, well, I was hoping to join the search inside the cottage," started Crawford.

"No. I'd like you to take charge of this search; take a couple of uniformed officers with you. There's gloves and protective gear in the support lorry."

"Yes, boss," said Crawford, moving off toward the van with a sour look on his face.

Moss and Peterson looked away, suppressing their grins.

CHAPTER 35

As Crawford tramped through the undergrowth surrounding the cottage, accompanied by two young uniformed officers, he reflected on his life. He was a decent copper. He'd worked hard, too hard at times, but he'd never reached the heights he'd aspired to, or felt he deserved. He'd dreamed of reaching the rank of superintendent, or chief superintendent, but his dreams had fallen short and he was still a detective constable at forty-seven.

He'd just come off a murder case where he'd had to take orders from a DCI fifteen years his junior, and it made his blood boil. Now he was looking for a septic tank. He paused at a ridge in the soil, a uniform line next to where a thin tree trunk had been hacked back, its pulpy inside glistening with moisture. He kicked at the soil, thinking he'd found the lip of the tank, but the soil flattened under his boot.

He sighed and looked back at the support vehicle, where Moss, Peterson and DC McGorry stood with DCI Foster. John McGorry was twenty years younger than him, and was in line for promotion; he could see it.

Crawford had lost interest in policing years ago, and did

just enough work to get by, but he still felt he was entitled to more.

He'd been involved in selling drugs seized from the street, for many years. It was a lucrative perk, he reasoned, a way of getting what he thought was owed to him, and he was careful to do it in moderation, careful to make just enough money on the side for a few luxuries, without drawing attention. It was Amanda Baker who had got him involved in it, fifteen or so years back. His wife had never found out that he'd been sleeping with her, and their relationship had fizzled out. But now Amanda was back on the scene, like a thorn in his side, calling in favors and threatening to betray him. He'd helped her out of several parking fines over the years, and had twice quashed a DUI which would have resulted in her losing her license.

His phone rang in his pocket, and he pulled it out. He saw that he had moved quite far from the two uniformed officers who were searching closer to the cottage, and was now on smoother, rocky ground. The phone showed it was the woman herself, Amanda Baker.

"Where are you? What's that droning noise in the background?" she said. There was no hello, how are you? Or any kind of deference in her tone. She still spoke to him like she did when she was his boss.

"I'm at work," he hissed. "I can't talk to you."

"Is she close by, DCI Foster?"

"No."

"Then you can talk. I need those videotapes, the ones from Trevor Marksman."

"We've had no luck tracking them down."

"That's why I'm phoning. I've been going back over things in my mind and I just remembered something. I had someone at the nick in Croydon look at those tapes, and they were sent over. Get someone to look in their evidence room. They might still be there. I want you to get them copied first, before you hand them over to Foster."

"What do you need them for?" he asked.

"I have a hunch. I'm not going to tell you what, but when I do get to the bottom of it, I will let you have it exclusively, and you can take all the glory...Maybe you'll finally get that promotion," she added with a mocking phlegmy laugh.

He looked back at the cottage. It had now been cleared, and a group of Crime Scene Officers had arrived and were shaking hands with Foster, Moss and Peterson. *Even that little idiot John McGorry gets to be amongst the action*, thought Crawford, *and she's got me looking for a bloody sewage tank*.

He gripped the phone, and turned his back on them.

"Okay. I'll see if I can get you the tapes," he hissed. "But it better be worth it."

CHAPTER 36

Forensics went into the cottage first, and the morning passed as Erika waited, pacing up and down by the water. The sun remained behind the clouds, but the water had an eerie beauty, framed by the dry reeds, and a bare tree. She watched as a light breeze pressed the water into creased patches, and as a group of six ducks landed on the water in unison, twelve neat lines trailing the flat surface behind them. She felt guilty enjoying the beauty of the quarry.

"They've found something; they want us inside," said Moss's voice behind her. Erika quickly wiped the tears from her eyes and then turned.

She suited up outside the cottage with Moss and Peterson, pulling the blue all-in-one paper suits over their clothes, and then putting on the face masks. A long sheet of plastic covered the front door, and Nils Åkerman, the Crime Scene manager, held it to one side for them as they entered. He was in his early thirties with a handsome face and a high Nordic forehead, and he nodded and smiled as they filed past him.

Erika was shocked at how gloomy it was inside. The door opened straight onto a small cramped room; the smell of decay was overwhelming, sweet and sour. She looked back at Moss and Peterson, and she could see it had hit them too. The floor was an uneven pattern of black and white and littered with broken glass.

"The floor, it's bird shit, tons of it," said Nils. "We've scraped a little away at the edges. There's parquet floor underneath." He spoke with a slight Swedish accent under his perfect English.

"Some people pay a fortune to get a floor to look like that," muttered Moss.

Above them, rotting beams were inlaid in a crumbling ceiling where water stains bloomed across the plaster, adding to the damp. A sagging lump in the center of the room was covered in more bird droppings, old newspapers, and broken glass. Rusting springs protruding in several places showed this was the remains of a sofa. One of the CSIs worked intently under a bright light, where she had stripped away a layer of bird droppings and the cover from a thinning cushion, attempting to examine the foam underneath. The sofa steamed lightly under the hot light.

In a corner next to a filthy, cracked window was a table covered in some old mugs, and the remnants of where someone had tried to light a fire. There were two other places where a fire had been lit; one against the back wall, and one by the front door. Black scorch marks streaked up the wall, and around them were the remnants of drug paraphernalia: slivers of blackened foil, a syringe, bent teaspoons. Erika moved across the sticky floor to where the wall was streaked with brown dots.

"Blood spatter, junkies most probably, but we've taken samples," said Nils.

"What's upstairs?" asked Moss, glancing at the sagging ceiling.

"No one has been up there yet. The staircase has rotted and collapsed on itself, and we're not sure how safe it is until we've done a structural check."

A shadow moved across the cracked window, and Erika jumped.

"Shit," she said when she realized it was just the outline of one of the uniformed officers working outside.

Nils led them through a low doorway to the back of the cottage. The kitchen was old and just as filthy as the living room. A low counter ran the length of one wall with its doors missing, exposing cupboards and, apart from a couple of old dusty saucepans and another blackened scorch patch, they were empty. Matching cupboards had been attached to the wall above the counter, but they had fallen off and lay in pieces in the middle of the room. The Rawlplugs still hung out of the holes in the wall. The light fitting was gone, just a few wires hung from a hole in the ceiling.

"What's that smell?" asked Peterson, putting the back of a gloved hand up to his face mask.

Nils tilted his head toward a small window over a stone sink. There was a sizable hole in the glass, blocked by dried blood and the rotting body of a pigeon that had tried to escape.

Erika moved closer and the smell became overpowering.

"Is that…" she started as she noticed the sink filled with piles of a dry brown substance.

"Shit," finished Nils. "Perhaps from the druggies."

The ceiling was slightly higher than the living room, and an exposed support beam crossed the length of the room.

"Could this be where Bob Jennings hung himself?" asked Moss.

"I can't be sure, but I've found this," said Nils.

He took them to a tall doorway in the back corner of the room; the door lay rotting on the floor. A strong lamp had been clipped to the doorframe, illuminating a cramped, filthy staircase leading down into darkness where thick dust swirled. The few stairs they could see were covered in piles of a hard brown substance, and mixed with bird droppings and rubbish.

Nils stepped through and pointed up with a gloved hand. There was a loop of frayed decaying rope attached to a hook in the ceiling at the top of the stairs.

"This could be from a hanging," said Nils. "I'm going to have what's left of the rope removed for tests. On finding a hanging body the police always ensure the noose is seized and cut with the knot intact for evidence." Nils went on: "I want you to follow me. Please mind where you walk, keep to the outside of each step," he said as they followed him through the doorway and down the creaking stairs.

The cellar was small and cramped with a low ceiling, and made Erika feel panicky. Another lamp on a stand was trained in one corner and, despite its brightness, parts of the cellar were in shadow. The walls were a dark brown and clogged in the corners with cobwebs. There was an uneven earth floor. From above they heard muffled creaks as Nils's CSIs worked.

"It's bloody warm," said Moss.

"As we approach winter the soil releases stored heat," said Nils.

As with the upstairs, there were several small scorched areas where fires had been lit, small piles of burnt foil and wood. The soil floor was a light brown and it was compact. Dotted around were several large blackened areas. Two CSIs were on their knees sifting intently where they had dug out some small sections of the blackened soil.

"These areas of the soil are saturated," said Nils.

He took an evidence bag full of soil and handed it to Erika. She put her nose to it, and even behind her mask she knew what it was.

"That's petrol," she said, handing it to Peterson. "You think there was a generator down here?"

"Perhaps. It looks like the junkies have been lighting fires too, could be lighter fluid," said Nils. Peterson passed the bag of soil to Moss. "If a generator had been placed down here, there's no ventilation, the fumes would have been over-powering."

A look passed between the three of them.

"I think I've got something here," said one of the CSIs, his voice muffled by his face mask. He turned to them with a small hard object held in a pair of tweezers. "It was embed-ded in the soil here."

Nils was ready with a small plastic bag, and it was dropped in. He held the bag up to the light and they all craned to look at the contents.

It was a small tooth. There was a moment's silence, and Erika looked over at Moss and Peterson.

"When we recovered Jessica Collins's skeletal remains, one of her front teeth was missing . . . I want this fast-tracked with toxicology," said Erika, trying to keep her voice even. Nils nodded. Erika looked around the dank cellar and shud-dered at the thought of being trapped down there. "If we can match that tooth to Jessica's skeleton, then we're close to solving this," she said.

CHAPTER 37

After the elation of finding the tooth, they had come back up and joined in the search with Crawford for the septic tank, but found nothing. The area around the house was overgrown, and over the years soil and all kinds of rubbish had been dumped there, on top of which trees and years of vegetation had grown.

After Nils had left with his team of CSIs, taking with them the tooth they'd found in the cellar, Erika felt they were so close and yet so far. The tooth could be a major breakthrough; it could also be from one of the junkies and squatters who had been in the hellhole cottage over the last twenty-six years. She would have to wait.

At 7:30 p.m. they called it a day. The convoy packed up and left the banks of the quarry. Erika rode back in a minibus with Moss, Peterson, John, Crawford and two other CID officers who'd joined them for the day. Her phone rang again. She pulled it out and saw it was the withheld number. She canceled the call, and rested her head against the window, not caring about the cold glass or the slow bumping as they moved toward the exit of the common. The bare trees rolling past.

*   *   *

Erika took her team for a drink when they arrived back at Bromley Station. They commandeered a long table in one of the pubs on the high street. It was busy, full of people unwinding after a hard day at work.

"It has to be the cottage at the quarry . . ." said Erika, tracing a pattern in the condensation of her glass. She sat at one end of the long table with Moss and Peterson. "Whoever grabbed Jessica had so little time. She could have been buried there first, in that cellar."

"And forensics are going to excavate it, boss. We have to be patient," said Moss.

Erika looked at the rest of the team, talking and laughing, and lowered her voice. "I want to talk to Crawford tomorrow. He was on the original case, he could potentially answer so many of our questions about missing files, and evidence. The problem when you don't take people seriously is that you don't notice them. I've dropped the ball."

"Don't beat yourself up, boss."

"Did you pull his file?"

"Yeah. He's had an unremarkable career. He's irritating, and he coasts, but there's no black marks against his name."

Erika took a long pull on her lager. "If that tooth doesn't come back as belonging to Jessica, we're screwed. Even if it does, I have to prove she was killed by a man with no prior violent behavior, who died twenty-six years ago."

"If it was him, think what you'll be saving the prison service," said Peterson. They sat and drank in silence for a moment. "Sorry, boss. Wasn't funny."

"That's okay. We should all be trying to unwind for a couple of hours. I'm not much fun."

"You're never much fun," said Moss. "That's what I like about you. There's no pressure to have a good time. I can be miserable around you. In fact, you have saved me from getting a hell of a lot of wrinkles. I look three years younger from lack of smiling."

Erika laughed.

"Dammit, here come the wrinkles," added Moss with a laugh. Her phone began to ring and she pulled it out. "Oh. This is Celia, will you excuse me."

She squeezed past them and went outside.

"For what it's worth, I love working with you. I've really missed you," said Peterson. Erika looked at him, feeling a little light-headed, and noted this was her third drink.

"You haven't. Have you?"

"Well, maybe just a little bit." He winked. He held her gaze for a moment and she returned his smile. He went to say something else.

"I think I'm going to use the bathroom," interrupted Erika, suddenly panicking.

She squeezed past him and went to the bathroom, locking herself in one of the cubicles. Sitting on the closed lid of the toilet she took a deep breath. She felt guilty that she was out drinking when Jessica Collins's killer was still out there on the loose. Guilty that she had lost her grip of the investigation. She also felt guilty that Peterson had been flirting with her...Had he been flirting? And did she secretly hope that he was flirting?

"You need to get a grip," she said to herself out loud.

"What?" came a voice from a cubicle further down.

"Nothing, sorry," she muttered. Erika pulled out her phone and saw two more voicemails from the withheld number. "Who is this?" she muttered. She dialed her voicemail, but had no signal. She sat for a few more minutes, listening to the sound of the toilet flushing and the hand dryer whirring.

Her mind went back again to Jessica Collins. She'd be thirty-three if she were still alive. What if she hadn't gone to that birthday party all those years ago? What if she'd left the house a few minutes earlier or later? She could be one of those women down in the bar, having fun, playing the "Who Wants to be a Millionaire?" machine, and laughing with her friends.

And then Erika thought about her past. What if she and Mark had decided to stay in bed the fateful day of the drug raid? Her life would be so different. She'd be at home with him, right now, watching TV, or making love, or talking about her day... *I'm a widow*, she thought. *But I'm only forty-four... I could still have children, couldn't I? I've heard of women having children in their forties.*

She grabbed at the toilet roll holder and pulled out a wad of tissue, dabbed at her eyes and made her mind up that she was going to go home. Three drinks were her limit.

When she came back out, Peterson sat alone at the long table with their drinks.

"How long was I in there? Did I enter a time warp?" she asked.

"No. John's girlfriend called, asking where he'd got to. Celia called Moss because Jacob has a temperature, and she's worried about him... The uniform lot just cleared out and went on to the Wetherspoon's."

"Right," she said slipping into the seat opposite. There was an awkward silence.

"I hope I didn't embarrass you earlier," he said. He sat back in his chair, his shirtsleeves rolled up and a lopsided smile on his handsome face. "I just wanted to say I've missed you. I don't expect you to do anything with it, I just wanted you to know."

"No, not at all. It's a compliment, so thank you." She

lifted her glass to him and they clinked, downing the last of their drinks.

"Would you like another?" asked Peterson.

"No. I should get going. I need to be in early tomorrow. I have to track down the video footage, beg forensics to move fast on the tooth…"

"Good point."

As they got up to leave, Crawford came back from the busy bar with a tray full of drinks.

"Where is everyone? I've been queuing for ages to get a round in."

"Everyone's gone, mate," said Peterson.

They paused awkwardly. "Thank you. I'm sorry, I can't stay," said Erika.

"Me either. Thanks mate, though," said Peterson. They said good night and left him standing with his tray of drinks.

"Arseholes," muttered Crawford. He sat at the empty table and picked up one of the drinks.

CHAPTER 38

When Erika and Peterson came out onto the high street it was buzzing with people moving between the pubs. They walked down to the train station in silence. A single black cab sat outside, its engine idling.

"Were you going to get a cab?" asked Peterson.

"Yeah. I'm over the limit."

"Me too."

They looked up and down the road. There was no other traffic. The first spots of rain fell, and quickly became a torrent.

"Are you going somewhere or not?" asked the driver, pushing down his window. He was a miserable-looking old man, with wispy gray hair barely clinging to his head. Peterson opened the door and they both got in and sat on the seat with a gap between them.

"Where to?" he asked.

"She's first, Forest Hill, then Sydenham," said Peterson.

"No, you're first, we need to go through Sydenham to get to Forest Hill," said the cab driver.

"Let's do her first, she's my boss," joked Peterson.

The old man rolled his eyes and pulled away. They rode in silence; the rain hammering down on the cab roof; the darkness slipping past. There was little traffic. Erika stole a glance over at Peterson. For once she didn't want to be weighed down by life, by grief and responsibility. She wanted to have someone to hold her as she fell asleep. She wanted to wake up next to someone without feeling desolate and alone.

He turned to look at her and their eyes locked. They quickly looked away again. Erika's heart was hammering as the cab turned in to Manor Mount and began to climb the steep hill to her building. The houses moved past so quickly, and then they were there.

"First stop," said the driver, coming to a halt. The automatic locks clicked open on the doors.

"Do you want to grab a cup of coffee? I mean coffee in my flat," said Erika.

Peterson looked surprised. "Okay... Yeah, a cup of coffee would be great."

They paid the miserable driver and got out, dashing across the car park. Erika could see that the lights were on in the communal entrance, and there was a blonde-haired woman inside with some kids.

At the door, she scrabbled in her bag for her keys, and Peterson slung his arm round her, pulled her against his body and kissed her cheek. She turned to him and smiled. She was about to say something when she heard a voice shriek.

"Erika!"

The door to the communal entrance opened, and a tall blonde-haired woman came dashing out. She looked similar to Erika, with a pretty Slavic face, and almond-shaped eyes. Her long blonde hair hung down wet over her shoulders, and she wore a long black coat over skintight blue jeans and a low-cut top. Behind her, a small dark-haired boy and girl hung off an expensive buggy where a baby slept. She grabbed Erika in a bear hug and then stood back.

"I'm so pleased to see you. I've been calling you all day!" she cried.

"Who's this?" asked Peterson, taken aback.

"This is my sister, Lenka," said Erika.

CHAPTER 39

Erika helped Lenka with the suitcases, the buggy, and with getting her niece and nephew into her flat. Through the window of the communal entrance she could see Peterson standing by the curb in the pouring rain, his suit jacket hitched up over his head, trying to hail a taxi. She'd asked him to come in and wait while he called for one, but Lenka was talking to her in rapid-fire Slovak, and then the baby had started to cry, so he left with a quick awkward wave.

Her niece and nephew, Jakub and Karolina, looked very tired, and despite everything, her heart lifted when she saw them. They were five and seven now, and she was shocked to see how much they had grown up. Erika switched on the lights and the central heating, and asked them to go through to the living room, saying she would be back shortly.

She rushed back out into the hallway and out into the rain, her head down as she ran up the gravel path, the rain pelting down. The pavement was empty, and she could make out the red lights at the back of a taxi turning the corner at the bottom of the hill. She stood for a moment, rainwater pouring down her face. She felt like she'd lost someone. But it was Peterson. She would see him tomorrow.

When she got back inside the flat, the bathroom door was shut. Jakub and Karolina sat on the sofa with the baby in between them, her tiny hand grasping Karolina's index finger and giving them a gummy smile. She wore a little pink hat with a cluster of colored buttons sewn on the front.

"How is little Erika?"

"We call her Eva," said Jakub. He sat back with his hands clasped over a Man United football top.

"Mummy's on the toilet," said Karolina, looking up shyly.

"How are you two?" said Erika, going over to them. Karolina let Erika give her a kiss, but Jakub shied away with a giggle. "I've missed you both."

"Is London always so rainy?" asked Karolina.

"Yes." Erika smiled, tickling the baby under her chin. Jakub pulled out his phone and started to expertly swipe through to his games.

"Is that new?" asked Erika.

"Yeah, it's the latest," he said nonchalantly. "What's your Wi-Fi password?"

"You have to pay for it," said Erika. "Two kisses for an hour's access."

"What?" he laughed.

"That's what it costs..."

He rolled his eyes and held up his face.

"Mwah, mwah!" said Erika, kissing him. "Password is, I'mTheDibble1972."

He wrinkled up his little face, and she helped him with the unfamiliar English words. Karolina pulled out her iPhone too, which Erika noted was the latest model, and she helped her put in the password also.

"Would you like a drink?"

They nodded. Erika went to the cupboard and found the blackcurrant cordial she had bought for them the last time they had visited. She poured them each a glass. When she brought it to the coffee table, she realized Jessica Collins's autopsy photos had been left out, and she managed to get the file off the table before they noticed. The toilet flushed, and Lenka came back. She looked pale and stressed.

"Why didn't you tell me you were coming?" asked Erika, picking up the baby and giving her a hug.

"I tried to, I called you, left you messages, but you didn't pick up!"

"Hang on, have you got a withheld number?"

"Yeah..."

"Why?"

"It's been withheld for a while now," said Lenka evasively.

"I have a job. A very stressful job, and I'd appreciate a heads-up. Have you seen how tiny my flat is and—"

"I did give you a heads-up, you didn't answer!"

"Even if I had answered you didn't give me much notice!"

"I'm your sister!"

There was a slurping sound as Jakub took a sip from the glass, his eyes still on his iPhone. Karolina took one eye off hers and asked: "Who was that big black man?"

"What? Oh, a colleague. He's a police officer. I work with him..."

Karolina looked to Lenka, who raised an eyebrow, saying, "He had his arm around you. It's almost ten o'clock..."

"Let's talk about this later, Lenka," said Erika pointedly.

"You bet we will. I want to hear all about him."

Erika grinned. Underneath it all she was glad to see her sister.

"Now. Who's hungry?" she asked. "Who wants pizza?"

The kids grinned and put their arms up in the air. "Good, I've got some menus in the drawer."

They ordered pizza, and then Erika made up the sofa bed in the living room and tidied up, while Lenka showered the kids and gave the baby a bath. Any annoyance she had with Lenka evaporated when she heard the shrieks of laughter as her niece and nephew helped to bath the baby. The flat felt different with the sounds of her family. The smell of her sister's perfume. It felt like home.

The pizza arrived an hour later, and the kids dug in, pulling out the steaming slices, leaning in to catch the strings of cheese in their mouths. Lenka had brought a DVD of *Tangled*, and she put it on and fed the baby sitting in the armchair by the patio window.

When the kids were fed, they settled back on the sofa bed and fell asleep in front of the film.

"I only saw them a few months ago, and already they look older," said Erika, watching their flushed sleeping faces. Eva had fallen asleep after her feed, and Lenka put her in the buggy under a blanket. Erika leaned over and kissed them all, pulling a blanket over Jakub and Karolina.

"Karolina has got so tall," said Erika.

"I know. I'm already arguing with her about wearing lipstick. She's seven."

"You can talk, you were putting on makeup virtually when you could walk," said Erika. "You went from Mum's tit to Max Factor."

Lenka laughed, then her face fell. "Can we talk?"

"Yes, we can," said Erika. She opened the patio door and saw it had stopped raining. They slipped on their coats and went out into the cold.

"Is this your garden?" asked Lenka, peering into the darkness.

"I'm renting, but yeah. Now are you going to tell me why you've shown up in London, on my doorstep?"

"I told you. I tried to ring but you didn't pick up the phone, or listen to my messages."

"I should have listened, I'm sorry. Why are you calling from a withheld number?"

Lenka bit her lip. "Things at home are tough. I needed to get away. And the kids haven't seen London in a while."

"Come on. This is term time. You've taken them out of school to come to London in early November? Where's Marek?"

"He, um . . ." Her eyes began to fill up. "Marek has had a bit of trouble, with business."

"His business being organized crime."

"Don't say that!"

"What do you want me to say? Mafia? Or are we just going to pretend that he runs the most lucrative ice cream kiosk in Eastern Europe?"

"It's a real business, Erika."

"I know it is. And why couldn't you just both be content with that?"

"You know what life is like back home. You left all those years ago, and you never came back."

"Where is Marek?"

"He's gone away."

"Where?"

"To the High Tatras. One of the local guys thinks Marek has been stealing from him."

"Local mafia guys?" Lenka nodded.

"And has he?"

"I don't know . . . he doesn't tell me anything. Last week he made me change the SIM card in my phone. This morning he told me I had to go, leave, until things have calmed down." She was now crying, tears pouring down her face.

"Oh, I'm sorry...come here..." said Erika. She put her arms around her sister as she sobbed. "You can stay here, no worries. You'll be safe and we'll sort something out."

"Thank you," said Lenka.

A little while later they were lying side by side in Erika's bed. Jacob and Karolina were fast asleep in the living room. Erika lay against the window so that Lenka could have the baby beside her on the floor.

"That guy earlier is a colleague. Peterson, James is his first name. I was going to invite him in for coffee," said Erika.

"Just coffee?" asked Lenka.

"Yes. Maybe...I don't know."

"He's handsome."

"I know, but it isn't that, isn't just that. I wanted to wake up with someone, not be alone every morning. I had a few drinks. I'm glad you were here. It would have been stupid to jump into bed with him. We have to work together."

"You worked with Mark."

"That was different; we got together before we joined the force. And we were husband and wife when we started out as police constables, everyone just took it as a given...Now I'm in charge of a murder investigation. I have to lead people. I don't want to be doing first dates and one-night stands with one of my team."

"I miss Mark," said Lenka. "He was a good man. The best."

"He was," said Erika. She wiped tears away with the back of her hand.

"I don't think Marek is a good man."

"He loves you, and the kids. He looks after you. Sometimes you find yourself in a situation, and you've got to make the best of it."

"Maybe me coming here is a good thing. You won't be alone. You get to wake up next to me tomorrow morning." Lenka smiled.

"Trust you to turn things around to your favor," laughed Erika. She turned and looked at her sister in the darkness. They looked alike in many ways, but Lenka was more daring with what she wore; she wore makeup and she'd kept her hair long whereas Erika's was cropped short.

"What's the case you're working on?"

Erika quickly told her all about the case, and Jessica Collins.

"Karolina's the same age. I couldn't imagine it if she was abducted," said Lenka.

It hung in the air, and it took a long time before Erika could go to sleep.

CHAPTER 40

The rain continued to fall on Manor Mount. The water coursed down drainpipes and alongside the curb, gathering speed as it moved down the steep hill. There was a hollow echo as it poured into the drains.

Gerry stood in the shadows across the road, sheltering under a large tree and the scaffolding of a half-built house. A long thick wax jacket covered his large muscular frame, and the hood was up, casting his face further in shadow.

He'd been prowling the area on foot earlier in the evening, a plan forming. It had been easy to find her address online from the electoral register. There was only one Erika Foster who spelt her name with a "k." He now had Amanda Baker under surveillance, and DC Crawford was feeding much of the important information about the case back to her, but Gerry could read people, and Crawford was an idiot. He was not in DCI Foster's trusted circle.

Gerry now had access to her phone. The text message hadn't raised alarm bells, it had been a stroke of luck that her sister had left those voicemails from a withheld number, but he needed her landline, and he needed to hear if she talked to anyone at home.

Earlier he'd seen a black guy, one of her officers from her team, getting into a cab. Moments after it had driven away, he'd been rewarded with a glimpse of Erika Foster when she had come running out of the building, a pained expression on her face. When she had seen the cab just turning the corner at the bottom of the hill, her shoulders had sagged. She'd stayed there for a moment, her smooth pale face turned up to the heavens, eyes closed.

Gerry had felt the first stirrings of an erection. The pain on her face, the smooth skin, and those red lips parted... The rain was heavy, and the blouse she wore had rapidly stuck to her skin. Her breasts were small but pert.

Gerry closed his eyes on the memory and focused. He had to find a way to get in and out of her flat quickly, but the old manor house building had bars on some of the ground floor windows. There was a communal entrance.

He'd stayed standing under the scaffolding after Erika went back inside, and stayed watching until the lights had gone out in her downstairs flat. He liked it: the dark, the sound of the rain in the empty street, the feeling of being hidden, hiding.

His phone vibrated in his pocket. He pulled it out and swiped the screen.

"Don't you ever sleep?" said Gerry.

"You now have access to Erika Foster's phone?" said the voice.

"Yes."

"What does she have?"

"Forensics found a tooth in the basement of the cottage by the quarry, and deposits of soil saturated with petrol..."

There was a pause.

"The tooth is human?"

"Course it's human."

"Whose is it?"

"They don't know; forensics are doing whatever they do...
It doesn't matter. Bob Jennings could have done all sorts of
stuff down in his basement with local kiddiewinkies...It could
work in our favor."

"You're acting as if this is a game," said the voice, low
and menacing.

"It's my happy-go-lucky Irish nature," replied Gerry,
unfazed. "And I know it's not a game."

"Just remember, if I go down, so do you...And you won't
get paid. Maybe the latter matters to you more."

The man on the end of the phone hung up.

"Fuck you," spat Gerry. He slid his phone back in his
pocket and stepped out from under the thick branches of the
tree. He turned his face to the sky for a moment, enjoying
the prickling sensation on his skin.

He then turned and walked off into the rain.

CHAPTER 41

When Erika woke, it was still dark, and when she saw Lenka pacing the small bedroom with Eva in her arms, it took her a moment to get her bearings.

"What time is it?" she asked, flicking on the light. Eva made small clucking sounds and gave a tiny sneeze.

"Five thirty," replied Lenka. "Sorry. I didn't mean to wake you up."

"It's okay. I need to be up early." Erika sat up and rubbed her face. "What are you going to do today? I've got a big day at work."

"You got some spare keys?"

"Yeah."

"Is there a park nearby?"

"There's the Horniman Museum just up the road, it's quite nice for a walk."

"Isn't that where you found the girl in the ice?"

"Well, yes, but there's huge gardens and a museum; it's got a lovely cafe... You could also go into Central London and see the Christmas lights..." Erika thought what a hopeless host she was going to be.

"We'll be fine. I think the kids will want to sleep in today, yesterday was exhausting. Can you take Eva for a few minutes? I'll grab a shower before it gets crazy."

Lenka transferred the bundle of blankets into Erika's arms, and went off to the bathroom. Eva was so warm. She reached up with a tiny arm, and she looked at Erika through large brown eyes and then sneezed. Erika gently dabbed Eva's tiny face with a muslin cloth, and a wave of love and sadness washed over her. Love for her perfect niece, and sadness that she would probably never have children of her own.

Erika left Lenka her work phone number, some keys, and showed her on the map where everything was. She kissed Karolina and Jakub on their sleeping heads, and then stole out of the flat just as it was getting light.

She arrived at Bromley Station just before seven thirty, and went up to the incident room. She stood in front of the whiteboards with her coffee and looked over the evidence. After the discovery of the tooth, she moved the photos of Bob Jennings and Trevor Marksman to either side of the photo of the cottage, and using a whiteboard marker drew a line linking the three.

Then her phone rang, and she saw it was Nils Åkerman.

"We've had a chance to compare the tooth recovered from the cellar with Jessica Collins's dental records," he said without much preamble. "I'm sorry. It's not a match. It's not Jessica's tooth."

Erika's heart sank. She had to sit down on the corner of her desk.

"Are you sure?"

"Yes. I was able to do the simplest thing and compare it with the broken off tooth in the jaw. It didn't fit or match. I then went through Jessica's dental records in case the tooth had been exposed to fire, which can make the tooth shrink, but it doesn't match those either. I've sent it off to a colleague of mine to see if any pulp can be extracted, and if we can pull any DNA from it, but it's not Jessica's. We've also been back into the cellar and excavated the soil, and we've conducted tests with a methane probe. There's nothing more than dirt."

"Dammit!"

"Sorry."

"OK, not your fault. And it now gives me more questions than answers... What was a child's tooth doing in Bob Jennings's cellar?"

There was silence on the end of the phone.

"Sorry, Nils, I know it's not your job to find out..."

"I don't envy you," he said.

"Okay, thank you for letting me know," said Erika despondently.

She came off the phone and went to the whiteboard where details of the quarry were pinned up beside the map of the common. It had been a clay quarry. She went to the nearest desk, logged on to *Wikipedia*, looked up "clay quarry, kent" and found a short paragraph:

London Clay is a stiff bluish clay, which becomes brown when weathered. The clay is still used commercially for making bricks, tiles, and coarse pottery. It is infertile for gardens and crops.

She carried on her search and found that Kent is made up of a mix of chalk, sandstone, and clay.

"What am I doing? This is so broad and random," she muttered.

"Yes, Kent is a huge county," came a voice behind her, making her jump. Erika looked round and saw Crawford standing behind her, peering at her computer screen. "Sorry," he added.

"Don't creep up on people like that," snapped Erika.

"I thought we knew what the quarry had been used for?"

"We do. I'm just struggling to find a link, struggling to work out the juxtaposition..."

"That's a big word for early in the morning," he joked. She didn't smile.

"Jessica goes missing for years, yet shows up less than a mile from her home." She went on to explain her conversation with Nils. Crawford perched on the corner of her desk, and nodded along as she spoke. When she finished he was silent for a moment.

"Did you know that the Kent coast, the Strait of Dover, is only 21 miles from Europe?"

"Yes, I just read that on the screen," snapped Erika.

"Hang on," he said, standing up. "What you said earlier, about the clay being used commercially for making bricks and tiles. Do you think that could be a link with Martin Collins? He's a builder."

Erika found his nodding face irritating. "Crawford, the quarry stopped being excavated for clay before the First World War. Martin Collins and the family didn't move here until 1983. And it's a bloody common; the quarry was a local landmark."

"Oh," said Crawford, blushing.

A few officers came through to the incident room, followed by Moss and Peterson. Erika suddenly felt all her anger and frustration bubbling up inside her, and Crawford was the perfect outlet.

"This is a complicated enough investigation without you creeping up behind me and pulling stupid theories out of your arse. It doesn't make you look clever, and it pisses me off. Now, unless you've got anything of actual value to say, bugger off."

The other officers were creeping over to their desks and taking off their coats. Crawford was now bright red, and his eyes were filling up.

"And I have no time on my team for crying," she said. "What can you tell me about the septic tank at the cottage?"

"Um, I'm still waiting to hear," muttered Crawford, trying to keep hold of himself.

"Well, stop twatting about trying to be clever, and chase it. Do your fucking job!" she shouted. More officers were now arriving, and there was an uncomfortable silence as they took off their coats and turned on their computers. "Does anyone else have any useless theories about who killed Jessica Collins?" she added to the room. Everyone was quiet. "Good. Now, I've just heard back that the tooth we found in the cellar at Hayes Quarry doesn't belong to Jessica."

There was a groan from several of the officers.

"Yes, my feeling exactly. So we need to redouble our efforts."

She went into her office and slammed the glass door, hating the fact that her team could still see her. She sat at her desk and tackled the growing pile of paperwork, and updated the case files on the Holmes system.

An hour later there was a knock at her door. Moss stood outside, waving a small white tissue.

"I come in peace," she said, opening the door.

"What is it?"

"The nick in Croydon have managed to track down Trevor Marksman's camcorder tapes in their evidence store," said Moss. "They've just arrived by courier. John's trying to track down something we can play them on."

CHAPTER 42

Crawford stood by a line of rubbish bins at the back of Bromley Station, sheltering from the rain under a small plastic awning. He had slipped out of the incident room, and was having a heated phone conversation with Amanda Baker, struggling to hear as the rain clattered down on the plastic above.

"Didn't you think you should get to work early? Or at least make the effort to intercept the tapes?" said Amanda.

"I did get in to work early," said Crawford through gritted teeth.

"Well, not early enough, obviously. What were you doing last night?"

"That's none of your business," he said indignantly. He had carried on drinking alone in the pub, and was now nursing a terrible hangover.

"I still want the tapes, Crawford."

"It's going to be a bit more difficult to get them. They've become the hottest piece of evidence; DCI Foster is now in one of the viewing suites watching. I can't get near them."

He heard the click of Amanda's lighter as she lit a cigarette.

"They'll be digitizing them as they watch. All you need to do is copy them over to a USB stick. Easy."

"Easy for you," he muttered.

"Anyway, I thought you'd requested the tapes. Why aren't you in there watching them? You should be there."

I'm sick of all these bloody women bossing me around, he thought. The wind changed direction and began to pelt rain horizontally, soaking him under the plastic shelter.

"I have other things to do," he replied, pressing himself against the stinking row of blue bins.

"Like what?"

He ignored her and went on to outline that the tooth they had found in the cellar didn't belong to Jessica.

"The child's tooth in the cellar is leading us toward Bob Jennings as a suspect, that he could have been the one that Trevor was working with. Perhaps they targeted other kids in the area before Jessica."

There was another pause; he could almost hear the cogs turning in her head.

"There's something I remember from those videos…" she said, finally. "I'm not quite sure but it's a gut feeling, just out of my grasp. Now go back inside, don't rouse suspicion, and get me a copy of those tapes."

She hung up.

"I bet you've got something in your grasp right now. Your third glass of wine," he said petulantly, noticing something greasy and brown had transferred itself from the bin to his jacket.

Gerry sat in his small flat in Morden. The curtains were drawn against the wind and the rain outside.

His laptop was open on the desk, and he pulled out the headphone jack, and played back a snippet of the conversation. Amanda's gravelly voice echoed around the small room.

"There's something I remember from those videos... I'm not quite sure but it's a gut feeling, just out of my grasp."

He picked up a phone and dialed.

"It's Amanda Baker. She's getting close. Do you want me to take it to the next level?" asked Gerry.

"No. Keep listening," came the voice. "If we move on this, we have to be sure."

CHAPTER 43

Erika and John were crammed into one of the small viewing suites in Bromley Station. In the interests of being frugal, Trevor Marksman had used 120-minute Hi8 camcorder tapes on long-play mode, which meant that each tape ran for four hours.

"And now, tape two," said John, switching them over in the machine.

Erika sat up and stretched out her arms.

"Did he ever think he was going to watch that back?" she yawned.

"What are you talking about, boss? Four hours of windy walks in gray empty parks, traffic on the ring road, and a grainy firework display filmed from his bedroom window, this is box office gold," replied John. He wore latex gloves as he pulled the first little Hi8 tape from its case and reached for the next.

"What's he written there?" asked Erika. John held up the case.

"**'GARY B'DAY PARTY, APRIL 1990,'**" he said, before slipping it out of its case. He held the small black cassette up to the light. "The magnetic tape looks in good nick."

He dropped it into the VHS adaptor and slid it into the machine. Checking the feed was being uploaded to the laptop, he pressed play.

The small screen in front of them on the desk burst to life with static, and then the interior of the television lounge in the halfway house appeared. The image was in black and white, shook a little, and then became color. Twenty men of different ages, most dressed scruffily, stood around on the polished wood floor. Several couches and sofas were dotted about, old and ripped, and a small TV was bolted high up on the wall. A large picture window looked out onto gray sky and a patch of grass. For a few moments the light outside whited out the camera. They heard some voices, and the camera turned to a mirror. Staring back was the reflection of Trevor Marksman holding the video camera. His skin was smooth; he hadn't yet been burnt.

"Here we are on the second of April for Gary Lundy's twenty-fourth birthday!" he said to his reflection.

The camera whipped round to show a thin man sitting on a fraying sofa. He had elongated features, and his hair was greasy and parted flat to the left. His nose was huge, and he had one of his fingers buried in his left nostril up to the knuckle.

"What are you doing?" asked Trevor's voice from behind the camera.

"Looking for something decent to eat," replied Gary, pulling his finger out of his nose. "Now fuck off," he snarled.

The image spun away as the camera moved across the room, past a sad and creepy group of men hovering around a saggy buffet table covered in plastic bowls of crisps, and a small round iced cake studded with smarties. One short round little man wore a party hat; the elastic dug into his three chins, and his long gray hair flowed from underneath.

"Jesus, all these bloody nonces were living just up the road from the Collinses," said John as they watched.

Back on screen, the fat little man in the party hat was looking into the lens: "Can I have a go?" he asked, reaching up, smiling, showing he had only two teeth.

"No," said Trevor, his hand appearing in shot and tartly slapping the fat man's hand as it grabbed for the camcorder.

"Go, on I've never seen one before—"

"Get your fucking hands off!" whined Trevor.

His hand swooped round and clouted the small man hard around the head. He went down on the floor, the elastic snapping on his party hat. He got up and charged at the camera. There was a jerky tussle and then the image went black.

"Bloody hell, we're going to have to watch the whole party aren't we?" said John.

Erika nodded grimly. The screen then burst back to life, the party again, but a little later. Music was playing and some of the men were dancing awkwardly. The camera swung back over to Gary, still sitting in the corner, picking his nose. He pulled out his finger and put it in his mouth.

"That's disgusting," said John, turning away from the screen.

"It's all right, he's gone," said Erika.

The camera swung round to show the small fat man, wearing a new party hat, and sitting in a corner by an old upright piano. He was stuffing his face from a plate piled high with food. Another plateful waited on the lid of the piano beside him.

"What's up with him?" asked a voice out of shot.

"He's being a dick, wanted to use my camera," said Trevor's voice as he cruelly zoomed in close on the fat man's feasting little mouth. "He's got two fucking thumbs. I don't let anyone touch this camera."

The image blurred in and out as he stuffed a forkful of quiche in his mouth, crumbs catching in his beard.

There was a high-pitched girlish laugh, and the camera panned round to a close-up of a tall, bald red-faced man with crooked rabbit teeth.

"You'll let me have a go, won't you?" he asked.

"NO!"

There seemed to be another tussle, and the image flicked forward to later in the afternoon. It was now growing dark in the television room, and the only light in the room was the candles on a cake being carried across the room by a tall man. Trevor followed behind him as they took the cake to Gary, still sitting in the armchair.

"Go on, give it a blow!" cried a voice. Gary protested and then blew out the candles.

"What did you wish for?" shouted another voice.

"To fucking die," said Gary, sitting back and folding his arms.

The man holding the cake turned to the camera for a moment, and then walked out of shot.

"Hey," said Erika. "Hang on, run it back."

"I can't. I'm doing the digital transfer," said John.

Trevor followed behind the man, over to the long table.

"I know that man," said Erika. "He was at Trevor Marksman's the other day. Pause it, now!"

Erika dashed out of the viewing suite and up the stairs to the incident room. Peterson was just coming off the phone when she grabbed him and told him to come downstairs. When they got back to the viewing suite, he watched with them. On the screen, Trevor now focused on the familiar man who was talking to the camera, joking as if this party was a red carpet event.

"That's the guy we saw when we went to visit Marksman: Joel isn't it? Joel. He's got hair in the video, but he's got the South African accent," said Erika.

"He's got the same strange milky blue eyes," added Peterson. "And that scar, running down from his temple to behind his ear."

"He said his name was Joel, but didn't give a surname. I want a list of everyone who was in that halfway house during 1990," said Erika.

They looked back at the screen where one of the other men in the halfway house had taken the camera, and as "Careless Whisper" boomed over the sound system, Trevor and Joel were slow dancing together.

CHAPTER 44

Erika and John watched two more of the videotapes in the afternoon; they were shorter, recorded using standard play. They consisted of several spring days spent in the park local to Avondale Road. Trevor Marksman had filmed lots of local children, often encouraging the parents to smile and wave at the camera as they pushed their children on the swings and caught them at the bottom of slides.

Jessica Collins made her first appearance in one of the videos in a clip which was dated "06.11.1990", playing at the park on a see-saw with another dark-haired girl. They laughed and bounced up and down, and in the background a younger version of both Marianne and Laura sat on a bench in the shade of a large oak tree. Laura was smoking, and barely listening, as Marianne leaned in to talk to her.

The camera watched Jessica play for several minutes, zooming in from the other side of the park. Erika was struck how beautiful and carefree she was, dancing with her friend, swinging from the climbing frame... Her feelings turned to revulsion when she remembered that she was watching all of this through Trevor Marksman's eyes.

The camera then cut to a shaky view of a thin path at the back of the park, moving past a battered rubbish bin and an old bench to a man trying to lever a spade full of leaves into a refuse bag. He was having no luck in the wind.

"Having fun are we?" said a voice. The man turned, and with his wild brown hair and gnomic face they saw it was Bob Jennings.

"Faak awwf you two bitches," muttered Bob, gurning weirdly.

Then there was a curse as the low battery sign began to flash in the corner of the screen. The image wobbled, and just before the battery died and the picture went black there was a brief flash of a familiar face as the camera was passed to someone else.

"Bloody hell, that was Bob Jennings, and that other face, just as the tape ended . . . Can we run it back?"

John took out the tape, and pulled the laptop toward him on the desk. They now had a digital recording. He found the last few minutes of the tape and ran it back, past the encounter with Bob, and then as the battery signal flashed in the corner of the screen. It took a few attempts, as the face was only on screen for a fraction of a second, but when they had the image—it was Trevor Marksman.

They stared at it for a few moments.

"This means that the camera was passed from someone over to Trevor; he wasn't filming in the park all the time. In the previous investigation he had stated that he was doing all the filming," said Erika.

"And he flipped out at that party that he wouldn't let anyone use the camera," said John.

He played the section back again: the camera approaching the gate; the flash of Trevor's face.

"Listen, can you hear? A voice says, 'There you go.' It sounds South African."

There was a knock at the door, and Peterson returned. "Boss. I've found Joel Michaels. I had to work back from his records attached to his original name, which is Peter Michaels. He changed his name to Joel in 1995. He's fifty-three years old. He was in the halfway house after his release from prison. He served six years from February 1984 until his release in March 1990 for the imprisonment and rape of a nine-year-old boy."

A look passed between Erika and John. Peterson went on: "Peter Michaels was interviewed in 1990, along with all the residents of the halfway house, and like Marksman, he had an alibi for the seventh of August, 1990. However, he was never placed under surveillance in the weeks after Jessica disappeared."

"Nor was Bob Jennings," said John. "I can't find anything about him in our case files. He was never interviewed, never a suspect…"

"And look, we have them all here on camera, interacting. They knew each other," said Erika.

CHAPTER 45

It was late when Erika called Commander Marsh from the incident room. She had sent her team home after a long day.

"Erika, I've warned you about going near Trevor Marksman," said Marsh. "We don't want another lawsuit."

"Sir, with respect, you're not listening. I don't want to bring in Marksman. I want to bring in Joel Michaels and question him about his association with Trevor, and Bob Jennings who keeps cropping up. He squatted in the cottage where we found a child's tooth in the basement."

"Which is, as yet, unidentified."

"But alarming nonetheless!"

"Yes, but there could have been other people squatting in the past twenty-six years, junkies who could have had children, who in turn could have lost milk teeth."

"We also found petrol deposits soaked into the soil in the cottage basement. Bob Jennings's sister has confirmed he used to use her lead petrol generator, and we discovered high levels of tetraethyl lead in Jessica's bones, indicating exposure to lead petrol fumes. Now I have video evidence linking Trevor, Bob and Joel..."

Marsh was silent on the end of the phone for a moment. Erika went on: "Sir, Bob is dead. I can't go near Trevor; I want to have a crack at Joel Michaels."

"Obviously this is your call, Erika," he said.

"I know, Paul. But I'd like your support. Your advice. If I'm right, we could be looking at a pedophile ring."

"When do you want to do this?"

"Soon."

"Jessica Collins's funeral is tomorrow morning. I would advise waiting until afterward. I am attending, and I think it would be wise for you to attend too. Good PR, and as we know, it's all about PR."

"Okay."

"You have to realize too, that Trevor Marksman is now a very wealthy man. I presume that he will have a good lawyer on hand to help out his friend when you make the arrest."

"I'm not worried about that. I'm more concerned that I've spent the day watching hours of video showing convicted pedophiles being thrown parties, taken on trips out to the seaside, and all of the video Marksman took of Jessica Collins, and several other local children. I'm angry that she is just a pile of bones, and somewhere out there whoever did this is running free. I want to question Joel Michaels. That's all, and I have evidence to support my suspicions."

Marsh was silent on the phone for a moment.

"Keep me posted, and before that, I will see you at the funeral tomorrow."

"Okay, thank you." Erika put down the phone and started to gather her things together to go home. She went into her office and packed her bag, then realized she had left her notebook down in the viewing suite.

CHAPTER 46

When the team left the incident room to go home, Crawford hung back and went to the men's toilet, and sat in a cubicle for twenty minutes, sweat pouring off him. When twenty minutes had passed, he washed his hands and came back out. Checking that he wasn't being followed, he took the stairs down to the viewing suite, where Erika and John had spent the day watching the Trevor Marksman tapes.

It was on the second floor, tucked in at the back of the station, at the end of a long corridor. There were several copies of the key, and earlier in the day he had taken one from John's desk when John had been distracted on the phone. Crawford slipped it into the lock and was relieved that it opened the door. He flicked on the lights and saw that the laptop was still on the desk, connected to the video machine. He closed the door and locked it behind him. The room was small, cramped, and windowless. A set of shelves held a mixture of leads and wires, manuals for the DVD and video machine, and there was even one for a laserdisk machine.

Crawford worked fast, booting up the laptop and pulling out the USB keys he had bought from Maplin's further up the high street. He was concerned that they wouldn't have enough memory. They only had 16Gb of memory, so he'd bought three. The sweat dripped off his face as he wrestled with the large square of molded plastic packaging, unable to release the tiny USB key inside.

He searched the shelves, but there were no scissors. He took his car key from his pocket and started to gouge at the plastic. After a long few minutes he got the USB keys out, and wiping the sweat from his eyes, he slipped one into the USB port on the side of the laptop.

It started making whirring noises, and he started up the Windows desktop. Finally, the icon appeared for the USB driver. He clicked through to the video files created earlier in the day by John, selected the first and dragged it across to the USB driver on the desktop.

The hard drive began to whirr again as a little box flashed up reading:

Copying 2 items to USBDRIVE1
11.8Mb of 3.1Gb—about 9 minutes

"Come on," he hissed, a drop of sweat landing on the keyboard of the laptop. It was then he heard the door move, stopped by the lock, and the handle turned.

CHAPTER 47

Erika tried the door handle to the viewing suite and found the door was locked. She took out a bunch of keys and tried to put one in the lock, but it wouldn't fit. She felt resistance on the other side. She was about to try the handle again when she heard her name being called, and Peterson was moving toward her down the corridor.

"Boss, I've got your notebook," he said, holding it up.

"Thank you," she said, taking it as he drew level.

"I thought everyone had gone home?"

"Yeah, I went to grab some stuff from the Waitrose over the road, came back to the car park and saw I'd picked this up by mistake," he said.

"Thank you."

There was an awkward silence.

"About last night, I really didn't know my sister was just going to show up," she said.

"It's cool. How is she?"

"She's great."

"Great." He smiled. There was another awkward pause. "Okay, well, I'll catch you tomorrow," he said.

"See you tomorrow."

He nodded and walked off. Erika pretended she was looking for the keys, and when Peterson was gone she slumped against the door. She waited a few minutes then set off down the corridor, home.

Crawford pressed his ear to the door and strained to listen, but the voices had receded. He quickly switched the USB keys and started to copy the next batch of videos over.

His shirt was soaked with sweat.

CHAPTER 48

Erika arrived home just after nine thirty. When she opened the front door to her flat, Lenka was in the hallway. Erika started to speak, but she put her finger to her lips.

"Karolina and Jakub are asleep," she whispered. "It's so late. Where were you?"

"At work," whispered Erika, sloughing off her shoes and putting down her bag.

"Is everything okay?"

"Yes, of course."

"You left at seven this morning!"

Erika pulled off her coat. "I usually work like this."

"What did Mark have to say about that?"

"Lenka, can you let me get inside the door!"

"Shhh! I've only just got them settled."

Erika peered through to the living room. She could just see the tops of the kids' heads as they slept under the blankets on the sofa bed.

"Lenka, my computer is nearly dead, and the charger is in there," she whispered.

"What does it look like?"

"What do you mean what does it look like? It's a char-ger," hissed Erika, moving into the living room, but Lenka held her back.

"No. You'll wake them up. Karolina has been really upset all day, and I've only just got them to sleep."

"Lenka, I need my charger."

"Did you eat?"

"I had lunch."

Lenka crossed her arms and rolled her eyes. "You should at least eat. I cooked. You take a shower, and I'll look for your charger."

Erika went to protest, but Lenka pushed her into the bath-room and closed the door.

When Erika emerged from the shower, she was hit by the delicious smell of smoked meat, potato and pickle. The microwave beeped and Lenka came out with a steaming plate of Francúzske Zemiaky, a dish of potato, egg, gherkin and smoked sausage, sliced very thin, stacked in a casserole dish and baked.

"Oh my God. It smells delicious. Just like the one Mum used to make," said Erika, her mouth watering.

They came into the bedroom, which was stuffed with Eva's buggy, a pile of nappies, and the dressing table had been converted into a changing table. The gilt-framed photo of Mark had been pushed to the back. His handsome face stared back at her with its perpetual smile. Erika sat on the bed and tucked into the steaming plate of food.

"My God this is amazing. Thank you."

"I went shopping," said Lenka. "It's nice round here, but lots of different people, Indian, Black, Chinese. The kids were a bit scared by everything... Your garden is nice, and we met a couple of neighbors. A woman upstairs with two little girls. Jakub went knocking on all the doors until he found them, and they came and played."

"They did? How did you talk to them?"

"I know a few words in English; the mother was nice. What's her name?"

Erika shrugged.

"You've lived here for five months and you don't know your neighbors?"

"I'm busy," said Erika through a mouthful of food.

"What happened today with the handsome guy, Peterson?"

"Nothing, really. We didn't talk about it."

"Do you think anything will happen? He's lovely."

Erika shrugged.

"You could invite him over. I'd cook something…"

Erika gave her a look, and through a mouthful of food said: "Give it a rest."

Lenka went to the dresser and pulled open the top drawer and started to stuff in the mat from the changing table and several blankets.

"A man called today, to read the meter. I think that's what he came for. I was busy with the kids in and outside; it was when the girls from upstairs were here. He left that letter," she said, indicating a piece of paper on the windowsill.

Erika scanned it and saw it was from the letting agent, confirming that the gas certificate had to be checked and updated.

"The food here is very expensive. What kind of things do you buy?"

"Lenka, can you just give me a minute to breathe? I've had a stressful day and you're just jabbering on!"

Lenka carried on patting down the blankets in the drawer.

"What are you doing?"

"I'm making Eva a bed."

"In the drawer?"

From the buggy, Eva woke up and started to wail.

"You woke her up," said Lenka, squeezing past Erika and picking Eva up. "There, there, it's okay. Shush, shush." Lenka pulled her shirt down and gave the baby her breast, but she shrieked even louder. "Can you go and shut the living room door?"

Erika shoveled in another mouthful of food and squeezed past, juggling her plate as she came out into the hallway and closed the living room door. Eva's shrieks rose to a higher octave so she closed the bedroom door. Erika sat on the carpet by the front door, with her plate on the floor, and finished eating.

What she couldn't see above her, fixed to the inside of the housing around the electricity meter, was a small listening device.

Just after 11 p.m., Amanda Baker was snoozing in her armchair. A half-finished mug of tea sat on the table beside her amongst piles of printouts and two notebooks. The living room wall above the sofa was now covered in papers, pinned up crookedly, and each one was filled with her black spidery scrawl. In the middle of it all was an A4 printout of Trevor Marksman's mugshot, along with photos of Joel Michaels and Bob Jennings. On the opposite wall, next to the television, was a picture of Jessica Collins.

There was a soft knocking, and she woke up from her doze. Heaving herself up and out of the chair she came to the window. Crawford was standing outside, his face red and glistening with sweat. She pulled up the window, and a cold draft rushed in.

"I've got them," he said, turning to look at the road behind, which was deserted.

"You've got all of them for me?" she asked.

He nodded and shifted on his feet. "Can I come in?"

"It's late, and I need to get my sleep. It's Jessica Collins's funeral tomorrow," said Amanda.

Crawford peered past her and saw a black dress on a hanger waiting on the back of the living room door. "You're gonna go?"

"Yeah," she said. She held out her hand.

"Can I come in, just for a drink…It's been a hell of a day," he said.

"I'm not drinking, and I don't want you to compromise my sobriety," she said, her hand still outstretched.

"You're kidding; you've given up?"

"Three days and counting."

He pulled a small envelope from the inside of his jacket and handed it over.

"Thanks," she said, taking it. She closed the sash window and pulled the curtains across.

Crawford stood outside for a moment, staring at the back of the curtain, and then trudged back to his car.

CHAPTER 49

The vigil for Jessica Collins was held in the Church of the Holy Virgin Mary in Bromley. The small room was decorated simply; it smelt of incense and floor polish, and candles flickered in the gloom.

Jessica's coffin was the finest dark mahogany that Marianne and Martin had been able to find. It sat on a wooden frame. Not small enough for a baby, not big enough for an adult.

Marianne had arrived at first light, to be there when it was delivered from the funeral home. She sat and stared at her daughter's remains; the bones neatly placed, small and vulnerable, on the satin inlay of the coffin, covered by a thin layer of lace gauze. The red coat that had been Jessica's birthday present was neatly folded and had been placed beside the satin pillow.

Martin, Laura, and Toby arrived a little later. They knocked softly at the heavy wooden door, and Marianne rose to open it.

They halted at the doorway in stunned silence.

"It's an open casket," said Martin, staring at the skeleton, which had been arranged as if Jessica's bones had just climbed in and settled down to sleep. "I thought we agreed. It would be closed."

"We didn't agree. You told me," said Marianne darkly. "I want to see my baby. I want to touch her. I want to be here with her."

Toby looked at his father and then Laura. "Dad. It doesn't seem right," he said. They moved to the thin lace gauze covering, and Martin put out his hand.

"Oh, Jessica," he said, pressing his hand against the lace to touch the skull.

Laura remained with a hand up to her mouth, her eyes filled with a look of horror.

"Come over. Touch her," said Marianne. "It's Jessica... Your sister."

Laura moved closer, her eyes still wide. Marianne leaned over and took her hand. She tried to pull away, but Marianne's grip was strong, and she placed her hand so that it lay on the forehead of Jessica's skull. "Feel her hair, Laura. Do you remember how it felt to brush her hair?"

"No!" shrieked Laura, yanking her hand away. She ran from the room. Marianne barely noticed what had happened, and kept staring at the coffin.

"Toby, I want you to touch her. I want you to touch your sister," she said.

"No, Mum...I want to remember her differently. I'm sorry," he said. He looked at his father, who seemed hypnotized by the skeleton in the coffin, then followed Laura out into the corridor.

"All I ever wanted was another daughter. And all I wanted was for her to be safe and happy," said Marianne, looking up at Martin. "Was this our punishment for what we did?"

"We said we'd never talk about it," said Martin, looking back at her.

"I agree. But this is the end, isn't it?"

"No, it's not. She was taken from us, but she's with the Lord. And we'll see her again. We shouldn't question why he took her when he did. Just take comfort that now we've found her, and she can rest in peace."

"Oh, Martin," said Marianne. He came round and held her tightly in his arms, in a way that he hadn't for years, and they cried out their loss and their guilt.

When Martin was gone, Marianne was left alone. The candles burned down, and a square of colored light cast by a small stained glass window slowly moved across the wall.

She spent the day in prayer, hunched over her daughter's tiny skeleton. Her prayers were well versed, almost automatic after years of practice. But when she uttered the words "Forgive me father, I have sinned" it always felt as if she was saying them for the first time.

CHAPTER 50

After the Mass, the congregation and the coffin moved to the vast graveyard for the burial.

Erika and Marsh attended this last part of the service, joining the large group of mourners by the freshly dug grave. The air was crisp, and it looked as if a storm was moving in. The sky was slowly turning dark blue in the distance.

Erika always found attending the funerals of murder victims uncomfortable; they were technically on duty, and finding the balance between being respectful and looking around at the mourners was difficult. It was often the only time you got everyone in the same place at once.

The priest stood by the grave where the coffin waited to be lowered, decorated with a vast spray of lilies, and started to speak.

"God of endless ages, through disobedience to your law we fell from grace and death entered the world..."

Marianne sat at the front of the semicircle of mourners, next to the grave, swathed in black with a large-brimmed black hat. She wept openly and quietly, her rosary clenched tight in one hand. Martin held her other hand, and she occasionally broke his grip to blot her tears with a white handkerchief. On her other side sat Toby. Laura was seated next to him with her husband and her two little boys. Tanvir, Erika noticed, had been relegated to the back row.

In the row behind sat Nancy Greene, the Family Liaison Officer. She was head-to-toe in black also; the only splash of color was the small white bandage still covering her healing nose. Oscar Browne sat a little way down with a tall, elegant black woman. His eyes locked with Erika's, and he tilted his head a little. She tilted hers back, unsure of what the tilt had meant.

The priest's voice was rich and seemed to soar over their heads: "In a spirit of repentance we earnestly ask you to look upon this grave and bless it..."

Erika looked over to Marsh to see if he had noticed Oscar, but he was transfixed by a photo they'd had enlarged, which sat on a wooden easel beside the heap of flowers. It was the picture of Jessica wearing her red coat that Marianne displayed in the hallway. It was unusual for a British funeral to do this.

"I keep thinking it could be one of my girls," whispered Marsh. "I keep thinking how I would cope."

They had traveled to the funeral together, and in the car, Marsh had told Erika that Marcie's lawyer had proposed a court date for their custody hearing.

An image of Mark's funeral flashed into her head: the moment his coffin had been loaded into the hearse and it had shifted, the weight of his body inside...

Erika turned to Marsh and grabbed his hand. As she did, she noticed Amanda Baker was sitting further down, on the end of their row. Amanda was watching her, and her eyes went down to where she rested her hand on Marsh's.

Erika nodded her greeting and went to subtly pull her

hand away, but Marsh clung on. Amanda noticed this too, and she raised an eyebrow. There was something different about her. She looked less bloated and puffy, her dress was elegant, she was wearing makeup and her hair had been dyed a soft brown.

The priest came to the conclusion of his blessing: "So that, while we commit to the earth the body of your servant, Jessica, her soul may be taken into paradise. We ask this through Christ our Lord. Amen." The congregation intoned: "Amen."

Erika looked back to Marianne and saw her distress: the realization that this was the moment when she would have to say goodbye to Jessica. Martin gripped Marianne's hand, and Erika noticed for the first time his girlfriend. She was placed a couple of seats down from Martin, their two small children used almost as a barrier. The little girl fidgeted on her chair in a billowing black dress, which she'd pulled up to show a pair of black tights. Her little brother wore a neat suit, and stared up at the sky above as thunder started to rumble.

Marianne stood unsteadily and moved to the graveside as the coffin slowly descended out of view. She picked up a handful of soil and held it for a moment. There was a crash of thunder and then it started to rain—within seconds, escalating to a downpour. Marianne shook her fist at the sky, and then her body seemed to go limp, and she fell into the open grave.

The rain was now hammering down and the graveyard lit up with flashes of lightning. There were screams and chaos as everyone rushed forward to the graveside, where the earth piled up beside it had quickly become a saturated quagmire.

CHAPTER 51

The rain continued to fall, pounding on the roof of Erika's car as she sat inside with Marsh and Amanda Baker. In the chaos and the rain there had been no taxis, so Erika had offered Amanda a lift. They had pulled into a McDonald's car park to grab a bite to eat, and they now sat drinking their coffee in silence. Amanda was in the back seat.

"God almighty. Talk about gallows humor," said Amanda, breaking the silence. Marsh turned and gave her a look. "Well, come on. She falls in the grave, and is pulled out by the priest, screaming and covered in mud. It was like a horror film...She's spent years trying to get closer to heaven and she ends up six feet under!" She started to laugh. It was a deep chuckle. Erika glanced at Marsh but he remained stony-faced. "Shit, I'm sorry," said Amanda, brushing crumbs off the front of her black jacket. "It's just years of pent-up frustration and despair." She caught sight of the look on Marsh's face and collapsed into giggles. Erika turned away and bit her lip.

In the chaos, the congregation had crowded around the grave as they were pelted by the torrential downpour. When

Marianne had been pulled out, she'd been taken into the church by the priest and the rest of her family. The rest of the congregation had scattered to the four corners in the torrents of rain.

It hadn't been until Erika was pulling out of the car park that she'd seen that Laura and Oscar had remained outside, and were deep in conversation under a large tree set away from the church.

"Well, I'm glad *you* find it so funny, former DCI Baker... Some of us are still working on this case, and from where I'm looking, it's not remotely amusing."

"No, no it's not," said Amanda, calming down and wiping her eyes with a napkin.

Marsh looked at his watch. "Right, Erika. It's half twelve, we'd better get going for the..." His voice tailed off. He opened the door and made a dash over to where he'd parked his car.

"Where can I drop you off?" asked Erika.

"Bromley Train Station will do. Can I ride in the front though? I'd hate people to get the wrong idea," said Amanda.

When she was settled in the front seat, Erika pulled out of the car park on to the main road.

"So where are you off to? What's the thing you and Marsh are up to? Afternoon in a hotel?"

"No," said Erika, shooting her a look.

"I saw you holding his hand..."

"It's not what you think. And, I don't care what you think."

"Everyone cares what people think of them. Are you off to arrest Marksman?"

"No."

"Then who? You can trust me."

"No. We don't discuss the case with civilians."

"Ouch," said Amanda, wiping the condensation off her window. "You know, I still share your ideals. I still want to uphold the law, catch the bad guys... Can you tell me if you think you're close? Have you any suspects?"

"What did you make of Laura and Oscar Browne?" asked Erika as they came to a stop at a set of traffic lights. She could see Marsh's car up ahead.

"Are they suspects?"

"No. I'm just trying to work the family out."

"Good luck with that. I couldn't work out if Laura was dating Oscar to wind up her parents, or if she really loved him... Although their relationship was over the second Jessica went missing. He dropped her like a hot brick. This was according to Nancy Greene."

"He didn't arouse suspicion?"

"No. He had an alibi with Laura, and Martin and Marianne liked Oscar. A young lawyer going places. He was on a scholarship. I think his desire to achieve made him drop Laura. It was terrible what happened but it was a mess. The family's grief, the media attention. He didn't want to be associated with it all."

They were now outside the train station. Erika pulled in to the taxi rank.

"Thanks," said Amanda, unclipping her belt. "Look, there's something I remember from those tapes seized from Marksman. If you'd like I could come in as a non-paid adviser. I'll sign whatever. I'd like to help you solve this."

Erika looked at her; she was bursting with enthusiasm. "Today is not a great day. Let me think about it."

"Okay. Thanks, and thanks for the lift," said Amanda. She grabbed her bag and left the car.

Erika watched her walk into the station, and wondered

if it would be crazy to take her up on it. And if so, how she would sell it to Marsh.

She pulled out of the taxi rank and drove down to the police station car park, steeling herself for the afternoon ahead.

CHAPTER 52

When Erika knocked on the front door of Trevor Marks-man's penthouse flat, Joel Michaels opened the door. He wore smart jeans and a shirt, and was carrying a coffee cup with a straw and a dirty dinner plate. In the background, Marksman was having what looked like his afternoon nap, tipped back in a reclining chair next to one of the floor-to-ceiling windows.

"What is this?" he asked, his eyes moving between Erika, Moss, and two uniformed officers. "Why didn't you use the intercom? Who let you in?"

Erika stepped forward. "Joel Michaels, I'm arresting you on suspicion of the abduction and murder of Jessica Collins. You do not have to say anything when questioned, but anything you do say may be used in evidence against you in a court of law."

He looked at the warrant card Erika held up. In the background Marksman shifted under his blanket and came to.

"What's going on?" said Marksman, fighting his way out from under the blanket and moving unsteadily to join them.

Joel put the plate and cup down on the coffee table and

went to take his arm. One of the officers grabbed him, and he turned and pushed him away.

"Hey, hey, easy," said Moss.

"I'm his carer," said Joel. His bald head was now glistening with sweat; the scar twisting around his ear was red and angry.

"Joel hasn't done anything, take me instead," said Marksman, who was now level with them, holding on to the back of the sofa for support. He looked at Erika. "I'm serious. Take me instead." The raw skin around his eyes creased in pain. "I admit it. I murdered Jessica. I took her on the way round to that party. I grabbed her off the street and—"

"Trevor, stop," said Joel, placing a hand gently on his chest. "Call Marcel, right now . . . Tell him I've been arrested. Where are you taking me?"

"Bromley Police Station," said Moss.

"Tell him to meet me there."

"This is madness!" cried Trevor. "You police must be scraping the barrel." He watched as Joel was handcuffed and taken away by the uniformed officers. "Why won't you arrest me? Are you too scared!?"

"We'll be in touch," said Erika, and they left.

It was growing dark when they arrived back at Bromley Police Station. Joel Michaels was booked and placed in a cell. His solicitor arrived shortly afterward. He was a graying, elderly man with huge glasses. They went through the process of telling him why they had arrested Joel, and then arranged for him to be brought up to an interview room.

"You okay, boss?" asked Moss. They were in the observation suite, watching Joel Michaels and his lawyer waiting in the interview room. Joel seemed unperturbed and sat at the bare table with his arms crossed. His lawyer sat next to him with a folder and paperwork on the table, leaning in and talking earnestly, gesturing with his pen.

"Yeah. This doesn't feel right though. I don't feel like I'm going in there with enough—"

"When have any of us ever felt like that?" said Moss.

"Let's hope he's caught off guard after so many years away from the police. The bastard never had to sign the Sex Offenders Register. He's never had that pressure on him."

Erika nodded. "Until now."

They went into the interview room, and Moss sat opposite the solicitor. Erika sat in front of Joel, laying her folder on the table.

"It's 5 p.m. on Thursday, the tenth of November. In the interview room is DCI Foster and DI Moss," said Erika. She sat back and regarded Joel for a moment.

He locked eyes with her and didn't flinch.

"I went to Jessica Collins's funeral today. She'd have been thirty-two years old if she'd lived."

"That's very sad," said Joel.

Erika opened her folder and took out a photo of Bob Jennings and slid it across the table. "What do you know about this man?" Joel kept staring at Erika. "Look at the photo, please."

Joel glanced down. "Never seen him before."

"Are you sure?"

"Yes."

"His name is Bob Jennings. He was squatting at the cottage by Hayes Quarry when Jessica Collins vanished."

"That's interesting to hear," said Joel.

"I have videotapes belonging to Trevor Marksman. He liked taking video, didn't he?"

"No comment."

"He won it in a competition. And he liked to video young children at the park in Hayes."

"No comment."

"You took video for him too, of young children, and like him, you also took video of Jessica Collins. It's not like you just caught her on camera, this was hours and hours of footage. Obsessive stalking behavior of a seven-year-old girl."

"No comment."

"Video taken by you, using Trevor Marksman's camera, also features Bob Jennings. Bob Jennings who you mention by name and say hello to."

Joel shifted in his seat and rolled his eyes. "No comment."

"When you were interviewed in August 1990, you said that you and Trevor Marksman didn't know one another."

"No comment."

"Well, I would like a comment on this, at least. You lied to the police."

"I must have been mistaken."

"You like small children, don't you? You find them sexually attractive."

"We both know my client has been convicted of child sex offenses. He has served his time," interjected the solicitor.

"And how lucky he is that he doesn't have to sign the Sex Offenders Register…"

"That wasn't a question." Joel smirked.

Erika sat back, trying to remain calm.

Three hours later, Erika and Moss emerged from the interview room. They watched as Joel was taken the opposite way down the corridor and back to the cells.

"Shit," said Erika. "We've got everything and nothing… I haven't got enough to go near Marksman; Bob Jennings is dead. Jesus."

"It's coming up to eight thirty," said Moss, checking her watch. "Let him spend a night here in the Bromley Hilton. Let's have a crack at him again tomorrow."

Erika nodded. She saw that Moss was trying to put a brave face on it too, but she agreed. They had nothing.

CHAPTER 53

Erika spent a claustrophobic night in her flat, tossing and turning, sleep eluding her. She loved Lenka and the kids, but all of them living on top of each other was becoming too much. She left very early the next morning, before they were awake, bought a chocolate croissant and coffee on her way to work, and took them up to the incident room.

She then sat on one of the desks, staring at all of the case evidence. The photos of Jessica, the quarry, of Bob Jennings. The case seemed to move further from her grasp.

Just before 9 a.m. the incident room was filling up, and Erika was working at her computer in her office, when Moss came rushing in without knocking.

"Sorry, boss," she said with a gulp, catching her breath. "You need to come downstairs, now."

"Shit, is it Joel Michaels? I thought we had him on mandatory suicide watch."

"It's not Joel, it's Trevor Marksman."

Erika got up and followed her downstairs.

When they reached the foyer of the police station, they saw that a large black minivan was parked illegally on the double yellow lines outside. Erika and Moss came out onto the steps. It soon became clear that someone had tipped off the media. A large group of press and photographers were congregating at the bottom of the steps outside the main entrance, and Trevor Marksman was standing by the car, wearing a long black coat, black trilby, and leaning on a gold-topped walking stick. He was addressing the waiting press in his gravelly voice.

"Arresting Joel Michaels, merely for being my carer, is once again a bullying tactic by the Metropolitan Police… Joel is innocent, but as you are aware, this means nothing to the MET police. I took them to court in 1995 after one of their officers leaked my home address to a vigilante group who put a petrol bomb through my door. The court ruled in my favor…"

With a flourish, he pulled off his hat, which showed the full extent of the skin grafts over his bald head.

"What the hell?" said Erika as she and Moss watched this from the doorway of the station. "Can we do anything about this?"

"I have to live with this face for the rest of my life!" he cried, the skin crinkling around his eyes. "The death of Jessica Collins was a tragedy, but I maintain my innocence! I was released without charge. I was not responsible. Now the police have arrested Joel Michaels, a man who has stood by me for twenty-six years. He is also my full-time carer. He is innocent, and this is a desperate plea from the police to intimidate me and punish me for successfully winning a case against them."

A voice was then heard from amongst the crowds of people and journalists who had gathered outside on the pavement, and Marianne Collins appeared, wearing a long winter coat. She swayed unsteadily, pushing her way through the crowds of people, flanked by Laura.

"Child killer!" she shouted. "You lying piece of shit murderer!"

There was a commotion, as she had to get past some of the news cameras and journalists to where Trevor stood.

Erika moved quickly over to the front desk and picked up a phone. "We've got a situation developing outside the front entrance of the station, yes Bromley, this station. I need all officers who are on site to attend urgently at the front desk."

When Erika came off the phone she went back to the front entrance. Marianne and Trevor stood very still a few feet from each other. Marianne had a wild-eyed hatred in her eyes. Trevor had both of his claw-like hands up in front of him in a gesture of peace.

The crowd had swelled in size, and as well as the press many of the younger people in the crowd were videoing it all on their phones.

"You took my daughter, and you killed her with your disgusting friends, and now you're laughing at us!" Marianne shouted, her voice cracking.

"Please listen to me," said Trevor, "I have always wanted to have the opportunity to talk to you—"

"Don't you tell me to listen! You never get to tell me anything!" screamed Marianne. "You killed her, you evil bastard! You killed my girl and you dumped her in the water! I had to bury her yesterday, and all that was left were her bones!"

Tears were now pouring down Marianne's face. The crowds around watched in rapt silence. They had now swollen, spilling off the pavement and into the road. Cars started to honk at them blocking the two lanes.

"Come on! Where are the fucking officers?" shouted Erika. The woman behind the front desk picked up her phone again. Erika turned back, and she noticed Laura by

Trevor Marksman's car. Standing silently, tears rolling down her face.

The atmosphere changed in the crowd, as suddenly Marianne was wielding a large kitchen knife. The crowd scattered as she held it up, spilling out into the main road amongst the traffic, which was now honking madly.

Marianne lunged at Trevor Marksman, slashing from side to side with the knife, gouging into the flesh of his forearms, which he raised instinctively to protect himself. Laura's eyes were wide, and she was now screaming at her mother to stop.

"Shit!" cried Erika. "Where are my uniformed officers?"

She and Moss dashed outside and pushed their way down the stairs. Seconds later, they were joined by six uniformed officers.

They managed to grab Marianne Collins and knock her to the floor. Her face was wild and covered in blood, three large patches were soaking into the front of her white blouse, and a splash daubed her left cheek. A young male PC, wearing an anti-stab vest, managed to get hold of Marianne's arm and twisted it so she dropped the knife. He kicked it away where another officer trapped it under his shoe.

Marianne was now screaming, a terrible raw scraping sound. A female PC placed her boot in her back, and Marianne fought her as she handcuffed her hands behind her back.

Erika ran to Trevor Marksman, who lay on the pavement. He was covered in blood, which pumped out of the three gaping wounds in his forearms. She could see that one was slit right down to the bone. Erika sloughed off her thin suit jacket, knelt down beside him and started to wrap it around his bleeding arms.

"We need an ambulance! This man is bleeding!" she shouted above the mayhem; crowds were gathering on both sides of the pavement, as people streamed out of the train station on the opposite side of the road and found themselves caught up in the drama.

Marianne Collins was dragged away screaming and covered in blood, just as an officer came running from the main entrance of the station with a first aid kit.

Throughout all of this, the press cameras took photographs and recorded video of the chaos.

CHAPTER 54

The Assistant Commissioner, Camilla Brace-Cosworthy, turned from the large television on the wall in her office to where Erika was standing in front of her desk.

It was early the next morning, and she had just played Erika and Marsh a two-minute round-up of the previous day's events. Marsh sat to one side of her in stony silence.

The incident outside Bromley Police Station had been headline news the previous evening. The two-minute round-up was edited highlights from the Sky News app designed to show the maximum chaos. It mixed the professional press video, taken when Trevor Marksman spoke outside Bromley Station, with shaky mobile phone footage taken up close of Marianne Collins wielding the knife, climaxing in her arrest where she had been handcuffed, face down on the pavement, covered in Trevor Marksman's blood.

Erika shifted uncomfortably. She hadn't been invited to sit, which was a bad sign.

"What part of bringing in Joel Michaels quietly for questioning did you ignore?" asked Camilla, peering up at Erika over the top of her glasses. "This was our advice when you spoke to us about making this arrest?"

"Yes ma'am. We couldn't have anticipated this chain of events. We believe that Marianne Collins was tipped off, just as the press was tipped off," replied Erika.

"I suggest you spend your time finding the leak, and then plug it, with ruthless force."

"Yes, ma'am. My officers are looking into this with urgency."

"So where does this leave our case?"

"Trevor Marksman is in hospital; he lost a great deal of blood but will make a full recovery. Due to the nature of his skin grafts he will have to spend time in intensive care."

"What about Marianne Collins?"

"She was arrested and charged. She was released on bail."

"And Joel Michaels?"

"I have two more days until I have to release him," said Erika.

Camilla sat back and stared at Erika for a moment. "Of course, DCI Foster, this is your case, but if I were you I'd release Joel Michaels."

"But, ma'am, I have evidence that he was involved in stalking Jessica, videoing her. He is a convicted pedophile. He lied about knowing Bob Jennings. I believe that Jessica was kept in captivity in the Hayes cottage cellar."

"You found a tooth in the cellar, but it doesn't match Jessica Collins."

"That's correct, but it was a child's tooth. And the petrol deposits we found in the cellar floor are leaded petrol. There were high levels of lead found in Jessica's bones."

Camilla put up her hand. "What you need is solid forensic evidence. Can you place Joel Michaels or Trevor Marksman in that cellar?"

"No, but—"

"Can you place, without question, Jessica Collins in that cellar?"

"No." Erika struggled to keep eye contact and not to look down at the floor.

"We were planning on doing a television appeal with the Collins family," said Marsh, speaking for the first time. "But I don't think this will be something we can pursue. The image of Marianne Collins wielding a knife is looming large in people's minds…"

"Yes, we need grieving mother, not knife-wielding maniac," agreed Camilla. She took off her glasses and chewed on one of the stems for a moment.

Erika could feel the sweat trickling down her back.

"You've been here before, several times, haven't you, DCI Foster?" she said.

"I've been here once before, ma'am."

"I'm talking metaphorically," she snapped. "You seem to lurch between brilliance and bone-headed stupidity."

"In my defense, when Marianne Collins pulled out the knife, I had officers on the scene immediately—"

"It happened on the steps of your nick, which is manned by anything between five and fifty uniformed officers each day. Don't give me bullshit!" shouted Camilla, slamming her hand down on the desk. "On the same fucking steps where Superintendent Yale launched his knife crime initiative and knife amnesty!"

Camilla composed herself and put her glasses back on. Erika opened her mouth to speak, but she put her hand up. "I'm in no doubt of what a good officer you are, DCI Foster, but we now have the media spotlight firmly on a tricky case. Do you believe you could find enough evidence to nail Joel Michaels, Trevor Marksman or Bob Jennings for Jessica Collins's murder?"

"Yes. I would like to put forward that we exhume Jennings's body."

"Absolutely not," said Camilla. "After twenty-six years underground what would you expect to find?"

"Toxicology, and evidence of broken bones, foul play, which could prove that he didn't commit suicide."

"And then what? The forensic evidence would be negligible, and forensics have already been over the cottage and found virtually nothing."

"We found the tooth," said Erika, but she knew she'd lost; she just couldn't stop and back down.

"It could have been knocked out, or fallen out. People who spend their time squatting in abandoned properties aren't prized for their oral hygiene. I strongly suggest you release Joel Michaels. Now, I'm going to leave you on this case for the time being while I look for a suitable replacement. Perhaps this will work in your favor. It seems when the chips are down you deliver results."

When the meeting was over, Marsh caught up with Erika at the lifts.

"It could have been far worse."

"How could that have gone *any* worse?" she said, turning to him.

"It could have been Oakley," he said with a shrug and a smile.

"I could deal with Assistant Commissioner Oakley. He was a bigoted old git. He rose to the bait; I could outsmart him. She's...She's bloody good."

"Yes. Speaking as your friend, and not your superior officer for a moment, she does make my testicles leap into my abdomen."

The lift doors opened and they got in. Marsh pressed the

button for the ground floor, and Erika felt her stomach lurch as they zoomed down the twelve floors of the New Scotland Yard building.

"Paul. This is the first case where I feel..." She stopped herself and looked down at her feet.

"What?" he asked.

"Where I feel I'm not going to solve it."

Marsh looked as if he was going to put his arm around her, but the lift came to a stop and a group of officers got in. Erika turned to the wall and tried to keep her emotions under control.

When they came out of the building onto the pavement, traffic was roaring past, and the sky was threatening rain again. They started to walk toward the tube station.

"I keep going back to that day, all those years ago: the seventh of August," said Erika. "I keep looking at the witness statements, the hundreds of people who were in the area, the remaining neighbors. How can one little girl have gone missing?"

"Children go missing all the time, every day, in every country," said Marsh, buttoning up his coat against the cold wind. "Over six hundred children went missing in Kent during 1990. Almost all of them were found alive. Eight of them still remain missing."

"So you're saying this is linked?"

It started to rain; they moved to shelter in the doorway of an empty office block.

"No, Erika. What I'm saying is that this wasn't an isolated incident. There are eight other children out there who vanished in 1990. Who is looking for them? Jessica Collins was white and middle class with blonde hair. The media grabbed hold of her story, pulled at our heart strings, and magnified it, and quite rightly too. But what about those other kids? Like Madeleine McCann, Jessica is the girl who stuck in people's minds. I hate to say it, but we can't solve every case. Please don't look on your inability to solve this as a personal failure."

Marsh put his hand on her shoulder and smiled.

"That's all very easy to say, Paul. The only thing I can do is be a police officer. I'm not a wife; I'll never be a mother. This is my life."

"And what happens in ten years when you're being pushed toward retirement, Erika?" he said. "You need to find a place for yourself in the world; a place where you can be happy that doesn't involve being a police officer."

CHAPTER 55

Erika watched from the window of the incident room as Joel Michaels walked out of the station a free man. He crossed the road and stopped on the pavement in front of the train station. He turned and looked, staring at her in the window. She resisted the urge to duck out of sight and matched his gaze. He smirked and then turned back, disappearing amongst the crowds that began to stream out from under the station awning. Erika wondered where he was headed. *Was he going to see Trevor in hospital?*

"You still think he did it?" said Moss, joining her at the window.

"That's the problem. I'm not sure," said Erika.

She spent the rest of the afternoon in her office, trying to focus, trying to make sense of the case, and if she even had one. At five thirty, after spending a couple of hours listlessly flicking through the case files on her computer, she grabbed her coat and left.

Erika found herself driving toward Hayes, and then she pulled in to Avondale Road. It was quiet, there was no one around, and just a couple of cars parked. She stopped outside number seven. Locking her car, she walked down the long sloping driveway, and saw there was a short round-faced woman at the front door, and a gray-haired man with a camera slung around his neck. A muffled voice from inside was telling them to go away.

"This is private property. Who are you?" she asked, pulling out her warrant card.

They both turned. "Eva Castle, *Daily Mail*," said the woman, looking her up and down. "We're only asking to get her mother's side of the story . . ."

The door shot open an inch, stopped by the chain. "My mother isn't here! She's in hospital," said the voice, which Erika heard was Laura's.

"She did slash a local pedophile with a knife, in public . . ." said Eva, leaning in to the gap in the door. "Where is she? The loony bin? This is your chance to tell her side of the story, and we'll pay."

"Come on, piss off," said Erika, putting out an arm to move them away.

The photographer lifted his camera and started to fire off some shots. Erika reached out and pushed the lens down.

"I think that's police brutality!" he said with a glint in his eye. His voice had a high raspy register.

"I could arrest you both for harassment. You're on private property," said Erika, her hand still holding down his camera lens. "And I can make sure we take up plenty of time processing you, taking DNA swabs, the works. I'll also confiscate your camera. What with all the bureaucracy, you probably won't get it back for quite some time."

"Come on, Dave," said Eva with a sneer. She pulled out a business card and pushed it through the gap in the door. "Call me if you change your mind, Laura."

Erika watched them until they had moved off and up the driveway, then turned to the door. Laura's face stared through the gap.

"Can I come in, and talk?" asked Erika.

Laura took the chain off and opened the door. "What about?" she asked, her face sagging fearfully. She was dressed in tight blue jeans and a white blouse tucked in at the waist, showing off an enviable figure. Her face was bare and free of makeup, and Erika was shocked how old she looked without it.

"Your mum, and what happened outside the station."

"I gave the police a statement."

"Please, Laura. It might help us with the case. I've just had to release Joel Michaels."

"Okay," she said, standing to one side.

Erika wiped her feet and came through the door.

Laura led her through the hallway and into the kitchen. "Would you like some tea?" Erika nodded. Laura moved and filled the kettle, and her hands were shaking. "What's going to happen to Mum?"

"She's been charged with attempted murder, but as you know, she's also been detained under the Mental Health Act at Lewisham Hospital. She'll need to be assessed by doctors. She doesn't have a previous criminal record so she may be tried for ABH or wounding. I would think the courts might show some lenience. It's a very sorry state of affairs."

Laura carried on making the tea.

"Where are the rest of your family?"

"Dad's with his girlfriend and the kids at my place in North London. I just came back to do the last of the tidying up after the wake."

"Laura. Who tipped you off about Trevor Marksman being in Bromley?"

"Mum had a phone call," said Laura, placing the kettle down.

"When?"

"Early yesterday morning."

"Who was the phone call from?"

"I don't know. I was outside in the garden."

"So your mother answered the phone?"

"Yes, she answered the phone, and then she came through here to tell me." Laura opened the cupboard and pulled a couple of teacups out.

"I thought you just said you were out in the garden?"

Laura dropped one of the cups and it shattered across the floor. "Sorry..."

"It's okay," said Erika, spying a dustpan and brush on the radiator by the door. She retrieved it and kneeled down to help clear up the pieces.

"I was out in the garden. I meant to say that she came out and got me," said Laura, carefully picking up two long shards of broken china.

"And it was her idea to go and confront Trevor?" asked Erika, sweeping the tiny bits of cup into the dustpan.

Laura nodded. She picked up the last of the big pieces and stood, moving over to a pedal bin.

"And you thought that was a good idea?"

"Of course not!"

"Did she say who the person was who called?"

"She said it was a journalist," replied Laura, emptying the pieces into the bin. "I don't know his name."

"The journalist was a 'he'?"

Laura became flustered again. "She didn't tell me the name of the journalist, or if he was a he or a she...There's been so many over the years, spying, and fishing. They're usually male."

Laura filled the teapot with her back to Erika.

"Did your mum explicitly say what she was going to do?"

"She said she wanted to see Trevor, and she wanted to ask him once and for all if he did it."

"Didn't you realize it was a bad idea, Laura?"

Laura placed her hands on the work surface and bowed her head, nodding. "It was the day after the funeral, and the wake…She'd had a lot to drink, and said she was going to drive into town with or without me."

"Where was everyone else?"

"They'd gone home the night before. I stayed with Mum here, to keep her company."

"Did you know your mother had picked up a knife?"

"No, and I wouldn't have taken her if I knew what she was going to do! Okay? What's going to happen to her?" Laura started to cry.

"Have you been in touch with Oscar Browne?"

"What do you mean?" she answered sharply.

"He's an excellent barrister. I presume he could help your mother's case."

"Yes. I see what you mean," said Laura. Her hands were still shaking. "No, I haven't heard from him. Well I saw him at the funeral, obviously."

"How is your relationship after all these years?"

"We don't really have one. We broke up, he's not on my radar really. I have my kids and my husband. He has his…"

"Okay. I'm going to request your phone records. We'll see if we can track down this journalist," said Erika.

Laura nodded, her brow furrowed. "Do you still want tea?"

"No, thank you. I need to get going."

They moved through the living room where the curtains were drawn, and to the front door. When Laura opened it,

Oscar Browne was on the doorstep about to ring the bell. He was surprised to see Erika.

"DCI Foster was just here to ask about Mum," said Laura, quickly.

"Ah. Right, of course," he said. He seemed to stand taller and become more formal. "That's what I'm here about. Laura got in touch about her mother's legal defense."

"Yes, I did," said Laura quickly. "Sorry, my mind is like a sieve at the moment."

There was an awkward pause.

"Okay, well look after yourself," said Erika.

"Thank you for checking in on her, DCI Foster," said Oscar. He moved inside and held the door open for Erika.

When Erika came back up onto the street and got into her car, she was confused by the interaction between Laura and Oscar. The case was making her head hurt. She was bombarded with information, but still couldn't get a hold of it all. She needed a good night's sleep and a drink.

She started the car and drove home.

CHAPTER 56

When she came through the front door, Jakub and Karolina were playing a game of chase, yelling and running through the flat.

"Hi, Aunt Erika!" they shouted on their way past. The baby was crying in concert with the screaming washing machine, and the television was on full blast, playing the MTV channel. Lenka was dancing around with Eva leant against her shoulder, trying to get her to calm down.

Erika's heart sank. After a terrible day, all she wanted was some peace and quiet.

"*Zlatko*! You're home early!" cried Lenka. "So you did what I told you for once."

Erika went to the fridge and opened the freezer, and Karolina and Jakub came tearing up and circled her legs, trying to catch each other.

"Where's my vodka?" said Erika.

"I moved it, for the frozen vegetables. I was worried the bottle would break," replied Lenka, transferring the screaming Eva to her other shoulder. The video for "Spice Up Your Life" came on MTV, and the kids ran up and over the sofa bed.

"Please can you just calm them down!" said Erika.

"You're their aunt who's never here, you can talk to them a bit you know," snapped Lenka.

"I've been at work! And why do they have to run over the furniture?"

"It's a bed, you know, it's okay for kids to jump on a bed—"

"It's a sofa bed, not a bed, Lenka."

"When it's open it's a bed, Erika."

The kids carried on jumping up and down, going mad to the music.

"Why did you take the ice out too?" said Erika, seeing the ice cube tray had been dumped in the sink.

"It's the middle of November, what do you want ice for?" snapped Lenka, transferring the screaming Eva back to her other shoulder.

"I just wanted a cold drink. Just one!" Erika took a deep breath and went through to the bedroom. It was a tip; the bedclothes were bunched up in a ball, there were toys all over the floor, and a bag of dirty nappies was warming by the radiator, giving off a nasty stink.

Erika squeezed past the baby's buggy in the doorway, and saw that her photo of Mark had been placed flat on the dressing table, and resting on the glass was a bottle of baby oil. She grabbed the frame and unhooked the back. The oil had gone inside and stained the top of the photo just above Mark's head and down to his hairline.

Erika marched back into the living room, holding up the photo, and nearly colliding with the children as they ran past.

"Who the hell do you think you are?" she shouted.

Lenka turned with Eva and stared at the photo. "What?"

"You put the baby oil bottle on my photo of Mark…"

"Sorry, Erika. I'll get you another one; have you got it on a USB key?"

"Lenka. I don't have another copy of this photo... I took it on an old film camera," said Erika, her voice cracking.

"So you have a husband who you miss more than life itself, and yet you have a photo of him which only exists as one copy! Why didn't you get it scanned?"

It drew her up short. She was right. Why hadn't she had it scanned? It was so simple.

"You are fucking careless and messy!" she shouted.

"You lord it over us all that you're this amazing detective, but you have one copy of the most precious photo in the world! I moved it from the changing table, and you put it back there! You knew I was using it to change her nappy! You tell me it's okay to stay and then you get all territorial!"

"How the hell is my photo in my house territorial? And look at this place! I'm pretty sure this all looks like YOUR territory!"

Lenka turned away to the TV. Eva had stopped crying, and was staring at her with big eyes.

"How much longer are you staying? Or is it all dependent on your stupid husband?"

"At least I have my husband's back!" shouted Lenka.

There was a horrible silence.

"What did you just say?"

"Erika, I didn't mean that," said Lenka, turning back, her face dropping.

"Right. I want you and everything gone by tomorrow morning. You hear!" shouted Erika. She left the living room, carrying the photo of Mark, grabbed her car keys, and left the flat.

It was pouring with rain when Erika got into her car. She started the engine and pulled away, unsure of where she was going to go.

CHAPTER 57

Amanda Baker didn't notice the rain hammering against her window, she was absorbed with her computer, watching and re-watching the camcorder videos taken by Trevor Marksman. Crawford had been good, providing her with copies of case files to help her fill the gaps in her memory.

The papers on her living room wall had multiplied, filling the back wall above the sofa.

Amanda had always enjoyed research, solving puzzles, piecing clues together. Without the pressure of answering to top brass, or even the pressure to leave her house, she felt in control. It was almost as if she was back on the case.

She leaned closer to her laptop, bathed in the glow of the screen. She had come to the part of the video where Marianne and Laura Collins were together in the park. It was a bright sunny day, and they were sitting on a bench under the canopy of a huge oak tree. The camera panned round from where Jessica and another girl were on the swings, their long hair flying as they pushed back and forth in unison, higher and higher. Marianne and Laura's discussion was heated, the camera zoomed in with interest, losing focus for a second before their argument became a sharp image. There was a little wind interference on the sound, but Amanda heard clearly what they were saying. She paused the video, and reached out her hand to the bowl of caramel popcorn she had on the floor beside the armchair. It was empty.

She heaved herself up and out of the chair and moved through to the kitchen. She was determined not to drink, and sugar seemed to help the cravings. When she opened the freezer she saw she'd eaten the last of the ice cream; the cupboard where she kept biscuits and chocolate was also bare. She went to the small pantry, pulled the door open, and using her smartphone as a light, she scanned the shelves looking for something to eat. The light played over the tins, spices, bags of rice and pasta. She was sure there must be something sweet in the dark recesses.

She looked out of the window at the back garden. The rain was lashing against the glass, and the messy square of grass lit up with lightning. She really didn't fancy going out on a chocolate run in that kind of weather.

She dragged a chair over from the kitchen table into the doorway of the pantry, and stood on it. She scanned the top shelves with her smartphone light over more tins, an old box of Weetabix, and her phone light came to rest on a box behind a small pile of OXO cubes. It was a very old Terry's Chocolate Orange. The blue box was covered in dust, and she could see through the little plastic sphere that the orange foil-wrapped chocolate inside had broken down and seeped through the foil. However, she didn't notice this: it was what was written on the box that made her stop in her tracks.

"It's not Terry's, it's mine," she said, reading the old tag-line. She picked up the box, stepped down off the chair and walked back through to the living room. "It's not Terry's, it's mine…" She repeated, almost in a trance. She moved back to her laptop, and played back the video a couple of times, watching the moment where Marianne slapped Laura across the face, and listening to the words she shrieked.

She reached for her phone and dialed a number, but all she got was voicemail: "Crawford, it's me," she said. "Jessica Collins's murder. I think I've worked it out... Call me as soon as you get this. I need help checking something."

Across town, in his high-rise flat in Morden, Gerry lay in front of the TV. The alarm signal he'd become used to hearing beeped out, and he paused the show he was watching, and went to his laptop to listen.

CHAPTER 58

Peterson stood in the kitchen of his flat, wearing only a small hand towel around his waist. He peered into his fridge. All he had were a half-full can of spaghetti hoops and some moldy bread.

His flat was a small ground floor rental in a decent area of Sydenham. His neighbors were mostly made up of office workers who left early and arrived home late, and a couple of old ladies who were always a little twinkly eyed when they saw him. They'd discovered he was a policeman a few weeks after he'd moved in, and they were comforted by the fact they had a man of the law in their midst, and as his mate Dwayne had remarked, they probably fancied him too.

As he sighed and closed the fridge, his buzzer went. He thought it might be one of the old ladies in question. He'd had a note pushed through his front door about coming to a neighborhood watch meeting.

However, when he opened the door Erika stood outside, dripping wet.

"Boss, hi," he said, picking up his underwear and socks, which lay on the floor by the bathroom door.

"Sorry, have you got company?" she asked. Her eyes flicked down to where a silver St. Christopher necklace hung between his smooth pectorals, and the dusting of hair on his washboard stomach.

"No, I'm just a slob." He grinned. "Sorry, I was just out of the shower," he said, pulling on the white T-shirt and nearly losing the tiny towel in the process. "Do you want to come in?"

"I'm sorry. I shouldn't have come," she said, turning to leave.

"Boss, you're soaked and it's freezing. Let me at least give you a towel...I've got another one," he added, looking at the one wrapped around his waist.

He showed her through to the living room as he went off to the bedroom. She looked around and saw it was very much a bachelor pad. There was a huge flat-screen TV on a low table with a PlayStation and two controllers hooked up to it. Two of the walls were lined with bookshelves and crammed with a mixture of books and DVDs. The furniture was black leather, and on the wall was a Pirelli 2016 calendar, still showing October. Peterson came back in wearing a white T-shirt and a pair of loose tracksuit bottoms. Erika thought how good he smelt.

"What's with the calendar?" she asked, pointing to the black-and-white picture of Yoko Ono sitting on a stool wearing tights, a jacket and a top hat.

"Yeah, my mates get me the Pirelli every year...This year it's gone all arty and conceptual."

"No birds with their tits out," smiled Erika.

"Sadly, no," he grinned. His eyes flicked down to the front of her blouse, and she followed his gaze, mortified to see that she was drenched, and her bra was showing through.

"Oh my God," she said, lifting the towel to cover herself.

"It's cool," he said. "You want a T-shirt? I can stick your blouse on the radiator?"

He left and came back with a dry T-shirt and went through to the kitchen so she could change. She went to a corner and quickly unbuttoned her wet blouse. Her bra was soaked, and she spent minutes trying to decide if she should take that off too. She unhooked it and pulled on the T-shirt. He returned with two small tumblers of whisky as she was hiding her wet bra under the blouse on the radiator under the window. Lightning flashed in the sky, and the rain was blown in sheets against the glass.

"Here, this will warm you up. It's just a single so you won't be over the limit," he said. She took a glass and they sipped. He indicated they should sit on the sofa.

"Is everything okay with the case? I know it was a bit of a shit day," he said.

"It's fine, well, not fine . . ."

"But?"

"I don't know why I'm here," she said, looking down at the amber liquid in her glass. "My sister is still here, the one you met."

"Haven't you got a one-bed flat?" he asked, taking a drink.

Erika nodded. "The tension came to a head tonight, and I stormed out."

"Sorry to hear that."

They both took another drink. The whisky was now warming Erika's stomach and making her feel more relaxed.

"Do I come across as a bitch?"

Peterson blew out his cheeks. "You've got to head up a team of coppers, you've got to be tough."

"That's a yes. Thanks."

"I didn't mean it like that, boss."

"Don't call me boss, call me—"

"Miss Ross," finished Peterson.

Erika burst out laughing, and he joined in. She looked down at her glass again, and when she looked up Peterson had moved closer. He took it from her hands and placed it on the table in front of them. He leaned over and gently cupped her chin and kissed her. His lips were soft and warm and sensual, and there was just a light flicker of his tongue. He tasted of whisky and man, and she began to melt.

Erika reached up and ran her hands down his firm muscular back, and hooked her fingers under his T-shirt. His skin was warm and smooth. His hands found their way under the T-shirt, and his fingers moved slowly up her back.

"You came here with no bra?" he murmured.

"It's on the radiator," she said indignantly.

He moved his hand round and gently squeezed her nipple. She moaned and lay back as he moved on top of her, their lips now pressed together.

Suddenly Mark's face came rushing at her. An image so clear, she cried out.

"What? Are you okay? Did I hurt you?" said Peterson, moving back.

She stared into his beautiful brown eyes, and burst into tears. She leapt up and went to the tiny bathroom, and locked herself inside. She sat on the edge of the bath and cried, huge heaving sobs wracking her body. She hadn't cried like this for so long, and it felt good and bad at the same time. When her sobs had subsided, there was a soft knock at the door.

"Boss, I mean, Erika. You okay? I'm sorry if I was out of order," came Peterson's voice.

Erika moved to the mirror, wiped her face then opened the door.

"You didn't do anything..."

"I did, I kind of grabbed your boob."

"I'm trying to be serious here," she said, closing her nose on a tissue. "It's hard to be a widow. Mark was my life, he was the love of my life and he's gone. He's never going to come back, and yet I spend every day thinking about him… and it's exhausting, it's exhausting grieving, and living with this huge gap in my life. But I'm only human, and I'd love nothing more than to just…you know…with you, but there's this guilt. Mark was such a good loyal man." She shrugged and wiped her eyes.

"Erika, we can just chill. Look, I can give you a minute. I'll go and whack off to that picture of Yoko Ono…"

She looked up at him.

"Too early for a joke?" he added.

"No," she smiled. "A joke is what I need."

She stood, and with a smile she looked at him leaning against the doorway. She grabbed him and began to kiss him again. They moved off, him stumbling backward, feeling their way together along the hallway, until they found the bedroom door and they collapsed onto the bed. And this time she didn't let him stop.

CHAPTER 59

Lenka lay awake in the darkness of Erika's flat, staring up at the bedroom ceiling and listening to the rain pelting down outside. Beside her in the bed, Eva clucked and snuffled in her sleep. She reached out a hand to check she was okay, stroking her soft head and fine hair.

The argument she'd had with Erika played heavy on her mind. She'd waited up until well after midnight, sitting in the dark living room with the children sleeping. Then she'd tried to call Erika's phone. It gave a muffled ring from Erika's coat hung on the back of the chair. Lenka fished it out of the pocket, but the battery died mid-ring, and in the darkness she couldn't find the charger.

Lenka sat back and looked over at Jakub and Karolina, and she felt very far from home. She knew that Erika had a friend who was a Forensic Pathologist, but she couldn't remember his name, and she knew Mark's dad was called Edward Foster, and that he lived near Manchester. She worried for her sister; it was unlike her to be so reckless and leave without saying where she was going.

*   *   *

Erika lay with her head on Peterson's chest and felt his warmth and the calm rhythmic beating of his heart. He stirred and pulled her close to him with his strong forearm.

She felt shock and a mixture of excitement and guilt that they'd had sex. Twice. The first time had been intense and fast, and then almost straightaway they'd done it again, slow and sensual. They'd fallen asleep soon afterward, but she'd woken an hour ago, and her mind had been whirring as she watched the digital clock in his bedroom.

It was now 3:04 a.m. She snuggled into the crook of his arm, closed her eyes and willed herself to sleep.

Lenka rolled over in bed, picked up her phone from the bedside table, and saw it was 3:05 a.m. She flopped back and checked Eva was okay. The little girl was breathing softly with her tiny thumb in her mouth.

Lenka froze as she heard a noise, like the cracking of plastic. It came again and then there was a clink, which sounded like something hitting the carpet in the living room. She moved swiftly out of bed and scanned the room; the vacuum cleaner lay in the corner, its pipe coiled round and the metal bar detached. She grabbed it and ran through to the living room.

The patio door had been pushed open, and she could see where the plastic had been removed to force it open. The curtains flapped in the strong breeze rushing through the gap. She turned with the metal pipe over her shoulder looking around the dark room, and unbelievably, the children were still asleep under the blankets.

There was a faint creak, and Lenka felt a pair of powerful hands encircle her neck. Without thinking she swung the metal pipe up and over her right shoulder. There was a crack and a yell. The kids then woke up and started screaming, and Lenka turned to see the large shape of a man coming at her. She swung the pipe up and hit him in the crotch. It wasn't hard, but he groaned and it gave her enough time to step back and really swing with some momentum as she brought it down with full force on his head, once and then twice. He fell to the floor, and she brought it down again and again, battering the man three times before he slumped forward and stopped moving.

Jakub and Karolina were now screaming and crying. Lenka told them to go and get Eva. She couldn't make out much of the man on the floor. He was big with lots of black curly hair. Keeping her eye on the figure on the floor, she grabbed the block of knives from the kitchen half of the room, and the landline from its charger, which she slipped in her pocket. She walked backward to the bathroom, still holding the pipe.

"Inside," she said to the children, who came out of the bedroom; Karolina was carrying Eva, who miraculously was still asleep. They went into the bathroom and Lenka locked the door, pulling a chair in front of it. She saw that the back of the chair was too short to stop the handle turning.

"It's okay," she said to Karolina and Jakub as they crouched like two little frightened animals in the bath. "It's going to be okay. Karolina, I need you to help me and keep hold of Eva," she said. The little girl gulped and nodded.

Lenka stared down at the phone and realized she didn't know any numbers; she didn't know how to call the police; she didn't know enough English to explain that they needed help. The only number she knew was for Marek.

She sat against the door and dialed her husband's mobile phone in Slovakia. Jakub was white-faced and pulling at her sleeve.

"What is it?" she said.

"Mummy, the lock doesn't work," he whispered, his face white and trembling. "Auntie Erika said it was broken…"

As the phone began to ring, Lenka heard a squeaking sound, and looked up. The door handle above her head was turning, and she felt the door start to give way behind her back.

A large hand reached through the gap, and this time Lenka screamed along with the children.

CHAPTER 60

When Erika woke the next morning, she saw Peterson had rolled away from her in the night, and slept on his side with all the covers bunched up around his bare legs. It was 6:01 a.m. So many emotions washed over her; guilt that she enjoyed being with Peterson, and a deep sadness that she was further apart from Mark. The memory of him had retreated a little; it was dimmer and further in the past now she had this new experience with another man. Her heart sank when she knew she would have to see Peterson today at work. She sat up and retrieved her clothes from the floor beside the bed, pulling on her underwear. Peterson rolled over as she pulled the curtain to one side. It was still dark outside.

"Morning. Don't you want to stay for breakfast?"

"No. I should go," she said.

"Come here."

"Why?"

He sat up. "What do you mean why? I want to kiss you."

Erika went to his side of the bed and perched on the edge. He put his arm around her.

"We need to lay down some boundaries," she said.

He raised an eyebrow. "There didn't seem to be many last night."

"I'm serious. I'm your boss. It would be easier if we didn't talk about this at work."

"Dammit, I was going to stand up and address the incident room and tell everyone how great you are in the sack..."

"Peterson."

"And you are great in the sack," he said with a wink. She looked at him. "I'm not going to say anything..."

"Good."

"Do you want to do this again?"

"I don't know. Can we just chalk it up to a great night?"

"Chalk it up?"

Erika stood and fumbled around for her socks. "What do you want? A relationship?"

"No."

"Good. Because I am nowhere near wanting to do that."

"You've made it clear you don't want one," he said, sitting up.

"Good. Then this was a one-off, we had fun and everything goes back to how it was..."

"Fine. Yes. I'll see you at work." He climbed past her out of bed and went to the bathroom, slamming the door.

Erika followed him out of the bedroom and went to knock on the bathroom door. She hesitated and then went to the living room and retrieved her blouse and bra. Leaving his T-shirt neatly folded on the back of the sofa, she let herself out of his flat.

CHAPTER 61

Erika went to the drive-through McDonald's in Sydenham, and ordered a sausage and egg McMuffin with a cup of coffee. When she came to pay, she saw that she didn't have her phone or wallet, and she had to use some spare change she kept for parking in the glove compartment.

Dawn was just breaking, cold and blue, as she pulled up at Manor Mount just after seven. Her heart began to hammer when she saw two police cars outside. She parked beside them on the gravel, and let herself in at the main entrance, feeling her heart race even faster when she saw her front door was open and a police officer was stationed outside.

A tall figure in a blue forensics suit emerged carrying a long plastic evidence bag containing the pipe from her vacuum cleaner. Blood was crusted on the metal tubing and smeared over the plastic. In his other hand was one of her guest towels: blood-stained.

"Sorry, who are you?" asked the police officer, putting out his hand to block her path. She saw he was very young with a thin face and had terrible razor rash.

"This is my flat. Where is my sister and her kids?" she said, feeling frantic and trying to move past him.

"This is a crime scene," he said, continuing to block her way.

"I'm a police officer, but I haven't got my warrant card. Why is there blood? Where are my sister and her kids?" She was now in a blind panic, out of control, heart racing, tears pricking her eyes. It was shocking how quickly she'd reverted to the role of the victim.

And then the last police officer she wanted to see emerged from the doorway wearing blue scrubs. Superintendent Sparks pulled down the hood of the scrubs to reveal a greasy helmet of hair combed back from his high forehead. His pale acne-scarred face regarded her for a moment.

"Erika?"

"Sparks, what's happening? This is my flat. Where are my sister and the three kids?" she said tearfully. She didn't care about their past differences, and only wanted to know the truth.

"Your sister and her kids are fine," he said. "They're upstairs with a neighbor. We managed to get a translator half an hour ago. They're shaken up, but unharmed."

"Oh, thank God," said Erika, wiping tears away with the back of her hand. "What happened?"

Sparks led her back out into the communal entrance.

"There was an emergency call logged at three thirty this morning from your landline...The operator didn't understand at first what was being said, but by a miracle one of the operators spoke Slovak."

Sparks went on to say that an intruder had broken in through the patio window, and Lenka had attacked the person with the metal pipe from the vacuum cleaner. "She locked herself and the kids in the bathroom and called 112, which luckily goes through to 999 emergencies. Whoever broke in was bleeding badly. They tried to get into the bathroom, left a lot of blood on the door. But for some reason they fled the scene. When we arrived just after 4 a.m. there was no one."

Erika slumped against the wall. "Was anything taken?" she asked.

"Not as far as we can see."

"Sparks, my bloody phone is in there, my warrant card, my bag...My laptop." She put her head in her hands. He stood over her, unsure of what to say.

"You know the score. It's a crime scene..."

"Sparks, I know we've got our differences, but can we put them aside just for a couple of hours? I'd do the same for you. Can you see if things can be fast-tracked?"

"I just told you. This is a crime scene. No one was hurt. You can wait."

"Why are you here, anyway?" said Erika. "I thought this would be a little below your rank."

"I came to a home invasion with a suspected dead body. Eastern European woman in distress."

"Cherry-picking the high profile cases still, are we? You always were a lazy bastard."

Sparks took a step back. "I don't think that's the correct way to speak to your superior officer, DCI Foster," he sneered.

"I'm just plain Ms. Foster this morning. The victim whose tax pays your wages. Now where is my sister?"

Erika had never met her neighbor on the top floor, a cheerful blowsy woman called Alison. She was in her forties and had a mass of messy curls.

"Hello," she said when she opened the door to Sparks and Erika. "Your sister and the kids are in the lounge, right shook up they are." She spoke with a soft Welsh accent and wore a flower print dress. Her flat was larger than Erika's, and comfortably decorated with rustic wooden furniture, books on every wall, and pictures of family. She took them through to the living room, where Lenka sat on the sofa with Eva sleeping in her arms. She was talking in Slovak to a tall thin man wearing a green corduroy suit, who was perched on the coffee table opposite.

Karolina and Jakub were at either end of a long sofa. Between them was a huge elderly Rottweiler, asleep with his head on Karolina's lap.

"Erika," said Lenka seeing her.

Erika went over and hugged them. "I'm sorry. I'm so sorry for leaving like that, and not coming back," she said.

"I'm sorry for what I said, I didn't mean it..."

"It's fine, we're all fine, everything is good and I love you," said Erika. They hugged again, and then Erika went to the kids and asked if they were okay. They nodded solemnly. Karolina rubbed at the dog's big ear, and Jakub tilted his head where Erika was blocking his view of the cartoons on the TV.

"Who's the creepy man? Looks like a vampire?" asked Lenka in Slovak, tipping her head toward Sparks, who stood in the corner, glowering, in his black suit.

"He looks like the man from *Hotel Transylvania*," said Jakub.

"What are they saying?" snapped Sparks.

The translator opened his mouth to speak, but Erika put a hand on his arm.

"It's fine. I can take things from here...I was just asking if they were okay." She turned to Lenka, and switching to Slovak, said: "He's the arsehole I told you about."

"You know we're in England and we should all be speaking English," said Sparks.

"*Kokot*," said Lenka, nodding in agreement.

"I'm smart enough to know that wasn't a pleasant word," said Sparks. "You obviously seem fine, and my officers have taken statements. So I'll be off," he said and excused himself. Lenka thanked the translator, who left shortly afterward.

"Do you want a cuppa love?" asked Alison.

"Thank you, yes," said Erika.

"Just give Duke a shove if you want to sit down," she added, indicating the Rottweiler. "He's harmless, spends all day sleeping and farting... He didn't hear your intruder."

"Thanks for letting them stay here this morning," said Erika. "Sorry I never came up to introduce myself..."

Alison batted her apologies away. "It always takes a crisis to bring people together. I'll get you that tea."

She left and Erika perched on the coffee table and grabbed Lenka's hand. "Did you get a look at whoever it was?"

"Just a glimpse of his face. Big bastard he was, with loads of hair," said Lenka. She sighed and went to speak, but stopped herself.

"What is it? Anything you can remember, however small..."

"You know I said the other day a man came to read the gas and electricity meter?"

"Yes."

"I can't be sure, and it *was* dark, but it looked like the same man."

CHAPTER 62

After the break-in, Erika's flat was a crime scene, so they booked into a hotel on the outskirts of Bromley.

Erika had stayed there previously, it was close to Bromley town center, but set amongst fields overlooking a golf course. Lenka booked a suite for herself and the kids, and an adjoining room for Erika, despite her protestations.

"No, it's on me. I've been restrained with Marek's credit card," said Lenka. "But he can foot the bill for a few nights of luxury. Did I tell you that I phoned him from the bathroom the night that nutter broke in, and that he didn't ring me back until the next morning!"

"It was the middle of the night," said Erika.

"I've been sleeping with my phone on, in case he needs me. I thought he would do the same, if not for me, at least to know the kids are okay..."

"Did you tell him what happened?"

"Yes. He was worried, but he didn't offer to fly over. He's too busy with lawyers, and trying to dodge bullets, metaphorical and real."

"The suite comes with an optional butler service," said the receptionist. Erika translated.

"Yep, we'll take him, and what's your most expensive spa procedure?" asked Lenka.

"She says the colonic irrigation," translated Erika.

"Good, book me one every day for the next week!"

"She'll just have the butler," said Erika to the receptionist. They took their keys and then checked in to their rooms, which were beautiful.

Erika managed some sleep, but she couldn't share the excitement of Lenka and the kids. She was still in case mode, and glad to get back to work on Monday morning.

When she arrived at the incident room, her officers had only just arrived and were taking their coats off and talking about what they did at the weekend. Everyone stopped when she came through the door.

"You may have heard I had quite an eventful weekend. No one has been hurt, apart from the intruder who was seen off expertly by my sister. It runs in the family..."

She looked around the room at her officers, at John, Moss, and DC Knight, who all gave her a nod and a smile, and then she saw Peterson, who just stared back at her.

"It's business as usual. We still have a case to solve, so let's get to it."

She went to her office. Moss followed after her.

"Boss, your iPhone is back from forensics, with your laptop and warrant card. They found nothing on it; no prints. Oh, and Sparks says hi."

Erika looked up at her.

"I'm kidding, boss."

"Very funny. I thought Superintendent Sparks would already be working some high profile case at Lewisham?"

"That's his problem, he's only on the lookout for the high profile ones, which is like an actor only wanting to be in the award-winning films..."

"So he's still good at palming the cases off that don't interest him?"

Moss nodded. "I think he was hoping to land something juicy when they answered your sister's emergency call but..."

"He ended up with my sister," grinned Erika. "Which reminds me, can you get one of our E-FIT artists to go and talk to her with a translator? There's something bugging me about this break-in."

"Yes, boss."

Moss went off, and Erika opened the clear evidence bag which housed all her belongings. She retrieved her warrant card and slipped it in to her pocket. The iPhone battery was dead, so she hooked it up to the charger she kept in her office, and switched it on. A stream of voicemails and missed calls came through. Several were from Lenka, but she was surprised to hear the first voicemail was from Amanda Baker, saying she had some important information for her regarding the Jessica Collins case, and to call her back urgently.

Amanda had called her a further five times, leaving other messages. Erika pressed call, but Amanda's mobile went straight to voicemail. She logged onto her computer and pulled up the phone directory and put in Amanda's address. She tried the landline number, but it rang out.

Erika opened her office door and called John over.

"Can you keep trying these two numbers. They're both Amanda Baker. When she answers can you put her through to me straightaway."

"Yes, boss," he said, taking the piece of paper where she'd scribbled down the numbers.

Erika went back to her desk and tried to get her head back into the Jessica Collins case. She looked through the notes she had made over the last few days, taking in the arrest of Joel Michaels.

There was a knock on the glass, and Peterson opened the door. He held a cardboard tray with two coffees from the Starbucks at the top of the high street. He moved to her desk and placed one in front of her.

"What's this?" she asked.

"I got you a coffee."

"I didn't ask for one."

"You looked like you could do with one..."

Erika pushed it across the desk toward him. "Peterson, what are you doing?"

"Can't I get you a coffee?"

Erika lowered her voice. "Are you getting me a coffee as your boss, or as your, I don't know, one-night stand?"

"That's not fair. I'm just getting you a coffee, read into it what you will. And for the record, the other night was special."

"We are not talking about that here in the bloody incident room!"

Moss reappeared at the door with a knock. "I was just going to run across the road for coffee, do you guys..." Her voice tailed off. "Oh. Did I miss the coffee run?"

"I've just been," said Peterson.

"You went all the way up to Starbucks?" she said, seeing the cups. She then looked between Erika and Peterson and grinned. "Oh... I see. Have you two...?"

"Moss, can you come in here and close the door behind you," said Erika.

She waited until the door was shut. "I don't know what Peterson has told you but this is not a dating game. I don't want to hear my or Peterson's private life discussed here. There's no office romance to follow or be a part of…"

There was silence.

"Peterson hadn't told me anything, but now I can see something *has* occurred between the two of you."

"Nothing has occurred," said Peterson.

"Really? Look at this Starbucks coffee. You've gone to the trouble of getting brown and white sugar, a napkin. You've even balanced one of those little stirrer sticks on the top. That's so sweet."

"Piss off, Moss," said Peterson.

"Your secret is safe with me…but, for the record, I couldn't be more pleased."

"Just get back to work, both of you," said Erika. When they'd gone she stared at the coffee for a moment and then relented and took a sip.

There was a knock at her door again; it was John.

"What? Did you get through to Amanda Baker?" she asked.

"No boss, but there's been an emergency call-out to Amanda Baker's house. It's the postman. He called 999 because he thinks he can see something through her front room window—"

"What?"

John swallowed nervously. "He thinks he can see her feet hanging above the floor in the hallway."

CHAPTER 63

A police car was waiting outside Amanda Baker's house when Erika and John arrived. Two uniformed officers, a man and a young woman, were talking to the postman Erika had seen on her previous visit. He looked shaken.

"Hello, I'm DCI Foster, this is DC McGorry," said Erika as they approached and showed their IDs. A couple of neighbors further down the street watched from their front gates.

"I'm PC Desmond and this is PC Hewitt," said the young woman. "No one has been inside the property. We did try to force the front door but it won't budge."

"She's got newspapers stacked up against it on the other side," said the postman, his face ashen.

Erika went to the front window and peered through the small gap left in the curtains. She could just make out a pair of feet in socks, suspended through the doorway from the hall. She felt a cold dread trickling through her stomach.

"I usually use the front window; it doesn't lock. I kept telling her to get it fixed," said the postman.

"This could be an entry point. I don't want to disturb any forensic evidence," said Erika to John in a low voice.

"But boss. It looks like she's killed herself," he said.

Erika peered back through the window. Something was wrong. Amanda hadn't seemed suicidal; she'd been positively brimming with life and enthusiasm when she'd dropped her off after the funeral.

"Let's go around to the back," she said.

They managed to get the side gate open, and then went down the passageway and into the garden.

The back door stood wide open.

"Shit," said Erika quietly.

She led, with John and the two uniformed officers close behind, and they went into the kitchen. It had been cleaned. Everything was neat and tidy. The door to the hallway was closed and they made their way toward it, slowly. The sound of a creaking floorboard made them stop. It was coming from the other side of the closed door. The uniform officers pulled out their batons.

"This is the police, come out with your hands raised," said Erika.

There was silence for a moment; the creaking came again, louder. Then there was a ripping sound, a snap, and an almighty crash shook the floorboards. It was followed by the sounds of debris crashing down the stairs.

They stood for a moment longer as the silence rang out. Erika looked back and gave a nod. She opened the door swiftly.

Amanda Baker's body lay at a gruesome angle on the hall floor at the bottom of the stairs. She wore just a white patterned nightgown with blue socks. Her left arm and shoulder were trapped under her back and her right leg was dislocated at the knee. Her body was covered in dust and chunks of plaster, and a square of thin wood lay nearby. It was the loft hatch. A fine dust rained down and filled the air.

"It broke away from the ceiling," said John, covering his mouth and pointing up to a gaping hole in the ceiling at the top of the stairs. Erika shielded her eyes from the dust and fine chunks of plaster still raining down. She moved close to Amanda's body, and saw her face was purple and bloated. Tied tight around her neck was a noose, and her eyes were still open.

CHAPTER 64

"Do you think this was suicide?" asked Erika. A few hours had passed, and Isaac Strong was attending the crime scene with Nils Åkerman and his team of CSIs.

Erika and John were standing in the hallway with Isaac.

"Death was by asphyxiation. The neck is elongated, and you can see the deep groove in the neck," said Isaac, gently tilting Amanda's head to one side. "My problem is that there's a glass tumbler on the carpet at the top of the stairs, with a residue of what smells like Coca-Cola. There's a corresponding splash on the wall," he went on. "If she was going to hang herself, she wouldn't do so holding a glass at the same time. We need to check that glass; it could have been that some kind of drug was dissolved in the drink..."

"Could she have been taken by surprise at the top of the stairs?" said Erika. "She's wearing a nightgown, which could mean she got up in the night. There was someone here, waiting in the darkness, and she walked into the noose?"

"That's for you to find out," said Isaac. Erika put her hand to her face. "You don't want this to be a suicide?" he added.

"She was one of us," said Erika softly. "And she didn't seem…"

"You never know what's going on in people's heads, Erika."

John moved to the loft hatch, which lay on the carpet halfway up the stairs. It was still attached to the other end of the noose.

"The rope was tied to the inside of the hatch, to a small metal bar," he said.

Erika looked around at the mess of plaster and dust in the hallway.

"Any chance of a time of death?"

"I'll know more when I've had a closer look," he said.

The crime scene photographer came through the living room door, and started to take photos. Amanda's open eyes caught the glare of the flash.

Nils appeared in the doorway behind him. "I think you'll want to take a look at this," he said.

They followed him through, and saw that the living room was tidy, but the wall behind the sofa was filled with papers tacked up. There were maps from Google, pictures of Jessica, Trevor Marksman, and some pictures that had been printed off of Marianne and Laura sitting in the park.

"This is the video; these are stills from Trevor Marksman's video," said Erika, looking to John. "How did she get hold of these? Where is her computer?"

"It was here," said Nils, moving to a metal computer stand in the corner. "There's only a laptop case and charger. There's an inkjet printer at the bottom," he said, indicating it on the base of the stand. "No sign of a mobile phone, and the landline in the hall has been removed," he added. "Her purse is still on the counter in the kitchen beside the kettle. It's got two hundred pounds inside and all her credit cards."

"So this wasn't a robbery."

"There's no sign of forced entry," added Nils.

"The kitchen door was wide open when we arrived," said John.

"But if the person came through the kitchen, they would have seen the purse there."

Erika noticed something on the top of the computer stand, and she went over, pulling a pair of latex gloves from her pocket. She picked up a small Terry's Chocolate Orange box. She saw that the chocolate inside was well past its use-by date; it had solidified and was oozing out of the orange foil.

"She hasn't opened it," said Erika. "And look, the slogan on the box has been underlined with a permanent marker."

"It's not Terry's, it's mine," said Nils, joining them and reading over Erika's shoulder. "This is very old. They don't use that slogan anymore . . . I eat at least one chocolate orange a week; I am an addict."

"How do you keep so thin?" asked John, looking up at Nils's tall slim frame.

Nils shrugged. "I have a very fast metabolism."

Erika ignored them and turned the box over. "'Best before end 11th of November 2006,'" she read. "Why underline the writing on the box?"

John and Nils looked back at her and shrugged.

When Erika and John came back out to the car, they sat for a moment, watching, as the body was brought from the house in a black body bag on a metal stretcher.

"I want her Internet history, access to her phone records. I want to see what she was looking at, and who she was talking to before she died," said Erika. "And I want to know about everyone who had access to the Trevor Marksman videos. Find out if someone had emailed her stills, or even given her the bloody footage."

"Yes, boss."

Erika looked down at the Terry's Chocolate Orange nestled in a plastic evidence bag on her lap.

"It's not Terry's, it's mine…" she repeated, looking at where it was underlined. "There's something wrong here. Amanda called me, several times. She left messages to say she'd found something, and I was to speak to her urgently."

Erika pulled out her phone and dialed her voicemail.

"You have no new messages," came the automated voice.

"What the hell?" Erika tried again, and got the same. "I had three messages from Amanda on here just a few hours ago."

"You didn't delete them by mistake?" asked John.

"No. No I didn't. They've been removed."

CHAPTER 65

Later that afternoon Erika was back in the incident room. Her mobile phone had been biked over to the MET's Cyber Crime department in Tower Bridge, and details of Amanda Baker's phone records and Internet history had been requested.

Erika stood over a laptop with Moss and Peterson, reviewing CCTV images.

"This is from last Wednesday afternoon, ninth of November," said Moss. The screen showed a static black-and-white image of the corridor outside the video viewing suite in the station. "This is you, boss, and DC McGorry going in to view the tapes," she added, as they zipped past in the sped-up video. "A few hours later Peterson makes a little cameo," she added, the minutes zooming past as she fast forwarded. "And there you are leaving just before seven and locking the door."

"That's just before I dismissed everyone for the day," said Erika.

"Right, now, this is just after 7 p.m., on the same day," said Moss. She now played the video feed at normal speed.

The corridor was empty, and then Crawford walked into shot and along, glancing around. He stopped to listen outside the door of the viewing suite. Then unlocked it and went inside.

"He could have gone in for an innocent reason?" said Erika.

Moss went on: "Okay, so he's inside, let me run it forward a few minutes...Here you are, boss, at 7:12 p.m. You go and you try the door—"

"And it was locked with Crawford inside," finished Erika, watching herself on the screen.

"Oh, and here is Peterson again; he's got some shopping and he's carrying..."

"That was my notebook," said Erika. They watched as Erika and Peterson were talking, awkwardly. "Can we run this forward?" said Erika.

"No worries," said Moss, giving her a look.

Back on the screen, the sped-up image showed Peterson leaving first, and then a few minutes later Erika walked off along the corridor.

"And here we are, 7:36 p.m., almost twenty minutes later, Crawford emerges," said Moss. On the screen the door opened a little at first, his head poked around the door, and then he moved swiftly out, locking it and hurrying down the corridor.

They all pondered this for a moment. Then John appeared from the back of the incident room. "Boss, I've just been going through Amanda Baker's phone records. There aren't many numbers, she didn't seem to call a great deal of people, but Crawford's number features on there a lot. She's been ringing him several times a day over the past two weeks."

"So this brings me on to the question: where is DC Crawford?" finished Erika. She looked around the room at her officers.

John shrugged. "I don't know, boss."

"Well, can you use your brain and phone him?" she snapped.

It was raining yet again, and the sky was growing dark when Erika and Moss drove from Bromley to where Crawford lived between Beckenham and Sydenham. They had tried his mobile and landline, but he hadn't been answering either. A call to his wife had come back blank. She hadn't seen him for several days.

"I have a bad feeling about this," said Moss when they arrived outside his flat.

"Is this it?" asked Erika, peering up out of the car windscreen. They were on Beckenham Hill Road. It was crammed with a long row of pound shops, newsagents, betting shops, a few crummy launderettes, and an Iceland supermarket. It was busy with traffic.

"I can't park outside. There's a couple of busses behind me," said Erika. She drove a little further up and pulled in to a McDonald's car park.

They hurried out and had to wait for a couple of minutes to cross the busy road. Crawford lived in a flat above a payday loans shop. It had a white front door, which opened directly on to the street. They found his flat number in the long row of doorbells and rang a couple of times, but there was no answer. A man came out of the door, and he held it open for Erika, and Moss slipped inside.

A staircase with a grubby carpet wound its way up four flights. Crawford's flat was on the top floor. When they reached the third floor, a door was open, and they could hear the sound of a Chinese lady shouting. A gray-haired man came to the door, followed by the lady, who was small and ferocious.

"You plumber, but you not fix this leak?"

"I told you, it's coming from the flat above, and the person isn't in," he said to her wearily.

"Hello, I'm DCI Foster and this is DI Moss," said Erika as they flashed their badges. "There's no one answering upstairs?"

"Thas' what he just say," snapped the woman. "There's leak in my kitchen, big leak. It spread since last night all across ceiling…"

Erika looked at Moss and then made for the stairs.

It took just two attempts for them to kick down the door. Crawford lived in a studio apartment. The bed was unmade under a window looking down onto the main road, and there were flies buzzing above dirty pots and pans in the kitchenette in the corner. On one wall was a picture collage of Crawford with two kids, a boy and a girl, who were in their early teens.

There was a large wet patch on the carpet outside a door in the corner. It was slightly ajar, and they moved slowly across to it.

Erika pushed it open. It was a tiny grotty little bathroom. Crawford's naked body floated in the water, which was stained pink. Gouts of blood splattered the wall behind the bath in a huge smear four feet high. And it had run down the opposite side where Crawford's arm lay limp, and mingled with the pools of water on the floor.

They could see he had slashed his wrists.

CHAPTER 66

The next day Erika attended the morgue in Penge. The air seemed chillier than normal, and the fluorescent lights appeared more stark; the brightness stabbed at her eyes. Amanda Baker and Crawford were laid out side by side on the stainless steel mortuary tables, and seeing colleagues, two police officers, brought back memories Erika would rather forget; her husband, Mark, and the four police officers who had all lost their lives on that fateful day.

She took a sharp breath and realized Isaac was talking.

"What disturbs me about both of these deaths is that, whoever did this, made a very weak attempt to pass them off as suicides."

"You don't think Crawford committed suicide?" she said.

"No, I don't."

He moved to Amanda Baker first. She lay on her front under a white sheet. Isaac gently folded back the sheet covering her body. Her head faced Erika, her cheek pressed against the stainless steel, and her long graying hair was brushed over the other shoulder to expose her neck, covered in a line of angry weals and bruises. It was still a shock to Erika; she had been talking to Amanda only a few days ago.

"What you can see here is the type of bruising I would expect to see from a hanging," said Isaac. "The rope has bitten deep into the skin around the neck and left a very clear and defined line of bruising." He indicated a purple line running around her neck with his gloved hand. "But see here, in addition to this, there is a series of small circular bruises at the nape of the neck. This indicates to me that the noose was placed over her head, and tightened, and then she fought or struggled. The knot of the noose moved during the struggle, creating this ring of welts... Also, note this bruise in the center of her back."

Erika saw a dark patch in the shape of an oblong.

"This could have been caused when she was shoved off the top step. Her neck is broken, which could indicate that she left the top step with great momentum and then the break occurred when the slack ran out... She may have fought her attacker. I was also able to swab some skin samples from under her fingernails. They have gone off to the lab."

"She was a fighter," said Erika.

Isaac paused, and then moved over to the body of Crawford on the next table. He lay on his back, his hair combed away from his forehead and, apart from his pale yellowy skin, it looked as if he could be sleeping.

Isaac folded the sheet over at each side, exposing Crawford's arms. He looked up at Erika and saw tears running down her face.

"Oh, are you all right to proceed?"

"Yes," said Erika, pulling out a tissue to wipe her eyes. "When it's one of our own it's bad enough, but two..."

"Do you need a moment?"

"I'm fine," she said, gulping back her tears and composing herself.

"Okay. If we look at the arms, you see here, two long incisions, one on each forearm. They are both around thirty centimeters, the incision is vertical up the middle of the arm as opposed to horizontal across the wrist. Each incision severed the radial artery, the main artery that supplies blood to the arms and hands. It was done with a straight razor, or what you might call an old barbershop razor."

Erika grimaced at the sight of the two long slashes in the arms, which had been neatly stitched up.

"The depth and length of these incisions would have caused rapid catastrophic blood loss. He also had high levels of alcohol in his blood, and traces of cocaine..."

"Yes, we found a small amount of cocaine in his flat... Isaac, I could understand if he committed suicide, more than Amanda. He seemed on edge the last few days he was in work. I didn't know, but he was just going through a nasty divorce; his wife was expected to get custody of their two children. She also said that he was depressed."

"He didn't slit his wrists," said Isaac.

"How can you tell?"

"The barbershop, straight razor, was found on the edge of the sink. It had been wiped clean, and there were no prints."

"It's obvious he couldn't have done that himself, isn't it?" said Erika.

"He could have, but there were torrents of blood when he sliced open the radial artery on each arm."

Erika closed her eyes again, remembering the scene, the gouts of blood splattered up the tiles and down the side of the white bathroom suite.

"He would have had to have used a cloth or a tissue to wipe the razor, and then place it on the edge of the sink. There were no bloody cloths or tissues found at the scene. The bloodletting was confined to the bathwater and the tiles surrounding the bath. Apart from a small spatter the sink was clean. Whoever did this wanted to make it look like a suicide."

Erika looked at them both side by side. "They were discussing the Jessica Collins case in the lead-up to their murders. Amanda Baker discovered something about the case. I don't know if it was a breakthrough or some new evidence. She was trying to get in contact with me," she said.

"And this was the same night your flat was broken into."

"Yes. I think I was a target too," said Erika.

CHAPTER 67

Gerry sat on the sofa, watching *Deal or No Deal*. He wore just a pair of shorts, and the dark-haired girl lay curled up beside him. She wore his white T-shirt; this time he'd relented and let her. She'd told him her name was Trish. She still hadn't asked for his.

Trish had knocked on his door the afternoon after his escape from Erika Foster's flat, when he'd been knocked unconscious. Trish had refused to leave until he unlocked the door and let her in. They'd stood on each side of the threshold staring. The bruise on her eye was a mere shadow compared to his.

"You look hurt, bad," she'd said, reaching out a delicate hand toward the swelling and crusted blood on his forehead. He'd done a rough job tacking together the three-inch cut on the side of his head with surgical glue, and the iodine he'd swabbed over it, against his cappuccino-colored skin, had a green tint.

He'd grabbed her hand, and pulled her inside, slamming the door. Lifting her up, he took her into the bedroom, where they remained for the rest of the night.

On the TV, the contestant playing the *Deal or No Deal* game was down to his last box. He was a thin man with a face like a potato with beady eyes.

"What's his name?" asked Gerry.

"It's written on his name tag," grinned Trish, tilting her head up from his chest. She went to kiss him, but he pushed her away.

"You think I can fucking see clearly with a bashed-up face?" Gerry snapped, pointing to the swelling on his face.

"His name's Daniel," said Trish quickly.

On the TV there was a pause as Daniel, the contestant, moved round and pulled the tape from the front of his box. The camera cut to his wife sitting in the studio audience. She wasn't well dressed. She didn't look lucky in life. The camera cut back to Daniel as he flipped the lid back on the box. "No!" he cried, his hands going to his forehead as he sank down on his knees. The camera cut to show the box was worth £1.

"Jeez, what a fucking eejit," said Gerry.

Back on screen Daniel's wife was invited down to join him. She was putting on a brave face.

"What did he say no to?"

"The banker offered him fifteen thousand," said Trish, putting her thumb in her mouth.

Gerry got up and went to the fridge. Trish sat up and rested her head on the back of the sofa and took her thumb out of her mouth.

"You got any juice?" she asked.

Gerry opened the fridge and pulled out a can of beer and a bottle of juice. A small round wooden table was between him and Trish where she sat on the sofa. On it was a Glock 17 handgun, and twenty-five thousand pounds in unmarked banknotes.

He stood for a moment with a bottle in each hand looking at her; her eyes glanced at the gun and the money, but she looked away quickly.

"Good girl," he said, "you keep your eyes on me."

He went back and chucked the juice on the sofa cushion beside her, and opened his beer. Trish sat up and took a long drink from the juice.

"Do you want to watch *Hollyoaks* later?" she asked.

His mobile phone rang. He picked it up off the coffee table and went out to the balcony, closing the glass door.

"Where the fuck have you been?" came the familiar voice. He was silent. "Are you there?"

"I'm here," he replied. It was now dark outside and the rows of orange stretched out below him in a grid.

"You were supposed to do all three of them. Two suicides and a home invasion. The Foster woman is still alive."

Gerry paused on the phone; he thought back to Daniel's face on *Deal or No Deal*.

"I'm out," he said.

"What do you mean? You're out? You need to finish the fucking job. I won't pay you a penny more."

"Keep the rest of the money. I'm out."

"It's not just the money, you know."

"You know what? You've been holding this over my head for so long, and I've had enough. Can you see what's happening? You're not going to keep a lid on this. The lid is off. And if I go down, so will you. I just realized I've nothing to lose by walking away."

With that, Gerry ended the call. He turned over the phone, opened the back and took out the SIM card, breaking it neatly into four.

He now had to move fast. He figured he had a day, maybe less. He downed the rest of his beer and went back inside.

CHAPTER 68

It was late afternoon, and Erika sat across from Superintendent Yale in his office. He looked exhausted. His face was pale, and he had large dark circles under his eyes. They were waiting for Marsh, who had called to say he was a little delayed.

"Sir. I don't need you to divert any more resources my way," she said.

He held up his hand. "Erika, I don't think that stationing a police car outside your hotel will break the bank. We've already had a stabbing in broad daylight on the front steps of the station, and one of my officers has been found dead in suspicious circumstances."

"It was two officers," said Erika. "One former, Amanda Baker."

"Yes," he said, reluctantly acknowledging her. He rubbed his eyes. "I take it you've heard about Jason Tyler?"

"What is it?"

"When he was refused bail they put him in Belmarsh, high security. People heard he was going to give evidence for a plea bargain, and they got to him. Last night he was shanked in the showers."

"How did someone get hold of a shank?"

"You're not going to believe this. Kit Kats."

"Is that some new street slang?"

"No," he said impatiently. "Actual Kit Kats, or should I say the foil the two finger ones come wrapped in. Some bright spark on a life sentence has been saving them up for months, and fashioned a lethal spiked shank with what must have been a few hundred foil wrappers. Tyler was stabbed in the thigh, bled out in the showers, and now his empire dies with him."

There was a knock, and one of the support staff came in with cups of tea on a tray; she gave Yale his *Who's the Boss?* mug and Erika a mug with a picture of the Cookie Monster on it.

"There we are," she said. "And I thought you could use something sweet." She placed two Kit Kats on the desk beside their steaming cups of tea and left.

"For Christ's sake!" he shouted.

Erika had a sudden urge to laugh; it took every bit of control to keep a straight face as Yale swept them off the desk and into the wastepaper basket.

There was a knock at the door, and Marsh entered.

"Sorry I'm late," he said.

"That's okay, take a seat."

"Bad state of affairs, losing an officer, very bad for morale," said Marsh.

"Two officers," said Erika, pointedly.

"Yes, of course," said Marsh.

Erika went on to discuss what was happening with the case.

"We've had DC Crawford's phone records back; they confirm he was in contact with Amanda Baker over the last few weeks. We managed to find Amanda Baker's phone. It had

fallen down the side of her armchair, so whoever was looking for it slipped up. The guys in the Cyber Crime unit have
given it the once-over and they found it was hacked in the
last couple of weeks using a Trojan horse program. This was
along with Crawford's mobile phone, and my phone. Someone has been listening in and monitoring calls. They have
also modified call records. Amanda phoned my mobile on
the night she was killed and left a message; she also phoned
DC Crawford. These voicemails were deleted remotely from
both of our phones."

"Jesus, Erika!" said Marsh. "So our whole investigation
could be compromised?"

"Yes, sir."

"I have to report back to the Assistant Commissioner..."

"And with respect, I have to live in a hotel because someone broke into my house. We are dealing with someone
who is strides ahead of us, and has been for the past few
weeks."

"So you don't think this is anything to do with Joel
Michaels?"

"Joel Michaels has spent the past few days at the bedside
of Trevor Marksman, who is still in intensive care. According to the nursing staff, he only leaves his bedside to use
the toilet. Marianne Collins may have appeared a knife-
wielding maniac, but she has been sectioned under the Mental Health Act, and remains in a secure ward. I can't go near
her. I can't question her... And the one bloody officer who
seemed to be ahead of us, well, she's dead... And as I said,
whoever this is, is steps ahead of us."

Yale and Marsh were silent for a moment.

"Oh, and I had some of my officers go back and search
Amanda Baker's. It seems she was working on case files of
her own; there was paperwork and printouts. We're going

through it all. They also found a small listening device in her smoke alarm."

"Who the hell are the Collins family?" asked Marsh.

"I'm not giving up on this," said Erika. "And I hope that you and the Assistant Commissioner will allow me to continue and refocus my efforts."

Marsh sat back for a moment.

"For now, yes. But I'll let you know what the Assistant Commissioner has to say when I brief her later."

After the meeting Erika went to the ladies' toilets and splashed her face with cold water. She looked at her tired face in the mirror. A toilet flushed, and a young woman came out of a cubicle and went to the sink. Erika recognized her as one of the officers who had been collecting money for Guy Fawkes. She was ready for her shift, and wearing a Kevlar stab vest over her uniform.

"You okay, ma'am?" she asked, moving to the sink and washing her hands.

Erika saw the vest, and immediately stopped feeling sorry for herself.

"Yes. It's just been a long hard day."

"It's been a long hard week, ma'am," she said. She dried her hands and went to leave.

"Be careful out there, won't you ..." Erika found herself saying.

"PC Claremont."

"PC Claremont, keep your wits about you."

"I always do. Thanks, ma'am," she replied and then left.

Erika washed her hands, and then went back up to the incident room.

CHAPTER 69

Erika briefly stopped by the hotel in the early evening to grab a shower, and a change of clothes. She then knocked on the adjoining door. Lenka answered it, holding Eva.

"Everything still okay with you?" she asked. "I'm sorry I've hardly seen you over the past few days."

"The kids are in their element: we've got room service and the pool, and the hotel is hardly busy. I've almost forgotten I have a husband waiting at home for me," Lenka replied, adding, "Are you okay?"

"Yes. I'm just taking a break, and then it's back to the station. Are you staying vigilant, keeping your eyes peeled?" asked Erika.

"Yes, we feel very safe here. And just in case." She pointed to an E-FIT image she'd worked on with the E-FIT artist.

"Why have you got him pinned up on the wall?" asked Erika, moving over to the eerie composite image of a man with thick eyebrows over glowering eyes, and a mass of dark curly hair.

"So the kids know exactly who he is, and what he looks

like. They've got copies on the front desk, and pinned up in the staffroom and in the kitchens."

"He was after me," said Erika.

"We do look alike, even if I am slightly better looking." Lenka grinned.

"Cheeky. Well, I don't know how long I'll be gone. I'm working late. There's still a uniformed officer stationed in the car park."

She gave Lenka and Eva kisses, and told her to say hello to Jakub and Karolina when they got back from the pool.

Erika arrived back at the station and went up to the incident room, where Peterson and Moss were unloading a bag full of takeaway cartons.

"Is that Chinese?" she said, when she opened the door.

Moss nodded, holding up a bulging white bag. "It's all the good stuff, too. Crispy chili beef, Chicken Chow Mein, crispy seaweed, prawn crackers."

"How did you know I wouldn't have any food in?"

An hour later, they had finished eating, and they were sitting at one of the long desks with the logs of Amanda Baker's phone calls, her Internet search history, and the paperwork she'd had pinned up in her flat.

They spent the next few hours poring over everything.

"There're two things that stick out. She's taken a screen grab from one of the Trevor Marksman videos," said Erika, holding up the printout of Marianne and Laura sitting on the bench. "And for me the other is the Chocolate Orange box, where she underlined the words, 'It's not Terry's, it's mine.'"

They looked at each other.

"God, I could murder a Chocolate Orange now we're talking about them," said Moss.

"Not the best use of words," said Peterson. "And you've just stuffed yourself with Chinese."

"Come on, keep the focus," said Erika. "I want to look at the section of video she's taken a screenshot from."

They logged into Erika's laptop and, after a fiddly search, found the video files where they featured. In both videos Laura and Marianne could be seen arguing; their voices were faint. Erika dragged the video back and to the same point and turned up the volume to full. The sounds of the kids screaming and laughing in the park boomed out; so did the squeak of the swings going back and forward. They strained to hear what they were arguing about.

"What's that Laura's saying? 'You don't get to boss me around...her either...'" said Erika.

"Yeah, her voice is louder; Marianne's is pretty inaudible," agreed Peterson.

They played it back again.

"You don't get to boss me around...not yours...mine..." came Laura's voice through the speaker.

"Again," said Erika. "And put the volume right up."

Moss played it back and the sounds in the park, and Laura's voice boomed out of the speakers: "You don't get to boss me around...She's not yours...she's mine..."

Erika stopped the video, and she got up, her mind whirring.

"What is it?" asked Peterson.

"She's not yours, she's mine...She's not yours, she's mine...The Terry's Chocolate Orange box, by Amanda's computer."

Erika scrabbled around for the photo from the crime scene. "She went to the trouble of underlining that tagline they used to use in the adverts: 'It's not Terry's, it's mine.'"

"You think there was someone called Terry involved?"

asked Peterson, watching Erika pace up and down, the cogs turning.

Erika stopped and stood still. "What if Laura is talking about Jessica when she's saying, 'She's not yours, she's mine'?" She turned to Moss and Peterson. "What was the age difference between Laura and Jessica?"

"Jessica was seven; Laura was twenty when Jessica..." said Peterson. "Hang on, you don't think...?"

Erika scrabbled at the papers on the table.

"What do you need, boss?" asked Moss.

"I saw something on the printout of Amanda Baker's Internet search history. A web address with the .ie domain, for Ireland."

"Here, give me some," said Peterson. They split the papers and spent a few minutes scanning each page of the tiny print.

"Got it," said Erika. She moved to the laptop and typed in the web address

www.hse.ie/eng/services/list/1/bdm/Certificates/

"Amanda was searching for a birth certificate. An Irish birth certificate. She wouldn't have had access to the records office like we do, so she went to this application page to apply for a birth certificate."

Moss peered at the website on the screen, reading:

"Due to a significant increase in orders for birth certificates as a result of the recent referendum in the United Kingdom (UK), the delivery time for certificates from this service will be up to thirty (30) days from the date of order."

"Amanda would have had to wait thirty days; you think that's when she phoned you?"

"Are we out on a limb here?" asked Erika. "Wouldn't someone have picked up on it?"

"The first investigation was a disaster, and why would anyone think of looking at Jessica's birth certificate? When do we look at birth and death certificates? Only when there is something fishy going on."

"Do you think it's possible?" said Erika, her face flushed with excitement. "Laura Collins wasn't Jessica's sister. She was her mother?"

CHAPTER 70

"Okay everyone, I want your full attention," said Erika to her team when they had all congregated in the incident room early next morning. There was silence as Erika went on to explain their hunch from the previous evening, and that they had reason to suspect that Laura Collins wasn't Jessica's sister; she was, in fact, her mother.

"We've put in a request to the Irish records office for a copy of Jessica Collins's birth certificate, and asked them to fast-track it the moment the records office opens."

"Boss, there's a fax coming through for you on the system," said John, indicating the screen of his computer.

"Well, don't just sit there, send it to print!" said Erika.

"Yes, boss."

Erika went to the printer at the back of the incident room; she could feel the eyes of everyone on her. It seemed to take an age for it to start whirring and printing. Then, very slowly, the scan of a birth certificate emerged. It was dated from 1983, and there it was: written in clear but legible handwriting. Erika couldn't believe it. She turned and read it out triumphantly: "Mother is Laura Collins . . . and, hang on, the father is on here too. It's a Gerry O'Reilly of 4 Dorchester Court, Galway."

Moss was already at one of the whiteboards and writing it up.

"Okay we need everything we can get on a Gerry O'Reilly. We don't know the circumstances of this, he could be old or young, but we have a name and an address."

The officers in the incident room swung into action.

Ninety minutes later, they had managed to track down two men called Gerry O'Reilly who were registered to the address at 4 Dorchester Court.

"They're a father and son who both share the same name," said Moss.

"Okay, how do we find out which one was the father?" said Erika.

"Gerry O'Reilly senior was born 19th of November 1941, which would make him—" started Moss.

"Forty-one years old when Jessica was born in April 1983," finished John.

"You're quick." Erika grinned.

Moss went on: "Gerry junior was born the same year as Laura Collins, 1970. He would have been thirteen when Jessica was born."

"Damn. Either of them could be the father," said Erika.

CHAPTER 71

It had taken Gerry O'Reilly a little more time than he'd have liked with his preparations. He'd thought about the risk, and what the police might have on him, and he came to the conclusion there was a slim chance he would be identified by the woman he'd attacked in Erika Foster's flat. She was the only one who had seen him, and that was during a brief struggle in the darkness.

The two police officers who had seen him were dead.

He'd debated killing Trish, and had spent several minutes watching her on the sofa in front of the TV, weighing up the pros and the cons. Then he'd made a decision, and gone to the kitchen cupboards, pulling out rubber gloves and a large plastic bag.

"What are you doing?" she'd said, fearfully, as he approached her.

"You're going to help me clean this place from top to bottom. I want every surface wiped down. No hairs left; no mess."

"Are you moving?"

"Yeah. And I need my deposit back."

They'd left the flat late that night, and he had been sorry to say goodbye to Trish at the railway bridge in Morden. She'd stood in the cold, vapor streaming from her mouth and nose, and watched as he walked away. If only he'd met her earlier, she would have been useful to work with.

He'd boarded the tube with a baseball cap pulled down over his face, and taken the Northern Line to Charing Cross, and walked up to Goodge Street where he'd checked into a youth hostel. All he cared was that he had a bed for the night, and decent Wi-Fi.

He'd worked on his computer in the small coffee bar, late into the night. Early next morning, he showered and had a clean shave. He walked up to Soho, and bought a fashionable dark skinny suit, a tight white button-down shirt and a pair of expensive black shoes. His next stop had been to a high fashion barber in Neal's Yard where he'd paid to have his unruly mop of curls cut short and blow-dried into a fashionable quiff. He'd then gone to Selfridges and bought an overnight bag, and taken it to a disabled toilet. He'd emerged a few minutes later in the suit, the new bag packed with his belongings. He'd shoved his old clothes and shoes to the bottom of the bin.

Gerry worked his way down to the ground floor, moving past the makeup displays until he found a young slim guy with bright red hair working on the MAC makeup counter.

"Hey," said Gerry, flashing the guy a smile.

"Hi," he'd replied, looking Gerry up and down.

Gerry pulled a picture out of his pocket of the American singer Adam Lambert.

"Can you make me look like him?" he'd asked, looking the young guy in the eye and deliberately flirting.

The guy had looked down at the picture and back up at him. He had a small leather apron slung over his slight hips, with several makeup brushes poking out.

"Course I can," he'd grinned, returning the flirt and selecting an eyeliner pencil. "I like your Irish accent. What brings you so far from home?"

"This and that. You think you can cover up my bruises? I have a job interview. A film company."

"You want to make an impression, do you?"

"Something like that. Do a good job and I'll make it worth your while," Gerry had said with a grin.

It was now just before eleven on Thursday. Gerry sat in a Starbucks at King's Cross St. Pancras station with his laptop. He swilled the last of his coffee down, and then finished the email he was writing. He attached a file, and then, activating the camera, he grinned, stuck up his middle finger and took a selfie, before attaching it to the email. He then scheduled it to send later that evening.

He dumped his takeaway cup in the small bin in the coffee shop and left. Crossing the concourse, he took the escalator stairs two at a time up to the Eurostar departure gate. His train was due to leave in seven minutes, and it was now or never. With adrenaline coursing through his veins, he placed his bag in the security tray. The twenty-five thousand pounds on his kitchen table had been exchanged for a mix of €100 and €500 notes which he'd divided between his carry-on bag, his wallet, and the pocket of his jacket.

He handed over his passport to a snotty-looking cow, she took it and glanced at the photo, taken a few years previously. He looked rougher, but she didn't bat an eyelid. She swiped his passport, and there was a long horrible moment where she stared at her screen, the passport held open in her tiny hand. The screen beeped and she handed it back with a waxwork smile, wishing him a pleasant trip. Next he had to go through the security gate. He joined the end of the short queue, made up mostly of business travelers, and looked to see who was stationed at the metal detectors.

Result, the guy on security looks like a textbook queer, he thought as he approached the end of a short line waiting to go through the metal detectors. He had been sure not to pack anything to rouse suspicion, and he'd removed his belt and anything metal. The thirty-five thousand euros he had was technically legal as he was traveling from one EU country to another, but he didn't want to be held up.

When his turn came, he breezed through the scanners, waiting another minute for his bag to exit through.

"Have a nice trip," grinned the guy on security. Gerry winked, and grabbing his bag he made it onto the train with three minutes to spare.

He located his seat just as the train started to move out of the station. Thirty minutes later, the train left the UK and started its journey under the sea, and into mainland Europe.

CHAPTER 72

Just as Gerry's Eurostar train left the UK and began its twenty-six-mile journey under the English Channel, Erika, Moss, Peterson and John waited impatiently by the bank of printers at the back of the incident room in Bromley. Out of the two Gerry O'Reillys, they had discovered that Gerry O'Reilly senior had died just before Christmas of 1981, just over a year before Jessica was born. There was a whirr and a beep, and then a red light started to flash.

"Who knows how to refill the bloody paper tray on this thing?" yelled Erika.

John moved fast and quickly stuffed a block of paper into the drawer. It whirred to life, and then Gerry O'Reilly's passport image emerged.

Erika picked it up and stared at the glowering eyes under thick eyebrows, the mass of dark curly hair. She looked at Moss and Peterson. "Where's that E-FIT from the other night when my flat was broken into?"

DC Knight came over and handed it to Erika. She placed them on one of the desks, side by side.

"Jesus. It's him. It's the same guy!" said Peterson.

"Okay, listen up everyone," said Erika, moving to the front of the incident room holding up the printouts of the E-FIT and passport photo. She stuck them in the center of the whiteboards. "This is our prime suspect: forty-six-year-old Gerry O'Reilly. I want an arrest warrant put out for him, contact the transport police, borders, airports, debit and credit card activity, you name it. We need to find this guy fast. He's murdered two of our colleagues. We also believe he is the real father of Jessica Collins...I want to know: what has he been doing for the past twenty-six years? Is he aware that he fathered a child? Laura Collins gave birth in Ireland in the early eighties, in a strict Catholic environment. I'm not saying that Gerry O'Reilly had a motive to kill his own daughter, but this is the most significant lead we've had so far. If he didn't kill his daughter, then he's been trying damn hard to stop us finding out who did. We find him, and we unlock this mystery. Now get to work."

The incident room burst to life as the officers started to work their phones and computers. Shortly afterward, Moss came through to Erika's office carrying a folder. "Gerry's criminal record has just been faxed through. It's extensive," she said.

"Hit me with it," said Erika.

"Okay. His first brush with the law was aged ten in 1980," said Moss, reading. "He was part of a gang of six kids who assaulted an elderly lady and stole her purse, arrest and caution...Arrested again aged eleven and twelve, for shoplifting, arson and stabbing another kid at school in the leg. Aged seventeen he was convicted of ABH after he glassed a barmaid during a pub brawl, and she lost an eye. He was sent to St. Patrick's Institution in Dublin for eighteen months... Then he seems to have turned his life around, joined the Irish Army in 1991. He was stationed in Kuwait following the Gulf War, for two years, then Eritrea for another year, and then spent time as part of the peacekeeping force in Bosnia...Then in 1997 he gets into a fight with another officer, nearly kills him, and leaves the army with a dishonorable discharge. He worked several security jobs over the years, and apart from a caution for marijuana, he's kept his nose clean and stayed off the radar."

"Jesus."

"I know."

"Okay, but the most important question is: where was he during the summer of 1990 when Jessica went missing?"

"John is just waiting on his passport records...What do you want to do with all this, boss? Do you want to bring Laura Collins in for questioning?"

"No. I want to confront her with this, catch her off guard," said Erika.

CHAPTER 73

Erika, Moss and Peterson drove the short distance from Bromley Police Station to Hayes, the revelations of the last few hours playing heavy on their minds.

When they turned the corner in to Avondale Road, there were no cars, no people, and it was silent, save for the wind, which slowly pushed a whirling pile of leaves toward them. Erika had spoken to Laura's husband, who had told them that the previous night she'd decided to stay at Avondale Road to sort some things out for her mother.

From the tone of his voice, it sounded as if this was an odd decision on her part, but Erika didn't press him further. They had also discovered as they were leaving the station that Gerry O'Reilly had been renting a flat in Morden for the past few weeks, but he'd told his landlord two days earlier he would be moving out.

Erika slowed the car to a stop by the curb, a little way from the entrance to number seven. Moss was beside her, and Peterson sat in the back.

"Okay. We need to be careful here," said Erika, turning to them both. "Laura's not a suspect, but we need to talk to her.

We can't rule out that Gerry O'Reilly is with her… We need to proceed carefully."

Just then a large black Range Rover with tinted windows pulled out of the driveway of number seven and turned left. With a squeal of rubber, it roared away from them along Avondale Road. Within seconds it had vanished over the brow of the hill.

"Who the hell was that?" said Erika.

"I didn't see. The windows were blacked out, but I got the license plate number," said Moss, writing it down in her notebook.

Moments later, a silver Range Rover emerged from number seven and turned right. As it came toward them, they saw it was Laura driving.

Erika flashed her headlights and opened the door, stepping out to flag her down. She slowed for a second, and then pulled past them, accelerating with a squeal to the end of the road.

"What the hell?" said Erika. She got back inside, started the engine, did a sharp U-turn and followed.

The Range Rover was still waiting at the junction at the end of the road, and as they approached it suddenly pulled out, narrowly missing an oncoming car, which had to swerve out of its way.

"What the hell is she doing?" said Moss. She and Peterson clung on as Erika pulled out after the silver Range Rover and set off in pursuit.

The road was single lane, and they streaked past houses, a small pub and a newsagent. The Range Rover was still gaining speed up a steep incline which stretched up ahead for a quarter of a mile. Erika stepped on the accelerator, closing the distance between them. The opposite lane was full of traffic speeding down the incline in the opposite direction, so Erika put on her lights and sirens. The car in front quickly pulled over, and Erika was able to overtake. Laura's Range Rover reached the top of the hill, and vanished over it.

"Why did she make a run for it?" said Peterson in disbelief.

They roared up to the brow of the hill, hitting eighty miles an hour; on the other side the car briefly left the tarmac as the road fell away and stretched out ahead with trees on each side, with Laura's car in the distance. Using her radio Erika called in that they were in pursuit of a silver Range Rover on West Common Road.

"She's not slowing," said Moss.

Erika could see glimpses of the common on each side through the trees. "Where does this road go?" she asked, flooring the accelerator.

Peterson was busy on his phone in the back seat. "This crosses the common and leads all the way back to the station," he replied.

Up ahead the Range Rover slowed, the brake lights flashed a couple of times and then the indicator.

"She's going left," said Erika.

"It's the junction with Croydon Road," replied Peterson.

The car turned left and again vanished from view.

Their sirens continued to blare as Erika approached the crossroads, slowing only slightly. Moss and Peterson braced as they shot out and turned left with a screech of rubber.

"I can see her, she's up ahead," said Erika as she started to accelerate again.

"If we lose her," started Moss.

"We're not going to lose her," snapped Erika through gritted teeth. Up ahead the Range Rover slowed, indicated, and then vanished behind a row of trees.

"What's she doing now?"

"She's pulling in to the car park on the common," said Moss.

They approached the gravel car park and slowed. Laura's silver Range Rover was the only car. They could see she had come to a stop, and was getting out.

Erika pulled in with a roar of tires on gravel.

"She's running," said Peterson incredulously, as Laura set off across the grass and heather in the direction of the quarry. She had on a thick black coat, leggings and lace-up black knee-high boots.

They crunched to a halt in a spray of gravel, and Erika jumped out.

"Laura! Stop!" she shouted, but her voice was carried away by the wind.

"Where's she gonna run to?" said Moss, jumping out, followed by Peterson.

They started to run after her. Peterson was in front with long strides, leaping over the thick heather, branches and rocks to gain distance. Erika was close behind.

"Jesus Christ!" yelled Moss from the back of the procession, breathless, with her hands clamped over her chest. "I should have worn my bloody sports bra!"

"Laura!" Peterson was yelling. "Laura, stop! What the hell are you doing?"

Laura turned, the wind whipping her long dark hair over her face. She brushed it to one side and then continued to run up and over the hill. Peterson and Erika were only a few meters away from her now. They reached the peak of the hill, and the quarry came into view. The water a little choppy in the wind.

"Laura! Stop!" cried Peterson as he reached her and grabbed her arm. She went wheeling round and lost balance, falling onto the gravel. Peterson went down too with a thump, and Erika nearly joined them. She came to a stop, her lungs screaming from having to pull in the freezing air.

Laura was scrabbling and kicking, her tights above one of her knees were ripped and she was bleeding.

"Laura! Laura!" cried Erika as she managed to subdue her and get her hands behind her back. "Christ, Laura, why are you doing this... You leave me no choice but to arrest you for evading a police officer."

"Three police officers," said Moss, coming to a breathless stop beside them. She pulled out a pair of handcuffs, and Peterson took them, cuffing Laura's hands behind her back.

"I'm arresting you on suspicion of assisting an offender," he started breathlessly. "You do not have to say anything but it may harm your defense if you do not mention when questioned something which you later rely on in court. Anything you do say may be given in evidence..."

Laura went limp, stared at the gravel and started to cry.

CHAPTER 74

They brought Laura back to Bromley Police Station, where her leg was cleaned up, and she was put in an interview room.

Erika, Moss and Peterson watched her from the observation suite. She looked small and vulnerable sitting alone at the bare table. There was a knock at the door, and John came in.

"What's Laura Collins said?" he asked.

"Nothing," replied Erika, looking at the bank of monitors. "She said nothing in the car. She's refused a solicitor."

"Do you think we need to do a psych assessment?" asked Peterson.

"If we call in a doctor, it will only delay me being able to question her," snapped Erika. "This is the closest we've got—"

"To what? She was obviously in distress. And it wasn't the sanest display of behavior when she drove her mother to attack Trevor Marksman in broad daylight with a carving knife."

"Peterson, when I spoke to her last Saturday, she said that

she didn't know her mother would be carrying a knife...She seemed lucid and capable of holding a conversation, right up until I left when Oscar Browne arrived..." Her voice faltered. "She's refused a solicitor, yet she knows Oscar?"

There was another knock at the door, and DC Knight came in holding a piece of paper. "Boss, the registration came back on the black Range Rover you saw leaving number seven Avondale Road. It's registered to an Oscar Browne QC."

A look passed between Erika, Moss and Peterson.

"Okay, thanks," said Erika.

"When did you say you saw Oscar Browne at the house, boss?" asked Peterson.

"Saturday. I asked her if he was helping with Marianne's defense, and she said no, but then just as I was leaving he was there at the front door, and he contradicted her. I want to talk to him. Knight, can you find out where he is?"

"Yes, boss," said DI Knight, leaving the room.

Erika looked back at Laura on the screen. "Right, let's see if Laura will start talking."

Erika and Moss went to the interview room, as Peterson and John remained watching from the observation suite. Laura didn't react when they entered and sat opposite, remaining slumped at the table with her arms crossed, her eyes staring straight ahead.

Erika read out who was in the room, and the time and date. She finished by stating that Laura had declined a solicitor.

Laura didn't break from her gaze, staring down at the table.

"Laura. How have you ended up here?" asked Erika. "You gave us no choice but to arrest you. Why were you running?"

Silence.

"On the day when your mother attacked Trevor Marksman, you told me that a journalist had called the house and tipped you off. We've had a look at phone records for the landline. There were three phone calls that day. Two that morning from your husband's mobile, and another just before 1 p.m. from Oscar Browne."

Laura remained silent, staring straight ahead. Erika opened a folder on the desk, took out the copy of Jessica's birth certificate and slid it across the table. Laura stared at it, her eyes widening.

"We know Jessica was your daughter. Why did your family hide this?"

Silence.

Erika took out the passport photo of Gerry O'Reilly and the E-FIT image. "We know that this man, Gerry O'Reilly, is Jessica's father. We also suspect that he is responsible for the murder of two police officers. What can you tell us about him?"

A tear spilled over from Laura's eye, and she wiped it with the back of her sleeve.

Silence.

"Have you seen him in the past few weeks... Why did you decline a solicitor?"

Laura bit her lip, almost defiantly, and she looked up at Erika. "No comment."

"You know what, Laura? I'm tired. We're all tired. For years, police officers have worked around the clock to try and bring your daughter's killer to justice. Although, they were allowed to believe that she was your sister. Police officers have worked hard and made sacrifices, they care deeply about finding her killer. Two of them have lost their lives in the pursuit... and you sit here holding on to important information and you say 'no comment'!" Erika slammed her hand down on the table.

"No. Comment," she repeated.

"Okay, Laura. You want to play it like that, do you? Have her taken down to the cells."

CHAPTER 75

Peterson was waiting outside in the corridor when Erika emerged from the interview room. Moss followed moments later with Laura, who was led past in handcuffs with a grim scowl. He waited until she was led past and out of earshot.

"Boss, Gerry O'Reilly boarded a Eurostar train out of London just before lunchtime."

"Shit," cried Erika, slamming her hand against the wall.

"And Oscar Browne has gone AWOL. He was due to appear in court this afternoon, but he was a no-show. His secretary says he's never done this before. He was defending a high profile client in a fraud case. She doesn't know where he is, nor does his wife . . ."

Erika looked at her watch. "Find out if Gerry got off the train at Paris or if he carried on, God knows where, fucking Disneyland for all we know. Get in touch with Interpol. I want an international arrest warrant issued for him."

"Yes, boss."

"And put out an alert to UK airports and train stations in case Oscar Browne tries to skip the country."

"You think he's going to skip the country?"

"God knows. We don't know anything, but obviously, don't say that. Laura Collins knows something though, and she's not leaving here until I get it. Even if I have to apply to detain her longer than four days. She can sit it out in a bloody cell."

"One more thing, boss ... Her husband and kids have just showed up. He's in reception and demanding to see who's in charge."

Erika and Peterson hurried downstairs and in to reception. It was quiet. The duty officer was working at her desk, and the long line of plastic chairs was empty, apart from Laura's husband, Todd, and their two small boys. Pooled around them were several shopping bags from TK Maxx. The boys were kneeling on the floor playing with toy cars.

Todd got up when he saw them approach.

"What is the meaning of this?" he said, his American accent full of nasal indignation. "I had a call from one of the neighbors in Avondale Road; there was a car chase? Involving Laura? I was shopping so I tried her cell, and your duty officer answered, and told me that you've arrested my wife!"

"That's correct."

"What about her phone call? And you better not be talking to her until she has a damn good lawyer ..."

The boys looked up from playing on the floor.

"Mummy's been arrested?" said one. Todd ignored them.

"Laura was offered a phone call, and the chance for legal representation, but declined both," explained Peterson.

"You gotta be kidding me?" he said, pulling at his hair. "Why was she arrested?"

"Earlier today we arrived at Avondale Road, wanting to talk to her, but she left in her car at high speed. We had no choice but to arrest her for evading a police officer," explained Erika.

"Why did you want to talk to her? Are you sure she knew that you wanted to talk to her?"

"We followed in pursuit for several miles with lights and sirens," said Peterson.

Todd shook his head. He had gone very pale. "But she has no record. She's never even had a parking ticket."

"Daddy, I'm scared," said one of the boys. Todd bent down and scooped them both up, one in each arm. Erika and Peterson were faced with three sets of confused brown eyes.

"Todd. What has Laura told you about Jessica?" asked Erika.

"That her sister went missing. I know the full story, and we've been over and over it . . ."

A look passed between Erika and Peterson. *He doesn't know.*

"I'm going to ask you to wait here, sir," she said, and left the reception with Peterson.

"Hey! You can't keep her locked up for nothing! You have to charge her!" Todd yelled after them, still holding the boys.

"What do we do now?" asked Peterson when they had swiped their IDs and were through the security door into the main part of the station.

"I want to see if she's willing to talk," said Erika.

They headed for the cells housed in the basement of the station, and accessed through a thick steel door. When they came close, they were interrupted by the sound of an alarm. They looked at each other and hurried down to the cells.

At the end of the long fluorescent-lit corridor of closed metal doors, painted green, and scratched and grubby, the door at the end was open. Two officers crouched on the floor. When Erika and Peterson came level they saw Laura lying on the floor, and one of the officers was frantically trying to unwind the thin black shoelace around her neck. The length of black lace ran up to the small hatchway in the door where it had been looped around the small metal handle.

Laura suddenly gasped, and the color swam back into her face as she coughed and spluttered. Erika ran to her and crouched down, taking her hand.

"It's okay, Laura. You're going to be okay," she said.

Laura gulped, coughed and whispered hoarsely, "Okay. I'll tell you. I'll tell you what's going on..."

CHAPTER 76

A little while later, Erika, Moss and Peterson were back in the observation suite. They watched as Laura sat with a duty solicitor.

"You think she's really going to talk?" asked Moss.

"When I told her that her husband and sons had been looking for her, and they still didn't know, she seemed to change her mind. I think she wants to be the one to tell them."

"Tell them what?" said Peterson.

"I hope we're about to find out," said Erika.

Erika and Moss came back into the interview room, where Laura now sat with a young woman who was the duty solicitor. They both had cups of steaming tea. Laura had removed her coat, but kept a scarf around her neck. Erika stated the time and the date for the tape and video recording, and then reached across the table and grabbed Laura's hand.

"It's okay, we're here, and it's going to be okay," she said.

Moss managed to hide her skepticism and smiled and nodded.

"No, it's not!" said Laura, tears running down her cheeks. "It's not."

"Start at the beginning," said Erika.

Moss handed her a tissue, and she took it, wiping her face. She gulped, a calm seemed to descend on her, and she began to talk.

"I loved living in Ireland. We had a small house in Galway, near the sea. We didn't really have much. Dad worked on various building sites, and Mum was at home with me, but we were happy. I met Gerry O'Reilly when I was thirteen."

"Where did you meet him?" asked Erika.

"At the local Catholic youth club. A little hut on the hill at the top of the beach. It was like a little church, that hut, filled with pictures of Our Lady, and there were games, sometimes they'd wheel out this ancient television and put on cartoons. The older kids would slope off to the beach, in couples, and hide amongst the dunes. I was the unlucky girl who fell pregnant."

"And this was with Gerry?"

Laura nodded and took a sip of her tea, wincing as she swallowed.

"Then what happened?"

Laura went on: "God, it was so long ago, and Ireland in the early eighties was like England must have been in the sixties. My mother went *crazy*. I managed to hide it from her for quite a long time, but one night when I stood up in front of the television she saw my silhouette and that was my childhood over..."

"Your mother was more religious than she is now?" asked Moss.

Laura nodded. "It's like a fervor in Ireland, competitive Catholicism, like keeping up with the Joneses, only it's not washing machines and house extensions that people are investing in. It's the accumulation of deities; it's time spent at Mass. I was sent away to an aunt...Aunt Mary. A fearsome, cruel old bitch. You must have heard of the type. She thought the whole Vatican II was an abomination. She's dead now, so you don't need to check, you can see I had the baby. I had my Jessica..." She broke down again and they waited to give her time to compose herself. The solicitor watched with as much interest as Erika and Moss.

"We moved to England a few months after I came back from my so-called holiday with Aunt Mary."

"What happened with Jessica's father? Gerry O'Reilly?" asked Moss.

"Nothing. He was a lad about town. He didn't know I was pregnant. It's not as if he'd have wanted a kid. So I didn't tell him. We did what was akin to a midnight flit from Ireland. We left without telling anyone. This was 1983, there was no email or Facebook, no mobile phones; my mother and father had recently both lost their parents. They cut themselves off. Made up their minds to forget. It was supposed to be a new start, and it was for my parents. We came to London with very little; we all lived in a youth hostel near London Bridge for two weeks. And we stuck to this story; my mother had given birth to Jessica a few months earlier. She was her daughter and my sister. The hostel was a dump, no one said grace before bed, they all took the Lord's name in vain, some of the women were shagging around...And you know what was fucked up? My parents were the happiest they'd ever been! No one would have cared that I was a thirteen-year-old single mother! They could have let me keep her. It could have been a fresh start for me too."

"How did you all make the leap from a youth hostel in London Bridge to that house in Hayes?" asked Erika.

"Within a few weeks of us arriving in London, my dad

got work on a construction project, an office block. They were behind schedule and they were throwing money at it to get it done. Overtime, four or five times what he earned back home. And once he'd started making contacts, the work kept coming. He'd never earned so much money. Within a few weeks we were living in a rented house in East London."

"And all this time you kept up the story that Jessica was your sister?"

"I fought them," said Laura, looking Erika square in the eye with a fierce expression. "I fought them hard, and I thought I was going to win—"

"But you didn't."

Laura shook her head, the tears coming again. "And I remember the day so clear. I was nearly fourteen, and Dad took me to work with him that day. We left Mum with Jessica. He was working on a big housing development, apartments for yuppies. A load of old buildings had been razed and there was a huge hole where they'd dug the foundations. The mud was dry, and you could climb down a ladder and walk around in the bits they hadn't started working on yet. Dad left me to mess about, and I got talking to this beautiful lad, he was a gypsy. He was searching in the mud for any scrap metal. I'd started smoking on the sly and I offered him a cigarette, and we got talking. He was clever, he told me what the word 'yuppie' meant: young urban professional. I didn't know. I told him I had a daughter and that I was going to bring her up well. The boy wished me luck, and told me I'd be a great mother, and then my dad started yelling at me to come back. He said he'd done a deal to buy a piece of land to build us a house. We left to go home to Mum and tell her; he was so excited. When we got home, my mother had registered Jessica for nursery school, the doctor, the dentist. She'd registered in all of them that she was Jessica's mother: she made it official, and after that I never told anyone again that I was Jessica's mother."

Erika and Moss watched patiently as she paused and took a sip of her tea.

"The land my father bought, it's the house in Avondale Road. After that it all happened so fast. Life changed, and I struggled to keep up with it all. We moved in to the big house, then Mum had Toby. I used to look at Mum and Dad with Jessica and Toby, they were the perfect little family, 2.4 children, and I felt the odd one out. My mother never let me forget that I was the sinner, a fallen woman. But it wasn't until I went away to university in Swansea that I realized I was living with a religious nutter for a mother. When I came back after my first year in 1990, I discovered my mother had started Jessica and Toby studying for their first communion. She was *my* little girl and I didn't want her to have to go through all that bollocks, having to go into confession as a child, learning all about original sin... It was around the same time that I'd met Oscar, in my first year at uni in Swansea. He was so handsome, and clever, and he loved me... he was a bit like my father, self-made. He was on a scholarship; he'd worked hard for it."

"That's who you went camping with when Jessica went missing?" said Erika.

Laura looked down at the table for a long time. A minute passed and then two. She finally looked up and said: "Jessica didn't go missing. I took her."

CHAPTER 77

TUESDAY, AUGUST 7, 1990

The air was warm, and a breeze floated off the seashore toward Laura and Oscar Browne as they sat on the sand beside a flickering fire. It was a cool night, and the sky was a vast canopy of stars above them. They were the only people for miles, sitting on the beach in the small, secluded bay in the Gower Peninsula near Swansea.

"She's sweet, your sister," said Oscar, poking at the glowing embers of the fire with a stick.

"Jessica has always been sweet. Even as a baby. Most babies are quite ugly."

"Objection, your honor!" he said playfully. "I was a very cute baby."

"I'm sure you were, and now you're a gorgeous, strong, sexy man…"

Oscar pulled Laura toward him and they kissed.

"You ever want kids?" she asked, looking up at him.

"Sure. Someday," he replied. There was a pause and he leaned over to a bottle of wine resting on a small rock. "Do you want some more?" he asked, holding it up. Laura leaned forward and let him top up her mug. She thought how beautiful he was, bathed in the firelight. He stood and stretched and went over to the pile of driftwood he had collected earlier in the day, with the help of Jessica.

"You didn't ask me."

"Ask you what?" he said, searching through the little pile and selecting a smooth flat piece which had been bleached white.

"If I want kids?"

"I take it you do," he grinned, chucking it on the fire.

"Course I do."

"I'll put it this way. When I get called to the bar, then we can think about babies," he chuckled.

Laura looked out to sea. He'd said it in a jokey way, but he was serious.

When they'd arrived in the secluded little bay, Jessica had been confused but excited to see the caravan with its view of the bay twinkling in the sunlight. The Gower Peninsula was stunningly beautiful, and this little bay was heaven itself; rolling grass and heather with rocks peeping out, which led down to a vast sandy beach where the sun glittered on the sea in the distance, and the wet sand was dotted with rock pools.

"Can we look for crabs and starfish?" Jessica had grinned, showing her happy smile where she'd just lost her first milk tooth.

"Of course. You go down with Oscar, and I'll get the caravan nice and cozy for us," said Laura.

She wanted everything to be perfect, and as Jessica and Oscar picked their way down to the beach with a little green net on a stick, Laura quickly set to work to make the caravan home. She made up the small bed for Jessica at the front of the caravan, under the window, where she could see the sea, and at night look up at the stars. She'd tucked her favorite teddy bear in under the covers.

Oscar had rented the caravan from an advert in the back of a guide book, and being a woman who loved her creature comforts, Laura was pleased to hear the caravan had its own electricity. However, when they'd arrived with the ice cream and frozen beef burgers they'd bought nearby, they discovered that the electricity came via a noisy petrol-powered generator, which had taken some of the romance from the air when it roared to life. But inside the caravan it was surprisingly muffled.

When Laura had finished, the caravan looked cozy, and she was secretly looking forward to snuggling up that night. She'd straightened up, brushed her hair from her eyes and peered out of the window. Oscar and Jessica were now far down on the sand in bare feet, poking around in a rock pool.

She jumped back with a scream and a giggle, holding up the net, and on the end of it was a large crab . . . Laura smiled. Then she noticed Jessica still wore the party dress, and a pang of guilt came over her.

She would need clothes; she wished she'd packed some of Jessica's things, but she hadn't wanted her mother to catch them and spoil the whole plan.

Laura had lied to her parents that she and Oscar were leaving to go camping on the sixth of August. And she'd lied to Oscar that her parents knew they were taking Jessica. These lies hadn't troubled her; it was how she'd engineered taking Jessica which made her uneasy.

Was *taken* the correct word? Collected was better. They'd driven up to the house on the afternoon of the seventh, and waited outside to collect Jessica.

Laura knew she was due at her friend's birthday party at 2 p.m. She was an independent little thing, and would want to go alone, like a grown-up girl. When Jessica emerged from the top of the driveway, Laura was waiting, feigning nonchalance as she perched on the bonnet of the car. Oscar sat inside studying the map.

"Hello! Surprise!" Laura had cried.

"I thought you'd gone away?" Jessica had said, squinting up at her, clutching the small gift under her arm.

"I've got a surprise for you. We're going to the seaside!"

"But I'm going to my party..."

"Oh, but this will be far more exciting. We can swim in the sea, and eat ice creams, and build sandcastles. And we're staying in a caravan right beside the beach. We can watch the sunset, and as soon as we wake up in the morning we can go down on the beach, we can watch the sunrise..."

Laura was trying not to let desperation creep into her voice.

"Does Mummy know?" asked Jessica, shifting the gift from one arm to another.

"Of course she knows! I told her I wanted to surprise you. Treat you. You can save that present for Kelly when we come back. I've told her you wouldn't be going to the party, and she was fine. This is a special trip... We're going to make a big fire on the beach tonight and toast marshmallows."

Jessica had finally relented, and become swept up in the excitement. She'd climbed into the car, Oscar had turned and grinned at her, and they'd driven away.

No one had seen them.

I didn't take her, I'm her mother, Laura had repeated over and over in her head. They'd go into Swansea tomorrow and get Jessica something else to wear, it wasn't a problem. The most important thing was that she had her daughter for a whole weekend, and she got to be her mother, a role she had been denied, and made to feel guilty about for so many years.

*   *   *

When Laura had returned from university a month earlier, the powerful maternal feeling she'd had for Jessica had returned. She longed to spend some time with her daughter during the summer. Laura had broached the subject one afternoon when everyone else was out. She'd approached Marianne in the laundry room at the back of the house, and asked if she could take Jessica out the next day, into London.

"No! Now, you need to get over this," Marianne had snapped, pulling clean laundry from the tumble dryer. "She's happy, if anyone is going to take her anywhere, it's her mother, and in case you've forgotten, I'm her mother!"

"You are not."

"Yes I am," Marianne had snarled. "You whine and moan about not seeing her, but you've been perfectly happy to take the freedom over the years, going out until all hours, whoring yourself with boys..."

"I have not..."

"Jessica is only a few years younger than you when you fell, but she's not going to make your stupid mistakes. You were nothing better than a common whore. I hoped it was a mistake, a one-off, but your behavior over the years shows me there's an evil in you."

"By that you mean that Jessica is a mistake! If I made a mistake, then Jessica is that mistake!"

Marianne had turned with real fury in her eyes and slapped her hard around the face. She'd reeled back and fallen over, hitting her head on the edge of the door to the laundry room. She lay there for a moment in shock and reached up to her head. Her fingers had come away covered in blood. She looked at her mother. She was unconcerned, and had gone back to unloading the tumble dryer, and was humming, actually humming, as she removed the rest of the clothes.

It was then that Laura had made her plan to take Jessica when she went away camping with Oscar. She'd lied to Marianne that they were leaving on the sixth of August, when in fact they were planning to go a day later.

She hadn't told Oscar the full story either. He'd presumed her parents knew Jessica was going away with them, so he hadn't been hard to convince. He loved children.

On the beach, next to the fire in the darkness, Oscar and Laura lay back on the soft dry sand. The fire crackled at their feet, and the air was fresh with the smell of the sea, and the far-off sounds of the tide.

His arm was slung loosely around her neck, and she felt his hand begin to move over her shoulder and under the neck of her blouse.

"What's that?" said Laura, slipping out from under him and sitting up.

"What? I can't hear anything," he said, pulling her back to him. "Come on, I really want to do you on this beach... There's no one around."

"Jessica, she's in the caravan; the lights are off," said Laura, pointing to it in the distance.

He saw that it was in darkness. "It's okay. The generator's stopped working. It's probably run out of petrol."

"But she's scared of the dark; she's all alone there in the dark!" said Laura, standing and hunting for her shoes.

"It's okay, she's probably fast asleep. She was exhausted after all day on the beach..."

"We should never have left her alone in there!" Laura shouted.

Oscar put up his hands. "Hey. It's not my fault, and it's

fine. If she was scared, she'd have come over to us. And you told her to keep the door locked," said Oscar, pulling the key from his pocket.

"Stop being clever. I want to go back," said Laura. She now had both shoes on and was marching off up the beach along the small footpath to the caravan.

Oscar hurried to catch her up. When they reached the door, he put the key in the lock.

"That generator really stinks," said Laura.

"It's the petrol fumes," said Oscar. When he opened the caravan door, the smell intensified, and thick smoke began to pour out.

CHAPTER 78

THURSDAY, NOVEMBER 17, 2016

Erika and Moss sat in horror as Laura continued her story.

"The inside of the caravan was thick with smoke and fumes...One of us had moved the generator because it was on uneven ground outside, and we didn't want the wind to blow it over, or for it to topple. What we didn't realize was that we'd moved it up against a vent near the front of the caravan. It was opposite where Jessica slept. She'd been locked inside with the windows closed, and the caravan had filled with fumes.

"Oscar flung them all open and tried to get the air circulating again, but when I went to Jessica...She wasn't moving. She was still under the covers. Her skin was this terrible purple-gray color, and she was dead."

There was a long pause. The solicitor removed her glasses and wiped the tears from her eyes.

"So it was an accident?" said Erika, in disbelief.

"Yes. We should have checked. I should have checked for things like vents and windows."

"What happened next?" asked Moss.

"We both freaked out. We couldn't remember who had moved the generator. I thought it was Oscar, he thought it was me...I then told him that Jessica was my daughter. He started going on about kidnapping, and manslaughter charges, and that he had signed the paperwork to rent the caravan, and he'd signed a legal thing about using the generator. He said he was a young black man at the start of a glittering law career... 'Do you know how they treat young black men in the justice system?' he kept screaming.

"Then I took Jessica and ran with her down to the beach, and I sat up all night holding her. Just holding her in my arms. She was so beautiful...Oscar didn't follow me. The next I remember was that it got light, and I heard the car start. Oscar drove away and came back a while later. He said he'd been to one of the camping shops a few miles away, and that it was all over the news that Jessica had been kidnapped. He freaked out even more then that I'd lied to him."

"And then what did you do?" asked Erika, hardly able to bear what they were being told.

"We buried her...we buried my little girl...we dug a hole and we put her in it. It was under a tree where she could see the sea. We were so scared. Oscar was threatening me. I hadn't slept..."

It was then that she broke down. Erika moved round the table, and took Laura in her arms. She looked over at Moss and saw she had tears in his eyes too. Laura managed to compose herself, and she pushed Erika away.

"Oscar was just able to switch himself off. We came back to Bromley, and he put it to the back of his mind, but I carried this terrible secret. I was burdened by it, and the thought that I had left my little girl...My Jessica. You know what the terrible thing is? I enjoyed keeping it from my mother. That bitch had taken my little girl from me and now she knew what it felt like! She can go to hell!" Laura shouted, slamming her hand down on the table. "I hate her!"

"How did Jessica go from being buried hundreds of miles away to resting at the bottom of Hayes Quarry?" asked Moss.

"I was going crazy; the police were searching for her, and then they arrested Trevor Marksman and it was sent from heaven. He was a pedophile; I was happy for him to take the blame for Jessica's death...But I couldn't bear the thought of her alone, buried all those miles away. I did something I never should have done, and I wrote to Gerry. I thought he had the right to know...I wrote Gerry a letter."

"Gerry O'Reilly? Jessica's father?"

Laura nodded. "I asked him to phone me. We got talking, and he said that he would be in London to see friends before he was posted out to Iraq. I went to his hotel, and spent the night, and I told him everything. I thought he'd go crazy, but I had to tell him, he was Jessica's father."

"What happened?"

"What happened is that I realized what a sick bastard he was. You know what he was more interested to hear? That a trainee lawyer was involved, that Oscar was on the way to becoming a fancy lawyer...He made me give him Oscar's phone number. He said he'd take care of it..."

"And he did?"

"He told me afterward that it was all sorted. That she was in the quarry."

"And Bob Jennings, the man who was squatting in the cottage?"

"Gerry told me that they'd been seen, but it had been sorted too. He told me to keep quiet, and if I did, I'd have a life. A future."

"Bob Jennings didn't deserve to die. It was made to look like he hung himself," said Moss.

The clock ticked through the silence.

"I used to go there sometimes," said Laura. "It was a comfort to me that she was there. I never told my family, my husband, or any of the friends I made. I blocked it out. When you live a lie it becomes so ingrained you almost think it's true. Until you found her again, in my mind, she'd gone missing on that afternoon on the way to the birthday party."

"So why has Gerry appeared again, Laura?" asked Erika.

"Oscar. It's been Oscar. You've seen what he's become, a leading barrister. There's talk of him being made a judge."

"Why has he gone along with all this?"

"A few years after Jessica died, Gerry got in trouble, charged with attempted murder. He made Oscar represent him in court. I don't know how he did it, but Oscar got him off. And then they started this screwed-up...association. Oscar became more and more corrupted by power. Gerry became like his fixer. Doing his dirty work. So when Jessica was found, Oscar had Gerry working for him again to keep track of what was going on with the case..."

"And when Amanda Baker got close to the truth he made it look like she'd killed herself, but she'd already told Detective Crawford, so he had to go, and she was about to tell me, wasn't she?" said Erika.

Laura looked up at her; her eyes held so much sadness and self-hatred. "It was supposed to look like a break-in, that you disturbed a burglar, and he snapped and killed you."

"My sister was there, with two small kids and a baby. Was there nothing you all wouldn't do to keep your secret...? Did you really think you'd all get away with it?"

"We got away with it for twenty-six years," said Laura.

Erika and Moss sat back in their seats. Their pity for Laura had evaporated.

"Do you know where Gerry O'Reilly is headed to?" asked Moss. "He boarded a train to Paris earlier today."

"He always said that one day he would make his move…
Take what's his, and he would have enough to vanish into a
puff of smoke."

"Be more specific," said Erika.

"He talked about Morocco."

"Why Morocco?" asked Moss, her eyes flitting to Erika.

"It doesn't have an extradition treaty with the UK," said
Laura.

CHAPTER 79

Gerry had now been on the Eurostar for over six hours, and he was getting anxious. He checked his watch as the green fields whipped past, and the first smattering of buildings started to appear on the landscape.

Seven minutes. In seven minutes they would arrive at the Marseille Saint-Charles Station. He felt a leg press against his, and looked up at the brown-eyed guy opposite. He was thin, with chiseled features and a pierced lip. His name was Pierre. He almost laughed at the generic French-ness of him. "Pierre from Paris," but the memory of their encounter in the cramped toilet dampened any laughter. He'd flirted with men in the past; he'd even kissed a few during drunken moments, and for a dare. But full on sex had left him feeling sick and angry. Pierre had enjoyed it, bent over the grotty sink... one foot up on the toilet bowl; the harder and angrier Gerry pounded into him, the more he enjoyed it.

"My hotel is close to the station," said Pierre, pressing his leg harder against his under the table.

"Cool," smiled Gerry. He'd figured that leaving the train hand in hand with Pierre would be a good cover. And they looked the part. Gerry hoped that he would be able to ditch the kid without too much of a scene.

There was a fishing boat waiting for him at the port in Marseilles. A friend of a friend who owed a favor would whisk him from Grand Port Maritime de Marseille across the Mediterranean to Rabat in Morocco; well, it was probably going to be a long rough crossing, but at least it would be a low-key arrival, under the radar.

He checked his watch again. Four minutes. He should have flown, he thought, but if they were looking for him it would be the airports where the authorities would be most vigilant.

The buildings grew thicker as they approached the center of Marseille, the darkness falling, and then the giant glass roof of the station appeared, glowing with lights.

Pierre smiled and got up out of his seat, reaching to pull down his bag from the overhead storage. He smiled and passed Gerry's bag down to him.

"I like it," he crooned.

Gerry grinned and nodded. It seemed to be one of the stock English phrases that Pierre had picked up, and he'd used it liberally throughout the journey: to describe his sandwich, a cloud shaped like a rabbit, the color of the seat upholstery, and repeatedly as Gerry slammed into him, bent over the sink, his head jammed up against the automatic hand dryer.

Gerry stood, and they made their way to the end of the carriage. The train was now under the large glass canopy, and the platform beside them was slowing. Gerry peered out of the window, but apart from a smattering of commuters, no police.

They stepped out of the train into the warm air coming off the Mediterranean.

"*Vive la France*," grinned Pierre, his brown eyes shining. He took Gerry's hand, and they walked along the platform and into the grand arrivals hall. The curved glass roof high above now showed the darkening sky: a deep blue with the first stars pricking through.

It seemed to take them ages to cross the giant marble concourse, past a huge electronic arrivals board, an elegantly dressed woman with a poodle, two young lads absorbed in their iPhones.

"You want to take a cab to my place?" asked Pierre.

"Yeah," said Gerry, his eyes flitting from side to side as the exit approached.

"You don't like?" asked Pierre.

"I do..."

They came out onto the street, and Gerry finally relaxed. There was no one, just traffic, people going about their business. They moved to the taxi rank, and Gerry stopped and turned to Pierre. He was about to say it had been nice, but I have to go, when there was a shout and a group of *gendarmes* were piling out of two delivery vans parked on either side of the taxis. They surged at him—guns drawn. There was no time to fight, to move, and Gerry was thrown to the ground along with Pierre, who began to shout in a stream of French he couldn't understand.

Gerry felt the muzzle of a machine gun in his cheek and he was pressed against the pavement by the boot of a dapper-looking *gendarme* with a clipped little mustache.

"Gerry O'Reilly? GERRY O'REILLY!" said the voice, pressing harder.

"Yes," spat Gerry.

"A warrant was put out for your arrest. It seems you are what they call an English bastard. A murdering English bastard."

"I'm Irish, you fucking French bastard!" he said, inhaling a mouthful of dust.

"It doesn't matter. You're still arrested."

As Gerry was pulled away and piled into the back of a police van, the last thing he saw before the doors closed in on him was Pierre, deep in conversation with one of the *gendarmes*, and holding his bag filled with thirty-five thousand euros.

CHAPTER 80

At the same time as Gerry was eating dirt outside the train station in Marseille, Oscar Browne QC sat at his desk at the Fortitudo Chambers Legal Firm, looking out over London. It was growing dark, and the rain was hammering against the large floor-to-ceiling windows.

He picked up his phone and tried to call Laura. Her number went straight to voicemail. He slammed it down and began to pace up and down his office, feeling sweat and dread prickling his back. When he'd left Avondale Road and seen the police, he'd panicked. He cursed himself for the fatal error. His nerves had finally got to him. He'd driven around for several hours, and to his horror, he had missed his court appearance.

He figured his chambers were secure, and he needed a place to think. He'd told his secretary to go home, and informed the front desk downstairs that he wasn't to be disturbed under any circumstances... This was an hour and a half ago.

The silence disturbed him... No, he'd been driving fast; he hadn't been pursued, and it was the first time in his career he'd missed court.

But where was Laura? Where was Gerry?

There was an email alert tone, and he moved back round to his desk. He didn't recognize the email address, but it had the title *"A CONCERNED CITIZEN."*

He opened it and read with horror.

"OSCAR,

DOSSIER ON ALL YOUR SCALLYWAG BUSINESS DEAL-INGS WAS EMAILED TO MET POLICE BIGWIGS EARLIER THIS AFTERNOON. **AND EVERYTHING I KNOW ABOUT JESSICA COLLINS.**

IF THE BOYS IN BLUE ARE DOING THEIR JOB PROP-ERLY YOU SHOULD BE HAVING A VISIT FROM THEM ANYTIME NOW.

I'LL SIGN OFF BY SAYING, CHEERIO.

I ALWAYS SAID I'D VANISH IN A PUFF OF SMOKE.

GERRY"

Oscar began to really sweat. Then his phone rang. He snatched it up.

"What is it? I said no interruptions—"

"I know you said no interruptions sir. But there is a group of police officers on their way up; they wouldn't take no for an answer...I checked their warrant cards and..."

His arm went weak and he dropped the phone back into the cradle. He looked at the photo of his wife and his two children, and then around the office, the career he'd built.

The double doors burst open, and DCI Foster stood with DI Peterson and three uniformed officers. Before they could say anything, Oscar grabbed his wallet, keys and phone and dashed through the door to the right and locked it.

Erika moved to the door and bashed on it with her fist.

"Open the door, Oscar. It's over. We know everything.

We've spoken with Laura. She's now in custody at the station…Gerry O'Reilly has been arrested for the murders of Bob Jennings, Amanda Baker and Detective Constable Crawford." She bashed on the door again. "Oscar, with every minute you keep us locked out, your future becomes more and more bleak."

The secretary rushed in after them, breathless.

"Where does this door lead?" demanded Erika.

"Um, I—"

"Where?"

"It's a small bathroom, an en-suite with an area for dressing…and it leads out to a small balcony," she said.

Erika looked at one of the uniformed officers and gave him the nod. He moved forward and charged the door. It splintered easily and opened. They moved through into an elegant bathroom; beyond it was a door to a small room with sink, a fridge, a low sofa, and French doors. The doors led to the balcony, and they were open, flapping in the wind and rain.

They moved out onto the balcony, and Erika looked down over the edge. It was a perilous drop; the rain fell away in sheets down to the road thirteen stories below, lit up with rush hour traffic. They looked up, and saw an iron rung ladder with protective hoops on the back wall of the balcony leading up two stories. Oscar was halfway up, climbing toward the rooftop.

"God I hate heights," said Erika.

She looked at Peterson, and they went for the ladder; she pulled herself up first, and he followed.

One of the uniformed officers followed Peterson, and the second stayed with the secretary.

"He's almost at the top," shouted Erika, trying to quicken her pace, but the soles of her black shoes had very little grip, and she had to climb carefully; the rush hour traffic stretching out far below them, a carpet of lights. There was a crack and a peal of thunder, and a flash lit up the sky.

"That's all we need, thunder and lightning when we're climbing up a metal ladder near the top of a skyscraper!" shouted Peterson.

"It's not a skyscraper, it's an office block," shouted Erika down to him.

"Either way it's bloody high!" he shouted back.

She glanced down at Peterson for a second, and saw the road far below him. She blinked the water from her eyes and turned back, trying to stop her hands and legs from shaking.

Oscar made it to the top of the ladder and climbed over onto the roof, vanishing from view. This spurred Erika on. Moments later, she reached the top of the ladder and eased herself over the concrete lip of the building and onto the flat roof.

Oscar was slumped against a fire exit in the center. When he saw Erika he rose to his feet.

"Oscar. It's over," she said. She was joined by Peterson, and finally the uniformed officer.

"Come on, man," said Peterson. "Where are you going to go? We know everything: about Jessica's death in the caravan, about you and Gerry, just give it up and come with us."

"You doing the brother act on me?" snarled Oscar. "You think cos we're both black I'm going to give up, out of solidarity?"

"Yeah, because we're both that stupid," said Peterson.

Suddenly Oscar moved quickly across the smooth asphalt, and ran to the opposite edge of the roof. He placed one foot on the raised edge.

"Stop!" said Erika as she and Peterson moved closer.

"My life is over!" he shouted. "What have I got to look forward to?"

"You've got kids and a wife!" said Peterson.

As Peterson spoke, Oscar's body sagged. "My kids, my wife," he said, bowing his head for a moment and wiping his eyes. "My kids..."

"Please, just come with us," said Erika, inching closer and putting out her hand.

"I never meant any of this to happen," shouted Oscar above the sound of the rain and thunder. "I know it sounds trite, but I didn't...I'm not a murderer. Things just got out of hand."

He looked over at the drop and took his foot down off the edge. He turned to them.

"Okay," he said. "Okay."

"Okay, good, just come toward us," started Erika. The uniformed officer reached around and retrieved a pair of handcuffs.

Suddenly Oscar seized the raised edge of the roof and hoisted himself up. He stood with his arms outstretched.

"My wife and kids, tell them sorry, tell them I love them," he said. Then he leaned back and threw himself off the edge.

"Jesus! No!" cried Erika. They rushed forward to the edge of the rooftop, and looked down at the road far below.

The traffic had stopped, horns were honking, and there was a faint scream. Below, they saw the small broken body of Oscar Browne lying in the road.

EPILOGUE

The sun shone brightly as Erika, Moss and Peterson emerged from the church in Honor Oak Park. It was a beautiful day in early December. The air was crisp and the sky blue.

This was the second funeral they'd attended that day. The first funeral had been in Bromley, for Crawford. They had learned that his first name was Desmond, and that prior to his separation he'd kept tortoises. There had been a small turnout, and he'd been put to rest respectfully, even if the congregation was sparse.

Superintendent Yale delivered the eulogy, and had struggled at times to paint a picture of who Crawford was. Then Crawford's daughter, who was no more than ten years old, went to the lectern and read a poem. Her mother and younger brother looked on, silent in their grief.

If I should go tomorrow
It would never be goodbye,
For I have left my heart with you,
So don't you ever cry.
The love that's deep within me,

Shall reach you from the stars,
You'll feel it from the heavens,
And it will heal the scars.

The poignancy of the poem took Erika off guard, and it touched her that this young girl was able to express so much in this short verse.

The second funeral had been a brighter affair. The church in Honor Oak Park was beautiful and the service livelier. They sang "All Things Bright and Beautiful" accompanied by the organ, which never failed to lift Erika's heart.

Amanda Baker had been more popular than they thought, and her funeral service had drawn a large crowd of old friends and colleagues. Erika had been touched to see that outgoing Assistant Commissioner Oakley had attended, sleek and smart as ever, as had his successor, Camilla Brace-Cosworthy, who had delivered an amusing heartfelt eulogy. She'd ended by saying: "Amanda Baker had a checkered history with the MET police, but sadly, her finest moment came just before her untimely death. It was thanks to Amanda that she never gave up on the Jessica Collins case, even when others thought that all was lost. She kept going, kept asking questions and, in the end, she delivered the breakthrough that ultimately solved the case. I would like to publicly pay tribute to Amanda for her years of service in the Metropolitan Police."

It was followed by a round of applause, and as Erika looked over at the coffin at the front of the church, she imagined that Amanda would feel incredibly proud.

After the service, Erika, Moss and Peterson walked through the graveyard to the road below.

"What a case," said Moss. "Three dead bodies and a

suicide, all to cover up the death of Jessica Collins. Why didn't they just come clean?"

"They were scared," said Peterson. "And then that fear turned on them; it made them do things they'd never have dreamed they'd do."

"Such a waste," agreed Erika.

When they reached the gate and came out onto the road, they were surprised to see Toby Collins waiting for them with Tanvir. They were both dressed in black suits, and Toby held a bunch of red carnations. He looked so young and vulnerable.

"Hi." He smiled weakly.

"Hi, Toby," said Erika. "You're a bit late. You've missed the service."

"No. I didn't think it would be appropriate to attend. We brought flowers, though..." His voice trailed off and it hung in the air. "I really didn't know," he added, tears in his eyes. "How stupid was I? What's going to happen to my sister?"

A look passed between Erika, Moss, and Peterson.

"I don't know," said Erika. "It's up to a court to decide. We have her story on record, and it's clear that, in the beginning, Jessica's death was an accident. What she did afterward with Gerry is what the court will have to decide on when they go to trial."

Toby nodded. "I've lost my whole family. Tan is all I've got," he said. Tan reached out and took Toby's hand. "My mother is still in a psychiatric unit... It's not looking good. Dad's just buried his head in the sand; gone off to Spain with his new family... And Laura's in Holloway, awaiting trial. I have to wait a couple of weeks until I can even see her, and I don't know if I want to."

"Your dad will have to come back. We'll want to talk to him too."

Toby nodded. "What do I do now?" he asked. He stared so intently at Erika that she was lost for words.

"You don't get to choose your family. Hold on to each other, and don't let go," said Moss, putting a hand on his shoulder.

"Okay, we will. Thank you," he said.

They watched as Tanvir and Toby walked away and down toward the train station.

There was a mad honking and Erika's car came zooming out of a junction on the wrong side of the road.

"Is that your sister?" asked Moss, peering. "Does she know she's driving on the wrong side of the road?"

There was another honk as a car heading toward them screeched to a halt, then Lenka lurched over to the correct side of the road.

"She does now," said Erika.

Lenka pulled up beside them at the curb, and wound down the window. They peered in and saw Jakub and Karolina sitting in the back with baby Eva in a car seat between them.

"Hello everyone!" said Lenka, over-pronouncing her English.

Moss and Peterson said hello and waved at the kids.

"Where are you off to, boss?" asked Moss.

"Winter Wonderland in Blackheath. Lenka's heading back home in a couple of days; it seems things are back to normal," said Erika, rolling her eyes.

"You'll be sad to see them go," said Moss, looking at Peterson, who was pulling faces through the window at Jakub and Karolina, and making them laugh.

"I will," she smiled. Lenka honked the horn and Erika got in, adding, "See you soon; let's have Christmas drinks."

"Give us a call," said Peterson.

The car shot off along the road, swerving dangerously across to the other side, before moving back into the left lane. Moss looked at Peterson as he watched the car vanish round the corner.

"You know she probably won't call us," she said.

"She might."

"You've fallen for her, haven't you, Peterson?"

He sighed and nodded.

"You poor deluded fool. Come on, I'll buy you a pint," she said.

Moss put her arm through his, and they set off toward the nearest pub in search of warmth and cheap lager.

A NOTE FROM ROBERT

Hello and a huge thank you for choosing to read *Dark Water*. If you did enjoy it, I would be very grateful if you could tell your friends and family. Word of mouth is one of the most effective ways of recommending a book, and it helps me reach out and find new readers. Your endorsement makes a big difference! You could also write a product review. It needn't be long, just a few words, but this also helps new readers find one of my books for the first time.

I've written in the back of the previous Erika Foster novels that I would love to hear from you, and you've done me proud. Thank you for all your messages! You can find out more about me at www.robertbryndza.com.

I'm thrilled to say that Erika Foster will be back very soon in *Last Breath*.

Until then...

Robert Bryndza

ACKNOWLEDGMENTS

Thank you to Oliver Rhodes, Natasha Hodgson, Natalie Butlin, Kate Barker, Kim Nash, and the wonderful team at Bookouture. Special thanks also to Claire Bord, my brilliant editor, who is always there with expert guidance throughout the writing process, and to Beth deGuzman, Lindsey Rose, Kirsiah McNamara, Nidhi Pugalia, and everyone at Grand Central for bringing the Erika Foster series to a whole new audience.

Thank you to Amy Tannenbaum Gottlieb, Danielle Sickles, and the fantastic team at the Jane Rotrosen Agency.

Thank you to Sergeant Lorna Dennison-Wilkins, who answered all my questions about police diving and shared stories about her experiences heading the Specialist Search Unit for Sussex Police, and to retired Chief Superintendent Graham Bartlett for the excellent advice on police procedure and ensuring I tread the fine line between fact and fiction. Any liberties taken with fact are mine.

Thank you to my mother-in-law, Vierka, whose fried chicken always appears when I'm flagging with the last few chapters. A massive thank-you to my husband, Ján, and Ricky and Lola. I couldn't do any of this without your love and support. Team Bryndza rules!

And lastly, thank you to all my wonderful readers, all the wonderful book groups, book bloggers, and reviewers. I always say this but it's true, word of mouth is such a powerful thing, and without all your hard work and passion, talking up and blogging about my books, I would have far less readers.

ABOUT THE AUTHOR

Robert Bryndza is the author of the #1 international best-selling Detective Erika Foster series. In addition to writing crime fiction, Robert has published a bestselling series of romantic comedy novels. Robert's books have sold more than two million copies and have been translated into twenty-seven languages. He is British and lives in Slovakia.